SPARK OF OBSESSION

ENTICE SERIES BOOK ONE

VICTORIA DAWSON

PAPER HEART PUBLISHING LLC

Spark of Obsession

Publisher: Paper Heart Publishing LLC

Cover Designer: Sarah Kil Creative Studio

Editing: Happily Editing Anns

ISBN (Paperback): 978-1-959364-01-6

ISBN (ebook): 978-1-959364-00-9

AUTHOR NOTE

Spark of Obsession is the first book in the *Entice Trilogy* that follows the same two main characters throughout the entire series. It is advised to read the books in order. This series is intended for mature audiences. Sensitive topics discussed could be triggering and not meant for anyone under the age of eighteen.

This book is dedicated to my husband and children.

Thank you for believing in me, when I convinced myself my dreams were impossible.
I hope I make you proud.

PROLOGUE

Some people describe the moments before being pronounced dead as a bright tunnel, flashes of light, or floating through space. I suppose the lack of oxygen will do that to one's mental state. But who am I to judge?

Here's the thing about death, though. Comforting words suck.

One hundred ninety-six people told me they are sorry. One hundred ninety-six people. I counted. And fake sympathy always oozes from the people who have somehow finally managed to bring themselves out of the woodwork. I mean, seriously, what the hell are you actually sorry for? And who the hell posts stuff like, "James, you will be missed, man. RIP!" on ConnectMe when you probably can't even remember whether he was in your class or not?

I have no idea why some people choose to finally make conversation after the time of death. It's the guilt talking. Or just a lame cliché.

Either way, I hate it.

The ground crunches as I am wheeled through the herd of people to the little building adjacent to the cemetery. Annoyingly gentle hands pat my shoulders like I'm an invalid. Hushed voices echo in the cold cement room, filled with old-person smelling flowers arranged in a horseshoe shape around the wooden casket. Even my nose wants to throw up from the strong perfume scent.

Thank God the director closed the casket for this portion of the ceremony. I am not sure I can look at James and not wish with every ounce of my being that it was me inside there instead. There is no part of me that doesn't wish that he was spared and I was the one who died.

Three people pass me a tissue, touching me on the back. One person with thick fingernails fixes my hair behind my ear. Another person adjusts my arm strap, where my sprained appendage lies limp inside. I couldn't tell you their names if my life depended on it. I want to throw up.

My eyes glass over as my dad weeps beside me, kneeling down on the dirty green twilled mat, burying his head in his hands. I feel like I should do something. Anything. But I can't bring myself to move.

The preacher stands near the decrepit podium, holding on to it as it wobbles back and forth. My glassy stare only makes his pitiful beady eyes droop more.

Two men—neither of them related to me—help Dad sit up into the chair beside me. We haven't touched since the hospital visit when James was declared dead.

"Dearly beloved, we gather here together to lay to rest your child, James Andrew McFee. Please take him into your arms and reunite him with his mother and grandparents, as he enters your kingdom."

I bow my head to avoid the stares. "The Lord is my Shepherd" passage from the Bible is recited like poetry, and the vibrating regurgitation from the crowd is oddly comforting.

"We pray that James's father and twin sister find comfort in your embrace"—four hands pat my shoulders, two rubbing circles into my coat fabric—"knowing that while death and decay is the physical aspect of a human body, the spiritual body will live in your ever-powerful grace."

A clean tissue appears in my hands. I can't even turn to look or care to see where it came from. I just can't seem to care about anything other than the fact that at the age of eighteen, I have no will inside me desiring to continue living.

1

I wipe the dribble of melted ice cream from the corner of my lip, savoring the sweet taste of sugar. It is day three post-Russell, and I find vilifying him to be great therapy. Wearing my homemade Feminist AF T-shirt and drinking mojitos before the time even gets close to happy hour also has its momentary perks. I roll myself off the bed when I hear the sound of his stupid car—with his stupid spoiler and his stupid custom rims—pull up.

What an ass.

I kneel on the bench seat and spread the curtains to see Russell standing below. His preppy style now disgusts me; a couple of months ago it made him look wholesome. He rings the doorbell, takes a step back, and places his right hand in the pocket of his perfectly pressed khakis. I unlock the window and open it. The August air hits my senses for the first time in days. Russell's smug face tilts up toward the sound. His crooked smile now just looks creepy.

"I'm here for my stuff," he shouts up at me, while

cupping a hand around his mouth to help the sound travel. He tries the doorknob but it is locked. “Let me in.”

Piles of his crap have been infiltrating my room for most of the summer, and for the past three days, I’ve been waiting for him to show his arrogant face so I can deliver my message back to him—loud and clear. I should have known from the lack of genuine communication that he wasn’t that into me. Sure, I can blame it on my general inexperience, or I can accept the fact that I’m a poor judge of character.

Picking up a laundry basket full of personal items, I launch it from the second story. I feel alive again.

“Hell, Angie!”

I unload the contents of a cardboard moving box over the windowsill. I manage to hit him right in the head with the controllers for his Xbox. A few cables and gadgets decorate the shrubs that border the townhouse.

“Ouch! Stop!”

A smile cracks through my bitterness. “I’m done being your summer storage facility, you jackhole!”

Russell raises his palms up in peace. “Let me in and we can talk about it.”

“Heck, no.”

“C’mon, Angie! Be reasonable!”

I toss his favorite cologne bottle down at his head. He dodges just in time. The glass hits the sidewalk and smashes into tiny shards. I’m sure there’s a really profound metaphor about how hurt people hurt people somewhere in all of this. I just don’t care enough to overthink it.

For two months, I allowed this jerk to string me along with his bipolar dating habits. The last month was a complete waste with him visiting family in Europe. What started out as a week's trip ended up being a flipping month. Pretty sure that was the plan all along. False hope and sweet texts were enough for me to think there was a chance. I should have just sold his stuff on eBay and used the money to throw a bash.

"You mad over the breakup?"

"Mad you had to do it in the airport! In front of your entire family!"

A few people walk by the scene we are creating and snicker. One guy wearing his Gamma Delta Theta frat T-shirt snaps a picture with his cell. Russell flips him off. A skinny redheaded girl mumbles an exaggerated "dude" under her breath. I give them a wave and a big grin.

Next, I hurl out a plastic bin of his shoes—purposely leaving off the lid. I watch from above as he tries to pick them back up. Pretty sure the only flower we have is now smashed.

"Hell, Angie! What's your problem?"

My giggle is demented. "Just cleaning house."

Russell is my July-'til-August mistake. I have no room for distractions like Russell this semester though. Second chances are not always free, so maybe losing this type of boyfriend baggage is the best thing to happen to me.

Next goes his entire tennis racket collection. I throw each one down separately. All eight of them.

"You crazy bitch!"

I feel childish but oddly refreshed. Empowered. Invigorated.

I slam the window shut and sit back on my heels, watching him scurry to retrieve his briefs from the shrubbery and dig out his watch from the dead flowerbed. Serves him right. Bastard.

I drive past the dorms on my way to Harrison Hall to meet with Dr. Williams. The first-year new arrivals of River Valley University are busy unloading vehicles and hugging loved ones goodbye. Welcome to a life of ramen, Easy Mac, and the deprivation of Vitamin D.

It feels weirdly nostalgic watching the new herd start their journey, when I'm on the last leg of mine. Sure, it is taking me longer than anticipated, but I remind myself that life is too short, and worrying over it will only make it shorter. Some things are just out of my control.

I slow down as a group passes in front of me. I can't believe this is it. My last semester—the sequel. I park in the permit-only lot and clip my tag to my rearview mirror. For a Saturday, the lot is nearly full. With classes officially starting on Monday, the campus is buzzing with life.

I jog into the main entrance of the building and travel to the end of the hall where Dr. Williams's office is located. I dread going in but know that backing down now will be the death of my dream—before it even has a chance to take flight.

I give two light knocks on the door and am quickly greeted by a young bright-eyed girl in her upper teens. Her arms are full of file folders. A possible work-study student? This is a first.

"Hi," I say. "I'm here to meet with my advisor." Even though it's a weekend, many of the senior professors are in their offices. It is a tradition, and I imagine an excuse for many of them to get together for a celebration later.

Her smile is contagious. "Dr. Williams is free. Go on back."

"Thanks."

I walk past the shelves of books and find the door half open to his study. I give a knock.

"Who is it?" Dr. Williams's voice breaks. He gives a cough, and through the crack of the door, I see him take a sip from his mug.

"Me." I open the door and peek my head inside. "Is now a good time?"

"Miss McFee." He places his mug back on the ceramic coaster and straightens his posture. His leather chair creaks with the movement. "I wasn't expecting to see you."

Dr. Williams's mahogany desk is polished and clean of clutter. In the few years I have been a student here, his organizational skills—or ability to hire help—have improved tenfold.

"I decided to give it another shot," I volunteer with a shrug. "I want to try for an internship again."

He motions to the chair in front of his desk, and I take a seat.

"As you are well aware, Miss McFee," he says, adjusting his wire-rimmed glasses, "not every student who applies gets an internship." He pauses to emphasize the fact. "Just the cream of the crop. You can always have an English degree without any journalism attached, you know?"

I nod my head in agreement. I know this. It is the reason why I am repeating a semester after the disaster of my failed final project in the spring.

"And some are more prestigious than others," he explains, tapping his pen. "Some are looking to hire after six to twelve months of stellar performance. And I think that your piece last semester on the water treatment facility and their faulty testing would have put you ahead of your peers if—"

"I hadn't been naive enough to believe that my story couldn't be hijacked," I finish. I focus my eyes on the little tray of sand on the wooden desk in front of me. The sun is shining through the tiny stained-glass window, casting colorful shadows on the grains. Plaques and diplomas and photos of awards ceremonies line the wall. Dr. Williams did an amazing job aging with grace. The legacy he will leave here at River Valley when he eventually retires will be marked with his reputation of expecting excellence among his students and enforcing it by never allowing anyone to coast through their college career by being mediocre. Or in my case, overly trusting.

"It would have been a game changer for you, and I'm sorry that you were duped."

I clear my throat and swallow. "Thank you, Dr. Williams. Lesson learned."

"Channel 10 has been known to use shady antics to masquerade as concerned civilians just to hijack already developing stories. You were not the first, and you will not be the last. The industry can be very nasty and competitive. Always note your surroundings and never let anyone know that you are really doing an investigation. Appearing friendly and welcoming allows others to trust you enough to provide potentially valuable information."

I nod, soaking in everything he has to say.

The fabrication of water testing data by a facility forcing workers to "retest until results are within normal range" was discovered last year after I witnessed an influx in unexplained bacterial infections at a daycare. Finding a worker willing to confess was the type of story that would have launched my career and most likely earned me a paying internship at a prestigious news outlet.

Unfortunately, me sniffing around the facility to take pictures was the same day some reporters were out doing a segment on working-class rights. I must have sent some red flags that there might be a better story to be told. I do not blame them for further investigating and talking to parents like I did. They had the resources to do so, but I just cannot have my work swallowed up by the big players again. I need to keep my cards close to my chest and not make the same mistakes next time.

I focus my attention back on Dr. Williams, as he clears his throat. "Think about why you chose this particular career avenue in the first place."

James. This has always been about the lack of justice for James. When the driver who hit us fled the scene, only leaving a few broken parts behind, I immersed myself into my own investigation. It helped my mind cope with the tragedy of losing my twin by channeling my obsession into research. While I was unsuccessful in providing the police with any additional information, my love for investigative journalism was sparked, helping me switch from my previous major of general education.

"Use that desire as your motivation," Dr. Williams encourages, "to keep you in your lane at all times."

I nod my head in agreement. He is right. I need to stay focused.

He stares thoughtfully at me, studying me. "Your writing is very well done, Miss McFee. But you are toeing the line too much. Playing it safe. My advice to you is that if you want to have a breakthrough article, you need to absorb yourself. Investigative journalism isn't about following a story per se. It is about how you view your world. Your surroundings. You need to train your brain to see in color versus black and white. Sometimes it is the gray area between right and wrong where you find the best details. And there you might find a case."

He fixes his glasses on his nose and relaxes back in his chair. His hand makes a sweeping motion cutting through the air. "The world is your canvas."

"So no parameters? No requirements? Boundaries?"

"None. This is your make-or-break moment. You'll be graded in segments on what you have accomplished. You cannot just wait until the end to share your ideas. I'm your advisor, after all. Without my recommendation, there won't be an internship in your future."

I let out the breath I didn't know I was holding. "Okay."

"You have the tools that make for compelling story-telling. And you know the criteria and guidelines for being thorough. Now it is your job to find something worth investigating. And when you find it, Miss McFee, dive in. All in. And maybe, your story will be good enough to award you with the internship of your dreams. Or you can convert your degree to just English as a backup."

I frown at that realization. I worked my ass off after high school to get my life back in order. And now, I'm at a similar crossroad yet again—continue to work my butt off or settle for being mediocre.

"I have confidence in you, Miss McFee," Dr. Williams says. "You're ambitious, and I'm looking forward to seeing what you come up with."

"Thank you. I'll try my best," I promise.

"Here is the syllabus for this practicum course. I expect to see some progress and a sample draft by the date listed. A third of your grade is dependent on it. All dates on which we should meet for advisory discussions are listed as well. Do you have any more credits on your workload?"

"I decided to pursue a minor since I am just a handful of credits away."

"Well, good luck to you."

"Thank you." I hope my skill outweighs the need for luck.

I leave Dr. Williams's office feeling less than ideal. How in the world am I going to magically find something amazing to write about that has not been done before or done better?

I finish wiping down the counters at the Sugar Butter Bakery, bored with the lack of customers that usually fuel my entertainment on the job. If it's completely dead—like it is today—I pull open the campus blog I created called *Bad Advice*. What started as a project for a creative writing class sophomore year turned into a fun way for me to utilize my sarcasm to advise others.

Each week students submit questions via my special

email address, SuckMySatire@gmail.com, and I respond to a selected few using humor. I sit behind the counter and pull open my laptop to log into the email account. With the start of school back in session, I imagine that the blog will pick up again. I open the first email.

Dear Bad Advice,

My boyfriend of two years has been hounding me to get a tattoo. He says it is a symbol of commitment and trust. What should I do?

-Ink Virgin

I copy and paste the email onto the blog and edit the format to meet the criteria. I then type a response.

Hey Ink Virgin,

The only way to fully commit to your man is to get his name plastered across your butt—or to make a sex tape. He needs to know that his opinion matters way above your own.

-Bad Advice

I publish my response and nibble on a few of the oopsies samples. When it's time, I move toward the front door of the bakery to lock it and flip over the "Closed" sign. I remove my apron and fold it into my oversized purse that I keep behind the register.

"Angie, dear, may I have a word with you?" Edna asks from the back room. She wipes flour off her hands as I approach.

"What's up?" I ask as I make my way to the kitchen.

I've been working at Sugar Butter Bakery in downtown Portland since freshman year. Edna and her husband, the original owners, opened the street shop thirty years ago. While the pay is barely above minimum wage, the stress-free work environment and flexible hours have made up for it.

"My dearest Angie." Edna frowns, reaching for my hands. Hers are aged but yet smooth. She gives mine a squeeze.

I stare sadly at her distraught face. "What's going on?" I ask softly, knowing whatever she will say will be bad news.

"We need to close the shop, dear." Her voice cracks, and she pauses to collect herself. "We just cannot keep up with the big bakeries. Especially those growing in volume over in the southern section of the city across the river."

"Oh no, Edna." I step forward and wrap my arms around her petite frame. This place was her baby. She was unable to have children of her own, and Sugar Butter was her everything. "Please don't cry." I fight back my own tears at the realization that even if the shop was doing well, they would not have an heir to pass it to.

"We can pay you for the next two weeks. But today is the last day we can stay open. I'm just trying to use up the fresh ingredients to donate baked goods to the shelters nearby. No point wasting them. The lease has been terminated. I'm so sorry."

"Don't worry about me, Edna. I'm so sad for you both."

"I hope you can find another job, dear."

Me too. But part-time jobs for college students get swallowed up fast. "I'll find something," I say, just to ease her worry.

I give Edna one last squeeze, grab my stuff, and walk out of the cute little shop that was my place of work for the past four years. I slip my cell phone out of my bag and find Claire in my list of contacts.

"Hey, love," she greets me, out of breath.

"If you are in the middle of spin class, I'll call you back," I urge.

"Oh hush, or I'll put you on speaker."

I shake my head at her before I realize she cannot see me. "Then I'll just hang up."

"Just spit it out. You never call, you always text. So what's up, buttercup?"

"The bakery is closing. I might not be able to pay my portion of—"

"Ang, it's fine," she interrupts. Her breathing picks up and I hear her huff out, "Hey, not cool!"

"What's wrong, Claire?"

"I cannot believe this Gym Nazi is broadcasting my effort stats on the screen for everyone to see. Unfuckingbe-lievable."

I giggle. "You know that still counts as swearing, right?"

On a whim, Claire decided that she needed to work on her image and cut out public swearing. I can tell that day one is a struggle.

"You hush now. Anyway, I kind of figured the bakery was going to tank sooner or later."

"You always have a way with words," I say with a roll of my eyes—despite her still not being able to see my expression.

"It was inevitable. Granted, that totally sucks. But I have enough to cover your half this month. Plus, Mommy and

Daddy will be sending me a check soon. You know, guilt money, for never visiting."

In the years we've attended River Valley U, I have only met her folks once. The Northern Virginia restaurant owners seem to be more interested in expanding their chain rather than visiting their only daughter. Claire moving to the West Coast was a way to start a new life away from the constant reminder that she is second best. I only moved across the state but for an equally depressing reason.

"I'll figure something out with the money," I promise.

"It's fine. Really."

"No, it's not fine. I already owe you from summer when I came up short. I'll be looking for a new job this week. But I figure it might take a while since most of the positions on and near campus have been filled already."

I hear the beeping sound of the exercise bike and the gulping of water. "Come to work with me," she says simply.

"I'm not as in shape as you. Pretty sure I'd die trying. Or be upstaged by a fifty-year-old."

"Not at the gym," she whispers, her tone an octave lower. "This job here is a hobby, anyway."

I stop at the closest empty bench and sit down to rest. The bakery is four miles from our row of townhouses. "Then where, Claire?" I ask.

"My other job."

"What are you talking about?"

"Just meet me at home. I'll explain everything."

2

"So you live a double life?" I ask, plopping down on the magenta and pink wingback chair. If Victoria's Secret sold obnoxious looking furniture, this would have been a signature piece. The chair definitely does not blend in with the ivory sofa and the exposed red brick walls. The townhouse was built in the seventies. Our particular unit was used several years ago for the set of an Indie rock music video. It was a selling point. While the outside of the entire row got a facelift with the urbanization revival of the Eastside, the inside has kept its unique appeal.

I slide my sandals off and curl my feet under my thighs.

"Not exactly."

"Claire? Then what is it exactly?"

"Well, I get paid to keep filthy-rich men company."

"Which is a euphemism for…?"

Claire gives a shrug and lays her whole body across the sofa in our living room. She fans out her dark hair over the decorative pillow. "I pretend I am their girlfriend for the evening. We go out. I act like they are king of the world. Make them feel special or wanted."

"And…?"

"And I make crazy amounts of money in a short amount of time."

I play with my hair as I absorb this new information. "How did I not know about this? When did this start?"

She lets out a sigh. "Angie, I wasn't trying to keep this from you. You were busy with the whole Russell saga. Plus, you'd just had a really shitty end to last semester. You were distracted. I joined the agency at the end of May. Maybe early June? Can't even remember."

"Okay."

"There are rules that help with discretion. I had to sign papers. I really shouldn't even be sharing all of this with you. I could get fired. Or sued. Maybe both."

"Then why are you?"

"Because you're my bestie. Because I'm tired of keeping it a secret. Because you could use a distraction."

"No. I do not need a distraction. That is exactly what I don't need. I need to focus entirely on getting an internship."

She toes off her socks, letting them fall to the floor. "But you need money, right?"

Ugh. My job. "Yeah, I need money."

"Well, this is the fastest money you'll ever make. It's fun. I also have a budget so I can buy pretty things."

"Just for going out with some men? Boosting their egos. Then saying 'good night' at the end?"

Claire sits upward and rests her weight on her elbows. "Well…"

I groan. "Of course, there's a catch. Why wouldn't there be? Let me guess, you have to have sex with them too, don't you?"

"First off," Claire starts. "That is illegal in this state."

I give her a firm look and roll my eyes. She has never, ever been on the straight and narrow when it comes to rules. Why is she pretending now?

"But they are men after all," Claire says with a shrug.

I sit up straighter. "I'm not prostituting myself! Are you crazy? I mean, you usually have these off-the-wall ideas, but this one takes the cake even for you, don't you think? I am not auctioning off my body to the highest bidder."

"Then I'm sure the word will get out, and you'll only get men who solely want a date for a business meeting. I'm not a slut, Angie."

A pang of guilt hits me. "I'm sorry I implied that. You know I didn't mean it."

"It's fine, hun."

"So sex is not a requirement?"

"Of course not. But word on the street says the pay magically triples if you, you know"—she lifts her eyebrows—"entertain. After hours."

"Yeah, and then you go to prison because prostitution is illegal in nearly all fifty states."

"Girl, you watch too many TV shows. That never actually happens in the real world."

"And by TV shows, you mean world news?"

Claire shrugs and flops back onto the pillow. "Whatever. You should know better than anyone how those reporters like to embellish stories to keep the viewers in a panic."

"Really, Claire, really?"

"Joking."

"Umm, I don't know about this. Something seems off."

"Just come to the mixer event tonight. It's a recruiting event where employees bring a friend. Everything is so confidential that you have to be specially invited. They have these once a month."

"Tonight? Where's it at?"

"At a super swanky mansion on the west side of the city."

In the rich people district, I'm sure. "How were you going to sneak out tonight without me noticing you dressed to impress?"

I can tell she is thinking about it. "Probably would have gotten changed at a gas station. And then would need another STD test."

"Ew." I make a face. "Not sure how that is possible, but I'd rather not know."

"Oh, it's totally possible. All you would need to do is rub your—"

I cover my ears with both hands. "La, la, la, la, la."

Claire laughs. "Okay, fine. I'm back to being serious."

"How did you even get involved in this underground escort business?"

"Funny story."

I am not surprised. Claire always seems to find the humor in everything.

"Do share," I encourage.

"So, it was purely by accident. I was mistaken for someone else by a piece of jewelry I was wearing. The guy at the bar was so hot that I just kept up the facade and played along. Fifteen minutes later the girl who was accepting the 'job' arrived and well, let's just say I had a lot of explaining to do. So, the girl ended up staying on the date with me, which was a bit weird at first. But I loved the idea of dating men for money. A week later, I was vetted in and signed the contract. Rest is history."

"Did you two go out on more dates?" I ask. This whole secret society of women dating men who are rich blows my mind—especially in a city like Portland.

"With the guy or the other girl?"

"The guy," I clarify, not laughing at her attempt at a joke. Claire is most definitely straight.

"A couple more, yes. But then, I usually switch before things get weird. Date someone else."

"Huh." I let out the air from my lungs. "I had no idea you were doing this, and we live under the same roof."

Claire gives me an innocent shrug. "So what do you say?"

"You know this goes against my belief system when it comes to men."

"You build your views on a faulty system anyway," Claire huffs. "There's nothing wrong with being all about girl power and still letting a man into your life. Some men are into feminists anyway. C'mon, you have nothing to lose."

"Or"—I swallow hard—"I have everything to lose."

After knowing Claire for four years, I should have predicted that she would be swallowed up in the world of the rich and famous when given the opportunity. She has always been drawn to the elite class. Paying for a personal shopper or hiring a person to blow-dry her hair were the first warning signs. It doesn't hurt that her parents are entrepreneurs, and she is the only child. Having two people showering her with money is very helpful for maintaining that kind of lifestyle. Even if it is money motivated by guilt.

Claire screeches to a stop along the cobblestone driveway, nearly clipping the base of the water fountain with her bumper but managing to drive up onto the curb instead.

"Keep it classy, woman." The only reason I allowed her to drive this far was because she convinced me she would get motion sick if I decided to take the wheel.

"Aren't you glad I flirted with my driving instructor to secure my license?" she asks with an over-the-top smile.

I give her my side-eye before breaking out into giggles. To this day, I am never quite sure when she is joking versus being serious. She definitely keeps life interesting and balances out my type A personality. Everybody needs a Claire in their life.

She lowers the window of her sleek, cherry-red Nissan Maxima and gives a wink to the valet worker. He takes her keys from her manicured hand and returns the wink.

"Be careful with her, okay? I'm very touchy with my baby," she warns with a straight face.

"Yes, of course."

Men in tuxedos usher us toward the front entrance doors of an elaborate, three-story mansion. Each balcony is adorned with strands of elegant lights. Sheer white curtains cover each window giving the massive structure a calming aura.

The setting sun is beautiful over the rolling landscape.

Just fifteen minutes outside the city limits of Portland and it is like we are transported to a different time zone. The sound of the water fountain fills the air and competes for attention with the symphony of crickets and locusts. With each little breeze, water droplets brush against my bare skin and quickly evaporate.

"This way, miss," the tuxedoed man says, pushing gently against my back.

His touch feels weird. Sterile. As if my back is just one of the thousands he has touched. I pull away from his hand.

"You okay, Angie?" Claire asks when I stop from entering the mansion.

"I just want to have a minute to myself," I say.

Her eyes study mine. "Okay," she says, pausing. "I'll wait for you in the foyer."

Claire's smile tells me everything is going to be just fine. She wouldn't get me involved in something that is harmful. Her fiery-red dress fits her like a glove, making her look powerful despite her petite frame. The girl is the epitome of class and sass. Shoulder-length dark hair frames her face in the most disheveled, but strategically planned way. She is rocking her mixed-race—being part Filipino and part Caucasian—with the best of both worlds. It's a shame that her biological dad never got the chance to see her blossom like she is now. It's a bigger shame that the parents who raised her only care about themselves.

We are opposites, yet the best of friends. Where she is vibrant, I am pastel. She is strong, and I only attempt to be strong.

The old me was vibrant.

The old me was fearless.

But sometimes life's circumstances snuff out the light that once glowed brightly.

I watch as Claire's retreating form disappears through the heavy wooden doors. I stand off to the side and make room for the new arrivals to enter. The men must already be inside because the next three cars that pull up just have women in them. Beautiful women. Every color of the rainbow is represented in their sexy-yet-sophisticated outfits.

I regret not owning better party-appropriate clothing. Claire is four inches shorter than I am and a little less fluffy. So borrowing clothes can get tricky. I feel like her selection is suffocating me. The corset top is strapless and light pink in shade. The matching skirt, however, is loose and airy. My straightened brown hair is pulled back in a sleek ponytail exposing my neck. I feel vulnerable and open to be judged.

When my breathing returns to normal, I turn and enter the building. I find Claire waiting as promised. She is talking to a man whom she quickly dismisses.

"Want a drink?" she asks.

"Yes, please."

I follow her through a series of spacious rooms until we find the main social area that is set up with a bar. In the corner, a pianist plays soothing music. I recognize the sad melody of "Clair de Lune." It was one of Momma's favorites from her collection.

"Wait here and I'll get us drinks," she says.

I scan the room and notice that all of the men are in traditional tuxedos. Most are paired off with a lady or two. The buzz of introductions fills the air. I can distinguish between genuine laughs and the nervous giggles. I wonder if any of the ladies will accidentally confuse a waiter as a client. They are dressed the same.

"Cristal?"

I turn toward the deep voice. A tall, dark-haired man stares at me intently.

"No, my name is Angie," I clarify with a half smile.

From the faint wrinkles around his eyes, I would say he is in his late thirties or early forties.

"Well hello, Angie. I am Nolan. Would you like some Cristal?" he asks.

My brows furrow. Who is this Cristal? I do not know her.

He starts to chuckle, and I can feel my cheeks heat. I feel like I am the butt of some joke.

"Champagne," he responds. He turns to grab two flutes from the buffet table behind him. The glasses are arranged to form the shape of a heart. Now the formation looks a bit lopsided. "That is the brand name. Cristal," he clarifies.

My eyes close for a second to keep myself from passing out. Is this common knowledge? I feel so stupid. How embarrassing! He presses the glass into my hand, and I take a nervous sip. It is delicious. Best tasting bubbly I've ever had. Definitely not the two-for-thirteen deals that Linny's Liquors has for the weekend special.

I finish my drink in a hurry, making my nose burn from the carbonation. I excuse myself to find the nearest restroom. Meandering, I catch a glimpse of Claire's back at the bar. She looks to be in conversation with a cute but serious-looking man. I see a line of women on the other side of the room and make my way over. Where there is a line, most likely there is a ladies' room.

When I exit the restroom, I notice that on the rear side of the mansion there are double French doors open, allowing in the warm end-of-summer breeze. I make my way back and step out onto the stone patio that surrounds a majestic swimming pool. Water from the layered fountain cascades over the edge into the pool's basin. Beautiful orchids and tropical flowers add color to the otherwise blue and beige tones. The backyard is lush and professionally maintained. It is a peaceful haven.

Music escapes through the doors, joining the sound of trickling water. The pianist's rendition of Coldplay's "Fix You" resonates in my ears. It is my anthem. I sing the lyrics to myself.

It is the story of my life.

Always taking two steps forward and a dozen back.

I do not belong here. I am beer and peanuts. Small town. Everyone inside is champagne and caviar.

I open my borrowed handbag and find a piece of watermelon bubblegum. I pop it into my mouth and chomp down to bring out the artificial flavors. I slip off my light pink heels and dip my toe in the water. My nails are a matching color, courtesy of Claire. I feel feminine and pretty.

Looking back, I should have suspected something was up with Claire when she was gone nearly every night over the past couple of months. Stupid Russell took up too much real estate in my brain. He strung me along and fed me just enough of the right words to keep me with him. What a mistake.

The instrumental music switches over to another classical piece that I don't recognize. I grab a loose cushion from the outdoor table and chair set and place it at the edge of the pool. I hike up my flowing skirt just enough to avoid dampening the hem. My right shoulder burns with a sharp pain as I lower myself to the ground to take a seat. The physical discomfort is a reminder of the burden I bear. My life was spared. And James is gone.

While I no longer wish to die, I do wish with everything I am that I could bring him back to me. Walking through life without my twin is like walking through a desert without any water. He was my lifeline. The physical wounds are still healing, but the emotional scars will remain with me forever.

My calves rest against the interior wall of the pool. I lean back on my hands and relish the coolness of the water. I close my eyes and blow bubbles with my gum. The repetitive motion relaxes me.

How did I get here? At twenty-three years old, I don't have a mother, a brother, a boyfriend, or a job. My college experience has lasted a little longer than it should. And even that is in jeopardy. I have zero savings. Four years has not changed much. Even now, I don't have much to live for.

The smell of woods and citrus infiltrate my nostrils with the breeze. I am no longer alone. I breathe in the masculine scent as I turn to find its source. My eyes do a double take as they connect with a pair of steel-blue ones. They are cool and calculating, as they hold my gaze. I am not used to eyes being this vibrant, alive. If I don't look away, I fear I will be swallowed whole into their depths.

The sight of him disrupts the autonomy of my breathing. My bubble pops over my lips, and I quickly suck the gum into my mouth and swallow it. The man pushes his thick brown hair off his forehead with his hand, while the other rests in the pocket of his pants.

My heart has never met a man like him before. And it would know.

Even in just the light of the moon, I can tell that he is beautiful.

3

"Nice evening for a swim," Mystery Man says, pushing off the wall he was leaning on. He moves closer to me, and my pulse increases.

"Yeah," I mutter. I don't recognize my own voice.

I watch in awe as he leans down next to me and dips his hand into the water. He stays there for a second before standing back up. The smell of his cologne intoxicates my senses. I want to lean into him and breathe in his masculinity. He has organized scruff on his face. I find it sexy. Getting a closer look, his eyes look tired. Maybe he hasn't been sleeping well.

"Who are you?" I ask softly.

His eyes meet mine, and a frown mars his face. "Someone you should stay away from."

What does that even mean? I was here first. Why would he answer that way? He is the one who joined me. I need to get back inside to Claire. I try to gracefully get up from the edge of the pool.

"Here, let me." His voice is deep, yet smooth.

Warm hands grasp my elbow and waist and lift me from the cement with a carefree ease. His fingertips linger on me for a few extra seconds, sending tingles up my spine. I do not mind. I can feel the strength behind his hands. I bet he works out daily. Probably three or more times daily. He is that fit.

I offer a smile and a soft "thanks."

"Are you cold?"

I look down at my bare arms and see the goosebumps forming. His finger trails along my flesh, stopping at my elbow. I shiver but shake my head no. I do not feel cold. I feel electrified. He is grinning at me. My cheeks flame with heat. He knows his effect on me. I bite my lip to keep it from quivering.

I wonder if he is part of the event. He is not wearing a tuxedo like all of the other male clients. Instead, he has on a dark black suit with a charcoal dress shirt and black tie. Regardless, he looks one hundred percent like he belongs here and not as the hired help. He looks expensive. Too expensive for me.

I stifle a giggle at the thought that I couldn't afford him. As if he were the one for sale instead of me—if I accept the job. If I am even offered the job after the interview process.

"We should play some poker," he drawls. He fixes his hair and slips his hand into his pocket.

"And why is that?"

"Your face gives everything away."

I place my hands on my hips, annoyed by his blatant judgment. "Maybe I'm bluffing." What I am bluffing over, I am no longer sure. My brain feels like it got put into a blender.

He chuckles. “You’re bad at that too then.”

I huff. “I’m actually really good at games.”

“I am better,” he says. Even his eyes appear to be laughing at me.

“So you think.”

“Know.”

“I thought I’m supposed to stay away from you,” I counter.

“You should stay away. Doesn’t mean you will. Something tells me you like to do what you want.”

I take a half step back. “How would you have inferred that?”

“You’re the only one who has left a posh party to bathe your feet,” he says with a straight face, pointing at my damp toes.

I burst out laughing. As much as I can with a confining outfit. I suppose that is true.

I step into my heels and regret not drying my feet off first. Water droplets trickle from my calves and settle at the tops of my ankles.

His eyes stare through me, and I instantly feel naked. It’s as if he is studying me. Judging me. I smooth down my skirt just to have something to do with my hands.

“Nice meeting you,” I say, as I turn to walk back into the building to find Claire.

“You forgot this,” he calls out behind me.

I pivot and see my handbag dangling from his extended hand. Of course. I walk back to Mystery Man and retrieve my bag. As I step backward to walk away, I see a bubble form from his lips. The watermelon smell is so strong. I watch it pop.

"Yum," he says with eyes full of mirth.

Thief. Who does he think he is going through my personal items? I am relieved that there is nothing more in there than candy, lip gloss, and my phone. But still!

If I stay out here any longer, I might not have the willpower to leave. Or I might just hit him.

I hurry back through the open doors and nearly knock over Claire.

"Where were you? I was looking for you." Her animated hands are all over the place. "I ended up drinking your drink after you didn't text me back. It's going to be your fault if I leave here drunk."

"I didn't hear my phone. I was just getting some fresh air," I answer honestly. "Then I ran into some man."

"Who?"

"He is out there," I say, turning around to point out the doors to the patio. I look around the pool and outdoor furniture. But Mystery Man is no longer there. "He must have gone inside another way."

"What was his name?"

"He never said."

"Weird."

"This entire night has been weird," I admit.

"Come with me. I want to introduce you to a few men who might be interested in going on some dates with you."

I try to hold back my groan. I cannot handle another awkward encounter. I'm becoming more and more doubtful that this job would be a good fit for someone like me. I am way more introverted than Claire. And way less experienced. But I need the money, so I follow her obediently into the main room.

Claire makes her way toward a group of men standing near the bar. They appear to be in the age range of thirties to fifties. My stomach starts to turn. I count backwards from one hundred to try to distract myself enough for it to settle.

"This is my best friend, Angie," Claire introduces me.

A blond-haired man steps forward first. He reaches out his hand for mine. "Nice to meet you, Angie. I am Will Jenkins," he says.

"Hi, Will," I say politely. He seems friendly. Normal. Maybe this is not so bad after all.

Another man reaches out a hand. I give him mine. He kisses the top of it. I do not expect that. "Nice to meet you, hun."

"Angie, this is Ian Downs," Claire says.

I move to shake Ian's hand, but he moves forward for a hug. It is clumsy. "Pleasure to meet you, Angie." He appears to be older than all the others. And extra handsy. Lovely.

"I'm Mark," a black-haired model type introduces.

I reach out my hand for him to shake. "Angie."

His smile is contagious. "Pleasure to meet you." However, his professionally polished looks make me think he emphasizes appearance more than anything else.

"So, it's not official, right?" Will asks me.

I furrow my brow. "Official?"

"Your employment," he continues. "You're not wearing your bracelet yet, so I'm assuming you still have to go through the protocols?"

I quickly look at Claire's wrist and scan the room for

other females. Most of the women have on jewelry that looks like an identity bracelet. Some are silver, some are yellow gold, and some are platinum. I never really noticed this before. I grab Claire's wrist and turn the bracelet's smooth metal plate in my fingers. It is beautiful. When she originally told me how she got into the business, she said it was over being mistaken by her jewelry.

"I'll explain later," she whispers.

"I'm just a guest tonight," I inform the group.

"Well, for the sake of most men in my presence," Mark chimes in, "I hope that you follow through."

"Yes," Ian agrees.

I swallow. I have no idea if I can follow through. This all seems too much.

I excuse myself to the ladies' room again. I think the pressure from the corset top is punishing my bladder. When exiting, I take another look outside to see if I can see Mystery Man. It's as if he vanished.

I walk through the great room where a female singer now sits casually on top of the piano, singing "Skinny Love." I love Birdy's rendition, but this version is amazing as well. I sway to the music and hum along. The words haunt me.

I watch from the sidelines as a crowded room makes small talk. Dates get booked. Phone numbers exchanged. And I am sure nights will conclude with some women accepting offers of more.

I walk up to the bar.

"What shall it be, pretty lady?" the bartender asks.

I play with the ends of my ponytail while I try to decide. There is no menu. Just rows and rows of expensive liquors, and yet everything belongs on the top shelf. Pretty sure that asking for a margarita is out of the question. Although, I could really go for one.

I see movement out of the corner of my eye.

"Two martinis. One dirty. One clean." Mystery Man.

I turn to find piercing blue eyes watching me. "You," I exhale.

"Me." His smile is full.

"I see your mood has improved," I comment dryly.

"I see your snark is still intact."

"This is true," I mutter.

The bartender places both drinks down in front of us on the polished wooden surface. "Here you go, Mister—"

"Thank you," he interrupts suddenly, moving the drinks closer.

In the light of the room, I am caught off guard by the striking blue eyes looking at me with expectation. I am drawn to them and yet know that I could easily drown if I stare too long. I gaze back at the drinks.

"Which one do you want? The dirty one? Or the clean one?" he asks, wiping condensation from each glass.

"Very cryptic, aren't we?"

I stare intently at the cocktails. Somehow this decision is more than just about a drink preference. My hand snakes toward the one without the olives, and I swear I can hear him snicker. I am tired of his games.

"Thought so," he says, reaching for the other glass.

But I am too fast. I snatch the olive one in my other hand and leave him at the bar—drinkless and alone. I could use both. I move to the other room adjacent to the lobby and find a sofa. I place my drinks on the end table and text Claire to join me.

"What a night," she sighs, plopping down next to me. She takes the clean martini out of my hand and finishes what is left. "That is pretty darn good."

"Sure is," I say, chewing the last olive off the toothpick.

"Never would have pegged you for a martini girl."

I laugh. "Same. I guess tonight is about trying new things."

"So, what do you think? Interested in coming into the office with me next week to find out more?"

"Maybe."

"There's a chance so you're saying…" her voice trails off.

We both erupt in alcohol-induced giggles over the butchered *Dumb and Dumber* reference that we often recite.

"That's not how it goes," I laugh even harder. "You're making it sound like a drunk Yoda."

"You know what I meant."

"My head feels fuzzy," I admit.

Claire flags down a waiter holding an hors d'oeuvres tray of gouda-stuffed mushrooms and just hijacks the whole thing. The waiter's deer-in-the-headlights expression makes us laugh harder. She tosses one up into the air and catches it with her open mouth.

"Nailed it!" she coos.

We snack on the food and people watch. When we get bored, we transition to snapping selfies, which causes a few guests to stop and stare. We have to be the only ones having this much fun. Claire's volume is the least discreet out of the two of us. She is going to get us kicked out.

"So what's up with all the blings?" I ask, touching her silver bracelet.

"Just makes it easier to spot us when we are out and about. You can choose to wear it off hours. But you must wear it during hours."

"Why the variation in metals?"

"Ranks. Silver is starting rank, then gold, and then platinum. Incentives for racking up dates or money…whichever happens first."

"And this is something you enjoy doing? Going on dates?"

Claire pops another mushroom into the air except this time it hits her nose and falls to the floor. We stare at the round ball as it rolls under the end table.

"I love it. You will too." She holds up her finger to tell me to wait. She grabs a mushroom and slurps it into her mouth and chews. This has to be a cheat day for her. "It's great money, and maybe surrounding yourself with a bunch of business people will help you with your paper you need to do for Dr. Williams's class."

Hmm…I never thought of that. Maybe Claire is right. Maybe having this type of exposure to this underground society of socialites will bring to light something worth investigating. Or maybe I will get to make connections with those tied to some media outlets; sometimes it is less about what you know, and more about who you know.

"But you cannot write about the agency," Claire quickly interjects. "There is an NDA you will have to sign. It will be off-limits then."

Nothing is ever off-limits. There is always a way to work around agreements. There is a whole thing with whistleblowers and the protection of sources that needs to be respected. I can write under an alias but still use a mainstream publishing outlet. Loopholes.

We are so busy in conversation that we do not notice a girl in a green dress enter the room.

"Hi, Claire," she greets with a smile.

"Hey, Monica, this is my friend Angie. Angie, this is Monica. We met last month during the mixer event."

"Nice to meet you, Angie."

"Same to you," I say.

"How are the dates going?" Claire asks.

Monica is very pretty with girl-next-door vibes. She has long straight auburn-colored hair that hits her shoulders. She has a familiar face. Maybe we had crossed paths on campus unknowingly.

"They are pretty good. No regulars. Just one-offs. I have a week, however, of dates with a guy I met tonight. An Ian?"

"Ian Downs?" Claire asks.

"Yeah, that's it."

"Seems nice," Claire says. "A bit handsy though."

"That's what I'm nervous about. I'm just doing this job for the money. Nothing past what I need to make ends meet."

I raise my hand. "Same boat here," I add, "assuming I agree to move forward with the process."

"Just be honest and upfront early on," Claire advises. "Word gets out fast about which girls want more."

"Well, I'll see you guys around," Monica says, exiting the room.

"Gossip Diva alert," Claire whispers.

I furrow my brow, until I see who she is referencing.

"Well, hello Claire, good seeing you," the average height Madonna lookalike greets.

"Same," Claire says with a smile. "This is my friend, Angie, who might be joining the agency. Angie, this is Tracy."

"Nice to meet you, Angie. Can I offer some advice though?" Tracy asks but then continues, "Be careful."

I swallow hard.

"What's that supposed to mean, Tracy?" Claire demands. "What kind of gossip are you going to spew now?"

"It's not called gossip if it's true, Claire. Anyway," she says, turning her attention to me, "there's a rumor that—"

"Oh great, a rumor. This will be good," Claire huffs, crossing her arms.

"That some of the agency men are using blackmail as a coercion technique to persuade some of the girls."

Holy. Shit. Claire's eyes dart to mine, and I can tell she is not part of the Tracy Fan Club. But I cannot shake the feeling that maybe Tracy is right. That maybe something very shady is happening within the secret realm of the agency. And that I could be on the cutting edge of discovering what it is and having a story to capture.

"Really, Tracy? And did these girls come forward and report it to Dominic? Did any of them file a police report?" Claire asks.

"Well, no," Tracy admits.

"Of course not. Because let's face it, the other two supposed rumors you shared in the past were unfounded and just a bunch of gossip running its course."

Tracy gives me a sad smile. "Don't say I didn't warn you."

I nod my head and watch her retreating form as she departs.

"That was intense," I exhale, turning my attention to Claire.

"What an attention whore," she groans. "I'm all about girl code and such, but that woman has been trying to relive her high school cheerleader years where she was the most popular. And I was a cheerleader, so I can spot one without any effort. Starting over again in college has to be hard for some people who don't have the reputation preceding them. And gah, why do her breasts have to be perfect?"

I shift in my seat and smooth down my skirt. "What if she is right? What if some of the girls are being blackmailed into doing things they do not want to do? Perhaps sexual acts and such?"

"Why would these filthy-rich men need to even use blackmail techniques, when they can easily find willing participants if they just look?"

Claire waves over a waiter carrying a tray containing a variety of fancy-looking cocktail drinks. She snatches two up.

"These are special order drinks for some other guests," he says in a hurry.

"Oops," she says in exasperation, slurping one down in an obnoxious manner. She passes the other one to me, and I cannot hide my embarrassment.

"Sorry," I mouth. But damn, the drink is delicious. Way better than the martini.

"Ready to call it a night?" Claire asks. "Things seem to

be slowing down. And the liquor is starting to taste like water."

"Yeah, I'm ready." I get up from the couch and stumble in my heels. "I'm not equipped to drive," I admit. "Neither are you."

"Taxi it is," she agrees. She opens the app and orders us a ride home.

We walk outside and wait for our ride to show. The stars are visible here this far from the city limits with the light pollution. I stare up at them and savor these last few moments before the stress of the semester really takes over my life.

When we arrive home, I retreat to my room and change into pajamas. I fall onto the mattress and drift off to sleep.

"Tell me why I ever agreed to this?" I whine. My voice is staccato as I try to catch my breath. Sweat pours from my face as I pump the weights to the beat of the music. "In fact,"—I pause—"I never agreed to this!"

"Oh hush, Angie," Claire snorts. "You most definitely said you would accompany me."

"When?" I snap. "When did I say that?"

"Last night on the way home."

"I was drunk."

"Well, maybe next time you should be more responsible. There are consequences to your actions, ya know?"

I laugh. I feel like crying though. This body pump class was falsely advertised. In the description, it said beginners welcome. Lies.

For a Sunday morning, the gym is busy with the diehards. I look like a fool.

When the song ends, I rush over to the wall of mirrors and grab my water bottle and towel from the mat on the floor. I take a mini break. I am not overweight by any means. But I also am not the athletic type. My right rotator cuff throbs from my previous injury, and I cannot wait to get back to the locker room to take some much-needed Motrin. This type of workout is life for Claire. And if this was high school gym class, I would expect to be chosen last every time.

I move back to my spot and pick up the weights again. "I'm never agreeing to this again."

"Whatever," Claire sighs. "Maybe there is some room in the geriatrics water aerobics class."

I give her a big smile. "Now we're talking."

When the class finishes, we move to the locker rooms to shower and blow our hair dry. It does feel good to release the stress from my body through an intense workout, but I am pretty sure I will be sore for days.

Around three p.m., I drive to the airport to pick up Zander. I am a few minutes early as I wait at baggage claim. I see him moving down the escalator with his guitar case on his back. I know instantly that summer treated him well. His blond hair has even more natural highlights, and his skin is a golden tone.

I half run to him, and he greets me with a huge bear hug, lifting me up from the ground.

"So good to see you, Z."

He pulls me back to take a good look at me. I have on

cutoff jean shorts and a yellow tank top. "Gosh, it's good to see you, Ang."

"How was your flight? Do you miss San Diego yet? How is your family?"

"Good, just the waves, good," he answers with a laugh. He adjusts his case on his back. "I'm not ready for classes to start, that's for sure."

"Yeah. I'm not really looking forward to this semester," I admit.

Zander gives me a half frown. "You'll do great, Angie. I know you will."

He always has been a great support system for me. Always rooting me on. Even when I fail.

"How's your sister?" I ask.

"She is good. Might get engaged this year, who knows."

We move over to the conveyor belts and wait until his luggage comes down the ramp. For planning to live here for a full school year, he packs light. Just two big pieces and he has everything he needs. I pull up the handle and help him pull one of the cases toward the parking lot tram.

We enter the transit and find the only empty seats available in the back. I clumsily pull the suitcase through the narrow passageway and bump into a couple of elbows on accident.

Once seated, Zander turns to me with his crooked smile. "How was your summer, Ang? I'm assuming you were pretty busy since I haven't heard from you much."

I feel the pang of guilt. I have not been a good friend. "I had some drama with Russell."

Zander swipes a hand through his long blond locks and sighs. "Yeah? I never liked that d-bag."

"It's over now. I am so done."

"Good." His smile is warm.

The tram stops to let off a group of people at Section A parking as we continue to discuss Russell.

"So, enough about me. Tell me what has kept you busy lately."

"I released my first app and made it public."

"What? Really? That is awesome!" I reach for his hand and give it a squeeze. "So amazing."

"Thanks." I can tell he wants to talk about it but doesn't want to feel like he is bragging. That is Zander. Always humble.

"What's the name of it? What does it do? Why did you wait until now to tell me?"

"I called it Musix. It is an app for running chords or lyrics to double check for plagiarism when writing your own stuff. It compares words and combinations of music notes to create a percentage or line-by-line match with thousands of songs in the database."

"That sounds awesome."

I watch as Zander pulls up the app on his phone. He demonstrates some of the features as I watch on with pride that he was able to accomplish one of his dreams.

The tram finally stops at Section D, and we exit. The trunk of my older model Honda Civic is too small for both pieces of luggage, so we toss the other one in the backseat. I hop onto the highway and make my way back into the city. Zander and I talk about his family. I'm sure he sees through my deflections to avoid talking about what is left of mine but does not pressure me.

"When will your car arrive here? Your sister driving it up like last time?" I ask.

"It's already here, actually. My dad decided to drop it off while attending a conference up here. He ended up just flying back then."

"Oh, awesome. But what a long drive!"

"Yeah, he did it in two days though. Took him a total of seventeen hours."

"Craziness."

When I park beside Zander's car at his row of townhouses, we jump out and unload the trunk and backseat. Z lives roughly a mile from where Claire and I live, which is close enough to the university but still considered off-campus housing. Music is blaring from Zander's rental, and I wonder how long it will take before the neighbors call the police.

"Guess the roommates have arrived," I mumble.

"Yeah and they better not have trashed the place already," he says, knocking on the door. After a few seconds, he just tries the doorknob and finds it unlocked.

We walk inside and are greeted by his obnoxious roommates, who thankfully cut the sound on their system. They open up beers for us from a local brewery, as we celebrate the start to another year at River Valley U.

Settling in on the couch, I curl my feet up under my thighs. "You coming over tomorrow night, Z?"

"For the chick show?"

I nod. "And possibly to fix my laptop?"

"What happened now?"

"A week ago, I started having issues. It just randomly shuts off and restarts."

"Yeah, I can look at it."

"Thanks."

While the guys channel surf and chat about what has happened over the summer, my mind drifts to the man from the event last night who has captured my attention. I wonder if he is part of the agency. I wonder if he already has a person he goes out with regularly. I wonder if we would be compatible.

And I don't even know his name.

4

I manage to scrape myself off the self-pity bus in time to get ready. It is so easy to play the "why me" loop in my head. But I need a job and I need one fast. I have no time to sit and feel sorry for myself.

I take a deep breath and stare blankly at the floor-length mirror. *You have exactly what the agency needs.* Claire's words, not mine. Nope, my words would be—*You are in over your head, Angie, and you have not even officially been hired.* I'm dressed in a plain white sundress. This is what I assume a girl next door would look like. My skin is untouched, my hair on the frizzy end of messy. But apparently, this is the golden look to land a job. Who would have thought?

I learned during my first year at college that Claire isn't someone to piss around with. When her heart is involved, there really isn't any human being who would be able to exercise their free will.

What in the actual hell am I doing?

I make my way down the stairs into the living room. Claire is perched on the wingback chair, looking as dapper as ever. Her spiked, candy-apple-red stilettoed feet dangle over the arm of the chair. Her dark hair looks sexy and free. The black jacket she's paired with her tight black dress looks almost conservative.

"You okay?" she asks.

"Yeah, I had a minor moment of freak-out. But I can do this."

Her smile is warm.

I fidget, digging my fingernails into my palms.

"Were you second-guessing it?"

For months, Claire has conveniently hidden her job under the masquerade of having a nightlife. And here I am, ready to embark into the unknown. After signing a nondisclosure agreement, of course.

"Would you expect any different from me?" I ask with a smirk.

Like an obedient child, I follow her out the door with my twill coat in hand. It is the nicest thing I own, despite being found at the Secondhand Treasure store in the city, and is perfect for this cool and dreary day. I had switched out the dull buttons for a shinier finish and stitched the few holes that poked through the inner lining with my sewing machine. But other than those minor adjustments, it looks new.

The outside bushes still smell like the men's section of the Walmart fragrance aisle. I laugh every time I exit the townhouse thinking of Russell's shocked face.

Claire's driving borders on terrifying—especially as she merges onto Interstate 5. She is getting worse with age.

Maybe she did coerce the driving instructor to pass her after all.

"Watch! You are going to hit the rail," I warn. I hold my breath as we take the Marquam Bridge over the Willamette River to enter the downtown area of the city.

"It's these damn shoes," Claire explains.

"Swear word," I fake scold.

"Oh hellyfish, I am never going to stop," she whines.

I giggle at her attempt. "Hellyfish. Really?"

"Yes, really, Angie. I am obvi struggling and trying to ease my way into this without going completely cold tofu turkey and being miserable."

I look over at her and bite my tongue to keep from crying and making her snap. When Claire decided on a whim to do this type of challenge, I welcomed it. Mainly because I do not have to really be involved—unlike her previous ambitious ideas.

Claire cuts off an SUV and a horn blares. Her manicured middle finger flies out the window in a fluid motion. I really should have offered to drive. Downtown's buildings block my view of the sun but only temporarily. After growing up in the small town of Baker City, Oregon, I find Portland to be very livable. The air seems fresher and the greenery greener. It is a bit of a hippy city without a bunch of potheads. People are overall health conscious and environmentally friendly.

It is easier to make a new location home when you don't have the other one to go back to. The other benefit is that there are fewer reminders of what was left behind.

We arrive at the huge contemporary-style building in under fifteen minutes. I admire the glass and metal structure, standing glorious in the city's skyline. Claire pulls into the garage and swings into the first free spot she sees.

We are here.

My door pulls open, and Claire helps me out by my elbows. Her hands are in my hair, smoothing down the waywardness of the frizz.

"Oh sweetie, they are going to love you. You already have a bunch of fans from Saturday night itching to get a date with you. I'm sure those men put in a good word for you too."

I grumble something that even I don't understand. I have been in intense situations before and can usually handle stress; however, there is something about this potential job that has me about to fall apart.

My flats cooperate with me as I walk into the waiting elevator. The sound of soft piano music fills the silence as I fidget with the chipped pink paint on my polished fingernails. The doors open on the eleventh floor.

Sink or swim.

The warm aura coming from the track lighting soothes my rapid heartbeat. An expensive-looking white desk is the first piece of furniture that grabs my attention. Business cards—in robin-egg-blue—rest on the corner near a pen mug with the company logo printed across the side. *Entice.* Behind it, a beautiful woman smiles with perfect white teeth, red shiny lipstick, and expensive-looking long French-manicured fingernails. Her red suit only makes her look more legit.

"You must be Angie," the receptionist greets, stepping around her desk. "Dominic, our CEO, is in charge of your training and style. Follow me and I'll introduce you."

My thoughts are in overdrive. I shift my weight from foot to foot, turning my toes inward and outward as I bounce a little on my heels.

The receptionist grabs hold of my trembling hand and leads me away from Claire into a very spacious office with plants on pedestals near the obscenely large glass windows. Other than the green from the plants, the rest of the color scheme is strictly white, charcoal gray, and blue. We turn to go down a long hallway. On the door, the name Dominic Crawford appears with the words Chief Executive Officer scripted underneath in smaller capital letters. Two knocks indicating our arrival are all that is necessary for the door to be opened by a tall, smiling man in his upper twenties with short brown hair and blue eyes. Hot damn. His charm is plastered all over his pearly-white grin. His laid-back style of wearing black jeans and a white button-down dress shirt throws off the whole boss feel. I am not exactly sure what I was expecting but someone this level of attractive was not it.

“Ladies, if you would be so kind as to excuse me for a minute, I’m just finishing up with a meeting. My apologies.”

His eyes dance to meet mine as his words echo in my ears. I can’t tell if he just winked at me or if my excessive need to blink created an illusion.

Holy hell! What am I getting myself into?

The receptionist leads me back down the hall and we make small talk about the weather, the start of my semester, and Hollywood scandals.

We are almost to the waiting area when the sound of Dominic’s office door flinging open pulls my attention back toward a tall, strikingly beautiful man. It is Mystery Man. I stare at his rumpled brown hair and crystal-blue eyes. His attire is slightly above business casual, with charcoal slacks and a light gray dress shirt. I stand like a statue as his eyes float over me like he is seeing me for the first time. Does he even recognize me from the other night? I have no makeup on and my hair is wild. There's not much to look at but yet that is what he is doing. And unapologetically I might add. His appraisal makes me feel violated—like there is nothing I can do to stop it. I am wired with nerves.

He gives a nod in our direction. The receptionist says something softly to him. My mouth gapes and I quickly shut it, watching his retreating form exit down the corridor. So moody.

Although his escape takes seconds, his haunting presence lingers in the hallway long after his departure. The charge of the air crackles and sizzles with the energy that he exudes, making my nerve endings stand to salute the tower of a man who didn't have the time to address me with a single word.

What in the hell just happened?

We shared a moment at the pool and at the bar just two days ago. And today, it is as if I am invisible, as if I fabricated the whole thing.

"Ladies. Come," Dominic urges from his office, standing behind his huge desk.

I fidget with my dress and walk toward the opened door. Once inside, I marvel at the size of the office. Like outside in the main sitting area, large floor-to-ceiling windows outline the back of the room. Gray insulated drapes adorn the windows, most likely controlled by a remote control.

The fabric looks rich, and I resist the urge to walk over and touch them. The polished white tiled floor and spiraling metal artwork make the room feel comfortable with a homey atmosphere.

"You must be Angela McFee." The smile helps me relax my neck for the first time, realizing that all of my tension is being secured by the muscles there. "Claire raves about you."

I force a small smile as I reach out to shake his hand. Mine gets lost in his big grasp. I watch as he discreetly motions toward the receptionist. The door closes with a click. We are alone.

"Sit. Please." Dominic points to an upholstered office chair in front of his desk. "Angela, I—"

"Angie," I correct, interrupting his sentence. "Please. Sorry, sir, I mean Mr. Crawford."

His laugh is nearly contagious, though I remain pensive and quiet. "Angie," he tests the sound on his tongue. I am mortified that I made the unnecessary correction. "I like you."

Um, okay. That's a good thing, I suppose.

"What brings you here today?"

"I need a job. Claire suggested that I try this out. I was at the mixer event." I rummage quickly through my bag, pulling out the folded copy of the NDA. I place it on his desk. "I signed the NDA."

Dominic leans back in his chair, never moving his eyes off me. "Here at Entice Escort Agency, we try to fulfill every type of man's needs. And I have a good feeling that you are just what the agency is missing."

My face warms, and my hands fidget with the lace on

my cotton countryesque dress. My eyes move everywhere but to Dominic's. If I don't look at him directly, maybe he can't see me.

He clears his throat, bringing me back to the present. "Of course, the needs are in a platonic manner. You know, like renting a friend." He waves his hand in the air in gesture to his comment. "Ultimately, we are an escort service, and our business model is to cater to the most exclusive clientele in the Portland area. I see that Claire informed you to show up natural and that we will doll you up for the photo shoot."

Whoa, slow down, please!

"Assuming that you would like to be a part of the agency, we need to build an online profile for you that our customers can explore. Men are visual by nature." He gives a sheepish grin, while opening a drawer in his desk to pull out a file folder. Opening it, he scans the document inside. "I see here that you got a nice initial response from the mixer."

I shift in my seat. What does he have, a dossier started on me already? They don't waste time here, that's for sure.

He closes the folder, cupping his hands on the smooth surface of his desk. "I have already received requests for you via email."

"Oh." I do not even recognize my own voice.

"There are rules in the club, Angie, for all members. All of our male clients have been given a thorough background check, subjected to a physical done by a prestigious health professional, and have no documented criminal records. Mandatory health checks are done every three months to ensure overall well-being."

I relax my shoulders a bit at Dominic's comforting words and try to quell the fear that Tracy's words brought about potential coercion.

"The safety of our girls is our first priority." Dominic analyzes my face for a moment before continuing. "Here is the initial consent form." He hands me a file folder off the corner of his desk. I place it in my lap. "Of course, there's the assumption that the doctor's report will show that you are healthy."

Hold up, this is the part I do not understand. "If I'm not having any physical relations with these clients, why would it matter if I'm healthy or not?"

"Well, Angie. As you meet some of the men, you will learn that they are nauseatingly wealthy. I understand that we haven't talked about salary yet for employment. Just know that you will be well compensated for your services—platonic as they are."

That does not answer the question!

His hand slices back and forth through the air. "We can't keep you from making free will decisions after duty hours," Dominic clarifies, a hint of mischievousness present in his dancing eyes. "As a precautionary measure, we just ensure all clients that we have at least attempted to verify legal age, do a background check, as well as monitor for any major health concerns." He takes a sip of his coffee from his mug on his desk, showing me a glimpse of a large gold ring he wears on his middle finger of his right hand. "Angie, I know you are a bit skeptical of this process." He straightens his ring to face in the correct direction.

Damn straight.

I swallow uncomfortably, trying to shake the nervousness down into the pit of my stomach. Is this high-class prostitution? What am I getting myself into?

"Don't you have to interview me first?" I ask stupidly.

He gives me an unreadable stare. "I am. Right now."

I make a silent oh, trying to figure out what exactly is being done to gain insight on whether or not I am the right fit for the job. For such an exclusive entertainment business, surely I would be asked something of importance.

"I can tell you are nervous, and I don't want to rush you into signing anything today." Dominic rubs his hands together before placing his right one under his chin and rests his head into the palm. "I know this is breaking company code, but with you I need to be a little risky." Leaning over his desk, he hands me a folder. "How about you take the contract home with you and read over it tonight. We can reschedule your appointment for some time next week if that suits you."

"Yeah, er…yes. Thank you." I slouch a bit and then get up from the chair, tucking the folder and my purse under my arm.

"Miss McFee?"

"Hmm?"

"Can you just please keep that file in a safe spot? Although this organization is completely legal, we use discretion in regard to our high rollers. As you probably could already tell, there is a referral-only invite for girls. Keep everything that you know private, otherwise you will be in violation of the NDA you already signed."

"Will do," I say eagerly and walk quickly toward the door I arrived in. "Thank you," I call back politely over my shoulder.

I make my way down the hall and into the big office space where I see Claire lounging on a plush white sofa. As I shorten the distance between us, I can see she is not alone. Mystery Man is there—sitting adjacent to her on a matching armchair. His body posture tells me that he is tense. Both of his hands are on his thighs, shoulders elevated. Neither notice that I am now a few yards away from them.

He looks so different compared to the night at the mixer. There he looked tired, yet relaxed. Carefree. Now he looks angry. Standoffish. He could be bipolar.

"Again, none of your business," Claire snarls. "You're making a big deal out of this for no reason. And it's not about the money!" I rarely have witnessed her being this upset. The last time was when there was a recall on organic spinach, due to an e-coli outbreak. I cringe remembering that incident a few months ago, during the heat of summer. No one pisses with Claire's health food. Not even the whole farm industry. And definitely not the FDA.

"Oh, I think it is my business." The iciness to his voice sends chills up my spine. He rises out of his chair and creates the blanketing tower effect, prepared to not back down.

What is his problem?

I do not know whether to hide behind the spider plants or walk the other way. I strive not to put myself in confrontational situations. Kind of a life goal I have.

"Oh, love, there you are." Claire's eyes warm. Mystery Man pivots and stares at me blankly.

There's something very compelling—besides his piss-pot attitude—about him.

"Do I know you?" I ask sarcastically.

"Excuse me?" he asks coldly. His eyes trail down my uncovered legs. Instantly, I feel vulnerable. Exposed. I hate men who make me feel this way. He is basically checking all of the boxes of someone I do not want to be around.

His hair is longer than I remember. His attitude is more aggressive. He is definitely not the playful gum thief that I remember from just forty-eight hours ago.

"Sorry," I cough. "I just feel like I know you."

"Few people do," he answers impassively.

Claire's eyes dart back and forth between us. "Wait, you know each other?"

I answer "yes?" as he answers "no."

He gives a smile that skims the surface. Is he playing games with me?

I rock on my heels, feeling powerfully shy all of a sudden. "I'm ready to go home," I state quietly, sparing a glance at Tall-Dark-and-Dangerous. He graces me with another once-over, lingering this time on my lips. His eyes change ever so slightly, but I can't figure out if it is a good or bad thing. I shift my weight and lean into my hip, trying to get a read on this enigma of a man. His pained expression pulls at my resolve, plucking away the one ounce of confidence I mustered up specifically for this interview. Funny thing is, I didn't need any of it for the actual meeting to join the agency. Instead, I stand here before a piercing set of blue eyes, wanting to crumple to the floor in a heap.

"What about the profile?" Claire asks, concern and a hint of alarm present in her voice.

From the corner of my eye, I see a faint smile pull at his lips. Does he think I am not good enough for the database of girls? How dare he! He probably thinks I just got rejected!

"Not today." I flash the file folder to her. "I can make my mind up this week. Let's go," I push.

"That's against protocol," he mumbles under his breath as he saunters back toward Dominic's office, leaving us both without another word. The slam of the door resonates in the waiting area, causing chills to run down my spine.

"Um, what was that?"

"I have no idea," she responds, holding her hands over her head in confusion. "His reputation is apparently spot-on. Who knew?"

"Who is he?"

"That, my friend, is the elusive Graham Hoffman."

5

As soon as the doors close on Claire's Nissan Maxima, I turn to her in a hurry. "How do you know that man?" I ask. "What did you say his name was? Graham?"

"How do *you* know him?" she counters, while starting the ignition. She puts the car in reverse and backs out of the parking spot—nearly hitting the parked car behind her.

"Use your mirrors, woman!"

"Which ones?"

"Any of them!"

"No, they are distracting."

My eyes snap over to look at her. Is she for real? "Remind me why I let you drive?"

"Because you know I'm the way better driver. Now quit changing the subject and answer the question."

"He's the mystery man I met outside at the mansion. He was a lot friendlier that night, though. Tonight, he acted like he didn't even know me."

"That man is trouble, Angie. Trouble."

"He practically told me the same thing," I admit.

"Then listen. I don't know him well. But I've heard about him from some of the other girls in the agency. You do not need that type of drama in your life. And drama follows that man."

"Is he connected with anything Tracy was saying?"

"No, that girl just likes to rile everyone up for no reason other than she is bored. It's as if she walks around acting a fool in case someone is scouting out contestants for the latest reality show."

"Well, I don't need to worry about him, right? It is the man that chooses which girls to date from the database, not the other way around. And if tonight was any indication, I'm pretty sure Graham will be avoiding me like the plague."

"Maybe it's better that way," she says with a shrug.

"Yeah," I agree. It probably is better that way. I really do not need drama in my life right now. I need to focus. But what I really need is a reason to write.

"That was my first time coming face-to-face with him," Claire admits. "I have only heard about him. And I would have remembered his smug face at the mixer events. He mustn't typically go to them."

"Well, it's as if I met a completely different person tonight."

"Let's put this behind us and enjoy the rest of our evening," Claire suggests. "It's Monday night after all."

She parks the car in front of our townhouse, and we both hop out. The air feels considerably colder. I look up at the night sky and see nothing but hazy gray. I miss being away from all of the light pollution. I miss the stars.

Claire opens the door, and we make our way upstairs. Relieved to be home, I change into more comfortable clothes and freshen up.

At 7:30 p.m., the doorbell rings. I run downstairs and open the door to find Blake standing on the platform with a paper bag in hand. We haven't seen each other since last semester, as most students go home instead of continuing to work like Claire and I have always done.

"The party has arrived!" he announces, enveloping me into his signature bear hug. I show him into the kitchen area where the food trays are being set up. He slips past me and unloads all the makings for cocktails onto the counter.

"Looking regal in the gray sweats, Angie. I'm a fan."

I ruffle his black, professionally dyed hair, earning an exaggerated sigh. If only I was his type. What a catch! But, like most too-good-looking men, he bats for the other team. Most of the campus's broad squad have tried to turn him, as if it is an elective class.

Claire joins us in the kitchen just as the doorbell rings again. Pattering across the hardwood, I open the door, allowing Zander and Resa inside.

"We come bearing gifts!" Resa holds up a container of bruschetta and a loaf of pre-sliced Italian bread. Behind her, Zander dips his head in greeting and raises a six-pack of Sierra Nevadas. His hand behind his back moves and reveals a bag of limited-edition flavored Skittles.

"Contraband!" I squeal like a hyper teen, but quickly cover my mouth, making my giggles sound demonic. "You show Claire and I'll kick your ass!" I whisper-yell.

"You owe me."

I move to the side to let them through the door, cradling the bag of Skittles to my chest.

"So glad you two could make it! We have just fifteen minutes until the drama starts!"

Zander glances around the living room; not much has changed since he was last here back in May. "Let me see your laptop, Ang," he replies casually. "I'm sure the ad gave you absolutely no choice but to click on the words 'click here to claim your prize.'" His even monotone is perfectly implemented with just the right timbre to be laughable. Zander is one of those people that you can't help but feel good when you're around him.

"Oh, come on!" I slap his arm. "I know better than to click on things. Give me some credit."

Claire bursts through the living room, causing us to stop our teasing. "Show's about to start! Everyone sit." She turns on the flat-screen television, which was a gift from the ex-boyfriend. We often refer to it as collateral for fucking up.

Blake brings in a tray of fruity drinks, setting it down on the coffee table for us all to enjoy. The melon, strawberry, and pineapple garnish are details I definitely would have overlooked in the preparation.

Beside Zander's feet, I slump down on the floor as he rests above me.

"Sit here instead," he says, attempting to get up.

"No, it's fine. I'm comfy here," I say with a smile.

He finds my laptop on the end table and gets to work trying to decide whether I have a virus or not. Discreetly, he sneaks me a small handful of candies from the hidden bag that is stuck between the armrest and seat cushion.

The show starts, as we all settle into our Monday night

ritual. It feels good to be back in a routine after the unpredictable day I've had. There's something calming about hanging around people who can make you smile.

Once the show ends, everyone leaves. I put the last dish away, wipe the counters, and discard the Clorox wipe. The entire island is clean and back to its happy state. I make my way up to my bedroom. I need to sleep to be ready for my nine o'clock class. But I catch sight of the file on my bed.

Just read it.

I head into the bathroom and do the routine—wash face, tame hair, and brush teeth. There's a joy to lounging around in sweats on a chilly night. Back in the bedroom, I flop down on the full-sized mattress and pull the quilt up to my chest.

My phone buzzes, causing me to jump. I unplug it from the charger and check to see the number is one I do not recognize. Hmm.

Unknown: Thinking about our meeting today. Would love for you to join the agency. No pressure. :) Dominic

I smile at the message and save his contact information into my phone. I close my eyes and quiet my brain, squeezing the unopened file to my chest. I visualize what working for the agency might entail, including the whole dynamic of having such an attractive boss.

From everything that Claire had expressed on the ride to and from the city, the money is good. The clientele seem to just want the arm candy. The hours are flexible.

Making slightly over minimum wage at the bakery for

the past three years didn't keep me from falling into debt. My priority is to find a job. However, if my job involves spreading my legs to the highest bidder, then I am not interested. I would rather have collectors come knocking at my door than to have to submit myself to a lifestyle where money can buy everything.

I am not for sale.

I wake with a start. Sweat beads on my forehead as my breath chants in a shaky rhythm. My throat is sore, and I wonder if I screamed the house down.

Again.

My shoulder throbs.

I need to do my stretches again.

I need to go back to the doctor.

The lamp is still on and the clock reads 2:36 a.m. I must have dozed off. I press my palms into my eyelids and rub. The flashes are becoming more frequent. They feel more real and less like a figment of my imagination. I glance around the room, trying to catch my mind up with reality.

I reach into my nightstand and pull out the tiny prescription bottle that holds the relief for my pain.

There are eight left.

I pop open the lid.

My thumb and index finger massage and rotate the little round disk, marveling at the control at which something so tiny can produce. Every nerve ending begs for it. Every pore salivates for it.

Need.

Want.

Desire.

I swallow down the urge to give in and count this exact moment as a mini-accomplishment, putting the pill back into its holder for the inevitable usage later. I need to use them wisely and save them for when my shoulder pain is unbearable.

I roll out of bed and grab the laptop. I log on and double-click on the search engine and type "Graham Hoffman" into Google. I need to know more. The first five results show articles about his success in business. I click the second link and it takes me to *The Headliner* database. I find an article dated back from a decade ago. Skimming through the vast material, I discover that Graham has always been a high achiever—even during college.

Wow. He was very ambitious for being so young.

The next set of articles highlight his growing business adventures. A dabbler in real estate. An acquirer of all things shiny—including a small jewelry company called Jealousy.

None of the articles show a photo of him, except for one.

I do an image search but am hard pressed to find another photo where Graham isn't wearing sunglasses or a black ball cap.

Hmm…He looks quite sexy when trying to conceal himself.

By Thursday, I can no longer avoid the file. It's night by the time I gather enough guts to open the folder. With a mug of hot chocolate in hand, I lay back on stacked pillows on my bed and focus on the task. The first page of the stapled packet contains basic information about what Entice is about—nothing that hasn't already been shared. Then there is the second page.

1. **Confidentiality:** Employees are required to sign a confidentiality statement prior to employment and again every six months thereafter. Discussion of hourly rates is prohibited.
2. **Exclusivity:** Employees are discouraged from being involved in a romantic public relationship with any person(s) when the contract is binding.
3. **Bidding:** Clients will have opportunities to bid (and outbid) on available employees via the password protected online profile system or through mixer events.
4. **Appearance:** Clients can put in requests on hair, makeup, and wardrobe. Clients score escorts using a rating system.
5. **Availability:** Employees are to be available for at least twenty hours per month or risk termination.
6. **Salary:** Employees will be guaranteed no less than $200 per hour, for a minimum of two hours. A 35% cut ensures the upkeep of the profile, safety measures, and other amenities. Ten percent will be held in escrow.

7. **Benefits:** Employees have access to two different types of health and wellness packages designated through the HR Department.
8. **Bonus:** A one-time bonus of $5000 will be awarded to all new employees. A bonus of $1000 will be awarded for the recruitment of each new member after three months.

Holy hell. I place my mug on the nightstand and exhale. I rest the file on my quilt and try to absorb the information I just read. I don't even know what overwhelms me more—the money I could earn or the hoops I have to jump through to earn it. Two hundred dollars an hour? Wow. Five thousand dollars to improve my appearance? This is out of my league. Bidding wars?

Yeah, like that will happen.

6

I wait almost a week and channel my energy into my classwork before deciding to go back to the Entice office. Alone. The task of searching for other jobs has resulted in my continued unemployed status. Every part-time position has been filled with the influx of students moving back to the area. If the bakery had closed a month before it did, I would have had a chance to find something that did not shake my moral compass as much. It's already the middle of September, and before I know it, October rent will be due. The feeling of desperation feeds into my bad decision-making behavior.

Examining my closet, I settle for the simple gray knee-length sweater dress. When I purchased the dress, I decided to embellish the sleeves with thin white lace to give it more flare. The downside of living in the Pacific Northwest is the dreary weather in the fall. In the floor-length mirror, I reposition the V-neck of the dress and push the sleeves in place at just below my elbows. Kneeling beside my bed, I pull the plastic bin out and rummage through my collection of socks. I select a pair of black ones with little pink hearts on the sides. I slide them on and then conceal them with the zip of my black knee-high boots.

The townhouse is sans Claire. Her sneakers missing from the shoe rack give away her location. I take my pea coat from the hook, grab my purse, and lock up the place. The morning sun casts beautiful warmth to the trees and cars in the lot. I hop into my Honda Civic and back out.

It is an easy drive to the downtown office. I follow the same route that Claire did the first time she showed me the building. I park in the same lot. I take the same elevator up to the eleventh floor. And I am greeted by the same professionally dressed receptionist.

She escorts me back to Dominic's office after first phoning him.

My mind is anxious thinking back to when I was here last and how I was treated by Graham Hoffman. While the man intrigues me, I do not have enough mental space to keep up with him and his changing moods.

Dominic is all smiles when I enter his office. I can't imagine him ever having a bad day. He dismisses the receptionist politely and gestures for me to sit. It is now that I notice he likes his jewelry beyond the gold ring on his right hand. He has a sleek watch and a gold chain that peeks out of the top of his black collared dress shirt. His clean-shaven face shows no sign of razor burn. His skin is flawless.

"Angie?" he interrupts my thoughts.

"Hmm?" I cough, straightening my posture in my seat. "I'm sorry."

He purses his lips and studies me carefully. "I was just

saying that I'm glad you're back. The wait was killing me. Up until a day ago, I thought I scared you off."

"Thank you, Mr. Crawford. I—"

"Dominic," he corrects abruptly, stopping me midsentence. His smile warms his sudden knee-jerk reaction. "Please," his voice softens, "call me Dominic."

"Okay. I, ah, signed the papers." I hand him the file folder. "Except for the actual contract."

"Good. You have to get the physical done first for it to be valid."

Ugh. The physical…I forgot about that.

"Would you like to cash in on the benefit of the agency providing you with a doctor? It would cut down on the wait time drastically."

"Please." I clear the building panic out of my throat. "Um, Dominic?"

His eyes look at me expectantly.

I swallow hard and try to shove down the panic that rises. "Can I request a female doctor?"

His eyes squint ever so slightly, and the pulsing vein in his neck seems to twitch. "Of course." His gentle tone hypnotizes the butterflies in my stomach into a slumber.

I watch as he picks up his desk phone and hits one button. "Call downstairs and set up an appointment," he instructs with authority. "No."

I shift in my seat, further wrinkling the fabric of my dress.

"Does it matter?" Dominic responds in a clipped tone. "Well, then page Dr. Lambert. Pay for the on-call fee." He glances up at me with reassuring eyes and then continues. "Yes, of course. Thanks."

Dominic cradles the phone against his neck. "She has me on hold," he whispers.

I nod and cross and then uncross my ankles, unsure if I am to make small talk or sit quietly until the person is back on the line. I pick at my fingernails.

"Perfect," he states into the phone and then puts it on the receiver. "Done. You have an appointment today in thirty minutes. The office is on the third floor of this building."

Wow. That is fast. I find it a little weird that the doctor's office would be in the same building, but I guess big companies can have lawyers and such on retainer. So, I suppose it isn't that far-fetched.

"We have our shit together here." His eyes twinkle, and a smirk lingers at the curl of his lips. He read my thoughts.

I laugh—probably awkwardly. I can't tell.

"Okay. So, let's assume you are perfectly healthy…"

Safe assumption. If he knew me.

He takes a sip of his coffee. Then he pulls out a laptop from one of his drawers and sets it up on the center of the desk. "Let's start the profile now. You on board?"

I cross my legs at my knees. "Okay."

"What name do you want to use?"

"Umm." Do I need an alias? "Angie, I guess." I watch Dominic type, not sure why a secretary or personal assistant is not in the works for such a seemingly lucrative business. Surely they have the money to hire extra help.

"Okay to use your legal last name?"

I hesitate a second and still my fidgeting leg—a nervous habit I can't seem to break.

"The site is password protected, and members have to pay an initial entrance fee to even be part of the agency.

They, of course, have the routine background check done. All financial information done through payroll is encrypted using secure measures." Dominic focuses on me for multiple seconds, looking over the open laptop.

"Sure, McFee."

"Angie McFee. It does have a nice ring to it."

Um, thanks?

"Age?"

"Twenty-three."

"Birthday?"

"June tenth."

"Height?"

"Five feet, five inches."

"Eye color?"

"Hazel, I guess. There's green in them too."

Dominic shows his perfect teeth and types a few things into the computer. "Okay, got it. Next, describe your hair."

"Medium brown, mid-back length, naturally wavy."

"Weight?"

"About one forty-five." On a good day. On a bad day binge, well…add five?

"Bra size?"

Seriously? How can he even ask this with such poise? He doesn't even blush. But then again, guys don't blush, do they? I watch open-mouthed as his eyes move to the screen, and he clicks the mouse button. His attention cuts back to me, staring into my eyes for my answer. At least he has the decency to linger there.

"34 C."

He nods knowingly and glances at the screen, without typing anything additional.

How mortifying!

A feeling of being exposed makes me jerk my eyes down to make sure the V of my dress is in place. Strangely enough, Dominic doesn't seem the slightest bit fazed.

"Are you a student? Have a second job?" And just like that the topic of my breasts is done.

"Student, yes. No second job," I reply.

"Major?" he follows up.

"English." Because saying investigative journalism is not something I should be broadcasting online. If I plan to use the agency in my future work, it's best I do not tip anyone—especially my classy pimp boss—off with my secret agenda.

He stares directly at me but blindly types way more letters than the word "English" has.

"Just English?" he presses.

"Pretty much. With a minor in creative writing," I shrug.

"Nice. Our clientele request girls who are intelligent."

I smile, but I know the wattage doesn't even come close to Dominic's.

"Hobbies? Things you do for fun? Passions?"

I can't remember the last time someone has ever asked me such a question. I suppose I had to state something of the sort in my college entrance essay. "I like to bake. And I sew. I'm passionate about music." I used to like to sing. Dominic doesn't miss a beat typing. He's fast. "Travel. Although, I don't get to do it as much as I would like." I'm not sure the last part is necessary. Perhaps I am clarifying it to myself as to not delude my mind—or his—into thinking that I am a globetrotter or something. I wouldn't want some client to expect something that I am not.

"Do you have a boyfriend right now?"

I can't contain my huff. "No."

His eyes show approval, crinkling and returning to normal. "Good. If you did that could be a problem."

Nope, very single. And very okay with that fact.

"No crazy exes, right?" he chuckles.

Dickhead Russell is not even worth me referring to as an ex. He was a blip. A mistake.

"Angie?"

"None that survived."

"Ha, nice. I like you, McFee," Dominic says, glancing at his watch. "Well, I think the next step of the process is waiting for you on the third floor. I'll walk you to the elevator."

Dominic gets up and moves around his desk. He reaches his hand out to me and pulls me up. The feel of his warmth causes my stomach to flip-flop. Oh, how I miss that feeling—even if ever so brief. He is definitely easy on the eyes. I sling my purse over my shoulder, trying to hide my girly unease.

I walk through the door first at Dominic's old-fashioned insistence. We walk side by side down the hallway, in the opposite direction of the reception area. We pass many offices. One plaque says Human Resources, others say Technology Division and Marketing. One room looks like a conference room, with privacy blinds on the windows. Through the blinds I can see a big table with about a dozen chairs around it. A meeting is in session with about half the chairs occupied—all men in tailored suits, except for one woman with pixie-length red hair, elegantly attired in a conservative dress. Shouldn't Dominic be attending?

We stop at the elevators at the end of the hallway. Dominic hits the button to retrieve the car. "Whenever you are done, have someone page me and I can come down and get you."

"Okay. Thank you." I do not know how to address him. Calling him by his first name to his face still seems so unprofessional.

The elevator pings, and the doors open to reveal an empty car. I walk inside and push the button labeled with the three. I fill the idle time with thoughts of big fat needles and flashbacks to the time I was forced to watch the eighties horror movie *Hellraiser*. That pinhead guy was one scary dude. Surely I can handle a few needles and some blood tests today. I have been through much worse pain and trauma.

Upon the sound of the ping, I anxiously take a few steps forward, trying to force feed my mind with thoughts of puppies and rainbows.

Hell! "Ow…"

My hand flies to my forehead in Olympic speed, rubbing at the sore spot which will undoubtedly leave a noticeable mark. I blink and slowly move my eyes up the wall of muscle and settle on curious crystal-blue eyes. He is clad in gray dress pants and a baby-blue dress shirt, no tie. Hands steady my shaking body, my breathing erratic from the unexpectedness. And the blatant hotness that only a strong man can produce. Graham Hoffman.

"Shit, sorry," I mumble, my expletive slipping off my tongue in an instant. "I didn't mean to run into you."

"Don't be sorry. I'm not," he responds with a serious tone, rubbing his fingers along the lace hem of the sleeves of my dress. It is strangely intimate for him to touch something that I created with my own hands.

"You are Graham Hoffman." I sound stupid.

He chuckles. "Yes, Angela, I am."

The heat from his touch warms me from the inside out. His scent permeates my nostrils in the most delicious way. A mix of wood, spice, and citrus. Maybe even leather? I melt into the hold, intoxication taking over.

The sparkling blue eyes stare down at me—pierce into me—flaming the heat running through my veins. His hands move purposefully, yet are gentle. The touch is reassuring. And soft? He is a complete contradiction to the rough version of him I met last time.

"I need to get going. I have a thing to do. An appointment. Please excuse me," I say, trying to get around him. I am a blabbering mess. What is it about this man that damned my confidence to hell?

His stare penetrates my fuzzy thoughts. He looks less temperamental today. More carefree.

"I think you're confused," he says.

"Huh?"

"This is the seventh floor." A smirk of friendliness finally appears on his supple, soft-looking lips. I watch—stone-faced—as a hand leaves my arm to abruptly stop the elevator door from closing on my body. "I'm assuming that you are looking for a different floor? Perhaps the third?"

I narrow my eyes, trying to harness all of my concentration.

"How do you know?"

He chuckles. "Because you are looking a little pale. Afraid of needles?"

I nod and then quickly shake my head. I can't seem to get my mind caught up with the time zone.

He hunches down to tie his shoes, while stopping the door from closing a second time. Except, they are perfectly laced, symmetrical in form.

I stare in confusion as his hands right my half-empty purse. He slides a few of my stray folded bills inside, then starts to push loose items into a pile.

"Fuck," I moan almost incoherently, my mind reeling in a flutter. I didn't even realize that the thing exploded. How humiliating.

I swear I hear him utter something about my mouth, and I hear the whisper of the word "dirty." I shake my head at the picture-worthy scene at my feet.

Mints, hand sanitizer, a bottle of ibuprofen, a note pad, a pen, packages of gum, fabric boob tape, stain wipes, a hair clip, sewing kit, and my cell phone find refuge on the carpeting outside the confines of the elevator. I frantically scan the area again, half expecting to see a purple vibrator and some lube hanging out in the wreckage. Every other personal item seems to be here.

I slump down to my knees, ignoring the pulling of my sweater dress material. My trembling fingers race to grasp my tampon before Graham realizes what it is. It doesn't matter what new neon colors the factory puts on the wrapper, it still freaks out grown men and makes them thank God for being born with a pair of balls instead of a pair of ovaries.

The scent of coconut now permeates the small space from a travel size bottle of body spray that rolled along the edge of the elevator car.

"Here," he whispers softly, handing me a disheveled stack of semi-bent photographs.

I look up at Graham and watch as he unwraps one of my leftover chocolates. He places the Hershey's Kiss on his tongue and closes his mouth. The man keeps stealing my candy.

"Taking an impromptu snack break?"

"I got hungry." His words are simple but harbor more meaning than their face value.

He unwraps another one and rests it on my bottom lip. I open my mouth, and my teeth grab it and suck it inside. He holds out his palm, and I collect the little balls of foil.

I sigh over the smell of cocoa and sit back on my heels and let out what I had been containing for days. Laughter. A full-blown church-giggle fest. I laugh so hard I sound like I am crying like a demented clown. The imagery just makes me laugh even harder. This whole scene is too much for me to handle.

I can't look Graham in the eyes if I want to have any hope of stopping before the tears come. "I"—gasp—"am"—gasp—"sorry." It is all I can muster up. Tears wash my eyes at the sudden emotional break. "So, sorry," I exhale through giggles.

He joins me in the craziness and laughs. "Sorry? For what exactly?" Clearly he is amused.

I can feel his eyes bore into me, as I try to hide mine in a mop of hair. My teeth bite down on my tongue, bringing pain. A purposeful action to stop the freak show. "I don't know," I admit absently. "Everything? For hurting you with my"—I try to think of the body part—"head?"

He fake scoffs and continues to chuckle. From his weird

expression, I take it he doesn't laugh often. But I can't figure out any better way to respond than to just laugh at myself and ease the tension that I have been holding inside with a little humor.

When I am finally able to look up from my unraveling, his lips curl up, bewilderment evident. He hands me my pepper spray bottle and three fully wrapped chocolates. Two are raspberry filled, one is caramel filled.

"You might need it after the day is through," he suggests, standing with graceful fluidity. He leans down and pulls me swiftly to my feet. I yelp from the shock of his strength.

"The chocolates or the pepper spray?" I ask, watching him place items into my purse.

"Plan for the latter, hope for the former?"

Moving in closer, he plucks a sliver of paper from the sleeve of my sweater dress. A fortune cookie message. Where did that even come from? He hands me back the white scrap after examining the words—*Power is derived from knowing what you can and cannot live without.*

"Hmm," he says, tapping his jawline with the pad of his finger. "I'm not sure if I completely agree."

I mumble something that made sense only in my head.

Graham manages to look taller. He hands me back my restocked purse and guides me back into the confines of the elevator by pressing gently on the small of my back. His long finger presses the button to close the door and then presses the star for the lobby. The three is still illuminated from my previous failed attempt. He leans back against the wall, hands in his pockets, looking confident but relaxed.

The silence is unnerving.

We stand in opposite corners of the confined space. The speed of the elevator seems to take forever. It is as if the world around me knows that I am running out of oxygen if I don't get out of here fast enough and for some reason decides now is a great time to play a game.

"Goodbye, Angie. Please think this whole agency job through before you sign the contract. This line of work might not be suitable for you." His words come across as patronizing, rather than out of concern.

How dare he!

He dips his head down in a nod, moving his disheveled hair out of place. I have an urge to run my hands through it and yank it out at the same time.

I slip through the doors before they shut, turning to catch one more look of the man who very much is still a mystery to me.

I plop down on a sofa that sits at the end of the beverage station set up in the corner of the studio. I am spent. The men in charge of the superficial part of the day gather near the far end of the room. I am thrown a glance and a nod periodically, as if I'm being discussed but not actually part of the conversation. They appear happy, so I try not to obsess.

It took two hours to get my nails painted, my makeup applied, and my hair managed. Another hour and a half consisted of snapping photographs between changes in wardrobe and hairdos.

I kick off my borrowed platform heels and prop my feet

up on the sofa cushion. They ache from the infinite amount of pressure that they've endured. My head has a dull pulsing sensation right between my eyebrows. It is relentless. A couple of ibuprofens would taste so delicious right now. And a strawberry mojito to chase them down. Heaven.

"You look deep in thought," Dominic interrupts.

"Sorry." I slide my feet to the floor, blindly searching for the inside of the shoes. I am still technically on the job.

"No worries. Relax." He assesses my slouched posture with a smile. "Angie, the team is very impressed with you, as am I. You are phenomenal. We got some really great shots. You will be activated online as soon as the IT team arrives tomorrow morning."

"Cool," I nod, fighting back a yawn.

"Let's go sign the last of the paperwork, then you can change back into your original outfit and go home." Dominic reaches for my hand, as he did back in his office. He ushers me through a series of doors and into an elevator, and we head back up to the eleventh floor. "I had the physical results and the blood tests dropped off. You already signed the release for me to view those documents and verify that you meet the requirements of the agency."

I follow Dominic into his office, and he retrieves the contract from his desk. He spends several minutes reading through the papers, tapping his pen on the surface without ever glancing up. I stare at the backs of the documents, only able to see the reflection of black typed ink on the reverse side.

"You can sign here if you agree to be part of the agency. Your test results all check out, and you are completely healthy."

"Okay." I sign my name with blue ink and place the heavy pen back in its holder.

It is official. I am an escort.

"Oh, and Angie? You have your first date tomorrow night. I hope you are free."

"What? Really? Already?"

The air leaves my lungs in a rush, and I feel the light-headed wave of surprise cloud my vision. Of course I expect to have dates eventually, but not this soon. The ink is barely dry on the contract! Am I even ready? I swallow hard and feel the scratchiness of my throat contract with the dryness. No, I can't have an attack —not now.

I need a drink. And I need fresh air.

"With whom?" I ask, gripping the side of his desk for support.

"Me."

"Excuse me?" I cough-choke.

Dominic moves to my side as I try to catch my breath.

"We need to get you some water. Have you even had anything to eat or drink all day?" he admonishes.

I shake my head.

"Why did you not eat at the photoshoot? There was a whole buffet of food set up. Did my staff not allow you a break? Do I need to start firing people around here?"

So many questions! I need to breathe. *Breathe, Angie.*

"No! Don't fire anyone because of me," I blurt out, exasperation evident. Maybe this is what buyer's remorse feels like?

"Relax," he urges.

He rubs his hands calmingly down my back. It soothes

my freak-out without being creepy. As attractive as Dominic is, he gives off the brotherly feel to me.

"I'm starting to get self-conscious over the fact that you going on a business date with me makes you panic." I can tell he is joking.

Dominic moves back behind his desk. A chilled glass container of filtered water is placed in my hand with a look that could only mean, drink now. I take several small sips, willing my eyes to dry my pooling tears. I'm such a girl. And a traitor to my feminist views.

The easiest way to go against your feminist views is to go off and be an escort. I am the worst kind of hypocrite.

I glance at Dominic through my new fake eyelashes as he fishes out a small plastic bowl of fruit and a wedge of cheese from what appears to be a mini fridge. The fridge has the same finish as his desk. Very discreet and upscale.

"Here's a snack."

"Thanks."

I have a feeling that arguing is not the best strategy, especially on the first day of the job. I take the plastic fork that rests on the edge of the desk and poke a strawberry. I am hungry. The bustle of the day and distractions have caused me to not even register simple cues that my stomach and mind were sending me. The guys in the studio did offer me food in between scenes. But how could I eat with the bubbling anxiety of being center stage?

I shove grapes and pineapple into my mouth. I remember to chew. Everything tastes better than usual, as if the fruit was handpicked that day and diced to perfection.

"Now that we have your stomach taken care of…and the choking fits have stopped," Dominic says with a smile.

"Tomorrow night we'll go on a date." He pauses and looks at me closely.

It is not a question. Not one that warrants a yes or no. By signing the contract, I automatically make the date consensual. I assume Dominic's gaze is to see that I am not harvesting hives on my skin as an adverse reaction to the potential date. That will not make me a good escort, for sure.

Escort. Even in my head, I have a difficult time grasping what I just signed up for.

"I'll send a car for you at your place, say around seven?" Dominic's cool composure has little effect on mine. He oozes confidence, yet maintains the laid-back outward appearance.

I stare in disbelief. Is my boss really taking me out on a date?

Dominic shifts in his seat, rolls his gold ring around his finger, and stares straight into my made-up eyes. "Don't think I'm good for the money, darlin'?"

"No, um. That's not what I—"

"Angie, it is part of my job to make you feel comfortable and have a smooth transition. Something tells me that you have never done anything even remotely like this before. It will be a trial run. Like a test. I can go over the ropes with you and then set you free to fly."

"Okay. Seven. What should I wear?"

"The date will be business casual. We will just go and have dinner and a couple of drinks at a restaurant. A simple dress and heels should be fine. Speaking of which, I am going to go ahead and give you the gift card with the five-thousand-dollar allotted value. You can choose to spend this money as you wish and as often as you wish until it is used up. However, I advise you to save some for a potential picky client. Some men have specific needs and will expect you to follow through."

My eyes widen with a mix of apprehension and alarm. I take the gift card and copies of the signed documents and form a pile on my lap. I readjust in the seat and take a sip of the water, forcing it down in a gulp.

"Is Graham Hoffman a client?" *I need to install a filter!* My skin warms and I feel lightheaded.

Dominic looks at me thoughtfully. "You know Mr. Hoffman?"

I bite my lip. "I suppose you could say that."

He leans back in his chair and taps his long fingers on the marble. "He is part of Entice, yes."

"I ran into him today." Literally.

"He was here getting his file updated," Dominic explains. "All clients are required to update their health and personal information every three months."

The phone rings, stopping our conversation.

"Give me a minute, Angie."

I make a move to get up to leave, but he gestures with his hand for me to remain seated. He places the cordless phone on his shoulder and maintains eye contact with me.

"Dominic," he greets. "It's done. No." His once pleasant tone darkens. I guess he can be in a bad mood after all. "Yes, of course. Too late." Another pause. "You know that," he snaps. "Some things are just out of your control."

He is getting irritated. I want to leave. I really don't like confrontation—even if it isn't about me.

"I'm not being unreasonable. You are," he growls.

Dominic glances at his watch and then back up at me. "You know the deal. Why are we even having this conversation again? We can talk about this at another time. I have no doubt." He places the phone back on the charger and then props his elbows on his desk. "Do you have a smartphone?"

"No."

"Upgrade this week. The agency will reimburse you one hundred dollars per month for the service plan to ensure that it is made available for clients to contact you."

I nod. "Thank you."

Reaching into another drawer, Dominic pulls out a sealed envelope.

"A thousand dollars should cover the cost of the phone."

Cool. One less thing to pay for out of the list of bills.

"I'll text you tomorrow, Angie. I'll also bring you your bracelet that you are encouraged to wear during dates."

"Okay, sounds good."

"Looking forward to tomorrow."

I move to get up but am halted with Dominic's hand.

"I'm going to have security walk you out to your car."

"Oh, you don't need to do that. I'll be fine."

"It's late. And I'll have peace of mind knowing you got to your car safely. As for your outfit from the shoot, just keep it."

I watch as he presses a button on his phone. He must have someone on speed dial because it only takes a second for someone to answer. And within a minute, there is a knock at the door.

The guard's attire consists of black jeans and a gray long-sleeved T-shirt. He wears a Bluetooth device in his ear. Other than that, I wouldn't be able to tell that he is hired for building security. Although his face is young, the fortress of muscle screams "don't piss with me" just by the sternness of his demeanor.

The parking garage looks bare and a bit intimidating. Classic horror movies have scenes focused around such set designs. Lonely girl. Nighttime. Empty parking garage. Enter deranged serial killer. Part of me is happy Dominic insisted on a security guard escort. Irony.

"Thank you for walking me out."

"No problem, Miss McFee." He smiles genuinely as he shuts the door to my car.

I turn on my ignition and back out carefully.

At the corner of Madison and 2nd, my phone buzzes with an incoming text. Zander's surfing picture appears across my screen, his blond locks darkened by the Pacific.

Zander: Free on Friday at 10? Open-mic night @ Shack. Please tell me you can make it!? ;)

Zander: The fall schedule just got posted.

I press the accelerator as soon as the light changes. As the car coasts down the road, I see a bright red light illuminate on the dash. An oil light? I just had that changed.

I hit yet another red light and pluck my phone from the cup holder and reply to Zander.

Angie: I think I can make it. Looking forward. Any chance you are free in 2 Saturdays for a Cancer fundraiser thing?

Zander: Tell me more

Angie: Annual gala; expect some dancing and the serving of amazing food

I smile at Zander's confirmation.

When I arrive home, I pull into the numbered parking spot. It is eight fifteen, and lights are on. I trot up the cement stairs—feels good to be home.

"Angie!" Claire screams as I unlock the door.

She is on the phone but still makes a grand announcement of my entrance. It is a sure sign that she is looking for an excuse to hang up. I kick off my shoes and put my pea coat and purse on the hooks. I then move to the couch to curl up beside her. I pull down a fleece blanket from the top cushion and tuck it under my feet and legs.

"Listen, I told you I'm busy this weekend." I smile at her exaggerated sigh. "And next as well. Come to think of" —she pauses from being interrupted, pulling the phone from her ear so I can hear the pitiful sound of his voice—"I'm busy every weekend for the rest of the year."

My frown registers to Claire, earning me a wink and a hand squeeze in response.

"Busy next year too," she mutters. "We're done here."

I can hear the poor guy's desperate attempt to get her back. I feel guilty for being able to hear his pleas. If I wasn't so tired, I would move to avoid listening to the awkwardness and the loss of his manhood.

Claire rolls her eyes in my direction and gives me the "help" face. I know this look well because I am the one who taught it to her.

"Claire!" I yell, making her wince in pain. "I need you to come back to bed and finish what you started! Or I'll whip that—" I yell, stifling a giggle at her blank expression.

"Gotta go," she says abruptly, cutting me off by her increased volume. "Bye." She tosses her phone onto the end table. "Really? Out of all the things to say, you make me seem like I changed teams and am a pain slut?"

I burst out laughing. Every time she gives me the look, I laugh harder. "It worked, didn't it?"

"Still," she huffs. "That's exactly how rumors get started."

"Doubt he'll call back," I say with a shrug.

"No, instead he'll probably stop over, looking for a threesome," she groans. "And if he does, I'm sending him your way."

I laugh hard.

"So, is it official?" she asks, changing the subject.

"Yup. I signed everything tonight."

"Yay!" she exclaims, giving me a hug. "This is going to be so fun now that we can talk about it."

We head upstairs and shower in our own personal bathrooms. When Claire finishes, she knocks on my door in her pajamas. I am sprawled out across my bed with my sewing materials in my lap. Sometimes hand stitching some fabric is a great way to relax.

"I made you some homemade hot chocolate. Can I come in?"

"Yeah, of course." I poke the needle into the center to secure it and place it in my bin beside the bed. I accept the mug and make room in the bed for her to climb in.

I take a sip. I assume Claire made it with organic cocoa

and almond wish-it-was-from-the-cow milk. It is tolerable, but borderline too thick—and way too healthy for hot chocolate. This concoction is definitely not from the local coffee shop that has a version that will wipe out an entire day's calorie allowance. Not like I'm counting. Avoiding math is my hobby. Until my pants stop buttoning, I will keep doing what I am doing, because why fix something that isn't broken.

My sweet side still wants to sneak to my secret stash in the fridge and drop non-synthetic chocolate morsels into the mug, with a generous squirt of whipped cream. Cheers to empty calories—even if they are appearing only in my fantasy.

"So, talk to me," Claire starts.

"I ran into Graham today," I say. "Literally."

"Oh yeah? He seems to be popping up everywhere," she grumbles.

"Seems it. And there was a super embarrassing scene where my purse popped open and all sorts of junk fell out."

"But not his junk?" she asks, her face serious.

"No! But there were tampons and pepper spray rolling around. Oh, and I had fortune cookie slips sticking to my ass like labels of shame."

"And you had your battery operated devices buzzing about?"

"No. Those always stay home. Cannot risk being mugged."

She starts to laugh.

"But Graham helped me pick it all up."

"Probably the nicest thing he's done all year," she

mumbles. “Mark it on the calendar. May never happen again in this lifetime.”

Okay, what gives? “What is so bad about him again? Other than his mood swings?”

“I have just heard that he is a hit-em-and-quit-em type of person. And there’s a rumor…”

I give her a look.

“Yeah, yeah, I know. I’m not a big fan of rumors. But a good source—that is not Tracy—said that he started dating one of the agency girls and then broke her heart. And then she left and supposedly had to go to a facility. To get over him.”

“Ugh, that sounds horrible,” I say. “Maybe it was just that though. Rumors.”

“Maybe,” she says absently.

I take a sip of the imitation hot cocoa. “I Googled him.”

“Oh. My. Gosh.”

“What?”

“You like him, don’t you!”

“Intrigued, Claire. That’s it.”

“You lie worth shit. Your voice literally rises an octave higher when you lie.”

I slump down into my pillow. “You just think it does.”

“Find out anything interesting?” she pries.

I shrug. “Not really.”

We sit in silence for a bit and just focus on the warm drink. It’s nice to just relax on a weeknight.

Claire turns to me suddenly. “Back to biz. If he asked you on a date, would you go?”

I am not sure what I would do. Both Graham and Claire

warned me away. I do not need drama. "I'm not interested in having a Russell-like encore."

"Speaking of the d-bag, I saw him today at the coffee house looking as smarmy as ever."

"He hates coffee. Why would he be there?" I ask.

"No idea. But only two types of people hate coffee."

I laugh. "Babies and sociopaths."

"Fact."

7

The alarm clock blares its annoying siren at eight thirty. I roll out of bed to shut off the nine-dollar contraption. My vibrating phone starts next, setting off the second backup alarm, two minutes past the first one—right on cue. It is then that I notice a series of text messages. Wow. Three.

Claire: Feel free to borrow anything from my closet for your DATE.

I make the safe assumption that Claire is at the gym, basing my hypothesis on the fact that if she was home, she would just scream me the message upon any indication that I am up. The next message, I could have avoided reading.

Dad: This is dad. Tried your email and it said delivery failed. I need a little help with finances. Got myself in a jam.

I swallow hard at the words splayed across the screen of my cell. Figures. The man doesn't talk to me for months, except when he needs me to bail him out of trouble. I place the anger that is rising in another box in my brain to rest until I can deal with it in an appropriate manner.

Dominic's text fills my screen next.

Dominic: A car will be parked outside of your place at seven sharp. ;)

Does anyone sleep in around here? I stretch and head for the shower, leaving the texts hanging in the balance, not responding to any. I have about an hour until I have to leave for the only class of the day—Human Behavior. The two-hour class has a lab component as well, which involves experiments with human guinea pigs. I learned early on in college that the longer you attend, the better the professors get, as well as the classes. Being a senior—again—does have the whole scheduling first advantage.

I dry, brush, dress, and organize myself in under forty minutes. A quick breakfast of a fruit smoothie fits nicely into a travel cup. Claire would be proud—except for the powdered sugar supplement she never needs to know about. Sun beats in from the sliding glass doors leading out to a wooden deck, casting shadows on the walls. It's going to be a nice day.

Two stacks of mail rest on the island, one for me and one for Claire. She must have organized it sometime this morning. I weed through the fluff to find the signature white envelopes that could only be one thing—bills. There are several addressed to me. I cringe at the numbers and use a tiny calculator to figure the total. I owe $1,458, which needs to be paid within the next ten days. Can I make any more cuts and live comfortably?

Slurping my smoothie, I head out of the house, locking up.

The drive to campus is peaceful, as I allow for time to just think in the silence.

When my car settles into a commuter spot near Newton Hall, I am grateful that the oil light on the dash disappeared on its own volition. Maybe it's just a fluke, but at least it is one less thing to worry about for the day. I step out, grabbing my bag from the passenger side of the car, and make my way into the building.

My legs carry me into the room, and I find my usual seat in the middle of the auditorium. I don't know anyone in the class, and it seems late in the game to go out of my way to make study partners or friends. My workload this semester is light, with the exception of meeting Dr. Williams's top-notch standards. I just need to coast my way to finishing up my degree.

"Hey, Teach," a masculine voice calls out to me before class starts, causing me to turn in his direction. "Is this seat taken?"

I laugh under my breath because there isn't and hasn't been anyone in this row from the start. "It's all yours."

"I'm Bryce, by the way," he says smoothly, drawing in my attention.

I look into the friendly eyes of a fellow classmate who appears to be holding what looks like two iced caramel lattes—my love language. "Angie McFee." I eye Bryce's frat hoodie and try to think if I even remember him being in this class. Who knows, maybe he finally decided to show up for the first time. It's not like I'm very observant these days. Got too many other things on my mind.

"Before you think I have a date with diabetes, one of these is yours. Figured we could all use a little pick-me-up. Plus, I saw you drinking one last class. Just finally got the courage to make a move."

"Make a move?" I ask stupidly.

He hands me the beverage and an individually wrapped paper straw. As environmentally conscious as Portland is becoming, I wish the cardboard straws wouldn't dissolve midbeverage. I rate them a three out of five for design.

"Figure sweetening you up will make asking you to be my lab partner on Thursdays easier."

Adjacent to the room is the laboratory, where all the real fun is to be had.

"What do you say, Teach?"

The nickname is growing on me although I am not sure his motives for calling me by it. I think Bryce is just buttering me up by making me think I am a good teacher so I will share all of my notes with him.

I dispose of my straw wrapper into my bag, pop the straw in the bubble lid's opening, and take my first sip. I close my eyes over the taste; it is really delicious.

"We can be partners," I accept, sensing that getting rid of Bryce will be a challenge, so we might as well join forces. He will at least keep me entertained. "This drink is very good, by the way. I'll buy next time."

"Any chance you want to come to our frat's Welcome Back party in two weeks? Will be lots of fun."

Parties are not really my thing. The thing at the mansion

was enough stress with just trying to fit in. And parties thrown by the fraternities on campus are notorious for getting out of hand. "What night?" I ask, just to be polite.

"Saturday."

"I'm going to an annual Cancer fundraiser. Sorry."

"Sure, choose cancer over getting drunk and pregnant," he says with a fake scoff.

I give him an artificial look of disgust and relax back into my seat and wait for class to start. For once, I am early. Bryce pulls out the syllabus and starts leafing through it. My heart drops at the thought that I missed an important assignment. School has barely been in session for me to get very behind. I need to keep my focus.

"Bryce, we don't have an assignment due today, do we?"

"Shit, if we do, I didn't do it." He flips a page in the packet. "I'm looking to see when the sex chapter starts. That's the only reason I took this damn elective class in the first place."

I shoot him a look. "You know that there is this thing called porn, right?"

Bryce glares at me. "That stuff is unrealistic. I don't watch it."

"Rigggggght."

He gives me the most over-the-top smile. "I also took this class because the professor is hot. I have a weakness for pencil skirts."

"How about angry chicks in pencil skirts?"

"Cocktease!"

I slap Bryce on the arm to get him to quiet down. For two people who have just met, we seem to be hitting it off in the friend zone. Other classmates are starting to stare, making me feel awkward at the scene we seem to be making.

"Angie, you suck at being a feminist," he says, pointing to the button pin I have attached to the side of my tote bag that broadcasts my view. It is situated beside the other button that says "coffee whore" across the front in bubble letters.

"Yeah, pretty much," I agree with a shrug. "But being a feminist means I can be whatever the hell I want."

"Hell ya. Girl power! Run the world!" he chants obnoxiously while pumping his fist. He receives a few hoots from around the room, making me slither farther down into my seat. So much for keeping a low profile this semester.

Bryce is a catch for anyone who likes a slightly shorter, hilarious-as-hell, muscular man. What Bryce lacks in his five-foot-and-some-change height, he makes up for with personality.

"I just want—"

"Shhh!" Bryce hushes me. "Show some respect for my future wife." He gestures toward the front of the auditorium, as our professor makes her way to her podium.

Her red hair is pulled up in a bun, and her throat is wrapped in a decorative floral scarf. The students settle, and my time is now monopolized for the next two hours. At least I have a distraction from overthinking about tonight's date with Dominic.

Bryce leans into my shoulder and whispers, "Can't wait for this absurd scarf phase to pass."

I muffle my laughter.

It is going to be a long two hours.

I sip on a glass of vodka and orange juice per Claire's request as I finish the last-minute touches on my makeup. I don't know why my nerves are multiplying like rabid bunnies. Yes, it is a date—for lack of a better word—but it is with Dominic, the boss. The whole point of tonight is to help me relax.

"I think the vodka is making me more on edge."

"That just means you need to drink more."

"Um, no, let's not," I say, covering the top of my glass with my hand as Claire tries to pour more.

"This dress is smoking, Angie. Dominic might think twice about sharing you with the database."

I stare down at the dark blue, knee-length, cap-sleeved dress. I feel pretty as my eyes sparkle with silver undertones, showing off the green pigment in my eyes. Silver heels dress up my feet that are also freshly polished.

"It's not too much, is it?" I ask.

"Just the right amount. You look hot!"

My biggest fan. She is hopelessly biased, and I love her for it. "You think we will be going to the same place tonight? The city is very small."

"I have no idea where Ethan is taking me. I'm sure he has his regular venues." Her look turns serious as she thinks about the possibilities. "Watch it be some place really random. Like a strip club. Or pottery painting. Or axe throwing. Ew, I hope it's not one of those escape rooms."

Her giggling only causes me to reciprocate. A car door from below my window shuts, forcing my eyes to glance at the clock.

Eek! It's time.

I pull my curtains to the side to see a man with sandy-brown hair leaning against the door to the driver's side of the sleek black car.

"Wow, he drives a Mercedes-Benz CLA," Claire groans with approval, while pulling back the fabric more to sneak a peek.

"How can you even tell from here?" I ask dumbfounded.

"I know a sexy car when I see one. Driver's pretty hot too. If you go for the rugged, alpha-in-a-suit, strong-jawbone type."

He is dressed in a black suit with a black tie—very professional. His eyes scan the premises, doing a sweep of the area surrounding him. I'm sure he is trained under strict protocol. *We have our shit together here*, are the words spoken by Dominic that echo freshly in my ears. Maybe he is the security type.

"Whoa. He's one mighty fine specimen of a man!" Claire announces with a whistle. We are both kneeling on the window seat cushion, trying to remain concealed, although the moving drapes have to be some kind of tell. "He'd be worth my attention. Climb him like a stripper pole."

"Okay, I'm out," I interrupt her blatant ogling of the driver. I stand and straighten my hem.

"No, wait," she insists. "Here, take these." In my hand, she presses three wrapped Trojans—all in various colors and sizes. "Make sure if you use a safe word, it is anything but the word 'yes' or 'more.' And if you end up doing the sex, make sure you don't black out so you can remember it with details, just to tell me all about it later."

My eyes narrow at Claire's version of the "sex talk." This is her weird way of being nurturing, so I let it slide.

"I'm not going to sleep with my—correction, our—boss!"

"Take them anyway for the future. If you want to undress Venus, wrap up your penis."

"I don't have a penis."

"Yeah, you do," she declares. "It's just small."

"What?"

"You know we all start out with boy parts in the womb," she instructs.

"Thanks for the anatomy lesson." I mumble my fake gratitude. "You're the best." I humor her and place the contraceptives in my handbag, shaking my head at her comment.

"I know." Her stretching smile takes up half her face.

My three-inch heels clink down the stairs in unison with the frantic beat of my heart. My arms sprout goose bumps from my nerves. I wrap Claire's borrowed silver shawl around my arms, knowing full well that it will not suffice against the night's changing temperatures as winter is just a couple of months away. I open a spearmint Lifesaver and discard the plastic wrapper into my handbag. A nervous energy shivers through me; the anticipation of having my first agency date is messing with my head.

I step out into the cold air and turn to see Claire's wide eyes through the window above. I straighten my posture and take a deep breath, making my way down the concrete steps. I chomp down on the mint and make it dissolve. My hair tangles with the wind, and I resist the urge to pull it back into a ponytail.

The driver, who is now standing at full attention, greets me with a neutral expression. “Good evening, Miss McFee.”

“Hi. Nice evening, huh?”

His once confident stance turns a bit awkward as he fumbles to open the door behind him and maintain the conversation. “Yes, very nice.” I look at him expectantly, as he has a debate inside his head. He acts as if no one has ever made small talk with him before. “I’m Collins. I’ll be driving you tonight. Watch your head, Miss McFee.”

“Collins, please call me Angie,” I insist, as I duck my head into the backseat, finding comfort on the plush dark leather seats. My door is shut gently once my limbs are clear.

“You look beautiful. Stunning.”

The smooth, sultry voice dances in my ears. Warmth spreads from the tips of my toes, traveling up to ignite my cheeks.

I pivot in my seat, only to stare as my gaze meets his icy-blue crystalline pair.

“Graham,” I whisper.

“Angela.”

Heat rushes to the apex of my thighs as my name rolls off his lips. It seems to be a premeditated caress—strategically designed to throw me off my game.

“What’s going on?” My brain cannot keep up.

“Change of plans.”

Unexpectedly so. The date was arranged for Dominic, but now Graham is here in his place? My brain is having a hard time absorbing. “I don’t—”

Graham’s finger presses against my lips, and my heart stops, as well as my train of thought.

"I've been thinking about these lips since the elevator," he says breathily. "I can't seem to clear my head of thoughts of you. You probably have no clue how wound up you make me."

My heart picks up rhythm, and I feel dizzy with need. He makes me want things I know I shouldn't want. I need to focus. To not get swept away in the exciting world that is Graham Hoffman.

He gently pulls down on my bottom lip with his index finger. I exhale and fight the urge to give him a little bite.

"Tell me you want this," he insists. "Tell me I'm not making this all up in my head. Deluding myself."

He releases my lip, and my body mourns the loss of contact.

"I want this," I admit with a nod. "What this is, I'm not quite sure."

Graham's body moves closer to me as his hands cup the back of my head. I lean into him, and he presses his lips slowly against mine. His lips are warm. Soft. He is gentle and respectful. It is the complete opposite of how I would have predicted our first kiss to be. Our tongues brush against each other's, and I dig my fingers into his shoulders. I deepen the kiss. I don't know what has come over me. I am never this forward. But then again, I've never had a reason to be.

He pulls back for just a second. His eyes look into my soul as he studies me—what he's searching for I have no clue.

"So greedy." His words come out raspy.

A faint taste of cinnamon is on my tongue. I lick my lips, earning a wicked look from Graham. I want more.

I moan. “You taste like candy.”

“You taste like sin.”

Graham grabs my waist and pulls me onto his lap. The confined space in the backseat forces us even closer. I am losing myself. Our lips are like magnets. My hands pull at his hair. I grind my ass into his groin, trying to find the delicious friction that I desperately need.

BOOM.

Flashes of light fill the sky. I pull back from Graham’s lips.

CRACK.

My body trembles from the sound of thunder.

Rain pelts down onto the parked car. Collins opens the driver’s side door and rushes inside before he gets soaked. How much time has passed? It never even occurred to me that we hadn’t even moved yet.

I slip off Graham’s lap and instantly regret my moment of weakness. He adjusts his dress pants, and I can see the consequence of my lack of self-control.

“Angie?”

I retreat back into my shell. My safe cocoon. This was a mistake.

Something tells me that the longer I spend with Graham, the more we’ll repeat this mistake. He is dangerous to my willpower.

“Angie?” Graham repeats. “You can’t keep ignoring me.”

I can feel his eyes on me, but I refuse to look over. Instead, I watch the rain fall onto the ground, darkening the pavement, forming rippling puddles.

“What’s happening?” I ask. The sensation of the car

moving makes learning his answer all the more important, more urgent.

"Whatever do you mean?"

You know damn well what I mean. My attention snaps to Graham. He wears a modern black suit with a gray dress shirt. Everything about his look screams designer, one-of-a-kind, and expensive.

"I expected you to come in a Prius. And you brought this instead?" I ask, gesturing to the surroundings. I catch Collins's reflection in the rearview mirror, revealing a subtle smirk.

"Trying to emasculate me?"

I giggle loudly, covering my mouth with my fist to keep from pissing Graham off further. Good, he took it as I intended. There is something about this man that brings out a completely different side of me—one I am realizing I have partially buried over the years. Hanging around Graham is like introducing myself to parts of my personality that I have never met.

"You can fuck with me. But not the car, Miss McFee." His serious tone has my head doing loops as to whether or not I should take him at face value.

Fuck with you? Now that is an interesting thought. "Where is Dominic?" I ask, looking at Collins for an answer. My pressing inquisition of the taciturn man has Graham coming to his defense.

"Quit distracting my employee. Now, buckle your belt, or I'll do it for you."

It's not a request. The look he shoots my way tells me that our game playing is on pause for the moment. "So bossy." I snap the strap into place, while never losing focus of the confusing man adjacent to me. "Where is Dominic?"

"I heard you the first time."

"Then answer the damn question, or I'm out of here." My demanding tone surprises me enough to make the words sound semi-authentic and believable.

Nothing.

"Collins," I snap, "where's Dominic?"

"He isn't going to answer you," Graham growls. "And quit obsessing over another man. Your boss, might I add."

"So you would just take me somewhere against my will?"

He scoffs, a curve forming on his lips. His eyebrows scrunch into a V. "I would bet my life's worth that, when given the opportunity, you would consent to whatever I want to do. Your lips proved that fact."

"Pretty smug, aren't we, Mr. Hoffman? Hope your ego isn't compensating for other inadequate areas of your"—I look down his body, tapping a finger against my mouth—"life."

A smirk forms on his lips. "Everyone has a price." He swallows hard and lets his eyes trail down my body. "I'm not lacking anywhere, Miss McFee."

"I am not—" For sale. I want to say more, but the truth is this job is my ticket to financial stability.

Graham's left hand rests on the seat between us. He leans in to whisper in my ear, just enough to censor the words from Collins's ears. "You keep playing with fire, my little pyro," he rasps, "you are going to get burned."

I do a double take. I'm not his anything. He just called me a pyromaniac. How dare he! We barely know each other and now he is name-calling. My shock only fuels the flame burning brightly in his eyes. "Is this a warning?"

"Most definitely. Although, foreshadowing is probably the better description. Something tells me that you just can't help yourself."

"You drive me mad. Just tell me why you're here and Dominic isn't."

"He had to handle a family matter. So he called me to initiate you into the glamorous lifestyle of the escort business."

"Lucky you."

"I don't believe in luck," Graham answers, his tone serious.

I eye him suspiciously. "What do you believe in, then?"

"Taking chances where the benefits outweigh the risks, even if you fail."

"Life isn't always that logical."

"My life is."

My jaw clenches as I have nothing else to say. Graham has to rate as the most frustrating man I've ever met. I divert my attention through the tinted windows of the Mercedes-Benz, trying to distract myself with anything other than Graham Hoffman. The car is sexy, despite my earlier jab at his taste. I just will never give him that satisfaction of approval. I'm having too much fun playing the dangerous game of keeping him off-kilter, making him wonder.

We stop in front of a tall skyscraper in downtown. I don't even remember going over the river to get to this section of the city.

"Stay put," he orders.

I freeze as Graham exits the backseat in a fluid motion.

Collins hands him an oversized umbrella, and the two men talk in private as the rain pelts down around them. By the time their conversation ends, the rain is just a trickle.

Graham closes the umbrella and walks to my side of the car. He opens the door and leans into the doorframe, gazing at me for a moment before he reaches out a hand, waiting for mine. I stare at him blankly, weighing my options. My feet slide in and out of my shoes, fidgeting on the floor of the car. I can refuse to get out, or I can accept his hand and then bolt at the first sign of freedom.

I watch as a couple of raindrops fall from the sky and land on his forehead. I want to wipe them away. Nothing about tonight is how I envisioned. I definitely never expected Graham to be standing above me, waiting for me to make my next move.

"I'll explain once we are inside. Quit being so difficult," he says with exasperation, continuing to reach for me. "I'm sure you are toting a concealed weapon inside your purse." His head jerks to the side, motioning toward my silver handbag. "Feel free to use it on me if you think I'm being anything but a gentleman. Tonight is not the night to play."

I look up at Graham in confusion. "I don't own a gun."

"Good. But I was referring to the pepper spray," he says matter-of-factly.

My lips round into a silent O-shape. I do have it packed in my bag. Beside the condoms, no doubt. Smiling, I nod and take his right hand, which grasps me tightly, massaging circles into my palms. His left one flutters past my face and down into the seat near my behind. My eyes dart open wider, confused on what his digits are doing. I hear the release sound of the belt as it retracts.

Oh, that. I feel like an idiot, and not for the first time today.

After quick maneuvering of the strap and hand holding, I am pulled from the car and urged to the front door of the Parkhouse Plaza building. The structure is iconic and has been featured in several action movies. I have never had a reason to enter it before now. The damp autumn air bites at my flesh that peeks out of the shawl. I second-guess my choice of open-toed shoes for evening wear, although my nails look cute between the straps of the design. Graham wraps his arm around my upper arms, holding me close to the heat of his body. I shiver but plant my feet firmly to the ground as I study the tower in front of me.

The alluring structure harbors one of the most magazine-notable restaurants in the area—El Pastel—with top-of-the-line chefs from all over the world. The rest of the elite building shares space with luxurious offices and is topped off with ten floors of condominiums—most likely owned by the richest people in Portland. I stare in awe of the illuminated shrubs and bronze railing leading up to the full-glass doors that are guarded by a formally dressed doorman.

"Come."

The single word pulls me from my private show of observing the magnificence of such a display of architectural brilliance. I feel my blush warm my pale skin at my awestruck fascination.

"Mr. Hoffman. It is a pleasure to see you this evening."

The two men exchange a look that does not register to me as friendly or hostile. Graham stiffens beside me and then relaxes in an instant, as he ushers me through the open doors. The doorman's name rolls off his tongue without the reverence that seems to accompany my spoken name. Is he irritated about something? I start to theorize that Graham Hoffman has more high-maintenance tendencies than your average guy. I might need to consult Blake's expertise to get a read on this moody man. He does seem to know and understand his gender well.

The lobby is made of ivory and gray marble. In the center of the floor sits a round pool that has floating plants and underwater lights. A clear cylindrical column rests in the middle of the pool with water cascading down around the column. Every few minutes, color filters change in the column to light up the water that flows down in different hues. It is majestic and unlike anything I've ever seen.

To the right of the fountain, an area is designated for social gathering, with couches, chairs, and luxurious glass coffee tables with huge earthy stone masses forming the foundations. A group of people dressed in long gowns and tuxedos talk animatedly to each other. I stare down at my shorter blue dress that had an affordable designer label even though it came from a clearance rack at TJ Maxx. I am sure upon inspection any woman of wealth would be able to label me as a counterfeit within seconds.

"You look stunning." My chin is tilted up by two fingers. The sizzling crackle fills the air between us, and I can no longer divert my attention to anything else but his eyes. They captivate me and turn me into a melted puddle of goo. The words soothe my unease in an instant, igniting the slow burn between my thighs even more. Although exhaustingly frustrating, the sexual tension shared between the two of us is off the charts. I chalk it up to being deprived of attention for so long. Naturally, I would gravitate to confidence, mystery, and striking looks. It's a no-brainer.

"There's a theater that hosts concerts and shows each month," he says while making a gesture to the group of people who at first sight look overdressed. "Or perhaps there is a wedding tonight." I find that option only viable on a weekend. Nonetheless, I am thankful that I tried for more than just business casual—Dominic's suggestion—for attire this evening.

"Hungry?"

The simple question stirs the marinating desire deep in my belly. I look up through my lashes at the daunting tower of man. The Parkhouse Plaza has nothing on him. I teeter on one foot, tapping the other behind me as I try to collect my thoughts. I'm not hungry—at least not for a full-blown meal. The queasy unease of my stomach tells me that a heavy meal is not in my best interest.

"Not really," I say with a frown.

"How about you try?" He asks the question but does not wait for an answer. He guides my elbow with gentle pressure, coaxing me forward toward the other side of the fountain. Graham walks me past the concierge desk. As we go around a corner, we are in front of four elevators. A female worker presses the up arrow and eyes Graham pleasantly, earning a polite smile. She is dressed like a go-go dancer—except with slightly longer hems.

I wonder how many times Graham frequents this building. Perhaps he takes all his dates here. When I first met Claire, she was a serial dater and would sign up for the online match sites where she could screen the guys before meeting them. When I asked her how she kept track of outfits and such, she told me that she would have a specific first date outfit that she would wear for every first date she went on. Then she would have a second date outfit planned as well. However, only about two guys out of dozens ever got to see that ensemble. If Graham is practicing the same strategy, maybe El Pastel is his preference for every first date. The thought puts a nasty taste in my mouth, making me scowl at the sensation of the acid coming up my throat from my stomach. Jealousy? Is that what it is? But how? I don't even know him nor do I know his dating history. Plus, this is a fake date—one that was not even supposed to happen. Pretending this is anything more than a trial run will only confuse my brain even more.

The ping signals the arrival of the elevator car. Graham nudges me forth first and follows behind me, still with his hand on my elbow. He presses the button to the eighteenth floor. I marvel at the attention to detail, even in such a small space. Intricate designs are formed on the base of the car with tiny square tiles. Browns, whites, and green tones make up the color theme. The far back wall of the car is lit up with a rich blue formation of crystal translucent squares, leaving the other two walls with floor-to-ceiling mirrors. I try hard not to look at Graham's reflection, not allowing him to gain satisfaction that I want to sneak a peek. His ego does not need a massage. I feel his smirk without looking up. He knows something that I do not. I smooth out the layers of my dress in a nervous gesture; at least I have something to do with my restless hands.

The car stops short of the full journey, allowing a couple on board. They, too, head to the eighteenth floor. Déjà vu washes over me. The girl is a petite redhead with green eyes and a skinny frame. I have about four inches on her and feel like a curvy giant. The man is tall with medium-length black hair, styled with gel. His gray suit fills out around his gym body. He looks familiar.

"Hoffman."

I look up at Graham in response to the greeting. His eyes narrow into tiny slits as he regards the man with a nod of the chin upwards. "Tanner," he returns with venom dripping into a pile on the floor. Tanner's grin makes Graham stiffen at my side. I shift on my feet and attempt to remain indifferent to the unfriendly exchange.

The redhead gives me the once-over and smirks at my fidgeting form that earns a tighter grasp around my waist. Graham's fingers rub and smooth the fabric above my hipbone. His touch is proprietary, and in that instant I like it. Ironically, it is the rhythmic drawing of his fingers that causes the unease in my stomach to ignite, yet calm.

A bit possessive now, aren't we, Mr. Hoffman?

The man smiles at me and reaches a hand in my direction. I shuffle my handbag to my other hand and extend my right hand but quickly drop it at the sound of Graham's deep growl. His rigid stance cements me to the ground of the car, and I can feel the daggers shoot from over my head.

"Mark Tanner. It's a pleasure to see you again, Angie." I must have given him a confused look. "We met briefly at the last mixer," he clarifies.

"Oh, yes." I remember now.

"I'm happy to see that you're now part of the agency."

I mutter a timid "thanks."

Mark turns to Graham and gives him a sly smirk. "Glad

to see you back on the dating field again…you know, after—"

"Shut the hell up, Tanner," Graham snaps, stopping Mark's line of communication.

The ping of the elevator and the stopping of the car makes it easy to exhale and settle back into Graham's protective crook. I glance up at his face and see the tick of his jaw starting. He sends me a stern look that can only mean "not now, wench." My eyes dart to my shoes from the silent scolding.

Every cell in my body screams in revolt at this feeling of inferiority. What the hell am I doing here? Is this job worth the cost of my beliefs and values? I pride myself on being a warrior for women, and right now, I feel like the biggest traitor.

We exit the elevator after Mark and his date. Graham halts as soon as we clear the closing doors. I can instantly tell that he has no intention of getting close to Mark and his date.

"Hey, Hoffman?" Mark calls back over his shoulder, getting Graham's full attention once again. "Tell Penny I said hello. Oh, and Angie? I'll be seeing you around."

"Fucker," Graham spats as he stomps along the corridor. His expletive is wasted. Mark is already too far away to hear.

"What's going on between you two?" I ask as soon as I am sure that only he can hear. My curiosity wants to know more about Penny, but I decide to keep my mouth shut. Graham is not in any mood right now.

"Oh, just your everyday friendly corporate competition." He rubs his forehead and stares after Mark's retreating form. "It seems that the gauntlet has been thrown down tonight."

"Something tells me that the gauntlet was thrown down a while ago."

"You are very perceptive," Graham says, turning to me with eyes full of concern. His warm fingers run up and down my arms in a motion to soothe me, even though he is clearly the one who needs to relax. My skin prickles under the sensations of his touch. "Angie, can you please excuse me for a minute? I need to make a call. I would never do this if it wasn't time sensitive."

"Yeah, no problem. I'll just go sit over there," I suggest, pointing to a vintage wingback chair near the restrooms.

Graham nods and turns his back to me as he whips out his phone from his inner breast pocket and presses a couple of buttons. His left hand snakes around his neck, and his fingers assault his hair, grabbing angry fistfuls. On occasion, he glances over his shoulder as if to make sure I haven't disappeared. Several people exit the elevator, all nodding to Graham as if they are acquaintances. While I wait, I text Claire, even though I figure she is out on her first date with Ethan by now.

Angie: Hey. At Parkhouse Plaza with Graham! WTF? Dominic had to cancel. Fill you in later.

I delete some messages from my nearly full inbox and wait to see if Claire texts back her location or advice or a snarky comment.

"Handle it…taunting me…must be stopped…think of something…dammit. This is why I fucking pay you and five other people. Yes, you can give me counsel, but I am ultimately the one who gets to decide the action—even if we aren't in agreement."

I watch as Graham ends the call and starts another one.

"Guess who is back on the radar?" he asks the second mystery person. "Yeah, he saw her." There is a long pause. "No." Graham looks back at me and tries to smile. I reciprocate. "I couldn't go through with it."

I listen intently as his tone changes to even lower.

"I can't change the past, dammit. I know what—"

I strain my ear to make out more of Graham's conversation. He moves farther away when he can tell I am staring. Luckily the sound of an incoming text changes my focus.

Claire: There too! Some symphony thing. Not my jam. Meeting ex-wife. They have a kid together. Awkward! Meet up with you after for a drink? My treat!

I type out a quick "sure" and continue to channel my eavesdropping in Graham's direction. His pacing on the pristine floors causes my mind to play tricks, imagining a trough being created from his incessant pattern of digging. Something bad has him rattled and although I am curious, I am in no position to press him. I debate with myself on whether or not to text Dominic but decide against it—trying to highlight my flexibility as an asset. Maybe he is testing me. After all, he didn't even send me a warning text. I can prove to myself and to him that I can be easygoing.

Angie: Do you know much about Mark Tanner? He was at the mansion.

I wait for Claire to feed me information. She has a keen sixth sense when it comes to weeding out the bullshit and discovering the true character of a person. Her warning about Graham is not forgotten, and I have been on guard since getting in the car. Something tells me that Graham keeps his private life private—which ultimately leads to creative speculation.

Claire: Business mogul sexpot with shitload of dough. Hand in pharmaceutical sales? Gotta go, getting angry eyes.

I snap my flip phone shut and decide that I could use a freshen-up. I should not be surprised at the fanciness of the restroom. The floors are polished and shiny. The air is scented with a sweet vanilla fragrance. The individual toilet stalls are the size of my entire bathroom suite at home. After I finish and flush, I rinse my hands and take a look in the mirror. My cheeks are rosy. My eyes look rested and alive. Maybe all these rapid changes over the past week have done me some good. It is easy to fall into a comfortable rut and resist change.

When I exit, I see the same redheaded woman from the elevator and notice for the first time that she is wearing a gold identity bracelet. She is an agency girl. I say "hello" but am greeted with silence as she disappears into the restroom. I know she heard me.

I open my handbag and fish out my phone to distract me. I take a quick selfie even though the quality is grainy from the lack of pixels.

The air shifts in the room and warmth coats my skin. I

reach for my shawl and tug it around my exposed arms. I feel his presence before I hear his words.

"You should upgrade," he whispers against the back of my neck. His warm breath causes me to shiver. I resist the urge to lean back into him.

"Clothes, phones, or dates?" I retort, turning to look him in the eyes.

"Definitely just the antique device you call a phone," Graham laughs, straightening his posture.

He takes his phone from his jacket pocket and opens up the camera app. Switching it to the front view, he extends his arm to take a picture of the two of us. I squeeze in closer and smile as he captures the image. I look up at him, expecting an explanation as to why he decided to take a picture of us.

Graham's blue orbs stare down at me. I am enchanted for a second, hypnotized by the intensity they broadcast. I turn off my outdated cell and slip it back into the handbag. I see the trio of condoms and quickly snap it shut. They are taunting me. Nothing is going to happen on this date that will warrant their usage.

"Surely by now you're ready to eat."

I give him a half smile. "Yeah, I think I am."

Graham takes my hand in his, pulling me gently toward the restaurant. I flatten my dress with the other hand, more from nerves rather than from wrinkles. Ungracefully, I follow beside him down the corridor to the entrance of El Pastel, praying not to stumble or have another purse mishap.

I can tell by Graham's eyes alone that he is stressed. Something has him rattled.

"Are you going to lie and tell me everything is okay?" I ask.

He looks down at me and studies my expression. It's as if he is not looking at me but through me.

His brows crease and his eyes darken. "You know how I told you I was trouble?"

"Yeah, I remember."

"Now's a good chance to walk away," he says.

It feels like a test. As if this whole evening is some sort of training session to see if I am good under pressure.

"And miss all the fun? I think I'll stay."

8

It takes about forty seconds until we are seated in an elegant booth near the back of the restaurant. I slide into my side, facing Graham. The cushions are so upscale that my body instantly relaxes into them. Drinks are ordered without a single glance at the menu or a single remark from me. Food is chosen by a simple word—"tapas." Apparently, that is all it takes to get two waiters running. Two! Graham likes to be in control. And I don't know how I feel about that. Especially when I pride myself in being able to take care of myself and do things my way.

Before Graham and I can start down the path of a conversation that will hopefully lead to an explanation of tonight's events, Waiter One brings a silver tray with three decanters arranged in a line, full of colorful liquids. He looks to Graham as if for permission to speak but gets a nod of dismissal, walking away politely with a smile.

"I thought that you'd like to try each of the sangrias from the menu. Peach, berry, and the classic Barcelona. All top-rated and prepared fresh upon order." For a second, I think he is going to go all Claire on me and start rattling off the harmful side effects of high fructose corn syrup and how the common processed ingredient is taking over the United States, one obese child at a time. I am relieved when he doesn't.

"Sounds good," I mutter, feeling completely out of my element. For someone who is accustomed to drinking wine from a box, I am not even sure what my expectations are. I have nothing awesome to compare it to.

The flasks alone seem to be more expensive than my entire ensemble—shoes and accessories included. Graham pours the peach sangria into two crystal tumblers with beautiful frosted-swirl designs along the base. He passes the glass to me, brushing my hand tenderly with the pads of his long fingers. His waiting gaze tells me that he wants me to take the first sip. I part my lips and inhale the intoxicating scent of sweet and tart. I tip the glass between my lips and swallow the chilled liquid slowly, savoring the contrasting taste of deliciousness. When I make for a second sip, his chuckle alleviates some of the tension I was involuntarily holding in my joints, and I sit back into the cushioned seat of the booth. I relish in the extravagance of the atmosphere presented to me as if from a layout in a travel magazine.

Small-town girls like me could get whiplash from this type of mental transport across the globe to a city in Spain that I'll probably never get to visit in person.

I swallow what's in my mouth. "Delicious."

Graham's mouth curls with a smile. "I couldn't agree more," he responds, looking directly at my lips. He did not even take a drink yet, and he is definitely not being shy about his blatant staring. “But I would love another taste from the actual source.”

I realize that my unease is entertaining to him. Perhaps, I am a challenge. Although with me, it doesn’t take much effort. He likes to make me squirm and goes to extremes to elicit such a response. The blatant staring at my mouth. The brushing of his fingers. He has to know the effect he has on me. I’m sure I am very obvious and lumped into the same category as probably every member of the opposite sex. I can’t imagine a straight female not finding him attractive. The bad part is, I am nearly positive that he knows it and uses it to his advantage.

Graham’s eyes change to a darker shade of blue in the dim lighting of the room. He takes a sip of the sangria and smiles in response to the taste combination. “I’m sorry about earlier, Angie.” I glance up from my glass to gain insight on his meaning. “The phone calls,” he clarifies, patting his chest where his phone rests inside his breast pocket.

“It’s okay. I understand that things come up unexpectedly.” I debate on whether or not now is the best time to start the twenty-thousand-questions round. Knowing that there is a high probability that I will have to ask multiple times to get a clear answer, I start the session. “Why did Dominic choose you to accompany me tonight?”

“You don’t waste time, do you?” All amusement disappears from his eyes. Serious Graham reports back to action. He straightens his posture and throws back the rest of the amber liquid. “Because in this line of business, there are only a handful of people who can be trusted.”

“So he sent you? What are you, the Client-of-the-

Month?" As soon as the words roll off my tongue, I instantly feel pangs of regret at the sarcastic undertones of my pointed question. Despite all the warnings, Graham doesn't seem to be the "bad guy."

He snorts and looks off in the distance past my head. His eyes show sadness, and I stare down in embarrassed remorse. "Something like that," he mutters with a casual shrug. "You can trust me, Angie. I'm not trying to hurt you. On the contrary, I'm trying to keep you from being collateral."

"Then why tell me to keep my distance? Why give me so many mixed messages?"

"Because good girls like you do not need to involve themselves with—"

"Bad guys like you," I finish.

"Yes, exactly."

"But yet here we are. Together. Regardless of your cryptic warnings. Why is that, Graham?"

He takes a sip of his drink and rubs the back of his neck with his opposite hand. "This world that exists behind the scenes is darker than you can ever imagine. Your pretty little mind does not need to be tainted with those types of visions. Why would you want the black-and-white version, when you can keep seeing it in color?"

Unfortunately, I know just how dark the world can be. I lived in the darkness after James died. I know what it is like to not want to get out of bed. Or to eat. Or get dressed or shower. I know what it is like to have every ounce of joy sucked out of your life. I stayed in that dark place for months. I quit going to classes and dropped out of college just a couple of months into my freshman year. It took the rest of the year to come to terms with the fact that my twin brother was never coming back, that my dad had issues that love could not fix, and that my mom would never see me graduate from college or witness my future wedding.

What snapped me out of my own personal hell was finding comfort in trying to find the punk that caused James's death. Being from a small town, every local television station and newspaper featured the story. All with conflicting information. Rumors spread like wildfire, and the birth of a conspiracy was born as to what happened that horrible night. My traumatized mind could barely remember anything from the accident and the moments leading up to it. It was as if my memories disappeared. I remember waking up in the recovery room. I remember Dad telling me that James did not make it. It is funny how seeking revenge caused a spark of obsession in me that I desperately needed to survive. Someone hit our car. Someone got away without answering for the death of my twin brother.

"You seem lost in thought."

I look up and find the sea of blues staring at me. "So you and Dominic seem to know each other beyond just a business relationship."

"We are acquaintances, yes," Graham agrees. "Our paths cross from time to time."

I nod and take another sip of my drink.

He studies me for a moment. "You know there are other jobs more suitable for you, Miss McFee."

Excuse me? I glare in response to his blatant criticism. His words from the elevator at Entice come floating back; it is twice now that he has questioned my suitableness. Am I such a bad date? I am not even supposed to be his date!

Before I can defend myself, Waiter Two is back at the table with white rectangular porcelain trays of delicate finger foods. I have no idea what the ingredients entail. I stare at Graham, searching my mind for a clever retort, coming up short. The waiter walks back to the kitchen, leaving me sulking in response to Graham's confusing behavior.

Maybe I will just surprise him by not giving him the satisfaction of a retort. Keep him on his toes by doing something unexpected. I am certain that he wins most arguments with his roguish good looks—at least fights involving women. The directed looks of the other female patrons—obviously with companions of their own—have not gone unnoticed by my eyes. However, Graham has his focus on me. His sexy smirk unnerves me to the point of anger, making me want to strike my hand across his lips to wipe it off. He's too proud of himself, smug, and defiantly masculine. What a jerk. He knows exactly what he is doing to me. And I let him work me.

"Claire seems to think that I'm a perfect candidate."

"Of course she does," Graham huffs.

"What's that supposed to mean?" I demand. He has some beef with Claire. "She's my best friend, you know?"

"Miss Nettles thrives on drama and loves the thrill of dating strangers. Plus, she has more experience handling arrogant jerks."

"I seem to be handling you just fine." I give my best sultry smile and then I stick my tongue out. Like a first grader.

Graham belly laughs and holds up his drink. "Touché."

I am grateful that the restaurant doesn't have any mirrors for me to catch my appearance. I have to look hideous. He is bringing out my childish side and somehow enjoying it.

"Dominic thinks I'd be a good asset to the company."

"Dominic needs to get his head on straight and start thinking about bu—"

"Shut it, you"—I stutter—"asshole." That's the best I've got. His brows shoot up, widening his stormy blue eyes. Oh, shit. Did I piss off the beast? Luckily for me, I don't care.

"Oh, Angie," he groans, reaching across the table to drag his long finger up and down my lips, pulling at the soft slightly damp skin. I am surprised that I do not pull away. "There are roughly 171,476 words in the dictionary, and those are the only ones you can come up with to string together?" He gathers some residual wine from the corner of my mouth, removing his hand from my skin to stare at it longingly. "Such dirty words coming from such a pretty mouth."

It takes one endless minute for him to sweep his lips over his finger, making me swallow hard and plant my bottom firmly into the cushioned bench seat. One second he is insulting me, the next he is tantalizing me. I don't get this man. He is a mystery, a puzzle that has a few missing pieces.

My eyes glare laser beams at him, only making his gaze turn seductive. I have no idea what necessarily he is criticizing about me. My intelligence? My mouth? Or maybe it is a compliment. He did say pretty mouth.

"Surely you can think of a few more suitable descriptors for how you really feel. Something a bit more creative, perhaps."

The coolness of his words causes my shoulders to

square. Oh, he thinks he's some shit. There's that word suitable again. Gosh, I am starting to hate that word.

The way he says it makes him appear older than he probably is. Yes, I most definitely want to take that grin off his face with a swift slap. Hand pain as a consequence would be welcomed and worth it.

"How about you conceal your clenched fist until dinner is over. For my sake, at least." He coughs to disguise his chuckle.

"You seem to swear a lot," I acknowledge.

"I'm allowed," he shrugs.

I look at him in disbelief. "Because…"

"I'm a guy," he confesses.

I start to fume inside over the double standard and then catch his cheeky grin and know instantly that he is baiting me.

I close my eyes for a few seconds to clear my mind. When I open them, I face Graham holding a bite-size cracker-looking thing in his fingers, beckoning me to open my mouth. A throb starts at my neck and works its pulse up the back of my skull, indicating a headache on the rise. This man couldn't be more confusing even if he put forth more effort. One second he is angry, the next laughing. He changes to borderline rude, then back to being confrontational. And now he is feeding me?

His eyes soften to a beautiful sky blue. One hand rests under his chin, while the other waits for me to remove the food that is perched so elegantly on his fingers. Part of me wants to keep him waiting. I want to grind my feet into the ground and draw the line in the sand to show him what not to cross. But deep down I know that the line would prove to just be a challenge indicator—a green flag giving him a reminder of how far to push my buttons. He already knows how to push them. He is tempting me with food, hoping for an accidental graze of his fingers to pass over my skin in the process. Desire brewing, harvesting between words and simple skin-on-skin contact. I want more. So much more.

I submit to my hunger for nourishment and my growing need to please the man sitting across from me. I allow him to slide the colorful stack of greens, bread, and meat between my parted lips. My tongue slips out to catch the creamy sauce that wants to escape. I want his approval. The need originates deep within the pit of my core. As aggravating as Graham is, I am at his mercy. The man exudes power, and I would be stupid to continue with my taunting. I will switch gears as well. Maybe even play nice for a bit. I can do this.

"Very delicious, Mr. Hoffman. What is it?"

His eyes narrow at my formality. "Sautéed octopus—"

I cover my mouth to keep from spitting it out.

"And arugula on a pan-fried potato," he continues.

Octopus?

I swallow what I have, and the taste lingers on my tongue. Wow, I didn't expect it to be as wonderful as it is. I was expecting chewier. Saltier. Octopussier. Maybe it's best that I do not know what I am eating until it is too late.

"What do you think?" he prods.

I clear my throat. "It is very agreeable to my taste." I bring my finger up to my lips to clean more sauce from them.

"We are in public, Angie. Please." His moan is animalistic, full of carnal need. He hands me a spare linen napkin, making it clear that licking my finger is not suitable five-star restaurant etiquette.

"What?" I look up in shock, moving my head around the open space to see if anyone sees what apparently he finds inappropriate. He did it before. Why the double standards? I dab my finger with the fresh cloth. "Sorry if I embarrass you." I bite my tongue to refrain from attaching the word asshole at the end. A diluted taste of rust fills my mouth.

Graham leans across the table on his elbows. He looks relaxed and in his element—gaining the upper hand by inducing my embarrassment. "Don't be ridiculous. It is just that every man here is eye-fucking you right now, and giving them a free show is not in your best interest." His sapphire eyes bore into me, causing my insides to melt into a puddle.

Heat rushes to my cheeks as the blush spreads. I sweep my hair across my shoulder and reach for another morsel of food. This time I settle for what appears to be chicken and a colorful salsa on a decorative spoon server.

"That is called Croquetas De Puerco. It is a pork dish."

I smile as I chew, savoring every bite. The food is second to none. Despite being small portions, Graham had to have ordered one of everything from the menu, making sure we both had a taste of all the signature items.

"So tell me something about yourself, Angie. Something that a simple Internet search can't tell me."

The open-endedness of the question makes it difficult to answer. I have no idea what he wants to know. Is he admitting to Googling me? A lot of the information about me can be found on my Entice profile. "Um. What do you want to know?"

"Whatever you want to share."

I shift in my seat, not knowing what to say. I shove another bite of food into my mouth. I silently wish that he would go on some tangent about describing each organic ingredient, forgetting that he wants information about me. Graham pours from the second decanter of sangria, the berry. I snicker to myself about his intuition about me needing to be tipsy to talk.

"Tell me more about this type of sangria," I say with a smile.

"It's berry." He is on to me.

"What do you do for a living, Mr. Hoffman?" I ask boldly, taking a big sip from the fruity drink. "Hmm, this is very good."

"You don't like to talk about yourself, do you, Miss McFee?"

"I like to do it as much as you do."

He snorts. "Accurate observation." After a long pause, he sighs. "I dabble in real estate. Have a few side projects. Play with the stock market a bit. Own and run a company. Just your average businessman."

"For someone as cocky as you are, I'm surprised that you are describing yourself as average."

My use of the word cocky has Graham amused. He leans across the table, and whispers, "I'm not average in every aspect." His wink sends the message of the sexual innuendo straight down to the crotch of my panties. I have indirectly felt his erection. He is definitely above average—not that I have much hands-on data to compare it to. I squirm in my seat, trying to scratch the itch that is now causing havoc between my thighs. What is wrong with me?

I never act like this.

"Ma'am, this was sent over for you, compliments of the gentleman," Waiter One interrupts my dirty thoughts, warranting a murderous glare from Graham. The waiter places the tall blue beverage down in front of me. The ice is shaped like perfect spheres and the liquid reminds me of pictures I have seen of the Caribbean.

"Oh," I breathe.

"Courtesy of whom exactly?" Graham is fuming, anger radiating from his muscles. His eyes search the area coming up empty.

"I"—the waiter swallows hard—"I'm not sure."

"Find out then," Graham snaps.

He scurries off to the other side of the restaurant.

I stare down at the concoction and touch the dewy moisture along the outside of the glass.

Graham's hand grabs it and pushes it off to the side, liquid sloshing over the rim. "Don't you dare take a sip of that, Angie."

"I'm not." I hold my palms up in surrender. I never planned on drinking it, despite being curious about the taste.

"Ah, um," Waiter Two clears his throat to announce his presence, probably switching jobs with his coworker in fear of Graham's reaction. "A Mr. Tanner, sir." I see apprehension in his eyes.

Graham grasps the glass and pushes it into the waiter's hands. "Tell Mr. Tanner to save his energy. And his money. Oh, and to fucking mind his own business."

"What was that about? What does Mark want?" I ask, as the waiter retreats with his tail between his legs. Awkward.

"To prove a point. A moot point." His nonchalant shrug

hides portions of his brooding anger, his shoulders still tense. I stare in a trance at the ticking of his jaw, completely blindsided by the simple gesture that was made in ill taste. If it wasn't for the tension-filled elevator meeting earlier, I would think that Graham was overreacting. There's more to this pissing contest than meets the eyes.

"Thank you for being so clear and precise," I snort, embracing my inner sarcastic self.

Graham throws his head back and laughs heartily. "Funny and sexy. I like the combo, Miss McFee. But you do know that sarcasm is the lowest form of humor."

So now he's back to flirting. Great. I am not sure which side of him is easier to handle. I shrug off his comment and give him my best forced smile. "And you do know that flirting is the lowest form of foreplay." I cover my mouth quickly, as if doing so can retract the words that just flew out.

Shit. It's the alcohol. I have never acted like this in my life. Hell, I won't even play Cards Against Humanity with the gang because I'm too shy. There's just something about Graham that allows me to let my guard down and basically say whatever is flowing in my head. It's like he dissolves my filter and breaks down my walls.

"And the dirty mouth is back in play." The twinkle in his eye and the glow to his facial features tips off his mood. He likes my smart mouth. My smart—needs to cut back on the sangria—mouth. "But, Angie," he whispers slowly and purposefully, "I promise to make it good for you, when the time is right. I have good endurance. And a customer-satisfaction-is-guaranteed policy."

I swallow back the lump in my throat and reach for the last decanter. Why stop now?

We down the Barcelona sangria and finish the rest of the food as Waiter One appears at the table, on edge from what I assume his coworker divulged about the last encounter. Two cups of steaming extra frothy coffee get distributed. The smell of hazelnut fills the air with the sweet nutty fragrance. I marvel at the intricate leaf design in the foam. The waiter then places a tray of delicately sculptured confections in the center of the table, clearing out the empty dishes with graceful adeptness. I stare in awe at the chocolate structures. My mouth waters, and it takes a great amount of self-control to hold myself back from diving straight in, mouth first. A small chocolate pastry is topped with a dollop of chocolate mousse, with a milk and white chocolate straw resting against it on an angled slope. Beside it, a cylindrical iced cocoa gelatin rests, garnished with a diamond-shaped platform of checkerboard dark chocolate. Last, a series of truffle balls form a pyramid, dusted with raspberry infused powdered sugar.

I am speechless over the presentation and unable to move despite the magnetic pull that keeps drawing me closer to the confections. It is food porn.

"Don't be shy now. This is what you waited for, is it not?" His hand makes an all-encompassing gesture toward the tray. His eyes are smoldering—enjoying my fidgeting—knowing the exact war going on in my head. It takes everything in me not to face-plant. Images of the little balled up foil wrappers from my purse make an appearance in my thoughts. He knows my weakness and is exploiting it. He is an opportunist.

I suck my top lip into my mouth in an awkward attempt to rein in my girlish glee over the picture-perfect display. It looks too good to mess up with my fingers or fork or tongue. Or face. My eyes dart between creations, unable to settle on which I want to try first.

"For heaven's sake, Angie," Graham snaps, taking his fork and deliberately putting a dent into each of the perfect structures, making chocolate pieces crunch under the sheer force of his intentional ministrations. "There. Now eat." He rests back into the seat and crosses his arms over the table, waiting for me.

My face heats as I glance up and lock eyes with his hazy blues. I can't help but smile over his attempt to make me more at ease. I take my fork and poke at a truffle ball. I nibble off a chunk, sucking at the sugary coating. It is divine and perfectly sweet, leaving a lovely aftertaste that lingers on my tongue. I finish the treat, retaining the fierce eye contact with Graham.

I sip the coffee, enjoying the flavors brought out by the smooth European blend. Graham scoops up mousse with the chocolate straw, licking it off with long, sensual strokes.

"Cold, Miss McFee?" Oh, he knows exactly what he is doing to me. Why is he so smug?

My hands swipe over my upper arms, calming the goose bumps. Graham leans forward over the table, mere inches from my face. His hand touches my cheek, running warm fingers up and down my scorching skin. He parts his lips, swiping his tongue along the edge in a tantalizing rhythm. Is he going to kiss me again? Do I want him to kiss me again? My deprived body responds with a shock that shakes my sex drive into orbit. I feel intrigued and scared all at once.

Every nerve ending in my body charges with electricity, coming alive over the anticipation of more. In this instant, I choose him over chocolate. I'm out of my mind. What the hell is wrong with me?

Every romantic scene from all of my novels plays out inside my head on loop. It's my favorite part of every book. The first meeting. The anticipation. The first kiss. And then the desire for more. Every time I pick up a new read, I eagerly trudge through the pages until I can find these signature moments. It's in every book—like a clichéd rule or writers' code. The longer the author waits for the characters to give in to each other, the better. Right now, I want to slow things down. I want this desire for him to be bottled up and preserved so it doesn't have to come to an end—like basically every relationship I have had in the past.

You cannot get hurt if your heart isn't fully invested.

I turn my face into his hand as his body gets close, leaving my lips at an angle that is not conducive for a make-out session. With infinitesimal slowness, he guides my head back in place with his demanding hand, forcing me to face him. Every nanosecond of time causes my mind to slowly lose touch with reality.

My eyes blink hard, thinking that my imagination is playing tricks on me, as if I am making things up in my overly deprived head as I see fit. The pad of Graham's thumb is at my bottom lip, playing with its fullness. He wipes it across the corner of my mouth, gathering and showing me the evidence of the melted chocolate that he collects. I move away again, not wanting him to see the effect he has on me. He directs me back—coaxing me—to gaze into the aqua abyss, feeling the same thumb press against my lips, pleading for entry. I part them just enough for his thumb to slip through, urging me to clean it off. I oblige and run my tongue lazily over the firm pad. My breath catches in a near choke. I give him a tiny bite. Graham's mouth parts in response, and a low moan sneaks out, heard only by my ears. Wow. That is hot.

"Holy hell, Angie," he says with a rasp, causing my insides to stir. He pulls his hand away. "If I knew that your response to dessert was going to be this erotic, I would have —" He runs his fingers through his hair. Sweat beads on his forehead.

"Would have what?" I whisper.

"Fuck, Angie. You are driving me mad. I want you so badly. Even though the noble thing would be to get up and walk away."

I slouch back into the seat, forcing my shoulders to relax. My breathing is impaired and staccato. My eyes dart to my hands resting in my lap in an attempt to conceal my embarrassment—and my need. Graham's intensity is hard to deal with, and his eyes speak volumes as to his feelings. It is like he is mad at me for making him want me. I can feel him stripping away my exterior with his unrelenting gaze—causing me to mentally freak out with every passing second. This is not what I signed up for tonight. I expected to have a couple of drinks with my boss, Dominic, not his super-hot client. Graham is a man who has already learned how to push buttons I didn't even think I owned.

"Are you a noble person, Mr. Hoffman?" I ask seriously.

"Hell, no. I am a selfish bastard who takes what I want."

"Always?" I probe.

"Yes, Angela, always."

"What happens if what you want can't be taken?"

"Everyone has a price," he claims smugly.

"Don't you mean, everything has a price?" I clarify.

"Semantics."

I pick at the chocolate towers as a way to keep my mind and eyes off him. I can feel his stare piercing me the more I try to avoid him. I make conscious effort not to choke on my caffeinated beverage with every sip—as I hold tightly onto my faux-sophisticated aura to keep it from unraveling like a ball of yarn.

"What are you even doing in this line of work, Angie? Isn't there some work-study program you could be applying for?"

"Are you that far removed from reality that you expect some entry-level job to pay for years of schooling and my growing stack of bills? Surely, you cannot be that naive—even with your six-figure salary—to think that the thoughts of being debt-free would not be appealing to the average girl."

"It's seven."

"Excuse me?"

He rubs at his chin. "I make a seven-figure salary."

I resist scoffing. "Do you want a prize?"

"Depends what it entails."

"Cute," I mumble.

"You are not prepared for the ugliness that this world can bring to your feet."

Tears well in my eyes as I think about just how familiar I am with the ugliness of the world in general. How ugly it was to watch my mom die of cancer. How ugly it was to bury my twin brother. How ugly it is to have an estranged relationship with my dad. I know ugly.

I force my eyes to dry and refuse to make eye contact with Graham. But he sees. He knows that his words have affected me.

"Ready to go?" he asks softly.

"Doesn't someone need to pay? I want to contribute for my part." I think about how much money I have stuffed into my clutch and realize that it wouldn't even be enough to pay for half.

"They know me. I have a credit card on file here." He slides from the booth and stands expectantly at my side. He glares at me when I try to open my bag. "And you will never pay when we are together. Ready to go, now?" he presses.

I clear my throat, realizing that I haven't said anything for an indeterminate period of time. My voice is scratchy, despite my efforts to keep it hydrated. "I am"—I take a breath—"going to have a drink with Claire at the bar downstairs." I watch the tick form in Graham's jaw. "Whenever she is done with her symphony date."

Graham's brows scrunch together to form a V as he listens to my words. "I think you've had enough to drink, but if you want more, I can order you something else," he offers, sliding back down into the booth.

"It's for social reasons as well. You can leave me here, and I can get a taxi home with her." His expression shows that he is not on board with what I am suggesting.

"You two are roommates. Can't you be social at home?"

"Graham..."

"Angie, I would feel better if I was the one to get you home. You do have class tomorrow, don't you?"

Why does he know so much about me? Did Claire share information with him during their brief quarrel in the office? "Yes. I do," I answer, tilting my chin up in defiance. I keep myself from adding "so" at the end.

"Well, then, it is settled."

I never agreed. Nothing is settled.

Graham gets up, grasping my hand and pulling me up from the cushioned seat. He places his hand on the small of my back and leads me to the exit of the restaurant, passing by several tables of dinner guests sharing a meal over candlelight and expensive vintage wine. I allow him to guide me for the sole reason of not making a scene.

"Graham," I say, coming to a stop by the elevators, "did you misunderstand me?" I turn to look at him, making him sigh. "I'd like to stay."

"And I would like to have some peace of mind knowing that you got home safely." Something tells me the fact that Mark Tanner is probably still lurking in the building causes him some level of unease.

"So we are at a standstill in regard to my free will?" My voice is a bit harsher than I originally planned. What is the big deal? Why is he being so bossy and demanding? He's not my keeper.

Graham's hovering stance makes me quiver back in unknown fear of a man I barely know. I feel petite and vulnerable. I use my phone as a distraction, quietly digging it from the safety of my bag. I swallow hard when I see that it is after eleven. Where have the past four hours gone?

Ugh, he's right. I should go home. Do I want to give him

the satisfaction of winning? Or do I want to drill my feet into the shiny tiled floor and hold my own to prove a point? I glance at the text from Claire telling me that she is exhausted and that she promises to make it up to me for skipping out on our plans. I bite my tongue to keep from showing the results of the text in my eyes. Graham doesn't need to know that I have no choice but to go home. It will do him no harm to go on believing that I have options. Serves his arrogant self right.

"I'm pretty tired. Go ahead and drop me off at home, then." I can see his smirk forming on his lips, and I instantly ball my fist in retaliation. His "I won" face is almost the most annoying sight of all, second only to his I-know-how-to-make-you-squirm face.

"Good decision, Miss McFee. I'm glad you can be reasonable."

Oh, the nerve of him.

We take the elevator down to the ground floor and slip out into the night. The cool air bites my skin as it hits me full force as we leave the shelter of the building. Collins jumps to posture at the sight of Graham, almost like one of those cute show dogs, eager to please his master. I can picture him wagging his tail and leaping through hoops just to get thrown a treat. I wonder how much excitement he encounters on a typical workday. It can't be that much. I presume that the biggest challenge would be biting his tongue to keep his snarky comments to himself. At least that would be my biggest challenge if I were faced with the same type of job for someone as egotistical as Graham.

I feel the heat from his icy blues burn into me. I can

sense my blush multiplying all over my pale skin. What is his deal?

"I'll double the money that I owe you for tonight if you share what has you so entertained up in your pretty little head."

What the hell? Graham's words startle and awaken my sleepy body, more than the night air has accomplished.

"Wait," I stop midstride. "This was supposed to be a trial run with Dominic. Not a paid escort date."

"Regardless of how you spin it, you are getting paid to go on dates. Tonight—for lack of a better word—was a date. Correct? Dinner, drinks, dessert, and a safe ride home…" He lets the rest of his statement fade.

Yeah, sure, it sounds just like a date. Except, there is nothing safe about being in confined spaces with Graham. I didn't expect him to pay me specifically for tonight. My eyes dart to my shoes as I feel the pang of shame overwhelm my composure. If this is what cheap feels like, without any sexual activity, then I am screwed. I imagine this feeling will be replicated in future agency dates as well. I better get used to it.

Where is my mind right now? As much as I need the money—and am doing this solely for the money—I don't want it for tonight. Tonight was not work. It was fun. Every instinct that has been hidden behind the glamour of being wined and dined screams that not every suitor will be as…enjoyable?

There's something about Graham. Besides the obvious hotness that he exudes, he is mysterious. Dare I say, dangerous? He has me tied up in knots. Like a moth to the flame, I am drawn to him, even though I know I'll get burned. Even

Graham warned me in no uncertain terms that I am headed in this direction.

Getting too close to someone means sharing a part of me. That is something I have made a hobby at avoiding. I have spent too much time trusting the wrong people and ignoring the good ones right in front of me. Graham might appear like a good guy from the outside. He has all the right moves—chivalrous, charming, flirtatious, and a master at seduction. He knows exactly what to say to get me wired. But, unlike most men, he wants to strip away my hard exterior and find out what makes me tick. To discover my weaknesses and then use them against me to bend my will.

Not interested.

The only way to handle the situation is to appease him. I give him a nod and pivot my body back toward the waiting car. My heels click against the smooth concrete, following the same rhythm as my heartbeat. His warm hand interlocks with mine. He caresses the sensitive skin of my palm with his thumb, sending rockets of heat throughout my body. Massaging. Teasing. Pleasuring.

My body trembles from the sensations flowing through my limbs. I can feel Graham's wicked smile on the back of my neck. I pull my hand away and walk faster to the car.

"What was that, Miss McFee?"

His voice penetrates my senses, awakening everything in unison. His scent intoxicates the air whisking through my nose. My lower lip slips in between the cage of my teeth, remembering the feel of his thumb being there just minutes ago, the soft, yet hard, pad of his finger teasing my tongue and conscious thoughts into submission.

"Hmm?"

Graham pulls on my hips, turning me around in a flash. We are facing each other. His height towers over me and my eyes slowly travel from his chest up to his eyes. When they lock, I notice his visible swallow and see the smoldering heat reflected in his gaze. I inhale his scent and commit it to memory. He inches forward, making me back up. His fingers tease my side.

Another inch forward.

I move an inch back.

An inch forward again prompts my inch back…

It is as if we are slow dancing to an unknown song for the first time.

My butt hits the edge of his car. I am trapped. He releases my waist only to place both hands into my hair. The pads of his fingers press into the tense muscles of my neck. I tilt my head to move toward the pleasure he is inflicting on my senses. My butt melts into the side of the car. My feet shift in an effort to keep me grounded. Graham lifts the weight of my hair and allows the waves to cascade over my shoulders.

"Angie, do you have any idea what you are doing to me?" he asks solemnly. He plays with an errant strand of hair, rotating it in between two fingers. "You are making me do things I promised myself I would never do."

It is as if he is blaming me for something. As if this—whatever the hell it is—is my fault.

His body inches even closer, invading the only free space left between us. He looks conflicted, like he is battling internally with himself over his next move.

It is a seductive dance.

Push and pull.

Give and take.

His eyes lock with mine and study me. I feel like he is X-raying my thoughts. I fight to resist falling over the edge. It is as if we are both dangling by a frayed thread that holds our self-control.

"Fuck it," Graham snarls. He presses his knee between my parted legs, resting it right against my pussy.

My mouth opens wide and is quickly covered by his lips. He swallows my moan, capturing it and making it go unnoticed. His kiss is full of need. My tongue slips into his mouth, and his teeth nip at it playfully. We are so deeply connected that I can no longer tell if I am breathing on my own or if he is doing it for me.

The skirt of my dress rides up to accommodate him. I use my hands to anchor myself to the car to keep from falling over—breaking the seal of our lips. I take a breath. One labored breath.

My core grinds against his knee, and I mold my body against his. We fit together seamlessly, like water to the shore. My arms wrap around his neck, and I desperately shift my body to get more friction.

He leans down and chuckles into my ear.

"You want me, don't you?"

My eyes connect with his.

"Admit it," he demands.

His words snap me into the present like a band pulled too tight. He is testing my limits, mocking me. It is then that I hear the cars driving past and people chatting while exiting the building. I push on his chest to get him to back away from me.

"Yeah, I thought so," he huskily whispers, releasing me

from his grasp. I miss the warmth of his breath on my skin.

"It's okay to be shy about it, Angie," he says, raising his eyebrows. "I find that just as sexy."

"We need to go," I say quietly, changing the subject. "I have to get home."

I swallow hard and grab the handle to the rear door. Graham nods to Collins who efficiently moves to enter the driver's seat. Has he been standing on the sidelines this whole time? Watching us?

Disgust washes over me. I wonder just how many agency girls Collins has driven home or back to Graham's place. I wonder what number I am on his spreadsheet of names. I feel faint.

"My bag. I don't know where my handbag is," I say in a rush.

"It's here," Graham says softly, reaching for it from the hood of the car.

I have no idea how it ended up there. It's as if my mind is playing tricks on me.

Graham helps me to get situated inside, fastening my seatbelt for me despite my protests that I can do it on my own.

"I look forward to when we can do this again," he responds. He leans down into the frame of the door and kisses my forehead. "I'll be in touch."

"What?"

I watch in confusion as he gives Collins some nonverbal cue that manages to get some message across. He shuts the door and the car pulls out swiftly, leaving Graham on the sidewalk of the street. Alone. I stare out the tinted windows into the night, watching Graham walk back into the building, his cell raised to his ear. The silence in the car is suffocating as I decipher the reason as to why Graham isn't accompanying me home as well. His request to see me home alluded to the notion that he would be with me. Why does it even matter? Why should I care so much? It's not like I would have invited him inside my place.

You aren't his type.

I resist the urge to grill Collins with questions. The man is obviously quite nervous around me. I find it a bit comical, but I am in no mood to entertain that tonight.

At some point during the ride home, I must have dozed off because the sound of the back door opening startles me awake. I hear a cough.

"Sorry, ma'am," Collins responds.

I take a moment to regain my senses. I scoot off the seat and straighten my dress.

Collins clears his throat. "Mr. Hoffman would like to give this to you."

I take the envelope and small wrapped box from his hands and turn to walk up the steps to the townhouse. "Thank you, Collins," I yell back over my shoulder.

I dig for my key in my handbag and can't find it. Squatting down on the doormat, I empty the contents out until the jingle sound alerts me to its whereabouts. I pack up my items and unlock the door. Once inside, I hear the sound of the car driving away.

I plop down on the couch and slip off the lid on the box to uncover a beautiful silver bracelet. This is my way of signifying my place in the agency. I then open the envelope and find a folded note. Behind the note is a perfectly crisp hundred-dollar bill, along with nine more stacked in a row.

My shaky hands flip through the pile to recount. Graham has paid me one thousand dollars to have dinner with him. Holy crap.

I unfold the note to find in perfect printed ink—*Apparently money can buy everything. Thanks for giving me a taste and proving me right.*

9

I stare at Graham's message, as nausea bubbles in my throat. How dare he!

Needing to work and wanting to work are two different things. Since I started college, I have become accustomed to hard work without a quick payoff. Few things in life come easy. Nothing in life comes for free. There is always a price. Working at the bakery while studying for exams was tough to balance. Feeling like I was constantly competing for recognition for my writing or for a coveted internship placement gave me the feeling of being in a race that may be impossible to ever win. The agency job, however, is my easy ticket. I show up. I look pretty. I get paid.

And then I feel cheap.

Graham makes me feel cheap. Like he is lusting after me and disgusted by me all at once. His moods are unpredictable, and his sharp tongue can cut into my already fragile self-esteem. James always gave me confidence by cheering for me. When I met Claire, I instantly gravitated toward her spirit and natural ability to see me for me. I had my fresh start at River Valley to reinvent myself. No one knew me here as the girl from Baker City who had her face plastered on the front of every newspaper in a fifteen-mile radius for months. I was labeled as the girl who lost everything—including her will to live. No, I spent four years working hard at my studies. And it wasn't until a failed final project my senior year that my world was shaken once again.

What Graham doesn't realize about me is that I do not need a man. Men are distractions.

This job is simply that—just a job. It is a way to earn money fast enough so that I can focus on my long-term career goals.

I toss the note aside, determined not to let a bitter man ruin the rest of my night.

I wake with the sun bursting through the parted curtains, fourteen minutes before my alarm is set to go off. I sigh in rested bliss, loving the feeling of waking on my own. Thursday is better than Monday through Wednesday for the mere fact that my weekend starts at noon. I click off my dual alarm of the clock and the cell phone, stretching my arms and legs out across my full-sized bed. For being bought from Ikea, it is fairly comfortable. Thoughts of last night float through my mind as I roll onto my back and stare up at the textured ceiling. It was a night full of surprises.

I lean over and reach into the bottom drawer of my nightstand to retrieve the thoroughly abused paperback book that has captured my attention many mornings. Despite the cover portraying the typical cheesy lovers' embrace, this particular novel is decent in the heat department. I find the dog-eared page that marks a particularly steamy scene that left me hot and bothered. I glance at the clock and see that I have time to try.

I fluff my pillow behind my neck and place another under my upper thighs to elevate my hips a few inches from the mattress. I read online a few weeks ago that this could help with the angles. I hike up the sheet that is fully coated with the warmth from the rays peeking through the windows. I chose this room for the morning sun.

As I reread the scene that involves pool table sex, I slip my left hand down my belly to cover over my panty-clad mound. I move my middle three fingers rhythmically, in sync with the beat of my heart. My eyes close from the pulsing surge of blood flowing rapidly through my body, pooling at the place directly beneath my fingers. I need friction. Something harder than what my fingers can produce. I need a knee to grind on.

Hmm…

My attention flutters back to the book where the badass guitar player is having his way with the innocent bartender in the back room of the bar. Her skirt is hiked up over her hips, and her butt is at the edge of the billiard table, begging for him to enter her. The thrill of getting caught in the act makes the scene even more electrifying.

My fingers increase pace on my pussy, using the lacy fabric to soak up my now leaking juices. I am in a trance—a deliriously hypnotic daze of gyrating my lower body and arching my upper half. My hand slides up to the lace trim and dips below the confining layer, making flesh contact sodden flesh. My pointer finds the bundle of nerves and presses the engorged clit, expelling the stale air from my lungs. The pleasure radiates through my limbs, down into my toes, and up to my ears. My finger scoops up the moisture from my inner labia lips and spreads it upwards, leaving a slick path along its way. I bounce my hips upward in an involuntary motion of pure bliss, a desire of wanting to be filled. My confidence builds with each word read internally from the page, each passing breath, and each stroke of my wanton pussy.

As the male from the story finds refuge in the confines of the hotness of the bartender's saturated pussy, I make my finger find the same habitat within my folds. The tightness of my inner walls squeezes my soft digit to the point of desperate pain.

I need to get off.

I forgo the book, tossing it to the side of the bed, using my own imagination to finish the job. I slide my right hand down to the apex of my thighs and use two fingers to rub circles around my clit, while the other hand has a finger buried inside, two knuckles deep. I conjure up all my deftness to create a rhythm between the two separate hands, moving them in unison to create throb after throb of a slow-building tidal wave. My breathing turns staccato and frequent as I climb the wall to the top.

Almost there.

The victory line is nearly in view as I continue the rapid assault on my drenched flesh. More liquid seeps out of my slit, dripping down to the awaiting pillow. Still rising. Pulsating. And charging forward. Faster. Harder. My blood inside my lower region boils to a temperature that nearly makes it want to explode. I twist my trapped finger, hooking it upward. I circle my outer finger. Just a little more.

Almost there.

My legs push forward to straighten out as I prepare myself for the potentially earth-shattering orgasm. Almost. There. Just. A. Little. More. Then…

It all stops.

It always stops.

Every single time.

I slink back onto the bed in defeat. I am so wound up that I feel like a ticking time bomb waiting to detonate. It's as if something as light as a feather could push me over the edge.

Just not now. Without my brain silencing, I will never get there.

The mounting pressure of finishing this semester successfully weighs on my mind. I have to find a topic worth writing about—something that is original and captivating. The longer I wait to nail down a topic, the harder it will be to complete the story before the end of the semester.

I push my right knee upwards and use my foot to kick out the pillow. I throw my book back into the bottom drawer and sigh in frustration.

Getting jealous of fictional characters in a book is my sign that I need to get up and do something productive. I roll over and grab the phone off the stand and read through my numerous texts.

Agency: Date scheduled for September 17 at 20:00. Entice automated message.

My pulse jumps at the alert of another potential date scheduled tonight. Apparently IT activated my account.

I click to the next text message and find that it is from Dominic, time stamped at two in the morning.

> **Dominic: So sorry Angie. Had to leave town. Hope Graham treated you right.**

I snicker at the message. Oh, if only he knew, just how right and wrong Graham treated me.

I grab my laptop from the nightstand and login to my email account. After opening the agency email that explains the information pertaining to the setup of my profile, I am able to add the link to the website and save it under My Favorites. I type in my name, phone number, birthday, and the code from the email, which all allow me to have access to the site and change my password from the default.

The "My Account" hyperlink allows me to peruse my information and pictures that were gathered from Tuesday. Wow. There are twenty pictures total, and all involve either a different hair style or a different outfit. My featured picture is the one with my white short-sleeved dress, straightened hair, and gold-toned makeup. It is the best out of the bunch that were taken that day. The photographer snapped the photo right as I was laughing at the hair stylist, who was behind him goofily juggling cans of hairspray. I look genuinely happy and surprisingly sophisticated, despite Zander's comment about girls who wear white.

At the top right of the screen, a rating bar, date counter, and review blog is sectioned off. Surprise hits me that my rating bar now shows five hearts, date counter set to 1, and my monthly hours set to 4.5. Graham didn't waste time with the data entry. I wonder if clients get an email after dates to remind them to be prompt.

At the top left of the window, there is a pull-down menu that allows me to check my finances before the agency gets a cut, money gets put into escrow, and taxes are removed. My eyes bulge at the number that is bolded in the "total earnings box." One thousand, five hundred dollars.

What the hell?

I was already paid cash for my date with Graham. Now this? This is absolutely ludicrous!

Graham's over-the-top nature that seems to be custom built into his controlling persona is a bit much for my liking. I scoff at his deliberate rejection of the $200 minimum payment rule. He obviously is trying to prove to me that he has money to blow—especially when he was not even supposed to go on the date with me in the first place! Despite the rush of relief that financial security brings—on rare occasions in my life thus far—I have to squash the idea of Graham dating me. The amount of money he throws around scares me. What is he trying to hide? How far is he planning to take this?

And will I be able to keep up with the flippant mood swings?

Remembering that I have a scheduled date tonight, I search for the button that will transfer me to my booking calendar. My phone buzzes with an incoming text, and I pick it up to read it.

Claire: Want to start the weekend off with a bang?

Angie: Depends

Claire: On what?

Angie: What your version of a "bang" entails.

Claire: Shopping? I'll pick you up at 1 PM?

I smile at the request for overdue girl time. With her master's program, Claire has a pretty nice schedule. It is nice that she has Fridays off with the expectation to do research. Her love of all things designer originated from a trip to Los Angeles to do a summer internship at a prestigious health resort—the kind of place where celebrities gather to rejuvenate. Or detox.

I type out a response to her.

Angie: Only if you help navigate

Claire: Squeeeeeee I knew you couldn't resist my charm

I switch my attention back to the date at hand for tonight. I need to see if a shopping spree can be done with enough time for everything else. Back at the screen of my laptop, I find the block that states the date. Sure enough, the number is bolded and blinking on the calendar and a paper/pencil icon is attached indicating that a message is enclosed. I click to open a small box. The air leaves my lungs in an avalanche-force rush as I read the name of my suitor—Mark Tanner.

He doesn't waste any time. Unease washes over me. Graham hates the man. But Graham is not my boss. I am empowered to make my own choices in this life.

The message attached is lengthy and requires me to scroll to see the end.

> *I will pick you up at your place at 8 PM. I will pay you the required $200 an hour and will plan on the date ending at 10 PM unless we both mutually agree for me to purchase more time. The meeting will be with potential business executives. I need you to find time to complete the following requests:*
>
> - *short black dress, at least 6 inches higher than the top of the knees*
> - *sheer black nylons, thigh-highs, whatever*
> - *black clutch, satin if possible*
> - *4-5 inch stilettos in black, whichever is more comfortable for you*
> - *minimum of 15-minute tanning bed session; no spray tan*
> - *hair styled up, classy*
> - *French manicure; be sure it is professionally done, no DIY*
> - *fake lashes, lots of mascara in black*
> - *lipstick, no bright red or brown shades*
> - *get eyebrows professionally shaped at salon*

Well, fuck me sideways! Nothing about that sounds even remotely fun. What a picky bastard!

No wonder Graham was giving him an incredulous kill-dagger-death stare last night. Part of me wants to just say "screw it" to Mark and cancel. The other part of me needs to step out of my comfort zone and jump through the hoops, trusting that more proverbial doors will open—hopefully not revealing more can't-please-worth-a-damn pricks.

I hesitantly click confirm to accept the date, refraining from writing a nasty note with my stipulations on what Mark should do to prepare for tonight. I doubt that getting a full body wax and professional lessons in manners are on the top of his to-do list. With confirmation, I enter in my home address to indicate where the date should pick me up. The paranoid part of me worries that a bunch of men will now know where I live, but I am nearly positive a simple Internet search will also provide that information. Dominic assured that everyone is cleared of criminal offenses and is legit. Thus, in theory, Mark Tanner should be safe.

I type in my schedule for the next two weeks into the calendar on the site, allowing clients to know when I am busy with class, fundraiser events, and personal stuff. While typing, the machine beeps, and a red flag appears at the top of the main screen. I hover my mouse arrow over the rectangular flag and read the pop-up words stating that another date is scheduled. The phone buzzes and I look. Shit.

Agency: Date scheduled for September 18 at 17:00. Entice automated message.

Back at the calendar, I find the 18th bolded and blinking. I open up the attached message from Will Jenkins. This one is not so complicated.

Pickup at 5 PM at a location of your choice. Wear a nice knee-length cocktail dress. Nothing too flashy. Dinner and drinks with new hires at my company. I will pay $250 an hour and am expecting it to last 2.5 but will reserve and pay for 3 just in case.

I click confirm. Will seemed very nice at the mixer event. This date should be easy.

My head spins with the realization that my evenings are going to get very busy. I open my top nightstand drawer and pull out a notepad and pencil to jot down all the things that need to be done or bought before the weekend. Mark Tanner's requests will be the hardest to comply with, hands down. At least the date with Will Jenkins should be low-key and maybe even fun. He seems real and less politician-like.

I check the time and see that it is quarter after eight. I have a half hour to get ready and be in the car. I log off the site and put my laptop to sleep, plugging it in to charge. A quick shower and blow-dry top my to-do list, followed by my half-ass makeup application techniques. My River Valley University gray hoodie and sweat set with light consignment shop pink Ugg boots complete my look.

With five minutes to spare before I absolutely have to leave, I find myself in the kitchen digging through the freezer for my frozen fruit to blend into a smoothie. I open the cupboard to pull out the protein mix, only to see a note in Claire's handwriting attached with a frowny face sketch.

Dearest Angie,

I found this bag of protein mix that you bought and did a little investigating. You can thank me later. So, it turns out that this ~~shit~~ mix contains Soy Protein Isolate, also known as SPI. Okay, before you freak out at my ~~awesomeness~~ analness, I am placing the research on the coffee table in the living room for you to read at your leisure. But in short, this stuff is B-A-D! It has some sort of estrogenic properties and can increase growth and shit —and not the good kind of growth (like where boobies are concerned). This poison-powder is packaged and marketed to appear to be healthy...but beware! I am going to outlaw this from our humble abode upon confirmation that you read this. I will purchase you a replacement. Promise! Always looking out for you!

Your Sister from Another Mister,
Claire

P.S. The FDA is full of a bunch of clueless puppets who couldn't make a decision on their own if their lives depended on it. Conspiracy, I tell you, conspiracy. Maybe you should take down the entire FDA as your writing topic? Now that is something I could get behind.

I giggle at Claire's thoroughly thought-out letter. She is the damn nutritionist elf on a shelf. The woman never ceases to amaze me with her food dedication—also known as dictatorship. But between the texts, the date requests, and the random smoothie attachment messages, it is all too early for me to fight back. It's not even nine o'clock!

I allow Claire these small victories when it comes to food. I do this to keep her from conning me into joining her fad diets with her. Eight months ago, she convinced me that the Carrot Diet was all the rage. We bought ten pounds of carrots for the two of us to consume over a week's span. They had to be shredded and eaten raw. It was hell. And I am pretty sure they were to blame for my UTI.

I pull out my phone from my bag and text my crazy roommate.

Angie: You killed my breakfast, now you owe me lunch. And it can be one that the FDA does or does not approve of.

I smile as I click "send." It doesn't take long to make her bite.

Claire: Deal! Chicken wings (for you) and a cheese plate! Claire Nettles approved, nuff said.

I grab a bottle of vitamin-infused water and head out the door. I better enjoy every last drop of it before Claire finds something inadvertently wrong with it and outlaws it from our residence.

I smile to myself in the parking lot as I check my phone for any missed calls or messages. One missed call and voicemail. I don't recognize the number as I press the buttons to retrieve the message.

As soon as his smooth voice starts on the other end, I know instantly who it is. "Hello Angie, this is Graham Hoffman. I'm calling to see if you would like to join me for lunch today. You can save my number in your phone and call or text your response. I am flexible today and am able to be free until three p.m. I'm sorry I was unable to accompany you to your door last night. I hope that you enjoyed your prize."

I swallow the knot forming in my throat down to the base of my neck. A fraction of my girly side is disappointed that I have plans already. The more rational—less fun—side of me is pleased that I am genuinely busy. I don't need this type of confusion in my life right now.

I listen to the message one more time, laughing at the way he specifies his last name. Really, how many Grahams does he think I know? He's the only Graham I have ever met. I save the number to my contacts list and open a blank text message and start typing.

Angie: Plans with Claire. Sorry.

I hit "send" and wait for a response. He does not disappoint.

Graham: How about tonight for dinner? I'll clear my schedule. Pick you up at 6?

As savvy as Graham appears to be, surely he saw that I am booked for tonight with a nameless date. Did he expect me to cancel for him? I ponder a reply that will appease him, although it lacks creativity.

Angie: Busy tonight. Sorry.

Graham: What's his name?

I suck in a deep breath, although it does nothing to calm me down. As little as I know about Graham, this was not out of character. He appears to be a bold man who does not back down. I have zero experience dealing with persistence. To a typical man, the words "I'm busy" usually imply "I'm not interested." But do I even want Graham to give up?

Angie: I have to go.

I dash through the parking lot before I am any more minutes late to my class. Avoidance is a great coping mechanism. My phone buzzes in my purse indicating a call. I ignore it, knowing without looking that it is Graham.

He repeats the calling four more times.

I ignore him.

10

"Sounds like a complete douchebag," Claire responds in regard to my list of things to do before the date tonight with Mark. She rips off a piece of bread slathered with brie and shoves it in her mouth, moaning with each lick of her fingers—earning curious stares from every male above the age of twelve. "This is delicious. Worth every single calorie."

"I'm in agreement," I laugh, getting my fill of the food as well.

"Good, because I am rarely wrong."

We have a window seat at a trendy converted-warehouse restaurant in the Pearl District. We watch as boat owners take their vessels out on the Willamette River. In one of them, a middle-aged couple relaxes in the glass-windowed cabin, sharing a glass of wine.

"So, what can you tell me about Graham that you are holding back? And don't give me that look, I know you know more." I snort as Claire chokes a bit on her daiquiri. "I still cannot believe that you've worked for the agency all these months and never told me."

"I wanted to tell you, trust me, I did. Keeping secrets from you is the last thing I ever wanted to do. But I signed the NDA. Plus, I knew you would never join when you were perfectly content working at Sugar Butter. Just think, all that time, you really just needed a Sugar Daddy."

"Pretty sure that is false."

"Well, dating that sack of potatoes, Russell, didn't help."

I give her an awkward giggle. "Yeah. He was definitely a mistake."

"That's putting it mildly. The spud was an idiot for letting someone as amazing as you slip away. At least you didn't take things to the next level." Claire pauses and leans in closer to me over the table. "You didn't do the sex, did you?"

"No. Not like we were even together much for that to happen." I sigh. I don't want to talk about my ex. "What else do you know about Graham?"

She grabs a napkin and wipes her mouth. "Is he bothering you, Angie?"

I shake my head and respond, "No, well, not really."

"Getting under your skin, ah?"

I shove another messy wing into my mouth to avoid talking.

Claire sighs and leans her back into her chair. "There's really nothing to tell. It's just that at the agency, you get to make friends with some of the women. You know, through mixer events and such. It's actually quite a small world, and we girls stick together. You know, we talk amongst ourselves."

"Go on," I encourage, not sure where she is going with her train of thought.

"You don't fit his typical preferences at all."

What's his type then? I stare back out the window, trying to snuff out the rising feeling of inadequacy. "How so?"

"It seems he has a preference for hiring blonde girls. Whether they are natural ones or wannabes."

Well, I am neither of those. "Well, he paid me for last night—twice—but he didn't actually hire me. The date was supposed to be with Dominic."

"Which is another surprising thing."

I stop eating midbite and prompt Claire to spill.

"I ran into a couple of coworkers on campus this morning, and I didn't mention your name, but I hinted at a date with Dominic. Well, the girls were shocked. Because Dominic never reserves any of the girls or takes out new members. It's not protocol at all. I think he went through a nasty breakup recently and is staying low-key when it comes to public functions. And dating his employees would not be best for business from a financial standpoint. You would have been his first if it had actually worked out."

"But why would he break his pattern?"

"I have no idea. Maybe he likes you."

My attention moves back to the golden-haired couple on their luxury boat. The woman appears to have dumped a little wine on her cashmere sweater set, frowning deeply as her husband runs to get her a towel. Rich people problems.

I take a sip of my melting drink, bending my elbow and resting my chin in my hand. "Not smart to send gorgeous Graham as a placeholder."

Claire raises her drink to clink with mine in response. "He's nauseatingly hot, and I hate the arrogant bastard for it."

"Same," I mumble under my breath. Seriously, what is wrong with brown hair?

"Well, apparently Graham at one time hired a girl regularly to attend functions with him. Her name is Sophia." Claire pauses as if to contemplate whether or not she should continue with her story. I raise an eyebrow and give her the look that means I want full disclosure. "She was getting pretty wrapped up in his life. I am sure that he either convinced her or bought her for overnight dates. Well, one day out of nowhere he just stopped. Cut off all ties. At least that's how it appeared."

"You two were friends?"

"Nah, Sophia is the snooty high-class type of person who is only going to be more than just-friendly-in-passing to climb the social ladder faster. I had an ex-friend in high school who reminded me of her. Those types of people stomp on those around them to get to where they need to go. Anyway, because I'm not famous or the next Victoria's Secret dream angel or on the cover of Vogue, I barely existed to her. The only thing I like to climb is the StairMaster. Or onto some guy's—"

"Got it!" I announce, holding up my hands in surrender, knowing full well that I am blushing twenty shades of red.

"Wow, perv, I was going to say motorcycle." She giggles.

"Yeah, and having intercourse in Intercourse, Pennsylvania is not on your bucket list."

"That is correct. It is not on that list," Claire answers smugly.

I raise my eyebrow at her, not buying it.

"It's on my fuck-it list," she clarifies with a cheeky smirk.

I smack my palm to my forehead, shaking my head at her blatant gift of embarrassing me and detouring us completely away from the real topic of discussion. Claire grew up on the East Coast but definitely blends in well here on the western side. "I can see your reduction in swear words is no reduction at all."

"When I use it with a hyphen, it doesn't count."

"Sounds like you make up rules as you go."

"Hush, child, and let's get back to trying to figure out this man of yours."

"First off, I have no man. Second, Graham ditching Sophia is pretty harsh. But isn't this how the business goes? It's fake dating. Nothing real."

"Anyone who observed them could see that it was more than that. So maybe she was into him more than he was into her. That happens about ninety percent of the time. But the way he ended it appeared callous and cruel. Her heart was broken, says the casual onlooker."

"Is she still with the agency?"

"I don't think so. I haven't seen her in months."

"Is that why you warned me against Graham? Or am I not reading between the lines well enough?"

Claire shrugs and looks off to her left, avoiding direct

eye contact. "He's a charmer. You're an innocent. Those two types of people seem to inevitably attract and react."

"Or implode," I say with a shrug.

Her attention is back on me, her expression warm. "You know? He is searching for a girl he can use his charm on. If you were easy, his talent would be wasted. I just don't want him to do to you what he did to Sophia, Angie. You deserve better—fake dating or not."

"Well, I would have to allow him to get that close to me. It is free will. For me and for Sophia. Did she honestly think that a guy paying her money for her company would fall in love with her and they would live happily ever after? Who would want to be with a guy long term like that anyway?"

"It isn't as hard as you think. Some of these men you may encounter are experts at getting what they want—in both their business and personal lives—by using whatever resources are at their disposal. Graham seems like a man who is not used to hearing the word 'no.' I am sure that you are a challenge to him. Something new that the agency hasn't seen in a long time."

"A shiny new toy," I interject, slurping the last drops of my banana-flavored cocktail from my glass. Or fresh meat.

"Something like that. But seriously, Angie. Just be careful. Keep work professional and keep your personal life out of it. It's safer that way."

"Well, I have been encouraged not to have a boyfriend while working for the agency anyway. So for the next six months, I am automatically forced to be impersonal."

Claire nods. "I strive to do that too, but it isn't easy."

"How did your date go last night? We never got a chance to chat about it."

"So, Ethan. He's pretty cool. He's been married before but his ex-wife seems like such a bad match for him, a.k.a. a royal bitch. No wonder why it never worked. What I am saying is that I have done this for several months and have been able to keep everything separate. Until last night. I got that pang of something that I haven't felt in a long time."

"Wow. You really like him?" I ask the redundant question, mainly out of shock. "Even more than the last guy?"

"Yes," she states flatly. "That guy just had a huge—"

"Personality."

"Why yes, a huge personality." She accentuated the last word slowly into staccato syllables. "Too bad his skills at using it were lacking. But anyway, I'm wary and on guard. With extremely low expectations."

"Ethan has a kid?" I ask.

"Yeah. He has a four-year-old son."

Claire has always wanted a sense of security. Her parents in Virginia avoid taking any responsibility for her. I get that she is an adult, but their level of disconnect just seems very odd to me. I know that them sending money to her has helped her to maintain a certain lifestyle. But I also know she longs for the unconditional love that is lacking in her life from those who should in theory give it out freely.

"How did the actual date go?"

"Better than expected. Last night was about meeting his ex-wife and her new boyfriend. Ethan hired me to help even out the score. He is having a difficult time allowing another man into his spot with his son." Claire shifts in her seat and wipes her mouth with her napkin. "Okay, enough about me. Back to you."

I play with my straw wrapper, thinking about the voice

message and texts that were left for me this morning. "What do you suggest I do if Graham asks me out via the website?"

"If you see a red flag, then keep saying no. But be aware that he can still book you for a date if you are free." Her hands are animated while she punctuates each point with a sudden movement, a sure sign that she is passionate on the topic. "But you can reject him. It is just that rejecting him could cause a rift within the agency. You might get a bad reputation. And since he obviously knows Dominic on a more personal level—"

"Ugh," I groan.

"Pissing off the boss, despite how laid-back he seems, is never good for business."

"Yeah, exactly," I agree. Claire has a good point. I stare down at the last bite of my bread that rests on my plate. Is there really no easy way out? We are only speaking in hypotheticals, but I'm already starting to get a headache.

"Word spreads like wildfire among men of elite status. It is like some special code they live by. They probably profile us beyond our Entice account."

Man code. "Gotcha." It makes sense.

"Anyway, let's stay focused," Claire says, clapping her hands together. "For today's preparation, I created a vision board to help us stay on track."

"Of course you did."

Her smile grows while she digs in her bag to pull out a folded piece of paper. "It was made on short notice, so keep your expectations on the low end of the spectrum."

I watch as she unfolds her work of art. "Mission Angie

Impossible?" I read the title. "Sounds ominous. Maybe I want to back down already." I look over the paper and see a 2D mannequin version of myself, with scribbled notes written along the edges. When I see all of the things I need to do in print, I ask myself again if it is all worth it.

"You'll be fine. You're in good hands with me." Claire clicks her tongue and then scoops out an ice cube from her glass of water to chomp on. "It'll be fun."

"If you say so."

"As we accomplish each task, I have a cutout to add to your body on the vision board. That way, we make sure you are all complete."

I give her a weak smile. I am glad she is helping me navigate these details. I already feel so lost, and we haven't even started.

"Ready to go? We have a lot of shopping and pampering to do."

"Yup," I mumble, knowing that I will most likely be blowing through the majority of my Visa gift card to please one man for one night. Seems like a big waste when I put it like that. Parts of me surrender to the mere fact that I will still not be enough for Mark—regardless of following his orders to a tee.

I am not going to be enough.

With travel and date preparation time factored in, Claire and I have three hours to run through the streets of the Pearl District with our list of tasks and vision-board outline to accomplish. I follow Claire into the nail salon first, and we both get our fingernails and toes done. The foot bath and massage make the outrageous cost worth it. I mean, seriously, who can afford this luxury every two weeks? I relax in the chair until the sweetest employee ushers me to the back for a fifteen-minute tan in the bed. I strip and lie down in the coffin, vowing to never do this again unless it is absolutely necessary. Even though the experience was soothing, I regret exposing my body to the harmful rays.

Picky bastard.

I forgo the suggestion of professional waxing for my brows and agree to let Claire do them at home, as well as put my hair up. If Mark notices the difference, so be it.

It takes fifty minutes to finish up at the salon. Claire unleashes me to the cell phone store while she gets a head start dress shopping next door in a trendy designer shop. I give her the list of qualifications on what Mark wants me to wear, from head to toe, making sure we are on the same page.

"Just go to the junior section, because apparently he wants me to look like a whore," I half joke. If he expects me to act like one, then he is going to be disappointed. She scoots into the boutique while I enter the phone store.

It doesn't take me long to have my new device in my hand with a sparkly magenta case. At least the workers got a good laugh over my much-needed upgrade. Heading out of the store, I set out to find Claire.

Once inside the boutique, I follow the sound of the high-pitched giggles and discover her in the dressing room with a champagne flute in hand. I have been doing this all wrong. Target does not serve alcohol while shoppers try on clothes.

Pretty sure if they did, it would end with higher cases of buyer's remorse.

"Try these three," she insists, pushing me into the little room. She retreats into another room with a few articles of her own to try on.

It is daunting being surrounded by this many mirrors. I don't even know which one to look at.

As soon as I try the first option and realize that it fits, I decide to skip the other two and get this one. Shoes and accessories are a bit more difficult due to all of the variations in styles and details. Claire's capable hands make the selection for me. I don't care one way or the other. Once the ensemble for the Mark Tanner date is complete, we run through the displays of clothes, grabbing more stuff to try on to add to our wardrobes.

"Here, try this on; you look awesome in this color," Claire announces, handing me a cranberry intentionally-holed sweater.

"Um, you do wear something under this, right?"

"Of course." She giggles. "A bra."

"Classy," I grumble. I make a mental note to get a tank top.

"Or just accessorize with nipple jewelry." How she says that with a straight face, I have no idea.

"Oh yes, stupid me," I answer sarcastically. "Hoops or studs?"

"Um," she turns to examine the fabric more closely. I start to think that she is completely being serious. "I would go for hoops, personally. Studs might snag it. Or rip your nip."

I can't help but roll my eyes.

Thirty minutes later, I'm in line with three pairs of skinny jeans, two pairs of leggings, five shirts, three sweaters, four dresses, and all the stuff that I need for tonight. When the cash register lady informs me that I owe $3,465, I nearly pass out. Claire whoops loudly, pumping her fist in the air, as if her favorite sports team has won.

"I was expecting much higher."

"I guess there is a 'mega-sale' going on," I mumble, using overdramatized air quotes at mega-sale. I pass my Visa gift card to the worker and pray that I can use what I am purchasing on future dates—freeing up the need to go back to this wallet wasteland again. At least for a few months.

We walk along the sidewalk bordering the river and make our way to the car. We load up the trunk with our purchases and settle in for the drive back home. The new sound of an incoming text startles me as Claire enters the on-ramp that leads over the Fremont Bridge, nearly hitting the driver in front of us who is yielding appropriately.

"Whoa," I squeal, grabbing the above-the-door strap to brace myself. "Easy, Claire."

"I have the right of way."

"You clearly don't," I counter.

"Well, I should."

I look down at my phone as soon as the car stops shaking. When I see the name of the sender, I groan.

Dad: Angela, I would love for you to come home for a visit. I promise to be on my best behavior. I know you are still mad. Please call me. Love ya.

My pulse quickens at the words. I don't have a home. No, my home was sold without even my knowledge or opinion. Guilt seeps through me like poison, hitting every crevice available for the taking. He has texted two days in a row. It's a record for him. Part of me wants to believe that he has changed or is at least ready to seek help. The other part of me wants to withdraw, knowing deep down that pleasing me with his own good health is not his top priority. I pocket away my frustration and focus on mentally preparing for my date. If I don't compartmentalize all of my emotions, I will never be able to function.

Once home, Claire works her expert hands on my hair and makeup, dolling me up. "You know, it would be pretty funny if you showed up tonight wearing the exact opposite of what Mr. Picky Pants requested. You know, like thick leg warmers, a tacky tunic, and clown makeup."

I laugh at the thought, agreeing with a slight nod, careful not to mess up the progression of the twisted updo. "I'll do it, if you do it," I tease, knowing that her goal as of twenty-four hours ago is to reel Ethan into her net, whether she acknowledges it officially or not.

"Rain check. I'm totally game in the future," she agrees with a cheeky smile.

"I was joking," I state without fluctuating my volume.

"Too late." Claire gives a little shrug implying that I set myself up all on my own. "I'm holding you to that too. But, lucky you, I'll wait until it's not a first date to collect my entertainment."

She can't be serious, but she is. Claire smooths the final touches on my ensemble, making me twirl and practice walking. "Well, Legs, you're smoking hot. Even a guy with a broken penis and erectile dysfunction would be able to see that. I have a serious hetero-girl crush on you."

"Is that even possible?"

"Totally, you are a—"

"No," I interrupt, "the broken penis part."

"Yup. We'll Google Image it later. And you now have the luxury of doing it from your new phone. You won't regret it. Totally cool stuff."

I burst out with a full-blown belly laugh at her awesomeness.

"Okay, all done. You're good to go with five minutes to spare before the bastard is to arrive."

I wear my identity bracelet for the first time, and it surprisingly fits perfectly. I am packing my black clutch with the essentials when the doorbell rings. I skip down the stairs with my deathtrap heels in hand and peek out through the security hole. I verify that it is Mark—whose head takes up my entire view—and open the door.

"Whoa," he responds in a rush. His eyes flash with—

Approval?

The air leaks out of my lungs in record speed, as nerves get the best of me. I swallow hard, not really knowing what to say or do. I clear my throat, staring up into the dark brown eyes of my date. His jet-black hair makes him strikingly handsome, matching the shade of his three-piece designer suit. The deep maroon tie creates a dramatic effect of confidence and power. I shoot him my best charming-but-professional smile.

"Turn around."

"What?" I gasp. I could not have possibly heard him correctly.

He clears his throat. "Let me see you."

I stare at him in utter surprise. Is he serious?

"C'mon, do a little twirl."

I comply but feel the bitter taste of acid inching up my throat.

"Very nice." He hands me a large bouquet of red roses when I return to face him. "These are for you." Smacking his lips, he mutters something about me earning it.

He leans into me and kisses my cheek, lingering a little too long for my comfort level. His cologne is strong and burns the lining of my nostrils, making me want to sneeze just to clear out the scent.

"Thank you for the flowers, Mark."

"You look amazing by the way. Wow. Just wow. What am I going to do with you?"

Hopefully nothing but take me to dinner and back home safely. I'm already having regrets.

"Thank you." I examine the delicate flowers, bringing my nose up to the arrangement to savor the fragrance. "Give me a minute. I'm going to put these in a vase in the kitchen. You can sit down if you want." I gesture to the couch with a swing of my hand.

I walk into the kitchen and am glad for the chance to regroup my thoughts. My phone buzzes with a text alert, which I ignore. I quickly discard the tissue paper and cut the stems. I follow the care steps on the flower food packet and place the vase onto the island for display.

I hear muffled voices in the living room and know that Claire has joined Mark. I hastily dig out my phone from the clutch and see that Graham is the sender. I clumsily open the app, still getting used to the change in my devices.

Graham: Being a good girl?

My body heats at the sight of the words "good girl" on the screen. There is something very provocative about those two simple words. I type a quick message in response. On impulse, I slip on my stilettos and snap a picture of just my feet. I hit send.

Angie: Never.

Angie: Being bad is way more fun.

Graham: Fuck, Angie. I'm still at work.

I lean my butt against the island and type another message.

Angie: Same.

Graham: What do you mean WORK?

Angie: Gotta go.

I hit "send" and conceal the phone inside my clutch. I can hear the vibrations indicating a series of texts through the fabric of the bag. I ignore them and head back into the living room to join Claire and Mark who seem to be having a semiheated discussion on the new casino project.

As soon as Mark notices me, he rises and walks over to grip my elbow softly. I control my impulse to jerk away and try to present myself with grace.

"Ready to go?" he asks.

"I think so."

He steers me to the doorway. I grab my keys to shove in my bag and wave goodbye to Claire. She seems too quiet, as if something is weighing on her mind. I give her a look, and she shoos me off.

I am wearing all black—black dress, black thigh-highs, black clutch, and black stiletto heels. If it wasn't for the extreme shortness of the strapless dress, I would look like I was going to a funeral. Perhaps I am mourning the loss of my modesty, as I slip further and further into the escort lifestyle. All night I will be afraid of accidentally flashing someone my Hollywood. The sparkly barrettes holding my hair up and matching jewelry give the outfit flare and personality.

"You take direction really well, Angie. You look amazing."

I nod and give a shy smile. I wish he would stop making comments about my appearance. Despite the kindness to his words, I can't help but notice the condescending feel to their meaning. Our age gap is showing. He is treating me like a child.

Mark's intense stare makes my skin chill with goose bumps—but not in a hot-and-bothered kind of way. He ushers me to the limo, and we are greeted by his driver, who is a man in his fifties with salt-and-pepper hair. The hand on my lower back makes me jump. I try to settle my nerves at the physical contact, attempting to hide my obvious unease. I slip onto the leather seat, carefully grabbing the hem of my dress to keep it from riding up my thighs. It is obscenely short for the low limo seats. I groan, realizing I don't even have the slightest bit of wiggle room to cross or move my legs. My phone buzzes with an incoming message, and I quickly mute the device without even looking at it.

Mark breaks the silence of the quiet ride. "Tell me about yourself, Angie."

I inwardly roll my eyes at the cliché question.

"Well, I am in my last semester at River Valley. I am in the process of finishing up my English degree." It is a half-truth. "Then looking for an internship." Part of my subconscious wants people to know that I have a goal—that this agency job is temporary.

"Pretty and smart. A rare combination."

"Thanks," I answer timidly, only because I feel obligated to say something when complimented.

"How's the outlook? Have you delved into the search for potential internships? In writing, I presume? Teaching?"

"Writing," I clarify. "Not really sure of the prospects. It is an extremely competitive field with way more applicants than positions. By not getting an internship, I would basically be settling for some mediocre job that doesn't pay well and doesn't allow me to have freedom to do my own work. I would essentially be—"

"A slave."

"Pretty much."

Mark reaches into the minibar that is built into the seat bench and grabs a bottle of wine that already has the cork popped. He offers me a drink and I accept, knowing that it will help with my growing nerves.

"I might be able to help you out, actually. I have a few connections to some publishers and news outlets. An old college buddy, actually, works for Pacific Press."

"Wow, really?"

"Life is one big social web."

I perk up for the first time all night. The offer of help extinguishes the initial comments I was quick to make just hours ago. Maybe Mark isn't as much of an ass as I thought. "You would be willing to put in a good word for me?" I ask quietly, sipping the red wine that has a bit too much tannin for my liking.

"If you're good."

"How will you find that out?"

"First work on a resume or a portfolio of work if you have not started already. I'll touch base with some of my associates and put out feelers."

"I appreciate that. Thank you."

"No problem." Mark's smile shows his professionally whitened teeth. No human could ever have that white of teeth on their own. His polished look makes my instincts send a warning to be on guard. I can't start trusting freely just because of charm and possible bridge building toward a better future. My track record for trusting early has resulted in heartbreak nearly every time.

When the limo stops in front of a tall glass and steel building, I stare out the window in awe. Although I know there must be lights on behind the glass panels, the only lights that are visible are the ones shining externally up the sides of the building. Around the foundation, little spotlights are hidden between green shrubbery. The structure is striking and different from all of the surrounding buildings. It's as if the building has an angelic glow.

My eyes latch onto the concrete side of the building that has the name etched into the stone. The letters are covered in a gold paint. Or maybe it is actual gold. Bright lights are angled toward the name, showing it off in the dark of the night.

I gasp when my brain finally registers the words.

"Welcome to the Hoffman Hotel."

11

"Here?" I ask in shock. "We are going to the Hoffman Hotel?"

Mark's eyes twinkle. "Do you have a problem with the restaurants at this hotel?" He smirks, gesturing toward the building through the tinted limo window.

"I, um, I..." I stare blankly at Mark as I try to form a complete sentence. "I've never been inside before. Nor did I know it even existed."

While living on the outskirts of Portland during college has given me ample opportunity to explore, I never had a reason—or a hefty paycheck—to seek out the luxury that is abundant in the growing city. By blatant judgment on just the exterior grandeur, I doubt that I will ever have enough money to afford even a room that can be reserved by the hour.

"It was only six months ago that it became the Hoffman Hotel. Before that it was a commercial office complex.

More floors were added, the interior was gutted, and the exterior got a major face lift."

I nod my head at the history lesson in a nutshell. "This is Graham Hoffman's hotel?" I ask because of pure curiosity over the mysterious man. He intrigues me.

"It is a family property, yes. I doubt he has time to run it or be much of an influence. He has his hands in other dealings."

I make an O with my lips. I still can't figure out why Mark would take me to this hotel out of all the others in the city. He could have just taken me to a stand-alone restaurant. He better not want to book a room.

"Let's get inside." His smile reaches his eyes, making them dance with mischief. He is up to something. Obviously. He reaches for the door and hits a button on the panel. A moment later, the driver opens my door, reaching his hand in to pull me out in one swift motion. I quickly pull at the back of my dress, feeling the air hit the exposed part of my upper thighs. Mark slips out behind me, his face lighting up like a slot machine as he gives me a once-over. "Has anyone ever told you how great your"—he covers his mouth as he does a half cough—"how long your legs look?" His audible choke makes me frown. Can he be any more transparent?

I give an awkward shrug as a response to the not-so-creative flirting. Even though Mark barely looks thirty, his piercing looks and hidden messages give him the creepy-old-man vibe. I picture him with a glass of scotch, a cigar, and two stripper girls giving him a lap dance as he adjusts his suit pants in some underground club for the elite. I chuckle at the irony of my image. Entice is basically the same thing but aboveground.

I am the stripper.

I feel like a walking disaster—just one wrong bend and oops, nip slip. The outfit he encouraged is not meant for my height. The fact that he is so smitten with himself is what unnerves me the most, nearly pushing a panic button within my head. The comments and sly grins make me uncomfortable, and the night has just begun.

The hand at the small of my back makes me jump. I doubt I will get used to these touches. Mark smiles down at me and presses his fingers into my clothed flesh, rubbing it in little circles. I swallow hard, trying to push the rising knot down into my throat, silently thanking Claire for choosing a dress with back coverage. I can do this. We shuffle toward the main entrance. A doorman greets us politely, directing us inside the warmth. His smile is grandfatherly and contagious, without a hint of creepy. I can't help but contrast the stranger and Mark.

The opulent décor of the main lobby strikes me as soon as my eyes are able to adjust to the lighting. The shiny marble floors are white speckled with big rectangular black sections spaced in between to form a pattern. Rectangular prism columns attach to the ceilings, highlighting the impressive modern version of a chandelier. The light structure consists of clear glass vertical pillars, falling from the ceiling like crystal icicles, making a swirl pattern to cover the ceiling space of the entire lobby. Amidst the color monopoly of black and white, there are punches of blood red that cover the trims behind the information and registration desks. The same color floats into the sitting area. It is on a pillow, on the border of a rug, and on a table's centerpiece. Elegant signs portray arrows that point to the areas of the hotel. The spa, gym, mall, theater, and aquarium are the ones that catch my attention. All of the workers—regardless of gender—are behind the sleek black marble desks dressed in black pant suits, a crisp white shirt, and a red tie or scarf. Silver tags attach to the right side of each outfit, stating the name of the worker.

Sensing my infatuation with the layout, Mark mumbles something into my ear, making me pull back and look up at him. "Sorry. What did you say?" I really didn't hear him. But from the glint in his eyes, I brace myself for something less than respectable.

"I was saying that if you keep looking at this place like you are, I might need to consider taking it over."

I frown at the words, not knowing if he is joking or being serious.

"They have nice rooms here too," he says with a slow wink.

Eww.

"So you know of Graham and his family?" I ask to change the subject and retrieve information.

He thinks about the question, studying my face. His laugh fills up the silent tension between us. "Yeah, we go way back." The way Mark says the words makes my hairs stand on end.

"And you two can't stand each other?"

Mark sniffs and stares off into the lobby. "Everything is a pissing contest with Graham. Always has been."

"Why did you bring me here? Are you trying to goad him?"

Am I a pawn in your little testosterone game?

"Graham isn't easy to rile up. But trying is all the fun," he states matter-of-factly, making me shift on my heels to better my stance.

Well, you sure had him in a tizzy last night in the elevator. I am not the only one playing with fire. And you didn't answer the question. I resist sharing my wayward thoughts. Boys will be boys when it comes to sizing each other up in the locker room of the business world. Part of me wonders if seeing me with Graham last night inspired Mark to want to dangle me as live bait in front of him at his family's hotel tonight. I feel a bit queasy at being disloyal to someone who I have no loyalty to; I don't like the idea of being a chess piece at all. I shake my errant feelings and thoughts—trying to compose myself and relax. It is what it is—a paid date.

"Do you think that's the best idea—provoking Graham?"

Mark turns to look straight into my eyes, pushing back a piece of loose hair from my cheek. "You need to learn your place. Your job is to look pretty and do as you're told."

My eyes drop down to the little space between us. Every part of me wants to resist the conformity. I am not one of those women who submits to a man. My gender has come too far throughout decades in history to backpedal now. But as hard as it is to admit, Mark is right. I need to be agreeable. Now is not the time for my moral compass to find a voice.

I look up at his unyielding face and nod.

"Graham will break your heart anyway. You are best to remember that."

I blink rapidly and try to maintain my poise, but his

words affect me. I have been warned multiple times by three different people—one being Graham himself. Maybe I should start listening.

I follow Mark into the elevator to the seventh floor. Like the lobby, the elevator shares the same color scheme. On the mirror in the back of the car, white descriptive nouns are printed in different sizes and fonts. I smile at the words relating to love, freedom, and life.

"I should warn you that tonight you will be meeting three potential business associates. They own laboratories all over the United States. I need to gain their trust as a distributor and make a wickedly good first impression."

"So they make medicine and you pitch those brands to hospitals and doctor offices?"

"In a nutshell, yes."

"Got it."

"So, you will be meeting Benjamin, Samson, and Edward. Feel free to openly flirt."

"Excuse me?" I ask. My voice is hoarse. What the hell is wrong with this guy?

"I give you permission."

Gee, thanks. The blood rushes out of my face, leaving my cheek muscles numb. "Okay."

"They are men, after all, and if you can assist in getting them all to sign, then I would be indebted to you."

Is he for real? "Um, I"—my gaze stays fixed on the mirrored wall to avoid meeting his—"am not good at flirting." Or the unexpected politics behind pharmaceutical sales. "I wouldn't know what to do." It is the truth. I'm a horrible actress.

"That's impossible," he croons. "You are a young

female with all the working parts." His eyes scan up and down my body, lingering at my parts. "Just get up to go to the restroom often. A little cleavage and ass shake always goes a long way, doll."

The cheapness of the comments crawls into my pores. I am not a showgirl. My instincts on Mark were correct. He's a dog. Not the cute golden retriever type. No, he is the mutt that all the other female dogs try to avoid.

The elevator stops on the seventh floor, and Mark leads me to the doors of the Bleu Lounge. The posh French restaurant is adorned with deep blues and whites. All of the tables and chairs have sharp looking edges, crisp lines, and sleek cutout shapes. The huge oval bar in the center of the lounge creates a dramatic effect. Jets of blue water shoot up from the glass frame around the base. The lighting is dimmed, creating a sophisticated aura to the place.

Blue signature acai berry cocktails with floating berries are served to us upon arrival. It is a surprising treat from such a high-profile venue, especially one that overcharges for everything and still keeps the customers coming back. All of the workers are dressed in all white, despite the impracticality of a chance for their outfits being stained. They look impeccable, so the risk seems worth it.

I sip my complimentary beverage and allow Mark to guide me to the reserved table in the back of the room, specifically set up for this business meeting. The white table touches the wall of windows, looking out into the beautiful harbor. The sight is spectacular with the lights on the water. This hotel is definitely sitting on prime real estate.

The fully cushioned leather chairs are in a brilliant shade of aqua. My eyes look around the room. I have the weird feeling that I am being watched. Nothing is out of the ordinary, though. Just a bunch of finely dressed customers enjoying a Thursday night out.

Our waiter greets us, and Mark informs him that we are still waiting on three more people. He orders an expensive vintage red wine for the table and an order of canapés.

"So are you dating anyone?" he asks, completely out of left field.

"I don't date."

"And why is that, Angie?"

"Because work comes first for me right now." How do you tell someone who makes buckets full of money that you are in need of some of the overflow? That is, after all, why I am here, on a Thursday night, dressed like a hooker.

"Maybe you will change your mind after a few of these bad boys?" Mark jokes, holding up the blue cocktail that slips down my throat way too easily.

Before I can grimace, the other three businessmen arrive —apparently traveling together—and introductions are done. I turn my attention to each set of eyes separately and shake hands. When my gaze reaches the last man, Benjamin, my heart nearly stops beating. A nasty feeling rushes through my veins, but I cannot understand why. There is something about the way he looks at me that rubs me the wrong way, but I can't put my finger on it.

"What did you say your name was again, honey?" Benjamin asks me, his eyes twinkling like the boats out in the harbor. He reaches for my hand, clasping it in his meaty pair.

"Angie," I exhale, my lungs feeling like they are going to collapse. What is going on?

"Nice to meet you, Angie," he says, squeezing my hand suggestively, his hard thumb making pinprick sensations scratch at my insides.

I sit back down into my seat and try to remain calm as Benjamin finds his chair directly across from me. Every time I glance up from my drink, I find him watching me. His brow furrows, making me want to go home and take a shower. Gross.

All business talk rests on the back burner for the first twenty minutes, while we all snack on appetizers and sip semidry wine. I politely down the amount served to me, hoping that the taste grows on me; it is not my typical choice. I need to slip some sugar into it and stir.

Edward's warm smile puts me at ease. He appears to be in his midthirties and lacks the sleazeball persona that is present among his peers. Out of the men, he is the one who stands out for his impeccable manners and sensibility. "So, Angie, tell us about yourself."

I hate questions like this. Where do I even begin? For starters, this is not about me. This meeting is about Mark and his business ventures. "Um, well, I am a student at River Valley U, studying English."

"Nice," Edward and Samson answer in unison. One man genuine, the other unreadable.

"So, Benjamin and Samson have been doing business together for a while now," Mark interjects, turning to look at me. "Mostly in the states, although they have laboratories for experimental purposes and research internationally."

I nod in response and give a smile to each man.

Mark's hand rubs up and down my arm that is closest to him. It takes everything in me not to make a scene and tell him to take his hands off me. Benjamin's eyes follow the path of Mark's fingers along my arm, glancing up to give me a sly smirk. "I'm hoping that they're on board with my new endeavor. I'd love their support."

I nod again, only because I do not know what else to do or say.

Between Mark's blatant attempts at supposed nonchalant touching and Benjamin's sadistic smile, I find it easy to excuse myself to go to the restroom. As soon as I move to push my seat out, all of the men rise—just like gentlemen do in the movies. Mark helps me out, which I am actually grateful for, because the seats are not light. As I walk away, I feel all of their eyes boring into my back. Okay, most likely it is my ass.

I carefully make my way to the other side of the room, where the restrooms are located, trying not to face plant in my stilettos and show everyone my fine china underneath my scrap of a dress.

If restrooms could be described as luxurious, the ones at Bleu definitely fit the bill. The first thing I notice as I walk in is the smell. Yes, really. Sweet almond floods my nostrils, making me close my eyes as I inhale the scent. Hints of cinnamon and vanilla linger in the air. It reminds me of the flavor combination I would use for icing cupcakes at the bakery. My senses shoot to overload status, as I take in the décor and architectural style of the detailed trims and furniture selections.

Soft instrumental string music plays through the discreet speakers in the corners of the room. A plush white leather sofa rests against the wall, and I wonder if it would go unnoticed if I just lounged there for an hour. Fresh cut lilies are displayed in a rich blue vase. The stalls are private with huge wooden doors that actually have working locks and multiple hooks.

I enter the personal toilet room and get situated. The door outside creaks and the clicking of footsteps filters over the musical arrangement. I can tell the ages of the girls by the giddy chirp of their voices—definitely lower or midtwenties. Just like me.

"You're too uptight, Britt." I strain my ear to try to hear more, if only for something to do. "His game, not mine," the same girl responds. Drama. I seriously have a problem for being so entertained by even the slightest amount of it. "Ahhh, he is such a good fuck." Alrighty then.

"Deprived much?" the melodic voice asks her friend. A hint of an accent breaks through the spoken words. The sound of running water and clicking cases of makeup foundation muddles with the clarity of my eavesdropping. I edge forward on the seat, continuing to strain my ear at the gossip. I know that I should mind my own business…but I just can't seem to follow through.

"…slow…loves the chase…"

And then I hear it. The one name that changes everything. "Graham."

"Well, it doesn't hurt."

I hear the sigh on the other side of the wall. "It might be too soon."

"He might just need a refresher course." They both giggle, and the melody is like nails on the chalkboard. "I mean, most roadmaps for the female body are the same. He just needs a nudge to know you're interested in getting back to how things were."

Feeling territorial for absolutely no rational reason, I flush and make my way to the sink area in a heated rush—hoping to catch a glimpse of the competition that I logically shouldn't be worried about. We all have a past. Why is any of this bothering me?

My detective skills uncover that the tall, supermodel blonde is after Graham—again? Her look is enchanting—a classy Reese Witherspoon, with long Cinderella locks and huge green eyes. His type. This must be Sophia?

Sophia's friend, Britt, is the same girl on Mark's arm last night. Her skin looks even more flawless than the last time I saw her. Her red feathery hair complements her green eyes. Both girls are stunning and hard not to look at, for the mere fact that their beauty is so…

Pretty and porcelain and painstakingly perfect. It is definitely easy to hate on them.

I catch myself staring and draw unnecessary attention to my plainness.

"Dear, you would be a gem if I could bum a cig from you," Britt asks in my direction, her eyes glowing with need. Definitely European.

Is she really thinking about smoking in here? Surely there are rules against it, even in a place that caters to the customer's needs.

"Oh, um, I don't smoke." I focus on washing my hands, adding extra exfoliating soap to my palms to prolong the nosy investigation. "Sorry," I mutter. I feel that it is perfectly natural to keep my eye contact in the mirror now that I am being addressed, even if I am useless in the nicotine supply department.

"Wait, I know you," Britt announces, giving me a once-over.

I nod slowly. "I think we met last night."

"Oh yeah, you were with Graham."

Blonde Barbie Sophia darts her eyes to mine and then down to my wrist to see my identity bracelet. "Lucky girl. But I'm surprised he chose you."

"And why is that?" I ask, locking eyes with her in the mirror.

"Because Graham doesn't date for fun."

"Oh, yeah?" I respond.

"Yup," she chirps. "He dates for fucks."

Her tone is stiff. Her words hollow.

"How do you know I wasn't just that?" I ask cheekily. I mentally smack myself for even entertaining this line of conversation.

Sophia tilts her head at me, deep in thought, and then bursts out laughing. "Right," she exhales, out of breath.

I swallow hard and go back to focusing on my excessive handwashing.

"Britt, you should quit," Sophia suggests, changing the subject away from me. "I did a few months ago. It's the whole clean-up-my-act image I'm trying to portray. Hopefully it'll be noticed."

"How's that working for you, bitch?" Britt sneers, pointing at something concealed in Sophia's Gucci handbag.

The girls share a secret smile that I barely catch from the mirror. Trouble. They leave before me, and I loiter a bit longer inside before having to go back to the table of awkwardness.

A million questions invade my thoughts. Does Graham

know that Sophia is here? Why did she come back to Portland now and from where? Why the hell does it bother me so much that she is after Graham?

I exit the restroom and travel down the corridor that leads to the dining area. From behind, I feel a tug at my arm. I jerk back. My heels knock me off balance, and I start to fall. Strong hands steady me, and the clean woodsy scent awakens my senses—completely throwing my mind into a spin. I try to catch my breath. My view of the room goes upright and my gaze changes to the source of the support.

"What are you doing here?"

"Graham," I snarl. "What the actual fuck?" I ask in a heated rage. "You nearly killed me with your manhandling! What's your deal?" My words flood past my lips without a filter to contain the raw emotion that shoots through my core.

"Such a dirty mouth," he scolds patronizingly. The corners of his mouth curl up in the sexiest of grins. "Lucky for me, I like dirty."

Damn him and his gorgeous looks. His hair falls around his ears, giving in to the playful head tilts that he directs my way. I fantasize about how soft it would feel under my fingertips—but only for a moment. I am mad at him after all for his greeting. And what is he doing here?

"Really? You are going there? How about, 'Sorry Angie, I thought you were someone else'? Or perhaps"—my brow furrows—"'I'm sorry for grabbing hold of you, nearly knocking you down'? Or better yet, how about 'It will never happen again'?"

"I wouldn't have let you fall," he answers smugly, his

quirky smile full of mirth. "I would have thrown myself on the floor just to cushion you if I had to, princess."

Well, now. I fight to hide my wicked grin and the gushy feeling the word princess does to my insides.

"Besides," he says, "I'm not sorry about anything. You feel good in my arms." His eyes glow at my internal struggle to maintain my composure. He's having way too much fun at the expense of my amateur acting skills.

"Not the point." My teeth bite down on my bottom lip to keep from rattling off more swear words that beat against my tongue.

"You have not been responding to any of my texts, Angie."

"I probably won't after I decide to read them either," I respond matter-of-factly.

"Come with me. Let's get out of here."

"No." I shake my head to add emphasis and plant my feet.

He starts to turn me, never letting go of me. His pewter suit hugs him in all of the right places. The crisp, freshly pressed white shirt makes his hair look even darker. I want to tangle my fingers through it and tug. Instead, I play with the soft, expensive fabric of the wool blend, massaging his forearms as I examine the quality. "Unless you want to stand here in the middle of the restaurant and feel me up. No complaints from me."

"What?" I look at my fingers and quickly pull them away.

"I'm completely content with that option, although I imagine some old folks would have a heart attack at your expense. If you're willing to take that risk, by all means continue."

I gasp loudly before I can form anything coherent.

"You know that your reactions to me only make me want to scandalize you more. You are conditioning me. Positive reinforcement at its best."

My nose scrunches up in disgust, my frustration heightened at the exchange. Everything is happening so fast and my head is spinning. "Graham, I am working."

His eyes focus on my wrist as realization hits. A low growl vibrates from his throat, his eyes fierce with an indescribable emotion. What did he expect? Surely after meeting me that first day, my attire alone would indicate that I am an average girl just trying to get by. It should be obvious that the only reason I am here is because someone else is paying for it.

"I figured as much," he says, toying with my silver bracelet, "yet part of me still had high hopes for you."

"What is that supposed to mean?" I glare into his eyes, ready to spit venom. "The point of the job is to go out on dates. It is pretty hypocritical for you to look down on me for this line of work when you keep women like me in business by purchasing us as dates." He should know this! Besides, the cost of the dinner would probably be equivalent to my gas money budget for the next three months—not that I'm good at mental math or anything. Did he expect me to just saunter into an expensive French restaurant by myself, with college loans and all? Plus, eating alone usually would entail pretending to shuffle through a "long" list of nonexistent text messages or giving the illusion that I need to catch up on imaginary schoolwork. Solo dining only works at cafes, during the day, with reading material in hand. Not at French bistros—with ancient vintages and immaculate sateen napkins that I am afraid to dirty.

"Give me a chance to conclude my business dinner with some associates. Five minutes max. Then I'll take you home. Sit at the bar and order whatever you like. It's on me. Just give them my name." The wink that follows furthers my frustration. When did the wink come back into style as an acceptable form of flirting?

I stare in disbelief at the directive. Who is this man? And do I really want to hang around to find out? "I don't want to go home." Just saying the words make me feel vulnerable and wary of the reaction that I wait to observe. This man does not like to be told no. Well, this girl does not like to be told what to do, regardless of how good the intentions are.

"Well, then we can go on a tour of the amenities here. Or have dessert. Whatever you like." If I had my doubts before, I do not now. Graham wants to pursue me. Reasons, yet to be determined. The possibility of grabbing sweets is a low blow. He's playing hardball—dangling weaknesses in front of me.

I focus on Graham's steel gaze, his blue eyes turning to a brooding storm. It is the same blue as the main color scheme of the restaurant. I am enthralled by both.

The electrifying fingers remain in place—one on my waist, the other on my elbow. "What would I have to do for you to tell me why you are so amused right now?" he asks.

I am not sure what comes over me, but I want to create the shock factor—if only this once. "I was wondering how much a room here would be for the night."

"Easily affordable and worth every penny that I own," he grinds out between his teeth, obviously trying to maintain a certain level of control.

"Your family would make you pay?"

His eyes twitch. "I would choose to pay," he states quietly.

"I'm here with Mark."

"It's like you want me to get arrested." The sneer shakes me to the core. His fingers tighten predatorily on the curve of my back. For a split second, I question whether I did something wrong, besides dampening the mood with the utterance of another man's name. The energy in the room quickly turns foul. The influx of testosterone surges behind my back as I feel the presence of my date hot on my heels.

"Hoffman." Mark's eyes take in my stance. "Angie, I came to see if you were okay. You've been gone awhile." He stares at Graham and then shifts his attention between the hand on my elbow and the one on my lower back. His eyes darken possessively, making me cringe. Please don't let them hit each other. "I just ordered you another drink."

"Whatever he ordered, do not drink it."

"Let's go, Angie," Mark persuades.

"I mean it, Angie. Do not drink it."

I flinch at the showdown of the staring/pissing/sizing-up contest. Both men appear equally ready to pull at my arms to see who can win me first. It is a game to them, and I am the prize—whether it is just for bragging rights or hope of slipping into my panties. But seriously, plain-Jane-me? I haven't been on a real date in a long time. Russell was a user. The closest thing we had to a real date was him paying for a home movie, during which he groped me on the couch.

Why all of the male attention now? I look down at my dress, if only to ensure that all the naughty parts are fully covered.

Mark puffs his chest. "She's here with me."

And here it goes…

"In this restaurant? Are you trying to taunt me, you fucker?" Graham's eyes shoot daggers of fire at Mark's head. "I can pay you back whatever you owe her and triple her wages in return. For someone lacking instincts in the business world, I would recommend you take the deal." Graham talks to Mark as if he is a little boy—demeaning but casual. "Or do you need to consult your lawyer?"

"Hmm, let me think," Mark goads.

"Excuse me," I huff, trying to get in a word.

Graham growls, tightening his grip on me, protectively embracing me to his side. "Take the damn deal."

"I am right here!" I snap. I shrug out of Graham's hold, staying longer than I should have in the first place. I realize instantly that I am guilty of sending mixed messages. Both men stop the arguing and deal-making temporarily but never release any of the tension that fills the air.

Graham's attentive eyes fluctuate between a persuading gaze at me and an I'm-going-to-rip-your-throat-out gaze at Mark. What business does he have interfering in my work? I am a grown woman and can make up my own mind. Besides, I have a job to do, one that pays rather well that I would prefer to keep. Being that girl—the one who everyone avoids due to unnecessary drama—is not what I want to achieve as my reputation.

Behind me, a familiar voice sounds as I pivot my body to see if my suspicions are correct. Dominic.

Lovely.

"Graham, why don't you go back to the table before you do something you will regret?" he suggests, his laid-back demeanor never ruffled by the situation at hand. His black suit and lavender tie make him look simultaneously edgy and stunning. He is a great catch, although I have no idea of his attached or detached status. "Angie," he acknowledges me with a warm smile and nod.

"What are you doing here?" I ask, air rushing out of my mouth in relief. "I mean, I—"

"Graham and I have business matters to discuss."

I give him an incredulous look.

"See the bracelet you're wearing?"

I look down at the beautiful piece of jewelry.

"Graham's company designs and manufactures them," he explains.

"Oh." It is all starting to make sense. No wonder why I kept running into Graham at the Entice office.

Dominic nudges Graham in the shoulder, giving him a look that hints at a mix of respect and well-meaning advice. "I'll see to it that Miss McFee is taken care of," he offers, knowing that Graham's current state of irrationality is in full testosterone bloom. So the two men are more than acquaintances? They are business associates.

Graham reluctantly nods to Dominic as he leans in to whisper his warm breath into my ear. "If he does anything remotely disrespectful to you—and I mean anything, Angie —I will destroy him. So if you don't want another man's life ruined, I would advise you to be a good girl."

"Noted," I huff. I am mortified that he is doing this in front of my boss.

"He has you wearing scraps of fabric. Lingerie covers more than this," he snaps, his voice a harsh whisper.

Well, not exactly, but pretty close. I swallow hard as he continues his rant.

"If you change your mind and want a ride home, text me, come find me, or ask any staff member to locate me. Understand? I'll be watching him. He fucking touches you, and you can guarantee he will never be able to do it again. Do you understand?"

I nod slowly, confusion sweeping through me at the old-fashioned change in his behavior. I shiver at the overprotectiveness that vibrates through him with every spoken word. If I said it is not sexy the way he wants to keep me safe, I would be lying to the world.

Graham gives me one last reluctant nod and a warning with his eyes before returning to a table on the outskirts of the room. Besides being completely thrown off-kilter by the turn of events, something deep inside me knows that Graham would never hurt me. Maybe it is my naive, trusting nature or my delusional assessment of the situation. Nonetheless, Graham scares the piss out of me. I do not know his motives for being drawn to me, and I do not know why the feeling is mutual. I do not know his past or even his present. Although part of me is curious about the future, I keep myself from even wondering past the next day—unable to think farther ahead than the next twenty-four hours. Everything is happening too fast. My life that was routinely boring is now becoming a series of moments that will change its course forever.

The fact that my emotions are getting involved makes it easier to detach myself from the man who elicits such rare feelings out of me. I need to keep saying "no." Even a man with a sliver of dignity would eventually give up and find an easier prey. He cannot possibly have trouble finding women —whether they be free or agency-ordered—to occupy his attention. Why me? Apparently, I am not his type. Or am I? Baffling, exasperating, overbearing man.

Then there is always Sophia to keep him company. She is here somewhere eating dinner.

"Angie, I apologize for deserting you the other night on our trial." Dominic's words force me back into the situation in front of me.

"No need to keep apologizing, I understand." I smile timidly at his impeccable manners. I can still see Graham in my periphery, stalking me with his eyes, chipping away at my wall.

"Are you alright with returning to your date? If not, I can figure things out with Mr. Tanner in regard to a partial refund. It is entirely up to you, Angie."

I cringe inwardly over Dominic's offer, praying that the thoughts about him being my pimp go away. "I'll finish my date," I say meekly, avoiding Graham's piercing blue eyes like the plague.

I turn back to Mark and link arms with the one he offers to me. As I walk away, I think I hear a string of curse words muffled by the low baritone of Graham's haunting voice. My shoulders hunch at the awkwardness of the situation, and I resist the urge to do my laugh of unease just to fill the silence. Mark's contentment cannot be hidden by his swagger of a walk, sauntering over to our table, feeling like the heavyweight champion of the world. I am one of the ring girls, holding up the number signs between rounds. I suppose, in a way, he did win tonight.

"I'm sorry that you got caught up in the middle of this, but I have no problem telling you that I am glad you chose me."

I nod. Did I really have a choice with my job? My boss could fire me on the spot if I didn't please the client. As laid-back as Dominic appears, I am sure he does not want unhappy clients and insubordinate employees.

Back at the table, the conversation picks up easily, and a discussion about the sales forecast for some foreign suppliers takes off. Mark dominates the flow and expresses his passion, citing statistics and marketing strategies about how to increase profits over time. I offer opinions whenever Edward asks something of me. However, I stay dutifully biased in favor of Mark's point of view. Mostly, I sip my fruity cocktail and enjoy the nice buzz that is finally developing, calming every uptight nerve in my body. Whatever Mark ordered for me was top-notch and delicious.

After the last course is served, the men slip seamlessly into a conversation solely in a language other than English. I am shocked. It takes me thirty seconds to determine it is Spanish. I sit isolated, as I am the only one at the table who does not know what is being said—despite taking the course four consecutive years in high school. I reach into my handbag to grab lip gloss and carefully turn my phone onto video to record what is being discussed. It is obvious they do not trust me enough to understand what is transpiring.

I sit in silence, not offering any indication that I find their discussion bizarre. I play dumb. It is obvious they think I am. I play with my cloth napkin and listen intently to the voice inflections of Mark as he speaks fluently. The arrival of the waiter makes the men stop, flipping back to English easily.

By nine thirty, the dinner date is over and the business associates shake hands and decide on another time to meet again to talk about the fine details of the proposal.

As Mark and I walk around the filled tables in the restaurant, I peruse the floor to see where Graham is sitting for his business meeting. I do not see him. In the back corner of the room, I find Dominic with his back toward me at a table. I continue to search for Graham until I spot him near the hallway leading to the restrooms, right where we ran into each other tonight. His stance shifts, and as he moves, I see that he is not alone. He is with Sophia.

Bile rises in my throat as I watch him make out with her. I blink hard, trying to shake the image from my head. Player. Did they spend the evening together? Was she his escort? Are they on a date?

Turning back to Mark, I thank him for a delicious dinner and push myself toward the exit. My mind races over the confusion with Graham. We have already been on one date. He seems interested in getting under my skin. However, during the span of sixty minutes, he goes from having a possessive meltdown over me to slipping his tongue down another woman's throat. A woman who is my polar opposite. It just doesn't make any sense. If he is into her, then there is no way he would be into me.

I follow along beside Mark like the dutiful date and go through the motions. I feel like a zombie. I can't wrap my head around tonight's occurrences.

Once outside the hotel, Mark grips my exposed arms in

an attempt to provide warmth to my body. Why didn't I bring a coat? I can feel his satisfied smile on me without even sparing a glance in his direction. The driver opens the door for me, and I start to slide in but catch a man in a valet suit walking quickly in my direction.

"Excuse me. Ma'am?" he asks, out of breath.

"Yeah?" I step out of Mark's limo and wait patiently for the man to continue.

"Mr. Crawford has another way home for you arranged."

I glance at Mark who looks ready to explode. "She's fine with me," he snarls.

I guess Dominic follows through on his word. I feel relieved that I do not have to be locked inside the backseat with Mark for the twenty-minute ride back home, where he will spend his time undressing me with his eyes. I have had enough drama for the evening and need to take time to detox.

"I really don't want to create a scene, Mark. He's my boss," I plead. "It'll make me look really bad if I turn down his generosity."

"Fine," he snaps. "I enjoyed our night, Angie."

He leans in, and my heart stops. My palms sweat at the closeness of our bodies. My stomach churns at the unexpectedness of what he plans on doing. I swallow hard as he hedges forward, our faces a few inches apart. He hovers over me, waiting for me to make a move. To avoid a full-blown kiss, I tip up on my heels and lean my face sideways, my lips connecting with his cheek for a modest peck.

A smile plays on Mark's lips when I pull away. He grabs

my cheeks and presses his lips to mine. I try to pull back but his hands grip me tightly.

Mark breaks the kiss and smiles devilishly at me. "Looking forward to next time. I love a woman who makes me have to work for it. Adds to the fun."

I mumble something wordless.

I feel ill.

"This way, ma'am," the valet worker says. He seems so on edge.

I allow him to usher me into another vehicle. The driver is not into small talk. I am thankful. Emotionally, I am exhausted and can't help but fantasize about sleeping in on my morning off. My head starts to throb, and my hands start to shake. Maybe I had a little too much to drink.

When the driver pulls onto the side of the curb near the front of the townhouse, he opens my door to allow me out.

I walk to my front door, quickly unlocking it and shoving myself inside, glad that I made it through my first real date at the agency. The silence of the house settles my nerves, calming them down to get ready for bed. I kick off the heels and climb the stairs, making my way through the empty hallway to my room. I slip out of my clothes and do my routine of teeth, hair, and face. The ringtone of my phone makes me jump, startling me out of the quietness. I dig in my clutch to retrieve the device, sliding the green bar to accept the call.

"You home?"

It sounds like a bark rather than a human voice.

"Yes, Graha—"

"Safely?" he snaps.

"Yes, of course." My answer is clipped with my mood.

"Good. Do I need to put my fist through Tanner's face?"

"No, he was the perfect gentleman," I lie, softening my voice.

"You do realize that you're a horrible liar, right? Your voice rises half an octave every time you try to cover something up."

Wow. Pretty sure Claire said something similar. I need to work on that.

Graham's growl vibrates through my phone. "Stay away from Tanner, Angela. He is not the man he appears on the outside."

"Give it a rest, Graham. Seriously. You're going to get me fired."

"Good."

"No, dammit. Not good. I need this job too much." I settle onto my bed, pulling an already worn pair of pajamas from the floor to slip onto my naked body. Another tone sounds on my end from the phone, letting me know I am getting an incoming text.

"I'm sure if you looked hard enough, you would be able to find something else."

"I'm going now," I say but do not hit end.

"Can't you find someone other than Tanner to throw yourself at?"

Oh, the nerve of him. "I'm not throwing myself at anyone! Including you, buddy!"

"I would love to see your face right now. I can only imagine what you look like when you're this feisty. Send me a pic."

"Oh, hell no."

"Come on," he coaxes. "I need the upper body to go along with the legs pic."

"Why? So you have something to fantasize about later?"

"Maybe."

"You drive me absolutely insane. You know that?" I groan, knowing I gave him what he wanted—a reaction. Shit. He is playing me like a slot machine—except he is winning when the odds are stacked against him.

"Could you not find a dress in the fucking stores that covered more of you? I can suggest a few designers who relish in the use of fabric and sophistication."

Criticizing the dress again? Perhaps I am a disappointment? I frown at his judgment, feeling vulnerable and unsure of my appearance. Part of me deflates at his disapproval. Pleasing one man, displeasing another. How can I ever win?

His heavy sigh fills the growing silence of me not answering. "Angie, you looked amazing tonight. That's the problem. The sleaze was dangling you for everyone to see. I was not the only one feasting on you with my eyes."

"It didn't stop you from feasting on some blonde's lips."

I expect to hear a defensive comment, but he says nothing. We sit in deafening silence. His breathing is unsteady. He doesn't owe me an explanation, but I still expect one. A tear rolls down my cheek, and I am shocked at how badly seeing him with someone else hurt. That simple display of affection has affected me more than the breakup with Russell, and the realization that I am in deeper than I should be is alarming.

"You should be getting a text stating that Tanner wants to reserve you for a week. You need to reject him."

"What? How do you know?" I ask, confusion lighting up my face. I lean up in bed, bending my knees to my chest. I grab my laptop and unplug it from the charger. It powers up. "Is Dominic enlightening you on all of my dates?"

"Yeah, right. Dominic follows the rules too much as it is to ever help me out. I am trying to book you from your profile, and I see you are potentially booked already. You have a say in the clients you date. So, I am telling you to reject his offer. I can give you a better one."

"Graham," I huff. "I can't piss off clients."

"Well, what about pissing this client off?"

"You aren't one of my clients." *Go be with your blonde.*

"Because you keep pushing me away. Why, Angie? What are you scared of?"

I cough on the knot forming in my throat, choking it back down into the pit of my stomach. He's being too much. I type in my password to log onto the account. I click onto the calendar and see the blinking dates waiting for my confirmation. Mark wants me for five nights at two hours each, monopolizing my evenings. I lean back against the wooden Ikea bed frame, praying that I can sort out my job situation of juggling temperamental clients. Both of these men need to chill out.

I clear my throat, feeling bold enough to speak. "What do you want from me, Graham?"

"A chance."

The simple answer pulls at my heartstrings. I can see his face in my memory, his hand most likely resting under his chin in a suggestive way.

"I'm not going away, Angie. I'll fight for your attention."

I fidget at the warning tone of his words, allowing them to soak inside my brain. I believe him. He's going to crack through everything I tried so hard to build. A flood of resentment flashes through me. He needs to find someone else to hunt. Reese Witherspoon looked willing enough.

"I'm sure there are other girls in the database who can strike your fancy." Blonde ones. Red-haired ones. Your type.

"I want a chance with you."

"I'm busy though."

"It's your choice," he counters. "Choose me."

"I can't. I need to go. Good night."

I hear his exasperated breath leave his mouth. I imagine him straightening his posture, pacing around the room. The muffled sound of defeat fills the void. For some unknown reason, I am unwilling to hang up first. Part of me wants him to have the last word—if only to let me know that he does not take my rejection personally. But how could he not? I am telling him "no."

"I'll be in touch. I am not going to give up on you yet. I want you to get to know me before you write me off without giving me a genuine chance. I need to get to know you more as well." He pauses, taking a deep breath.

"I just do not understand you. At all. From the moment we met, you have been pushing me away. Now you want to spend time with me. Which is it, huh? This hot-and-cold attitude is making my head spin."

"I'm not a good person, Angie."

"So you say. For the tenth time," I huff, tossing my hands into the air.

"And because of that, I can't stay away from you. I have

tried. Trust me, I have tried. But I am drawn to you. And despite your better judgment, I know you are drawn to me as well."

"My track record with men has proven to me that I make horrible decisions."

"I would definitely be a horrible decision," Graham admits.

"So, I should say 'no' then, right?" I ask.

"Yeah, you should. But you won't. Part of you wants to know what we could be."

"A disaster, that's what," I say with a breathy giggle.

"A beautiful one."

I roll my eyes. "Good night, Graham."

"Dream easy, sweetheart."

My heart skips at the gentle tone of his words. The way the word "sweetheart" falls from his lips makes me melt into a puddle of goo. I whisper a goodbye and click the button to end the call. I slump back on the pillows, placing the phone and laptop on the nightstand. I shut off the lamp, curling up in the fetal position, my mind racing with thoughts of a tenacious blue-eyed man.

He called me sweetheart.

12

The smell of bacon wakes up my senses, making me stir in the warmth of my sea of pillows. It takes my brain a moment to comprehend that I am at home and not at IHOP. The unfamiliar scent of fattening meat throws me off as to my location. How much did I drink last night?

I grab my phone from the nightstand and remember the video I took from dinner. I set up my laptop with the audio translation tool and play the video at full volume.

Only Mark's voice gets picked up on the software since we were sitting beside each other. "Trials…must check placebo…sleeping pills…"

Hearing the interchange the second time makes me realize that the conversation is of a mixed language. Some words are definitely Spanish. Other words are of another language that I do not recognize. But why? Why the extreme attempt to keep the messages secret? And isn't it rare to have four multilingual men meeting for a business discussion?

Nothing from the staccato translation gives away anything of importance, other than the mere fact that they were trying hard to keep me and the wait staff from understanding what they were talking about. Maybe this is how business is usually discussed? It is not like I have that much experience in this type of world.

Also, Mark made it seem like he was meeting the men for the first time. None of the men shook hands at the table; they appeared to know each other.

Something is not right.

I send the video to my email and archive it under "research."

I pull up Google on my laptop. I type in "Samson" and follow it with "laboratory" to see if anything comes up. Having no luck, I try "pharmaceutical." I follow that with Benjamin, Edward, and Mark Tanner's names. Nothing. It would help if I knew some more last names.

I try just searching Mark Tanner's name but cannot find much information longer than six months ago. It is as if someone came and vacuumed out all the dust from the Internet. All of the current information is news reports of Mark at fundraisers and charity events.

Giving up, I open my private email for the *Bad Advice* blog and weed through some of the questions. I need a distraction. Time to clear my head.

Dear Bad Advice,

I think I might be attracted to my best friend's girlfriend. What should I do?

-Pretty Shy for a White Guy

I type out a quick response, taking little thought.

Dear Pretty Shy for a White Guy,

Kiss the girl and see if you like it. But take a selfie doing it and post it on social media.

-Bad Advice

After responding to a few more questions with my snarkiness, I crawl out of bed and go into the bathroom to assess my bedhead situation and wash my face. I fix my curly hair into a messy bun on top of my head, not even trying to undo some of the tangled chaos. I brush my teeth, choosing the cinnamon paste out of my stash of travel sizes. I think back to Graham's cinnamon kiss. Yum. Pretty sure my lips have not had better ones pressed up against them —ever.

I grab the fuzzy robe from the hook on the back of the door and throw it on over my pink sleep pants and white fitted tank top. Matching fuzzy pink slippers complete my look. I head downstairs.

At the sight of the half-naked man on my living room couch, I nearly stumble into the coffee table. I squeak out a "hi" and a cheesy grin.

He is the reason for the bacon. And for that, I fall a little in love with him.

"You must be Angie." The tall, brown-haired man places his coffee mug on a coaster and reaches his hand out to me for a shake. I accept it, trying to keep my eyes anywhere but on his ripped, tanned torso.

"Nice to meet you…" I let the "you" trail off, not ready to throw Claire under the bus by guessing a wrong name.

He chuckles to himself. "Ethan," he finally answers. He releases my hand and then relaxes back into the couch.

I smile and nod. "Of course."

Claire peeks in from the kitchen, dressed in a white collared men's shirt and a pair of indecently short booty shorts. So that explains why I am greeted with abs and pecs before noon.

"Hi," she mutters, almost shyly. She has a whisk in her hand and a frying pan in the other. So this is what domestication on Claire looks like. Her megawatt grin fills in every between-the-line assumption.

"Boy, oh boy," I say cheerfully, clapping my hands once and then rubbing them together. "Isn't today full of fun surprises."

Claire glares and bumps into me until I move into the kitchen.

"Stop looking at me that way, Angie!"

"Whatever do you mean?" My eyes dramatically blink.

"Shut up."

"So, um, I guess you enjoyed your night," I comment with a chuckle. "Bacon, huh?"

"Ethan is a big meat eater. And so am I." She winks.

"Ew, gross, Claire!" I whisper-shout. "So, no faux-turkey-tofu-torture?" I ask with a hint of sarcasm.

"No," she loud whispers. "That stuff tastes like Styrofoam. In the shittiest kind of way. Even I have standards."

I wiggle my brows up and down. "I like him already. Can he move in so that I can feel less guilty when I come back from the grocery store?"

"This is part of a cheat day experience," she whispers every word. "Shh, he doesn't know about my—"

"Food avoidance quirks?"

"Whatever," she huffs, throwing the drying towel onto her shoulder.

"One night with a man who likes real food and Commander Claire loses all of her inhibitions in regard to organi—"

"The pigs were pasture raised and organically fed. So stuff it!"

"They are also highly intelligent animals that could have—"

"Stop, please," she whines, holding her hands over her ears in horror. "I saw the documentary. Twice."

"Then obviously you are an expert." My tone is deadpan.

She flips me off, and I belly laugh loudly enough to be heard from the other room. I can't hold it back anymore. "If a man can get you"—giggle—"to relax your tyranny"—giggle—"of all things food"—giggle—"then he has to be a keeper." Seeing for the first time that Ethan's shirt is buttoned wrong on Claire's petite body only makes it next to impossible to stop the laugh attack, as I point out the error.

Claire props her hands on her hips as I finish up my shit show. "Poor piggies."

"I'm sure it's a fast ethical death with dignity."

"La, la, la, la!" she yells, recovering her ears. "Hush, please."

I pull her hands away from the sides of her head. "I had my fun, and I am done now," I promise.

"I like him," she says suddenly.

"I know." I smile and nod. "I'm sorry for teasing you."

"If you didn't, I would think you were ill. Want to have breakfast with us and channel surf? I need to order some As Seen on TV items that I'll never use."

I shake my head at her. "Sure. Then I have to go to the lab to work on some research."

"Don't forget about open-mic night," she reminds, scrambling the eggs in the pan over the stove.

"I won't. Pissing off my tech support isn't best for business," I joke. "Zander still needs to exorcise my latest malware STD from my laptop. It is running soooo slowwww."

Claire's bubbly laugh makes me smile. "Yeah, Z is very excited that you agreed to come." She gives me a knowing glance that I elect to ignore. With Claire, there are a lot of things I choose to ignore.

"I wouldn't miss it. Plus, he agreed to accompany me to the charity gala. At least I'll have someone to dance with this year. Surely, I can suffer through being stuck in a room with a bunch of drunken college students at The Shack, flashing fake IDs like they are going out of style."

"Sure is one busy week."

"And a get-busy one for you."

"Bringing the cheese, Angie McFee! I like it."

My Friday afternoon flew by fast. Between four hours in the computer lab and then an hour to get ready for the date with Will, my body craved a nap that there wasn't time for.

As predicted from the initial meeting at the mixer and the contact from the agency website, Will was a perfect date. At no time did he try to "handle" me, coax me into awkward conversations, or push his luck. The midthirties man simply wanted a companion for an outing with his new employees. Through a light dinner, I discovered that Will owns a construction company that he inherited from his late father. His compliments on my teal long-sleeved silk sheath dress were tasteful and gave me confidence in starting conversations with his workers.

Will basically reestablished my confidence in myself for doing this line of work. Some men just need a simple companion—nothing more. I desperately pray that more of those types of men come out of the woodwork and want my company.

Upon request, I have Will take me back to the town-house for me to change into something less formal for the night at the bar. A friendly hug is exchanged upon exit from the car. I actually had a good time.

I race up the stairs to my room, tossing the dress onto the bed. I skip down the hallway to Claire's room, taking her up on her offer to borrow an outfit for the evening from her closet. I push on her door and meet resistance. Dirty clothes are scattered on her floor in a wrinkled heap. Empty cups and plates are on her dresser stacked from the week. While this is her typical behavior, I am surprised she did not clean up a bit for her sleepover date with Ethan. If we get a rodent, I will blame her.

What am I thinking? She'd probably rescue it, name it, and call it her own.

I settle for a black sequined halter top that ties around the neck with a delicate satin bow, showing off my bare shoulders. A flirty pleated gray skirt with flared layers showcases the length of my legs and sits low on my hips. When I move certain ways, a small section of my belly gets exposed—probably because I have a longer torso than Claire. I go back into my room for a pair of sheer black thigh-highs and black knee-high boots with a two-inch heel. I forgo a coat, simply because The Shack is not the venue for such an amenity as a checking station. It will be a miracle if they have enough toilet paper in all of the stalls and some working soap dispensers. I layer on more smoky silver eyeshadow, add another coat of mascara, and put on some sparkly hoop earrings.

After a week like this week, I am ready to let loose and have fun.

I arrive at The Shack via a short cab ride, knowing that I will get a ride home with friends at the end of the night. The bar is standing room only with local patrons lining the space between wooden hi-top tables and surrounding wall booths. The rustic look of the venue creates a homey feel that could only be enhanced with the genuine energy of the crowd. Strings of clear, full-sized glass light bulbs drape from the ceiling, giving the place an open-air outdoorsy feel. It is like everyone is on a patio having a good time.

I squeeze my way through the semidrunk groups of people, trying to find Zander and the gang. Surely, Z will have a space reserved since he probably arrived earlier than the rest to set up the stage for the performances. I feel a jab against my shoulder as an elbow hits me, causing me to stumble backwards a bit. I steady myself and continue to search for groups of females to try to break through, because the guys won't budge. I stand on my tiptoes and stare in between heads to see if I can recognize anyone. Before I can pull my cell out to text Claire, I feel a tap at my shoulder and turn.

"Oh, hey you! I didn't know you were going to be here, Bryce!" I yell over the chattering going on around us. He is dressed in casual jeans and a green T-shirt. His backward baseball cap hides most of his hair, and he blends in with the rest of the male population.

He gives me a half hug. "Drunk, hot ladies. Need I say more, Teach?"

I chuckle at his comment. So predictable. "Your transparentness is oddly comforting."

His laughter only spurs mine on full force. It feels good to let go. "Where you heading?" he asks, throwing back beer from his bottle. He tilts it toward me in offering, but I decline. I need something stronger.

"I guess to the bar. I am supposed to be meeting friends here who are performing for open-mic night. I just don't see them yet." I do another scan of the room but am blocked by tall guys.

"You performing, Teach?"

"Um, hell-to-the-capital-no. You crazy?"

"Clinically, yes. Theoretically, no."

I giggle at his response.

"Well, let me buy you a drink," Bryce offers.

"Can't say no to that." I follow him through the crowd as he gently pushes through, grabbing hold of my hand to keep me from getting stuck behind in the chaotic cluster of people. When we arrive at the bar, I spot Zander and Blake shadowing the seated backs of Claire and Resa. "My friends are over there," I tell him, gesturing with my hand the direction to turn. "I'll introduce you."

"Either single?" His eyebrows wiggle up and down suggestively. Oh, boy.

"Um. Not committed exactly," I say slowly, pronouncing each syllable with thought. I didn't really know how to answer the question. Resa had a thing going on and off with her boyfriend. He is the reason she is on a diet campaign. She wants to impress him. Claire is sharing breakfast, white collared shirts, and bodily fluids with Ethan. And as much as I have a thing for bacon, Bryce cannot interfere with that phenomenon.

"Challenge accepted," he jokes.

"Hey guys!" I announce my arrival. Zander leans over to embrace me in a full-on hug, catching me off guard.

"Thanks for showing, Angie." His smile is so genuine that I can't help but feel a pang of sadness. Did he really think I wouldn't come tonight to support him?

I give him a nod and a look that means I wouldn't miss it. "This is Bryce. We have human behavior class together on Mondays and Wednesdays. Oh, and a lab. Bryce," I say, pointing to each of my friends, "This is Zander, Resa, Blake, and Claire. Claire is my roommate."

"Nice to meet you guys." He sets his empty bottle on the bar and then raises his hand out—as if to catch a cab—in the direction of the bartender. "Ladies, what are we drinking? I got this round."

Resa bounces in her seat at the mention of more alcohol. From the looks of it, I am not quite sure she needs more.

But who am I to judge? Claire smiles warmly in Bryce's direction and mouths a "thank you."

"L.I. Teas?" I suggest, knowing that something strong would settle my thoughts that have been flying all over the place this week. Time to unwind.

"Vodka diet soda for me," Resa says sadly. "I know, boring."

The bartender moves over to our group. "Two Long Island Iced Teas and a Vodka with Diet Coke. And three beers on tap?" Bryce asks, eyeing Zander and Blake for approval. He passes over his card to pay for the order, smacking hands with the bartender, who he obviously knows. I am not sure if Bryce works while he studies, however, buying everyone a drink can't be healthy for his budget.

"Thanks, man. I got it next time," Zander insists.

"I have appetizers coming," Blake chimes in. "I put in the order about twenty minutes ago." I whoop at the thought of a fun evening with friends, drinks, and pub food.

"So, when do you go on, Z?" I check my cell and see that it is twenty minutes till ten.

"I'm like the third act," Zander responds. "But, I am getting a bit nervous because Kendra isn't here yet."

I mouth an oh, hoping that he is not disappointed if she flakes last minute. My heart flutters at the thought of him being let down, as excited as he has been for this night. The once-a-month occurrence sparks a liking among the locals. The place probably is barely making fire code right now. I doubt any more people could fit inside this shoebox.

As soon as the seat beside me is vacated, I sneak up on it joining the girls while the guys chat behind us. Our drinks arrive, garnished with lemons, limes, and oranges. I take a sip and cough. Holy shit, these are strong.

The appetizers arrive ten minutes later. Boneless chicken bites, breaded mushrooms, cheese sticks, carrots and celery, and burger sliders are arranged in two oversized foil-covered plastic baskets. Everyone grabs a tiny paper plate to fill.

The first act takes the stage at the front of the restaurant to set up and prepare. The elevated bar area is prime for viewing and the easiest place to order food. It is amazing that we even scored a spot here.

As the alcohol infuses my blood stream, I feel light, carefree, and topic-less. My thoughts frantically bounce from one idea to the next. The high-pitched giggle fits from the girls only harmonize with my own.

I turn my swivel stool to see Zander leaning over me, his elbow resting on the bar. His eyes glance between my drink and my face, his look amused. "Okay, Ang, I think you need to pace yourself. You're going to fall."

"I's good." My lips feel a bit numb.

He chuckles and fixes a stray hair behind my ear. "You's good?"

I nod my head quickly and instantly feel nauseous. "I's not the best."

"Eat some more food, please," he suggests, passing me his half-filled plate. "Here's some water. Drink it all."

I smile at his thoughtfulness, but really cannot figure out why he is treating me like this. Something changed over the summer. I just cannot put my finger on it.

I didn't even finish my drink, and I feel just lovely. And light. And lusciously liquefied.

"I love words that start with L."

"Do you now?" he asks with mirth in his eyes.

"Yuppers. And all the rest of the words that have letters that start in the alphabet from our beautiful dictatorary."

"Pretty sure that word doesn't even exist."

I shake my head back and forth over the nonsense that spews from his mouth. I am coherent enough to know that what I am saying sounds ridiculously accurate. I sip on the water and douse a mushroom in honey mustard. I lick off the dip and ignore the mushroom entirely. So good. "You know, the place where all the words go to mingle."

"Sounds pretty magical, if you ask me."

"Oh, it is!"

Why is Zander single? It's a thought that I can't shake. Since knowing him, he has been on, like, two first dates. That's it. The girls were lame though and a little too dorky even for his technical brain. Kind of alternative punk too. Not really the type of girl I would set him up with. No, Zander needs an artsy type of girl with beautiful long skirts and a love for puppies. And bird houses. I perch on the edge of my stool and spin from side to side, never taking my eyes off him.

"You okay, Angie?"

I ignore him and just go with the track my mind is taking me down.

"Okay, so my friend from high school…"

"Wait." Zander halts the flow of my fluttery speech. His hand is in the air, a few inches from my mouth.

I stare at his fingers, confusion making my brow wrinkle. I give the look that translates to *what don't you under-*

stand. I wonder if he is trolling me. I chuckle at my own thoughts, proud of myself that I even can talk.

He taps his finger along his jaw. "Are you trying to set me up with your friend?"

No. Yes. "Maybe."

"Maybe?"

"Well, I'm not exactly sure she is single," I blubber out in a rush of breath. "We aren't"—I sip more water to keep my mind clear—"weren't close."

More people move to the stage for the sound check. The crowd continues to grow. Claire and Blake are deep in thought. Resa and Bryce are laughing. The bartender is tossing bottles into the air, enjoying the whoops from his growing audience.

Zander's voice cuts through the drone of sounds. "Focus."

"Trying to," I groan.

"What are you trying to say then, Angie?" The V between his brows shows his confusion. He has to be messing with me. He's never this serious. Running his hands through his golden wavy hair, he leans in closer to me. "Be direct. When have you ever filtered your words?"

Pushing some hair behind my ear, I smooth out the locks. I chew the stir straw from the drink until it is tattered and worn, no longer capable of sucking up liquid efficiently. "It's just that you are a good catch and—"

Zander's smile stops my words. It could light up the dark corners of the room.

I point at his chest and press my finger into his pectoral muscles. "I just want you to be happy."

"And you think getting me a girlfriend will do that?"

"It's a possibility." I mumble over the rim of my glass, as I take sips of my drink. Ice rattles while I use the straw to unsuccessfully slurp the last drops. "B'tender! Refill, stat!" I demand in the best authoritative voice that I can muster.

"Cancel that," Zander intervenes. "This little lady has had enough for now. Coffee instead. Two creams, one sugar," he counters.

I frown at my empty glass of spiked tea. It was only one drink. I sip again at the melting ice producing an obnoxious sound. The stuff is lethal, but I still feel like I deserve another something-something. I'll have a designated driver. What is the problem?

"What color is your friend's hair?"

"Um, blonde," I reply, trying to picture her in my head. We were more of acquaintances than friends.

Zander's eyes focus on mine. "I like brunettes. Tall ones."

At least someone does.

The coffee arrives, and I take small sips to check the temperature. The smell is sobering and probably what I need at this moment. It tastes decent for coffee made from behind a bar.

The first act does the honor of introducing what open-mic night is all about. The all-male musical group consists of a drummer and two guitarists. The crowd goes wild and those standing jump up and down to the rhythm of the harder-rock anthem of some group unknown to me. My eclectic taste did not branch out far enough to recognize the song. However, everyone acts like they do—or are too drunk to care. I suppose that a song from *The Sound of Music* would produce the same reaction. Everyone is amped and ready for a good time—liquid persuasion flowing heavily through their veins. Feeling alive.

Zander pulls his cell out of his pocket and looks at the screen, his frown wiping away all of his happiness.

"Uh oh, flaking?" I guess. His nod and downward eyes cause my stomach to turn. "What are you going to do? You still going to play?"

I have heard Zander jam many times at his place with his roommates. However, none of them showed up tonight. I feel horrible just looking at his eyes. He is sad.

"Can your roomies meet you?" I press.

"No, they have a gig this weekend. For pay."

"Well, then, what are you going to do?"

"I don't know. I'm not mentally prepared for a solo act. Even after all of these years playing, I still get—"

"Nervous."

Zander sighs. "Yeah. I just wish Kendra had a legitimate excuse. I was counting on her."

"Can you reschedule?"

He shakes his head. "No, the owner considers it a cancellation. A last minute one, at that. I will lose my reserved spot for months as a penalty." He throws back his beer, placing the glass bottle on the bar. Claire and Resa are teetering on the edge of the stools, waving their hands in the air to the beat of the drums. Bryce and Blake chat about all the times they have nearly been arrested and the magic it takes to get charges dropped. Who would have thought that Blake had a bad-boy streak? Bryce is a bit easier to imagine.

"Angie?"

"Yeah?"

"Can I ask you a huge"—my heart stops—"favor that

will earn you several future favors? Please," he pleads solemnly.

No. I know exactly what Zander is going to ask before he actually does. Fear creeps into my body, possessing me from the inside out. I am paralyzed, immobile. His "please" rings in my ears, and my mind flashes to all of the times over the past couple of years that he was by my side to help me with my problems. He would never ask unless he was desperate, this I know.

"Z, I haven't done this in a long time. The memories, the feelings, everything. I just don't know if I can."

"I know, Angie. I shouldn't have asked. I'm sorry."

I frown and tilt my eyes to the floor. "I just—"

"No worries," he says softly. "Doing a solo act can be done, even if it is going to look pathetic."

His sadness and my feeling responsible for it stab at me. He can see that I am contemplating saying "yes." His mind churns with a sprig of hope, coming up with ways to bribe me into relenting.

"Add tech support for life to the multiple favors proposition. Oh, and I will detail your car. And stock your candy supply."

"Z, you know I would do anything for you. But this—"

"I know, Angie, forget I asked. I am selfish. And a jerk. I know it reminds you of—" His sentence cuts off, not wanting to say his name, for fear of upsetting me.

I swallow the saliva pooling in my mouth. "I'll do it."

"Really?"

"But you have to back me. And I mean it. Oh, and I get to pick the song."

"Anything you want, you get. I can Google chords if I

need to. Here, look at my playlist," he says handing over his phone. "Pick from here if you want or something else."

I scan through the hundreds of songs he has listed and finally settle on one that I like, pointing to it.

"Perfect," he says eagerly. "This is going to be fun."

I am so on edge.

"I'm going to run to the restroom to freshen up."

I slip off the bar stool and make my way through the crowd to the other side of the room where the restrooms are located. I have approximately six minutes before I have to be on stage. As I step into the hallway, my arm is tugged, jolting me back. Pain seers through my limb. The yanking inflames my old injury, making me wince.

"Hey! Ouch! Let go!"

The thumping background beat of the bass swallows my volume, making my throat sore as I repeat my words. I catch my balance and snatch my arm away. I rub at the soreness and turn to stand eye to eye with douchebag Russell. His polished appearance makes him look extra smarmy.

"You owe me five hundred dollars, bitch," he sneers.

"For wha—"

"For all my stuff you broke when you tossed it out of the window."

How dare he! He best be glad I didn't toss it into the river. The only thing that stopped me was the guilt over pollution. "You owe me that in storage fees, asshole. Call it even," I say with a shrug.

His eyes move down my body and settle on the patch of exposed skin on my stomach. I tug on my halter top to try to conceal my body more. Sweat beads on my forehead.

"Quit being so creepy!" I yell over the music, and his eyes finally meet mine again.

"Why didn't you dress sexy while we were together?"

Ew. "Because we were barely together, you ass."

"And when we were, you were such a prude."

"Get out of my way!"

"Remember, Angie, five hundred dollars. Not a penny less." He bumps shoulders with me as he moves past. "I'll see you around," he calls blindly.

I stare at Russell's back as he disappears into the crowd.

I make a dash toward the ladies' room and slip ahead of a group of oblivious girls waiting in line. Once inside, I dab my heated skin with a dampened paper towel. After washing my hands, I fish the plastic-wrapped pill from the side pocket of my skirt. I check the time.

Three minutes.

My mind races for a way out. I am in need of sturdy ground—a platform to hold the weight of my decisions when I am too stressed to stand on my own. Each breath that slips into my lungs feels like a bomb waiting to go off. The vibrations of the noisy crowd penetrate through the walls. They want a show, and I am part of the next act.

With the added knowledge of Russell lurking in the audience, my anxiety rises tenfold. Without a doubt, he'll be watching and wishing me to fail.

Two minutes.

I look down at the tiny pressed-powdered pill in my palm, rolling it with my thumb. I slide it across the trails of veins that pop with color through the pale clammy skin of my hand. My mouth dries and then salivates at the memory of the rush of relief that will soon follow. With no time to think, I toss the pill into my mouth and bite down hard and manically, a sure method to jumpstart the calming effects in record speed. I wash the nasty bitter taste down with handfuls of cupped water from the faucet, scowling at the chemical taste of the tap water.

I stare at my reflection in the mirror, disgusted. Helpless.

I don't even recognize this girl. It is like she is someone else, someone I'm not sure I like. She is the weak one. The lost girl who free-falls into the flames.

I slip out of the restroom, thankful that all of the occupied stalls stayed occupied during my desperate visit. I find Zander on stage and squeeze my way through the sea of people. I join him as he tunes his guitar and gives directions to a few of the night's helpers. He gives me a reassuring smile.

I stare out into the crowd, my toes contracting at the fear of making a total ass of myself. It has been over four years since I have done anything remotely theatrical—and I wasn't even the one with the talent. Nope, that was James. He was the actor and the star. I tagged along and had fun making memories with him, but it was more of a hobby for me than a passion. When he died, so did a part of me.

"Oh, come on, Ang. You know that the music teachers make everything a popularity contest. But audition anyway. For me. It will be fun, I promise. We can be the Dynamic Duo."

That was James. Always trying to include me. Always supporting me and trying to make me smile. I still don't know how I made it this long on my own without him.

The panic rises with the bile that erupts from my slow-churning stomach. I instantly regret the pig-out session of greasy, gooey, heart-attack-inducing food. The buzz from the spiked tea and pill gives me fleeting courage as the alcohol still filters through my system.

I want to crumble at the memories flowing rapidly through my brain; nothing is capable of shutting off the flashbacks. Not time. And definitely not a pill.

Guilt seeps in at the mere possibility that I could actually enjoy myself. I wrestle with the desire to keep some things sacred. I want to lock it away in an airtight box, never to be exposed again. But here I am. Touching and tainting the abandoned joy with the newness of a different time—knowing that an element is missing, never to be replaced or replicated.

God, I miss James.

I blink slowly at the layers of people awaiting the show. It feels like my head is submerged underwater, as my ears endure the echoing hollowed out sound. I can only hope it is a sign that the pill is working. Above all others is Claire's high-pitched squeal, cheering us on at full volume. Her wild enthusiasm becomes my focus. I turn to Zander who starts playing the introduction. His eyes lock with mine, as I perch farther on the end of the wooden stool. The track lighting illuminates the sheet music resting on a makeshift podium. A worker kneels down in front of my microphone stand and adjusts it with ease. It is go time.

The last song James and I performed in front of an audience was the John Lennon classic, "Imagine." It happened to be a tribute song to our mom, who would sing it to us whenever we were having trouble falling asleep as kids. It was also the song we both sang to her while she took her last breath. It wasn't until years later that we were able to find the strength to sing it again during a cancer fundraiser held in the Baker City town square. I can still feel James's hand holding onto my smaller one, trying to keep me from crying during the song. He was my rock, and since his death, nothing has come close to filling that void—not even a little pill.

Emotions overcome me, and I sniff back the moisture wanting to escape. I stare into the back of the dark room, trying not to connect gazes with anyone in particular. The less I realize I am being watched, the better. I need to detach. To treat this like a job. My breath is shallow and frequent. I fear that it can be heard through the mic, in a creepy horror-film kind of way.

I hear the same familiar tune echoing again in my ears. Shit. I missed my entrance. My eyes fill with tears as I dart them back to Zander. His soft smile and nod assist in me regaining my composure. His voice—a barely-there whisper—starts my part of the song. I inhale sharply and let it go. My lips part, and I get swallowed up in the music. I do not even recognize my own voice as it picks up where Zander fades out. It is the voice resurrected from the ashes of the old me.

The eruption of the crowd blasting through the air is quickly silenced by the slow tempo of the song's melody. My eyes hop from the back of the venue to Zander who plays the guitar like an expert. The words purr from my lips on their own volition.

I relax into the melody and find it easier to focus. In the back of the venue, I see a tall man in the shadows. My stomach lurches at the possibility of seeing the crystal blues that have been hijacking my recent resting thoughts. I feel crazy. Why would someone who has an exorbitant amount of money go to a no-cover-charge pub that doesn't make any food that isn't coated with a week's worth of fat and where the average age is twenty?

I go back to the page of lyrics to make sure I don't blunder the words. Zander's skilled blending of our voices and the sound of his guitar surprise me at how we turn the solo song into our own version of a duet and actually make it sound good.

I vow to myself that this is a one-time deal—a favor for a friend who I am indebted to for multiple rescues. Singing on a stage is a slingshot ride back to a past that I buried when James died.

As the ending of the song fades out, Zander is on his feet, pulling me from my stool into an all-encompassing hug, spinning me around as the volume of the crowd is at ballistic-level again. The irony of what a romantic song could do to people who are drunk is impressive. Cheering, cells waving, beer splashing over the edges of glasses. A. Damn. Good. Time.

"Encore!" is repeated on loop. Zander lets go of me and holds his hands up to the crowd to shush them. He looks down at me and asks, "Want to do something upbeat?"

The ice has already been broken, and I have a new sense of bravery. I give him a nod.

I forgo the stool and grab the mic from the holder so I can move around the stage some. Zander starts playing "Don't Stop Believin'" and we get the entire venue to participate in the anthem.

When the song ends, I am physically exhausted from bouncing around the stage.

"You killed it, Angie!" Zander says while picking me up once again.

I laugh my trademark nervous laugh as I return to the wooden floor. Zander leads me down the stairs. Claire and Resa join in the reunion, hugging me and telling me how good we sounded. Zander earns some handshake rituals that only guys can manage to make look cool and some pats on his back. Blake follows with two drinks in hand. He must sense my unease of the whole situation now that I can process it and my need to debrief. He clinks the glasses together before placing one in my right hand.

"Thanks, Blake!"

"That was a firecracker performance. You were amazing! Both of you were. Had no idea!"

"Neither did I," I admit quietly. I don't even sing to the radio in the car or while getting ready for school. It's something I did in my old life. But not any longer. Tonight was…

Surprising.

"When did you learn how to do that?" Resa asks, making me gulp air as if it would run out.

I blink hard and glance to Claire who covers for me instantly. "Well, our girl Angie has many talents. Why do you think I keep her around?" The cheeky comment puts the innocent interrogation at bay for the moment. I do not need to talk about James right now. I do not need to cry.

I slurp the frothy mudslide drink, getting drizzled chocolate sauce and whipped cream on my nose in the process. The feeling of relief and adrenaline produces a pleasure surge of endorphins through my system. For just a moment, I feel invincible.

"This drink is awesome!"

"Goes down like a milkshake!" Blake announces, making our glasses clink together again.

I make my way back to the bar with the gang and find that Bryce is saving our seats, earning everyone's praise. Blake stays back near the stage to prepare for his poetry reading act.

"Well done, Teach."

I sink into the bar stool, knowing that my work is done. Time to relax and get my drink on. The mocha drink is way easier to down than the wicked lethal teas. I swallow the last drops in record time and place the empty hurricane glass on the waxed wood.

The bartender saunters over to our corner and places a glass down in front of me with a little cocktail napkin underneath the base.

"What's this?" I ask in confusion.

"A gift."

"From whom?"

"A customer." He is being so cryptic that I want to scream. Then he smiles at me and continues, "Oh, and you killed it tonight. Going to add yourself to the future lineup?"

"Ugh, no. One-time deal." The rosy heat brushes past my outer cheeks, causing the global warming effect through the rest of my limbs. My embarrassment lingers longer with the liquor that penetrates my awareness. Who's the customer? I look around to see if I recognize anyone. I contemplate whether or not to interrogate the bartender about the gift giver but he is off serving the next person before I can decide.

I take a sip of the fruity drink and rest farther into my stool.

My flesh chills and warms in unison as I pivot in my seat, sensing the presence of someone behind me.

"You really shouldn't accept drinks from strangers."

13

"You." One word is all I can muster up at the moment. I blink hard and swallow at nothing. My response produces a smile in return and a nod of the chin. The eyes that once haunted me from the shadows were not a figment of my imagination. My instincts were right. He was watching me.

"Not all people are as trustworthy as I am," he says with a smirk, leaning against the bar, shamelessly staring at me.

Quit seducing me. It's working.

"Thanks for the drink, Graham." I stare into the reddish liquid, not having a clue as to what it entails. It is good though.

"You were enthralling up there, you know that?" His question caresses my insides, making me melt into warm goo. I glance at the stage to see a guy playing a piano solo. "Breathtaking."

"Yeah," I nod at the player.

"You, Angie." He turns my chin to focus on him. "You were"—he clears his throat—"are breathtaking."

I don't know how to respond. Graham leans his body into me, turning his back to the stranger sitting at my right even more. His perfect wash denim jeans were tailored to his exact body shape. His black thermal shirt tempts me enough to want to touch it. I want to run my hands up and down it, to feel the expensiveness of the fabric. It would be fun to sew him clothes. The man could sell the articles right off the bone. I think of how funny it would be if Graham took up modeling instead of whatever it is that he does.

I whisper a barely audible "thank you" and continue to ogle the male specimen standing inches away from me. From the corner of my eye, I spot Ethan making his way to the bar, surprising Claire with a full-on kiss. I try not to stare at the intense PDA make out session.

I look down into the top of my glass and shake it a bit to jiggle the ice, trying to hide my blush from witnessing my best friend in an intimate moment. My drink doesn't smell strong, which could be troublesome if I didn't have my fleet of friends floating about the place. I take a big gulp of the drink, trying to keep myself from saying something mortifying.

Graham signals the bartender and gets waited on right away—skipping the line completely. The place keeps getting more claustrophobic each passing minute.

"A shot of the best vodka you have."

"Grey Goose okay with you? It's not as smooth as Ketel One, of course." The bartender laughs with Graham, as if they are enjoying some secret joke. "Otherwise, it is all rail and lower-tier brands."

"Goose will be fine."

I watch in awe as Graham hands over his black credit

card—the kind that only an exclusive spender is privy to possessing. It is the first time I have ever seen one in person. No wonder he is getting the royal treatment in a dive bar. He's probably tipping outrageously.

"Why are you here?" I blurt out, turning his attention back from the bartender.

"Oh, I was in the neighborhood." His smile is wickedly devilish.

"Are you following me?"

His eyes study me. "Would you like that kind of attention, sweetheart?" The words roll off his tongue with ease. His sexy smile strengthens his facial features. He throws back the clear liquor, swallowing the contents in one gulp, never making a twisted face. His breathy gasp and the clink of the glass on the bar shake me.

I use my own drink as a distraction for my hands. Just twenty-four hours ago, we were bantering over the phone. Can I fight him off when I feel so compelled to submit?

The smell of his manly cologne penetrates my nostrils, making me want to burrow into his side and get high off it. It calls me to him. I lean into his body, nearly falling off my stool. One hand grips the wooden edge of the bar, the other clutches the red drink.

"Why you here?" I try again.

"I wanted to see you. You keep avoiding me."

"I not doin' that." I take another nervous sip. "I just saw you yes'day."

"Easy, sweetheart. Slow slips." His face is that of concern. Genuine caring? He gently pushes a stray hair behind my ear, dragging his fingers down my heated cheek.

The contrast in temperatures is soothing, and I lean into his cooler palm.

"Shtop," I mutter.

"Stop what?"

"Bein' perfect."

His full-on smile makes me groan. My head feels like a bowling ball. The alcohol and the aftereffects of the pill are causing me to lose focus. My gaze jumps around in random directions. I just want to lie down and snuggle into a warm blanket. It is so cold all of a sudden in here.

"Hey. Look at me," he prompts, using his hand to guide my face back into view.

I look at Graham and smile.

"Let's dance," I suggest, sliding down from my bar stool ungracefully.

"Okay, let's dance," Graham agrees.

It is so crowded that we basically just stand beside the bar, and I press the front of my body up against his. It feels so good. His arms wrap around my midsection and rub the exposed flesh of my back. I turn around so I can reach my drink and take a sip. Graham moves closer, and we sway to the Matt Nathanson song being sung by some dude on the stage. I can feel his erection on my back, and I rub my ass against him, earning a growl.

His lips are at my ear, and the warm breath tickles my neck as he murmurs, "Keep it up, woman, and I'll drag you into the restroom like a caveman and fuck you up against the wall."

Holy shit. Why is his dirty talk so hot?

"Hmm…"

"Is that what you want? That is how you want our first time to be?"

I reach for my drink and down it in a gulp, slamming the glass onto the bar a bit too hard. I lose my balance and fall forward, but Graham catches me.

"Shot of tequila!" I yell loudly.

"You've had enough to drink. I'm going to get you some water," Graham chides.

"I fine." My voice is hurting my ears.

"Fine? You aren't fucking fine," he huffs, and I giggle.

My mind finally clears, and I have an epiphany as I stare into the steel-blue eyes of beautiful perfection. "You so hot. It too late to cast my vote for wall sex?"

As soon as the words escape my betraying lips, I groan at my stupid-girliness. My hand flings up to my mouth, bumping the new shot glass full of tequila that magically appears in front of me. A few drops leak onto the polished wood. Shit. I need air. I am going to hyperventilate. I cannot look at him.

I throw the liquid down my throat like I am dying of thirst before Graham can stop me. I push off from the bar's edge and use my palms to plow through the maze of people, searching for an exit. Graham's baritone voice is in my ear, urging me to stop. I cannot tell if my imagination is playing tricks or if he is really there. I vow not to drink anymore for a long time. I have already had too much, and my rationality and mouth-to-brain filter are deteriorating at exponential speeds.

"Angela. Stop running," he snaps. His once encouraging voice turns angry, desperate. "You are going to get hurt," he warns.

I just want to get away from the source of my weakness. Graham does something to me. I can't put it into words. It is just a feeling, and it freaks me the hell out. I see Russell with a few clingy girls and bolt the opposite way. I have no time for his drama. I twist between a group of guys and feel my body shove forward with a jolt. I crash into the back of a tall man, earning me a glare and an expletive. I nearly hit the floor from the sudden force. I feel the pressure of my halter shirt being pulled as I try to regain my posture and stance. The sound of ripping alarms me to the point of looking back to the origin of the sound. A blonde girl reaches for me from her knees, trying to stand. She tugs at my shirt for leverage. I anchor myself and gasp at the hole being created, sequins falling like black snow to the floor. The smell of beer and stale cigarettes burns my nose. I reach down and yank the petite girl up from the floor.

The comments made by the male population as I move through the crowd cause my eyes to roll. The predictable hey baby, nice ass, and wanna have some fun come-ons make me queasy. I push my way forward to find that two guys refuse to move for me. They create a blockade with wide shitty grins and the intent to cause me harm reflected in their eyes. I try to hide my quiver, as to not show weakness. This place could really use a bouncer or two.

"Hey, sexy," the shorter one sneers.

The taller one puffs out his chest. "Wanna dance?"

"Excuse me," I try. "Move!" Not even the universal middle finger gets them to budge. Their evil snickers and grins make me want to vomit on their shoes. I toss around the idea of tickling my throat just to have a little revenge. Taking the option of fresh air motivates me to change directions and try again to break through another male barrier. This time, I feel a squeeze on my skirt-covered ass, making me stop.

I see red.

Before I can even think, my right hand is in action, whirling past my head and connecting my open palm with the man who violated me. The smacking sound that it produces causes a searing pain to shoot through my hand. The feeling of empowerment outweighs everything—sending a charge running through my nervous system.

I do it again, this time hurting myself more than him.

He backs up and then bounces forward, ready for war. I clench my eyes shut in fear, knowing that I am no challenge, bracing myself for what he thinks I deserve. I scream as a reflex, cowering and trembling, attempting to shield my face.

Arms bind around me in a death grip, making my eyes flash open. I do not need to look to see who has me trapped in his arms; the woodsy citrus smell tells my brain that Graham has me safely cocooned. "Don't move," he orders, muttering a string of curse words under his breath. Something flies past my head in a flutter. The sound of a boxing bag getting beat is what enlightens me to the fact that Graham hit the man who was threatening me. His venomous voice toward the man causes shivers to pulse up my spine. Graham is in full rage mode. This is very different from all of the Mark Tanner encounters, where he reined in his anger and was just moody.

"We are going to do things my way," he growls at me, making me shrivel at the intensity of his sharp tone. "Quit moving!"

Graham continues to hold me around my waist, bulldozing through the crowd with ease. Apparently his scowl and bad mood are evident to those around us to the point where they just submit and part ways to create a path. My feet do not even touch the floor as I am zipped through the crowd, until we reach the side metal door to the outside.

Once the air hits us, Graham sets me down on my feet but does not let go of my elbow. He steers me toward the black Mercedes-Benz. "Get in."

I turn to him. "Are you insane?"

"Yes."

"I'm going back to get my friends," I scream as soon as I am able to catch my breath.

"No, you're not."

"Yes, I am!"

A group of girls exit the same door we did, huddle into a circle, and light up cigarettes.

"Get in the fucking car, Angie. I swear to God I am at my wit's end with you."

"I can take care of myself."

"Coming from the girl who just hit a guy twice her size?" he asks. "What were you thinking? He could have hurt you. Then what?" His glare says everything that his mouth doesn't. He's furious with me. But why? Why does he care so much? I am not his responsibility. Actually, I am not anyone's responsibility.

"He deserved it," I defend quietly, staring down at Claire's damaged shirt. I will try to sew it and add more sequins. If that doesn't work, I'll just have to try to buy her another. Hopefully it is a recent one that can be ordered online. I smooth out the ruffled gray skirt, still feeling the perv's hands on my butt. Maybe I am crazy.

"Not arguing that. But seriously, Angie, are you trying to get yourself killed? The thought of what could have happened if I wasn't there to…" Graham stops midsentence and shakes his head as if to remove the worst-case scenario from his brain. "I just don't want anything to happen to you. That's all."

"What happens if he calls the cops?"

"He won't."

"Why the hell not?" I press. "You assaulted him."

From my periphery, I see Collins make his way through the exit of the building, talking into the air at no one in particular. It is then that I see the communication device in his ear. He gives Graham a nod as they exchange looks before finding his seat in the front of the vehicle.

"Because having the police show up will blow his fake ID cover."

"Oh," I mouth.

Collins must have found the guy and checked his wallet for identification—just in case he was planning to try to come after Graham.

I shiver in the night's air. My exposed parts of my arms sprout goose bumps. What was I thinking not bringing a coat?

Graham opens the door to the backseat, pushing me gently to get inside. I do not budge. "Please, Angie, let me take you home."

"I have a DD."

"We are not going back inside that dive."

"Too seedy for you?" I joke to try to lighten the mood and melt away some of the tension.

Graham's chuckle is music to my ears. "Something like that. Now get inside before I have to put you in this car myself. And Angie?" He stares into my soul. "I will do it if you keep pushing me. Another mistake you can make tonight is underestimating me."

"So bossy."

"Be careful, little girl. I will lean you against this car and spank your ass for the stunt you pulled in there running away from me. And you will deserve every little sting that my hand can deliver. Get in the car."

My face flushes with heat over his tirade. Part of me wants to be a bad girl just to see what would happen. All this dirty talk is ruining my panties.

"You put your life in jeopardy tonight," he continues.

"I don't need—"

"Get. In. The. Damn. Car."

"Alright!" I swallow hard and comply with his wish. I slip into the backseat, loving the feel of warm air enveloping me.

"Collins, drive until I tell you to stop. Miss McFee and I have a lot of discussing to do." He clicks his belt into place, acting like ordering people around is the most natural thing.

I try to hook my belt, but my hands will not cooperate. Each time I almost get it, it slips from my grasp, going back into the keeper. I curse under my breath. He is enjoying my struggle.

"Here," he whispers seductively in my ear. "I'll get that for you." He reaches over the seat and pulls the strap, snapping it into place in under three seconds.

Damn him.

"Wait. My friends will wonder where I am." Claire and I have a code we follow when we go out together. Just leaving and not saying anything would be wrong.

Graham looks at me and rubs his hand through his hair, ruffling up the free-flowing locks in the process. He takes his phone out of the pocket of his jeans and dials a number.

"Claire, this is Graham. Yes Hoffman, how many Grahams do you know?" He sighs.

I giggle at what I can only imagine Claire is telling him. Graham turns to glare daggers at me, putting a finger against his lips to shush me. He is so not in the mood.

"Does it matter…yes…I have her…promise. No, of course I won't hurt her." He lets out another sigh. "If you or your friends need a ride, please call or text me at this number and I'll send someone…you too." Ending the call, he places the device in the holder on the door. So he has Claire's number? When did this develop? I stare at my hands, lacing and unlacing my fingers. "She was just as surprised as you are that I have her number. She works for Entice. I pulled it from the site. That is it."

He must have done that proactively since it was already saved. Collins pulls out of the parking lot and makes his way down the side road. He takes a direction opposite of where I live. "Um, you are going the wrong way, Collins." He ignores me, never even flinching.

"Scenic route, Angie. I have a few things I'd like to discuss with you. I'd be lying if I said the idea of having your full attention—by being locked in my car—wasn't appealing to me."

"Oh, is that so?" I ask with my best attempt at snark.

"First off, stay away from Tanner."

This again? Mark isn't even here and yet his presence is taking up room inside Graham's head. I turn in my seat to face him, ready for a showdown. He does not get to tell me what I can and cannot do. "When you say things like that, it just irks me and makes me want to do the complete opposite," I confess. The buzz of alcohol makes me bold and honest, while the pill makes me mellow.

"I am hyper aware, Angie. Trust me. That's why I'm just going to handle the situation myself."

"What situation?" What the hell is he talking about? It was a date. One flipping date.

Collins takes a right onto the entrance ramp and merges onto the highway.

"The one where you think catting around the city is appropriate. In my family's hotel of all places. Either he is taunting me or you are. Which is it?"

His comment on my behavior makes me cringe. I turn my eyes from him and stare out of the tinted windows into the night. This is not the first time he has hinted that I am being trashy. He really thinks that little of me? Tears well in my eyes for the second time tonight. I don't know if I can hold them back. I hate crying—especially in front of others.

"Work, Graham. It's called work. You should find some," I grind out, keeping my eyes anywhere but on his. Being angry is good. Anger helps keep tears at bay.

"Keeping you out of trouble is becoming a full-time job."

I turn my eyes back on him. I bite my bottom lip that is quivering from the sudden, unexpected fight. Graham's temper scares me. I stare out the window again and see that we are on the outskirts of the city. I want to tell Collins to just take me back home, but I know that when it comes down to it, his loyalty does not lie with me.

"I'm not your responsibility. I do not answer to you."

"Yet," he says. "That will change."

"Says who?"

"Me. You like me. You think I'm hot."

I snap my eyes to his, turning my body against the confines of the belt. "I like the job."

"Well, I sure as hell don't like it."

"Well, you sure as hell don't have a say in the matter."

"On the contrary, Angie. I do have a say."

"You would go to Dominic about me? Are you really that much of a bastard?" Fear creeps in that he would spread lies about me to get me fired. When the realization hits me, I am frozen stiff. I need this job. It is more flexible than any other job I have had, and right now I need that benefit in order to still focus my attention on landing an internship.

"If you like and value your job, I suggest you"—he rubs at the back of his neck—"first, stay the hell away from Tanner. He's using you. Find another date. Tell him to fuck off. Don't accept his requests and don't make side appointments. Second, quit making rash decisions that will only put you in a predicament that is less than admirable. And third, start looking for a replacement job in the meantime. I can assist with all three. Just say the word."

"You are just pissing me off!"

"I quite frankly don't give a rat's ass who I'm pissing off!" he roars.

"No shit! Message received!" My voice cracks with my screams. "I'm not quitting my job. I like it." Collins must be well versed in not making his presence known, because he doesn't even fidget at the yelling going on in the backseat. For someone who has so much money, he could seriously invest in a vehicle with a privacy screen.

"Your character judgment expertise is off. I'm here to help with that."

His smug look deserves to be wiped off his face with a sharp smack. I have it in me. I proved that to myself already once tonight. And for someone who witnessed it himself, why is he not more afraid of my potential?

"Mark is nice."

"Oh, I'm sure he can be. When, of course, his goal is slipping into your skimpy attire. He is so fucking predictable. He is playing you, Angie! He wants you superficial and fake. Quit tampering with your natural beauty." He runs his hand down my cheek bone. "You are perfect the way you are, baby."

I am not perfect. Tears well up and trail down my flushed cheeks in clear salty streams. Graham's hand catches them. He unbuckles my belt and pulls me into an embrace. I settle my behind on his lap, encased in warmth. His cooing calms me. His gentle fingers brush over my damp cheeks, collecting more tears and drying them. I feel exhausted and emotionally drained.

"Listen. I am fully aware that I am being unreasonable, irrational, and ridiculous. I just don't give a damn. You can do better."

"It's not your choice." My words come out as a whisper. I push off his chest to detach myself from my weakness. If I stay too long, I will get swept away, and all of my determination and hard work will be for nothing. My life is finally coming back together. I cannot allow it to explode at the seams over a man who deludes himself into believing he has my best interests in mind, when in reality he is working his own agenda. I move back over to my side and snap the belt back in place.

"Take me home, Collins, or I will call the police and have you both arrested."

Collins's eyes meet Graham's in the rearview mirror, and information is passed with their look and silent signal. These looks are really starting to irritate me. Not even my verbal threat shakes the two men. What is with them? They act like they are above the law. I remove my phone from my skirt pocket and pretend to call their bluff. I press a few buttons and—

"Hey!"

I stare blankly at my device gripped inside the palm of Graham's hand. He flicks it toward the front of the car, dropping the phone onto the cushion of the front passenger seat, out of my reach.

"Don't threaten me."

"You bastard," I grind out from between my clenched teeth.

I give Graham the silent treatment for several long minutes, sniffling and staring out the window. Realizing that I am done talking, he gives Collins the directive to start driving toward the townhouse.

A dizzy feeling swirls inside my head, making me queasy and weak. Every bump and turn of the car cause my stomach to rumble. I cannot tell if I am getting motion sickness or if the nausea is alcohol-induced. I squeeze my eyes shut, feeling unbearable heat flame from my toes to my head. Sweat forms in beads on my forehead, over my brow, and my upper lip. I feel faint and fuzzy. My breathing turns to harsh shallow breaths as I fight back the quaking urge to expel the contents of my stomach. Shivers roll through me despite my skin feeling scorched.

"Pull over," Graham orders suddenly, snapping the belt back from my body. His strong arms yank me around my waist when the car comes to a complete stop along the side of the road. He pulls me through the shale, pressing my knees into the guardrail, holding my hair in his hand and placing another on my back. "It's okay, Angie. Just let it out. You will feel better, sweetheart. You had too much tonight. Let it out, baby."

Within seconds, I am purging out the sins of the past four hours of overindulgence. Between the date with Will Jenkins and the food and beverages from The Shack, I have hit my limit on bad choices.

Violent tremors shake my upper body, as I heave and flail and double over in pain. Graham stays at my side the entire time, his soothing words comforting me in my state of utter embarrassment. The sky is dark, and the crisp clean air sobers me. Circles are drawn on my back over and over again, making me soften—my anger is completely dissolved, as my sickness comes to an end.

"Shhh, you're okay. I got you. Don't cry. You're going to be fine."

At the words spoken to me, I feel the cold dampness on my cheeks. With every cooed hush he murmurs, I sob even more, not even knowing that I had started to cry again. Graham's arms swing around me, holding me to his chest, standing on the side of the highway. His strength keeps me from flopping over and down into the ditch. My eyes burn from liquefied makeup draining into them. I rub my face against my arm. The sight of dead bushes and dry grass fill my vision in the illumination of the four-way flashers that Collins puts on the parked vehicle.

"Hush, now. I got you."

He turns his body to sit against the rail, pulling me into his knees to rest my butt. Strong fingers rub against my back as I lean forward, my face parallel with the ground. The worst is over.

Or so I thought.

Another wave of nausea overtakes me, and I flop over and expel the rest of my stomach's contents. My body dry heaves, and I fall limp into Graham's arms. He smooths my clothes and fixes my hair.

"Here, sir," Collin says, passing a bottle to Graham. The voice cracks over me. I am instantly mortified that not one, but two men have witnessed my demise.

Graham's legs tighten around me, keeping me upright as he removes his hands from my shoulders, ending the light massage.

I hear the crunch of plastic and feel the coolness of water fill my mouth as Graham tips the bottle to my lips. "Rinse and spit to clean the taste out." I obey silently—too weak to talk or argue. I wash the acidic taste of vinegar out of my mouth. The water is so cold and tastes so fresh. I have no idea why Collins is so prepared, but I'm glad that he is. Exhaustion takes over my body. I want to lie down on the gravel and be done with it. "Now drink the rest. You are going to be dehydrated if we don't get fluids back in you."

I grab the bottle and sip the refreshing water, feeling my

stomach settle to what it was before I entered the bar. I mutter a barely audible thank you at the tenderness of being taken care of by a man who drives me crazy. "I think I overindulged," I whimper softly.

"You think?" Graham eyes me incredulously.

"Justalitttt—"

"Angie? Angie, what's wrong?"

I feel as if I am stuck in a blender. My head is too heavy for my neck. My body feels boneless. All sounds are muffled. Distant. I just want to fall asleep.

I want to fall…down.

14

I feel like I am floating. My body is weightless but my head feels like it is encased in a ton of bricks. My mind drifts back and forth like a pendulum. I float. Back. And forth. The air is cold. I shiver and tremble. I am in pain. It feels as if my brain is bleeding. Even my arm hurts. Ouch.

"Stop!" I scream, bolting upright. My eyes snap open in a panic, and I search for stability. Something that will anchor me to present. I am in a bed. In a sterile, cold room.

"Angie, thank God!" Graham gasps, rushing to my side.

"What's goin' on?" I slur, my mouth feeling parched. I lift my arms to push hair out of my face and cringe with a searing pain. "Ouch." Monitors go off behind me, making my head throb.

"I see you're up," a middle-aged woman says while entering the room.

I guess privacy does not matter here.

"You pulled your IV out," she scolds. She turns and flicks a few of the buttons on the machines to make the beeping sound stop. The Winnie the Pooh scrubs only give the illusion of softness. "Lucky you, your bag has been done for the past ten minutes."

I look up in confusion at Graham, who has dark circles under his eyes. He gives me a half smile and gently squeezes my hand.

"What am I doing here at the hospital?" I whisper. "Am I dehydrated?"

"Humph," the nurse huffs. "That's on the list of many other things."

"Excuse me," Graham bellows, "if you want to continue with your condescending tone, I suggest polishing up your resume and getting ready to search for a new job. You do realize that the Hoffman family donates annually to this hospital? I'm sure the Board of Directors would not approve of someone this low on the food chain making waves with someone as influential as myself."

I sit in silence as they have a standoff over my prone body. This is what it feels like to literally be in the middle. I sink back into the bed and rest my head against the pillow until the custody battle ends. I can feel the stickiness on my left arm and can see the blood from the taped needle drip onto the bleached white sheets. The sight makes me queasy. I look toward the window, searching for any type of distraction.

"Maybe it is best that I send in the doctor," the nurse suggests, her tone a bit better.

"You do that," Graham snorts at her retreating form.

He turns his attention back to me. I can see the faint wrinkles around his eyes. He looks older, as if a day has aged him.

"You scared the piss out of me, Angie. You know that?" he asks. His eyes scan over my body. It's as if he is making sure all my limbs are there.

"Why am I here?"

"You had a seizure last night."

"What? Really? When? The last thing I remember is calling you a bastard in the back of your car."

Graham brushes hair off his forehead. "You don't remember vomiting on the side of the road?"

I shake my head no. "No." My voice is barely audible.

"You don't remember going back in the car?" he presses. "I was going to take you back to your townhouse and then you started acting really weird. I had Collins rush us to the nearest hospital. I knew something was wrong. Your eyes were glassy. It was as if your soul left your body. Then you twitched, and it was then that I knew you were seizing."

"I…I…" I start. My tongue feels like cotton. I motion to the pink water pitcher on the rolling table.

Graham pours me a Styrofoam cup's worth and lifts it to my lips. It is room temperature and tastes like chlorinated rust. I make a face.

"Want me to get you a bottled water from the vending machine?" Graham asks with a smirk. "A soda or juice?"

I take another sip of the stale water and cough to clear my throat. "I really just want to know what happened to me. Why am I here? What made me have a seizure?"

"I can answer those questions," a deep voice from the doorway answers. "I am the doctor assigned to you."

I watch as he walks inside the private room. He is short, roughly in his sixties, and wears wire-rimmed bifocals.

I hit the button on my bed to sit up straighter. Graham shakes the doctor's hand and then pulls up a padded armchair to sit on.

"So, Miss Angela McFee, your blood work came back suspicious."

"What does that mean?" Graham demands before I can even form together a sentence.

The doctor straightens his glasses on his nose. "Are you on any kind of depressants? Antidepressants?"

"No," I whisper.

"Prescription drugs?" the doctor quizzes.

"No." It is a white lie. I hate myself for it. It was one pill from an old prescription. A moment of weakness, drowned with an abundance of alcohol.

"Why the interrogation?" Graham huffs, raking hair off his forehead.

"Miss McFee," the doctor addresses, "you tested positive for benzodiazepines."

"Was she drugged?" Graham interrupts.

I sink into the abused mattress of the hospital bed. Part of me is relieved that he thinks this is not my own doing.

"It's hard to say when recreational drug use is so common these days."

"I'm not a drug addict!" I insist.

"Miss McFee, you had a seizure which was most likely the result of the drug's effect to your central nervous system. Regardless of whether it happened by choice or not, you ingested a potent drug."

I grab my water and take another sip, listening to the doctor explain the blood results in a bit more detail.

"Are there any long or short-term effects to the body?" Graham asks.

"Loss of memory from last night seems to be the biggest side effect. Research is still being conducted on long-term effects. It's not like clinical trials can be ethically conducted, especially with dosages like what was found in her blood." He clears his throat. "In addition, alcohol or other medications could alter the side effects. There are so many variables to consider. You should count your blessings that you were not assaulted," he says, giving me a stern look, "or left to choke on your own vomit."

Graham turns and looks out the window. It is a dreary, rainy day.

There is a knock at the door. I move my head to look past the doctor and see Claire and Zander walk in.

"Angie! I am so glad you're all right!" Claire says at full volume, pushing past the doctor to give me a hug.

Zander stays on the sidelines with a vase of flowers that has a little balloon sticking out of the top. "You had us all very scared," he says sadly.

"Not my intention."

"She was drugged," Graham explains. "I will find out who did this to her. That is a promise."

"Oh, Angie," Claire responds. "I'm so sorry."

"If you reject counseling, then you are free to leave," the doctor says. "Otherwise, you will need to wait for rounds."

"I just want to go home."

"Very well. I'll send in the nurse to detach your lines and handle the discharge paperwork." He turns and leaves the room.

"Are you going to file a police report?" Zander asks, moving closer to my side.

Graham gives Zander a once-over and looks back and forth from me to him. "Police reports are useless. To them, a real crime has not occurred. I will do everything I can to take care of this. I have connections and resources."

A pang of guilt hits my heart. "I just want to go home and rest."

Claire gives me a smile. "Let's bust out of here and go ho—"

"She's spending the rest of the day and night at my place," Graham interrupts. "I need to get a list of everyone she encountered at the bar last night."

"I can just text you," I say softly.

"Angie, you nearly gave me a heart attack. I would appreciate it if you would just come back with me. You can rest. I can drop you back off after dinner, if that's what you want."

Claire opens her mouth and closes it. I know she wants to argue on my behalf. I just do not have it in me to endure a fight.

"Okay, fine," I sigh. "Can someone please grab me my clothes, so I can change and get out of here?"

"They got destroyed when you arrived here," Graham answers. "Claire brought you something from your home."

"Here, Angie." She hands me a duffle bag. "All the essentials."

"Thanks."

Graham calls for the nurse, and she unhooks the tubes attached to me without saying a word. I retreat slowly to the restroom with my bag and change into a matching maroon sweat outfit. I brush my hair and pull it back into a messy bun. Washing my face brings life back into my skin. I brush my teeth and realize that I feel human again.

I decline counseling, sign my discharge papers, and allow Graham to escort me to his penthouse suite at the top of a luxurious building in the heart of the city. The silence from the car ride and the elevator trip is so loud that it is deafening. He is pissed off. At whom, I'm not sure.

The doors of the elevator open, and we exit into a black-tiled foyer, which is completely separate from the main living area. Looking through the open doorway, I can see white furniture arranged against the back wall. The ceilings are so high that it's hard to believe that we are in a multi-floor building. Black-and-white abstract paintings fill the space. Punches of vibrant colors add to the otherwise bland pieces. My eyes fixate on the contrast. There is such beauty in simplicity.

I turn to Graham and see his standoffish body language. "Can you just say something?" I plead.

He shoves his hands into his hair and stares into my eyes. He bends down and our foreheads touch. His skin feels so warm that it startles me. My arms slide around his back, and I wrap myself in his warmth. He hesitantly does the same. Here we stand in his foyer—wordless. Yet our bodies are physically touching more than they have ever been.

"Why are you not more upset over being drugged?" His shaky voice breaks through the silence.

I think about the question for a moment. "Because I knew my friends would never let anything bad happen to me."

He sighs and steps back from me, breaking our physical contact. "But something bad did happen to you."

"The story ended well, Graham. I am fine. Been through much worse."

"Let's go inside and make a list of everyone who interacted with you at the bar. I need to figure out who would slip something in your drink. Whether you were specifically chosen or just randomly selected."

It is a waste of my time other than keeping my little secret hidden. I am almost out of my stash anyway—without any means of replenishment unless I find a doctor who acknowledges my residual effects from the car accident. Until then, all of this will just be in my past.

"Okay," I agree.

I follow Graham past the huge double doors that lead to his home. I would be lying if I said I wasn't nervous. You can tell a lot about a man from his living area. I quickly kick off my shoes.

"You can keep them on," he says, passing by the kitchen and dining room into the open space with all of the windows.

"I would prefer to take them off," I insist. When Mom was diagnosed with cancer, we adopted a bunch of practices to avoid bringing in germs. Taking off our shoes was one of those things. The habit stuck with me.

"Make yourself at home."

My feet feel the chill from the tiles as I follow Graham into what appears to be the living room. He sits down on the contemporary sofa to remove his shoes. I continue to the edge of the room that overlooks the city. The view is magnificent. I can see the city park, the shopping district, and the mountains in the distance.

"Breathtaking, huh?" Graham asks, startling me by his close presence.

I turn to see his eyes smolder. "Yes," I breathe.

I can smell his masculine scent emanating from his body. It is unique and only Graham. My body shivers.

"I'm going to start a fire," he says, retreating to the opposite side of the room. "Why don't you relax on the couch? Put your feet up."

I move over to the sofa and sink into it, surprised that something so modern looking can be so comfy. I curl my feet up under my thighs to try to keep them warm. I regret not taking the pair of hospital gripper socks with me during discharge. I look around the room while Graham works at the fire. Everything seems very sterile and minimal. It's as if this is a house and not a home. No pictures, no personalized artwork. The décor of the room is in the grayscale; the foyer had more life. The only signature piece of furniture is the beautiful glass coffee table that has a rock formation as the center pedestal. It looks one-of-a-kind. Expensive.

"Would you like something to drink? Coffee, tea, soda?" Graham asks.

"Tea sounds good."

"Preference on flavor?"

"Surprise me," I say with a smile, "but please add honey if you have it."

Graham disappears into the kitchen, and I can see him over the high countertop. He turns on the lights, and I move from my perch to get a better view of the layout. I creep closer and earn a smirk from him in the process.

"What's with your gender and kitchens?" he asks with a chuckle. "And here I thought you were someone who cared more about removing the stigma of women belonging in the kitchen…"

I give him a sheepish look and continue to be nosy.

I move into the main area and admire the contemporary stainless steel appliances. The quartz island takes up the majority of the space but yet does not look hideous or over-bearing. I watch as Graham seamlessly removes teacups, a kettle, and loose leaf tea from the various cabinets. He fills the kettle with water, measures out the correct amount of tea for the diffuser, and places the device onto the burner.

Someone taught him well. I just hope it wasn't an ex-girlfriend.

His eyes twinkle with mischief as he catches me staring. "Amused by what you see, Miss McFee?"

"Yup."

"Is that so?" He shoots me an adorable smirk.

"Uh-huh."

"And what has you so intrigued?"

My eyebrows lift suggestively. I am too shy to admit that I find him absolutely sexy—especially when he catches me off guard. Witnessing him move around his kitchen being domestic is equivalent to watching chore porn for the first time. I smile to myself as I wonder the effect he would have on me if he decided to vacuum.

Graham moves closer. I back up. Closer. I sidestep. I feel like prey. We are moving around the island. I know I am asking for trouble—playing with fire—but it feels so good to taunt and be pursued. When I am cornered against the joining counters, I stare breathlessly up into Graham's hooded eyes. He lifts me at my waist and drops me onto the smooth surface of polished quartz. The chill on my bottom feels good against my building heat. He steps closer and presses his groin into the apex of my parted legs.

"Know how badly I want you?" he asks gruffly.

I hum a nondescript answer. If it is anything like the magnetic pull I feel toward him, I am surprised my clothes are still on. My fingers play with the waistband of his pants, touching the skin of his abs.

"Because I do, Angie. I want you so badly."

We stay in this standoff for a minute before Graham steps back, sighing. "But you were drugged last night. And I need to keep a clear head if I want to protect you."

He returns to the kettle and pours two cups of tea for us. I slither from the counter and feel a pang of shame that I came on to him.

I add honey. "Thank you for the tea."

I carry my drink back to the sofa and reclaim my spot. Graham joins me and opens his laptop. He sets his teacup on a coaster and takes up the other end of the cushions.

"Shall we get started?" he asks.

"Sure," I say with a shrug. "Not sure how much help I will be."

"Let's start by listing all of the people you knew last night at the bar. We can then ask them for a list of people they knew in attendance. Maybe someone will appear out of place or suspicious."

"Well, I came by myself but ran into my classmate, Bryce. The night is a little fuzzy but Claire, Zander, Blake, and Resa were there." I pause to think of anyone else I might have known.

"Anything else out of the norm?"

"Oh, I ran into my ex on the way to the restroom."

Graham shifts in his seat and looks sternly at me but keeps typing. "Anything happen, Angela?"

I am caught off guard by his sudden coolness. "Just a minor confrontation."

"What type of confrontation?"

"He thinks I owe him some money. But I don't. He is just butt sore."

"What's his name?"

"Russell."

"Last name?" Graham sneers.

"Fanitelli," I say softly. I really do not want Graham to get involved. I can handle Russell on my own.

"He touch you?"

"No," I lie.

"Ever?"

"Graham…"

He stops typing and looks at me with eyes of steel.

"I really don't think it's a good idea to talk about this right now," I say.

"Does he have any motivation to try to hurt you?" he asks.

"I doubt it. I just threw a bunch of his shit out my bedroom window after a summer breakup. I'll pay him his money if he keeps making a big deal out of it."

"Seems like it was a serious relationship if you two were living together, yes?" he presses.

I shake my head. "It's not what you think." *Nor is it any of your business.* I sigh. "He used me on a superficial level. We were never serious. It was a mistake."

I can tell Graham wants to ask more questions. He stares at his screen without meeting my eyes. "I will have him checked out," he replies curtly.

I take a sip of my tea and clear my throat. "Only other person I can think of was the bartender. I just know him by frequenting the bar. How is this even going to help? It could have been a completely random act."

I need to stop taking the pills to calm my nerves. That will end all of this nonsense and the cellular birth of a conspiracy theory. I just need to humor Graham while he tries to exhaust his resources and eventually gives up.

"Or you could have been targeted," Graham growls.

I pull up my knees and wrap my arms around them tight. "Why? Why would someone do that to me?"

"Don't be so naive, Angie. It will only get you into trouble. It is a big, bad, scary world out there with takers and users."

"I'll take my chances at that world, Graham. I can handle myself."

"Doubtful."

We stare at each other for several seconds before I break the deadlock and look away. Anger simmers in me. I am capable of taking care of myself. Been doing it for years. I do not need some man crashing into my life and barking orders. Women have come a long way living in a man's world, and while the territory may not be equally divided, at least our voices are less muted than they were decades ago.

I watch in silence as Graham picks up his phone and orders an outrageous amount of Chinese takeout.

"Expecting company?" I ask with a forced smile. I'm not even sure I want to stay to enjoy it.

"Peace offering." He takes in my body language and sighs. "You're obviously irritated with me."

"Seems to be a common occurrence."

"Just start lowering your expectations, and things should level out," he responds nonchalantly.

I burst out laughing. "Pretty sure they cannot get any lower."

Graham chuckles too. At least in the middle of an argument, we can find the humor.

The doorbell rings, and Graham gets up to answer it. It is way too soon for the takeout to arrive. I get up to put my teacup in the sink and to try to see who it is. I crane my neck over the side wall and hear Collins's voice.

"I got your email and will run the names through the search database. See if any names correspond to the list Penny has given."

Penny. Why does that name sound familiar? I know I have heard her name before. Oh yes! Mark Tanner said her name to Graham which set him off.

"It's a long shot," Graham says softly. "Now Angie is a victim. This has got to stop. I want all resources and available men working on this, Collins. I am done playing by the rules. I am losing patience."

"I know, sir."

"Go against the grain if need be; I can handle the fallout and repercussions."

"Undoubtedly. Do you still want me to move forward with what we discussed in the hospital?"

"Yes, of course," Graham answers. "Nonintrusive. She cannot find out."

Who cannot find out? Penny? Me?

Sensing the conversation is ending, I sneak back into the living room. I stand at the wall of windows and admire the amazing view. It truly is a beautiful city. While growing up in Baker City had the perk of having small-town intimacy, it lacked the boldness and inclusiveness that Portland brings. People here are accepting and way less nosy.

The glass fogs until I cannot see the details of the outside world. I turn around, and my eyes land on Graham leaning against the wall holding a remote. He hits a button, and the glass appears transparent again.

"Showing off your toy, Mr. Hoffman?"

"Only if you find it even remotely impressive."

"I don't," I clip, biting my bottom lip to keep it from curling up.

He gestures with the remote toward me. "Have I told you that you're a horrible liar?"

I shrug and hum. "Perhaps. I don't remember a lot of things that you tell me."

His eyes come to life with amusement. "Come eat."

The takeout boxes get arranged on the coffee table. We sit on the rug and munch on beef with broccoli, sesame chicken, cashew shrimp, and spicy pork rice. This is a definite upgrade from my typical dinners at home.

"Which is your favorite?" I ask.

"Hmm…probably the cashew shrimp. Yours?"

"Spicy pork rice."

"Like the heat?" Graham asks suggestively.

"And you don't?"

He gives me his full-on smile. He grabs a remote from the end table, and suddenly soft instrumental piano music starts playing through hidden speakers. It is soothing after a stressful day.

I stand to gather the leftovers.

"Relax on the couch while I clean up." Graham holds his hand up as I start to move. "I insist."

I feel spoiled. Pampered. The feeling has been foreign for so long that I forgot how good it feels. I rest my head on the pillow and grab a throw blanket from the back of the couch. My eyes grow heavy, and I see light in the darkness. A beautiful shade of blue.

It is hope.

The sound of typing wakes me from my slumber. I slowly pull myself up from the softness of the cushions. The instrumental music is still playing in the background. My eyes lock with Graham's. He is on the opposite couch typing on his laptop.

"How long have I been asleep? Why didn't you wake me?" I ask in a panic. "I need to get home. Is it still Saturday?" I glance out the frosted window, and it appears dark now. Maybe I slept through an entire day. In the past, that was common for me. Sadness can do that to a person.

"Just forty-five minutes or so. You looked so at peace that I didn't have it in me to disturb you. Yes, it is still Saturday. Any other questions?"

"Can I please go home?"

"Of course. Let me grab you a jacket to wear. It's cold out now."

I watch as Graham retreats up a set of stairs that I never

even noticed before. Within seconds he is back down, holding a plain black jacket.

"Here," he says, offering it to me, "this should fit well enough."

"Thanks."

I put on the fleece-lined jacket and relish in the warmth it delivers. It comes down to my knees but serves its purpose well. I follow Graham out into the foyer, slip on my shoes, and step into the waiting elevator. We travel down to the parking garage where he auto starts the engine of his metallic-gray Lexus.

"You a car hoarder?" I ask with a smirk.

"What's the criteria?"

My mouth drops a little. "Owning more than you necessarily need."

He gives me a shrug. "Highly likely."

I slip into the passenger seat. Graham pulls out of the spot, and the engine purrs as we exit the garage.

"Plus, the Mercedes is in the shop getting cleaned."

"Oh." Because of me, probably. "Sorry.

He glances over at me. "It's routine, Angie."

I am either extremely transparent with my emotions, or Graham is extremely intuitive. Both theories unnerve me.

He pulls onto the interstate with ease. The ride is really nice. Smooth.

"I should text Claire. Do you have my cell?"

He reaches into his coat pocket and hands over my device.

"You had it this whole time?" I ask.

"You didn't seem to miss it, did you?"

"That's not the point."

I turn it on and wait for the logo screen to come to life. I check my text messages and see that Zander messaged me to see how I am doing. So did Resa. There are two missed calls from Claire with a voice message. I listen to the recording. She is just letting me know that Ethan will be spending the night. I text Zander back a quick message.

When Graham pulls into the spot beside my parked car, he jogs to my side and helps me out. He pops open the trunk to pull out my bag of hospital toiletry items. The name McFee is written along the side with Sharpie marker, and the image causes a shiver to run through me. The last time I was in the hospital was when—

My heart feels like it is creeping up my throat.

Graham's hand touches mine gently. "Everything okay?"

"Yes."

I know he wants to say more but doesn't pry. We walk side by side up the stairs to the front door. When we get to the top, he turns to face me. He gently grabs the waistband of my sweatpants and tugs me closer to him.

"When can I see you again?"

I look up into his waiting eyes. They are hooded. Sad almost.

"I have a lot of schoolwork to get caught up on. But I might be able to get a break midweek."

Graham gives me a single nod. He leans down and presses his lips to mine. He lingers there with his simple kiss that is so sweet and gentle that I think I might faint. My heart races in anticipation of what he will do next. His fingertips play with the bare exposed skin under my waist-band. There is no denying how much I want him. I move my head back to catch my breath and release myself from his hold to unlock my door with the key. He stands stoically on the doorstep waiting for me to step inside.

"Bye, Graham."

"Bye, Angie."

15

For an entire week, Graham has made zero effort to contact me. I assume he has lost interest. Most men do. While part of me is sad over this occurrence, the other part—the more sensible part—is happy for the ability to focus. I submerge myself in schoolwork, making several trips back and forth to the campus library to retrieve journalism books, speak with past professors, and meet with Dr. Williams. I feel refreshed, productive, and ready to enter another busy weekend.

While waiting for my laptop to power up, I check my phone messages and find the one from the agency alerting me about potential dates. I accept the evenings with Mark Tanner, justifying in my head that I need the money and I want to figure out what he is hiding. Luckily, I am not given a list of qualifications with regard to my wardrobe and hygiene this time. Maybe he can trust me to dress myself this time.

I find the charity gala's website and remind myself of all

the things I need to know for the event. At least I won't have to go alone. Zander is so easy to hang out with and knows how to adapt to social situations better than I do. Plus, having Claire there for moral support always helps. I text myself the address, as it has changed locations from last year's event.

I hop out of bed and make a beeline for the stairs, ignoring my typical morning ritual. In the living room, I find what has become the new norm playing out in front of me. This time Ethan is rather decent, in a white undershirt and jeans, and Claire is on his lap, cuddling in his black buttoned-down shirt. She could easily model men's clothing for some swanky designer, showing guys how amazing their clothes could look on and off their bodies. It's perfect advertising on a real-life mannequin.

"Hey you," she says using my greeting, a warm smile playing at her lips. Oh, she is so smitten.

I give a quick wave to Ethan.

"Can we talk for a minute?" Claire asks. "In the kitchen."

"Sure."

I head toward the kitchen, while Claire follows me. "I'll bring back breakfast," she calls to Ethan over her shoulder.

"Ethan have a thing for servants, now, eh?" I ask with a huge smile and a curtsy.

"Oh, shut up," she hisses, "a man gets hungry in the morning."

I chuckle. "What did you want to talk to me about?"

She looks up at me with pity as she smears cream cheese on a bagel half. "Your dad called me last night."

"What? Really?"

"I think he is in some kind of trouble."

I feel the air rush from my body. "I'm sure."

"Yeah, I think he needs money."

"He always needs money, Claire. He's a chronic gambler. Do not give him any. It is just feeding his addiction."

"I didn't know what to say to him. I was put on the spot. I just said I would call him back."

I lean against the island and rub my forehead to ease my developing headache. "I'm sorry he reached out to you. You don't need to deal with my family drama."

"Angie, I consider you my family."

"Same. But you know what I mean."

"I mean it." She looks me directly in the eyes. "You're more to me than my best friend."

My throat constricts. "I feel the same way."

"If there's something you want me to do, just let me know," she says while fixing another bagel half and placing it on the plate. "I got your back."

"You always do." I move toward her and wrap my arms around her petite frame. "I appreciate it too."

After several seconds, I let go and grab an orange from the bowl to peel.

"Things seemed pretty uneventful this week for you," Claire says, changing the subject.

"Yeah, for once, I didn't have much going on. Ironically, no dates either."

"Not even from Graham?"

I know she does not particularly like him, but she is starting to strengthen her tolerance level of him since the hospital scene—or so it seems.

"Have not heard from him actually." I munch on a segment of orange. "It's not unheard of for a guy to suddenly lose interest in me."

"Maybe my threat to dump liquid nitrogen on his balls sank in. I actually figured he would need a few more warnings before he really understood my willingness to protect you."

I choke on the piece that I was trying to swallow. "Uh, what?"

"I just made it clear that if he hurt you in any way, he would feel the power of my wrath."

I lean my butt against the island, crossing my arms at my chest. "The price being genital torture?"

Claire shrugs. "Seems fair, if you ask me. I was even exercising restraint with that threat. Be proud of me."

I laugh hard over the image of her going to bat for me. Oh, how I love this girl with my whole heart.

We head back into the living room. Claire joins Ethan in a snuggle on the couch. I claim the adjacent chair.

"I hear you are attending a charity gala this evening, Angie," Ethan says, making small talk.

"Yeah. It's to raise money for cancer research," I volunteer softly.

"Wow, that's really awesome to be part of something so important. My mom is a breast cancer survivor."

I nod with a warm smile, fighting back the tears that want to start. My mom was a cancer victim. Clearing my throat, I look to Claire. "Zander is picking me up around 5:40 p.m. If you need a ride there, just let us know. Remember, it starts at six."

"Wait," Ethan says. "You're going? Why am I just hearing about this now? Hmm?"

He bends down to tickle Claire's sides. She squeals and wiggles, trying to free herself, nearly knocking her plate onto the floor. I laugh at her reaction. I am happy that she is happy. Everyone deserves love.

"You should come," I persuade. "There will be dancing though."

"Why am I getting invited by your bestie instead of by you? Huh?" he asks her with a smile. "Do you think I am incapable of moving my hips?"

Claire tries to get away from him, but he is twice her size.

"Stop," she playfully yells.

"Huh, is that it? Let me prove my point about my hips that you must be questioning."

Ethan places the half-empty bagel plate on the coffee table and swings Claire over his shoulder with ease, marching upstairs. She lifts her head to look at me on her ascent, giving me just enough time to implement our you-better-use-protection hand sign, consisting of three Girl Scout pledge fingers getting covered by the opposite hand. Of course, Claire mimics the gesture using just her middle finger instead of three. Either way, equally effective. The sound of a door shutting rather loudly and her muffled yelps make me flush.

I shuffle into the kitchen and busy myself with cleaning every surface, before moving into the living room to do the same.

By the time I am done, Claire and Ethan make their way down the stairs, a post-sex glow over their skin. Claire is dressed in a bright yellow dress with short sleeves and a black belt that sits around her tiny waist. She looks like a ball of sunshine.

"Wow, you look amazing."

"Thank you. I have to pick up my gala dress from the shop. I just hope it fits. Is it okay if we meet you there? We have a couple of errands to run."

"Yeah, no problem. I am going to throw in a load of laundry and then spend the rest of the day getting myself ready."

"Cool. I'll text you when we get there."

I watch as the happy couple exits, smiling at how good they look together. I can't help but wonder if that will someday be me—despite my own personal hang-ups when it comes to love. It's not like I don't know what it is. I just have more experience with what it isn't. It is more of a delusion. People in love put blinders on and take everything at face value, never reflecting enough to uncover motives or intent. Love takes work, and I have enough on my plate to avoid it at all cost.

Second chances are expensive.

Third chances are nonexistent.

By the time Zander picks me up in front of my townhouse, I'm already a bit exhausted from all of the primping I did to get ready for tonight's event. I am not into these big social scenes, yet I know if I don't attend, I will forever feel guilty over it.

"You look wonderful, Angie." Zander opens the

passenger door for me and helps me inside. "I love the"—he gestures toward the layers of chiffon fabric of the long flowing skirt—"I don't even know what color that is, but it suits you."

I laugh. "It's called champagne."

He mumbles something that I think is another compliment and then shuts the door gently. I take a deep breath and glance in the mirror at my wavy hair as Zander rounds the front of the car and gets settled behind the wheel. I second-guess if my eyelashes are too long or if my makeup is a bit much for the gala. Wanting to look my best and actually accomplishing the task are two different things. Plus, people will be too polite to tell me if I flubbed up.

"I appreciate you escorting me this year."

Zander shoots me a smile as he backs out of the parking spot and heads toward the main road. "Anytime. Plus, I'm pretty sure I'll forever be in debt to you for rescuing me from humiliation at The Shack for open-mic night."

I look over at him. "I'm glad my nerves didn't get the best of me."

"You sounded amazing, Angie." His soft-spoken tone pulls at my heart. He is such a great guy. Why is he single? "You stole the show."

I swallow hard. Singing for me is a painful memory of what I have lost. Some things are meant to stay buried. However, I have to admit to myself that I liked the duet that unexpectedly occurred. It was reminiscent and actually soothing—but only until my brain caught up with my heart. The void that remains in my life is not filled completely by that moment. It is just the start of removing a bandage that is meant to stay covered.

After about ten minutes of silence, Zander clears his throat. I can tell he has something on his mind and is reluctant to bring it up.

"Everything okay?"

"So, this Graham person. What is he to you?" His words shake with hesitation.

"A friend," I blurt out. Is that what Graham is? A friend? He definitely acts levels above an acquaintance, but classifying him as something with an actual label just seems—

Pretentious?

We definitely touch more than friends usually do. And there are kisses.

I can tell that Zander has internally battled with whether or not to ask. I wish he hadn't. The car is starting to feel claustrophobic.

"Are you guys dating?"

I turn to look at him. Why all these questions? "Not dating. He's just someone I met recently through an acquaintance." I feel pangs of guilt for being so cryptic. However, I'm still trying to figure things out on my own.

Zander pulls up to where the valet worker is waiting to take his keys. "Well, he seems like a pretty intense individual."

"Yeah, he can be," I whisper, opening my door and hoisting myself out. I shoot Claire a quick text letting her know we arrived. Luckily inside, the tables are all assigned to guests.

Zander jogs to my side. "I would have helped you, Angie."

I smooth out my dress and pull my shoulders back with fake confidence. I think all of the interrogation questions got to me, because I'm still trying to figure out what Graham is to me myself.

Gorgeous guys like Graham are dangerous for a girl like me. He is experienced and seasoned. Addictive. Then again, he has completely fallen off the grid this week, so maybe all of my internal analyzing is a waste of headspace.

The gala is held at a private resort on the water. Lights strung from trees light the path leading up to the main entrance, like magical lanterns in the night. Dozens of people gather outside the venue to talk about sponsors, take some photos near the backdrop sign, or to get interviewed.

Skipping some of the hoopla, Zander and I meander inside with linked arms.

"I'm not used to seeing you this dressed up," I say, smiling up at him. "A black suit looks good on you."

His smile calms my nerves.

The main entranceway of the building is set up with tables of champagne, a guestbook to sign, and a pledge to donate area. I try not to allow thoughts of inferiority to flutter through my head, but it's hard being around designer labels when I am wearing a rent-the-dress that made it into the consignment sales after being retired. Dozens of girls could have worn this very dress. Granted, I gutted the thing and made it extra special with my sewing skills. I doubt anyone can tell that it is semi-homemade, and I'd like for it to stay that way the whole night. It's not like anyone would ever ask me who I was wearing; I'm not special.

Instrumental music filters in from the main hall, where circular tables and chairs are arranged to almost mimic the scene of a wedding reception.

A man in a tux escorts us to our table, just in time for Ethan and Claire to come walking in from the side door.

"Oh, good, you guys made it," I say in relief. Having my bestie here will calm my nerves a bit, and at the very least will keep Zander from asking me more questions I don't really know how to answer about Graham.

"Are you participating in the silent auction?" Claire asks.

"I doubt I have enough money in my bank account to even hit the minimum bid. So, no," I laugh awkwardly. Sadly, I'm here mainly to honor my mom in spirit and not be an ample financial contributor. Sure, the sale of my ticket helps, but it is very meager compared to some of these bigger donations.

The host for the evening announces for everyone to sit down, while he goes over the reason why we are all gathered tonight. A slide show plays in the background featuring photos of passed loved ones. I wait with anxiousness for Momma's picture to appear.

I sip from my wine glass and fidget with the sheer layers of my gown. At least it has a halter top, and I can worry less about my boobs slipping out. Despite knowing that I belong here at this event, it still feels so weird being here to honor Momma without James or Dad.

When her picture appears on the screen, I let out a breath. Both Zander and Claire give me a half hug as my eyes well up with tears. I chose a happy picture. One long before the cancer really took hold and ripped apart a family I once thought was unbreakable. But like anything precious, being destroyed is always a real possibility.

I am thankful when the slideshow ends and the soup and

salad course is served. Doing something other than thinking about all I have lost is welcomed right now.

We chat and eat and enjoy the soothing live music. On occasion the host comes around and welcomes individual tables personally to the event while making small talk and schmoozing with the guests.

After all the food is served, the aura changes in the room, as the music becomes louder and people gather on the dance floor. This is why it helps to bring a friend, I remind myself.

Zander stands, places his cloth napkin on the table, and then extends a hand to me. "Will you dance with me?"

I smile up at him and nod.

He escorts me to the dance floor where there is a break in the crowd already gathered. Resting one hand on my waist and the other laced with my right hand, he turns me clockwise to the melody of the song, bumping feet with mine on accident. "Sorry," he says sheepishly. His height makes me stretch up to put my left hand on his shoulder, balancing myself from falling down.

I giggle. "It's okay."

Zander's arms around me are comfortable and stress-free. He is my best male friend, and we care for each other. I look over at Claire—with her knowing glances—and can only guess what she seems to think. I make a point to avoid eye contact with her.

Friends. Just friends.

Another song starts. Zander maintains his grip on my waist and hand. His fingers fidget with mine, drawing attention to the sweat forming from the close contact.

I barely hear the word "beautiful" breeze past his lips,

choosing not to comment or act like it registered. I keep my focus on his jawbone and not his eyes—trying hard not to have awkward staring between us.

"I'm really sorry that you lost your mom, Angie," he whispers into my ear.

"I know." My words come out choked.

"But I'm glad I'm here to honor her tonight."

It's hard not to draw comparisons between how sweet and tender Zander is and how intense and unapologetic Graham can be. Two men who seem to maintain a place in my life—yet are vastly different. "Sometimes I feel like I don't deserve you as a friend. You are too good to me." It is the truth.

Zander stops moving to level his eyes with mine. "Don't ever think that, Angie. There's not much I wouldn't do for you."

Precisely—this is why you are a better friend. I smile at his tenderhearted soul, hoping that he can find someone one day who will appreciate all he has to offer. He deserves someone good and baggage-free.

As we continue to move to the music, I see a shadow on Zander's face and look up to see Graham's tall statuesque features in full glory. What the hell? What is he doing here?

"I'm cutting in," he states.

It is not a question—just a demand.

16

Zander glances at Graham, and I can tell he is pondering whether or not to argue. Both men size each other up, but neither moves. Graham's steel eyes cement his order to the ground, and Zander eventually breaks our hold.

"I'm sorry," I whisper to him, not quite sure my words were audible.

"I'll catch another dance with you later, Angie," he promises, locking eyes with Graham in some wildly inappropriate showdown. If I wasn't in the middle of yet another pissing contest, I might find the whole situation comical. But I am in the middle. I continue to find myself in the same position in many areas of my life.

I smile at Zander and mouth a thank you to him for his good sportsmanship in dancing with me and for backing down to avoid a potential throw down. He retreats back to our table and finds a seat.

"There, that was easy," Graham says with a smirk. He

links his fingers around my waist and picks up the rhythm of the music.

"You do know that stalking is illegal in all fifty states, right?" I ask, glaring at Graham for his rude behavior.

"Is that so?"

"It is so. And thanks for being so nice to my friend." My words sizzle with sarcasm, as I stare at the ill-mannered man. "Such a gentleman."

"Don't spread rumors, Angie," Graham counters, pulling my body swiftly to his, making me grunt softly from the force of being slammed into his torso.

My body heats as we sway to the music. I can feel the familiar tingling between my thighs, and I know that I am wet. He makes me hot without even trying. The effect he has on me is intoxicating.

"I have a reputation to uphold." His face is expressionless. "Your smart mouth will destroy my street cred."

As soon as the words hit my ears, I howl with laughter. My lungs deflate as air pours out in a gush. My eyes squeeze shut harboring the tears from escaping. This man is a comedian. Street cred? Living in his gangster paradise penthouse. Who does he think he is? Some leader of MS-13?

"I'm so glad you find me so funny, Miss McFee. You surprise me with what you find humorous. Catches me completely off guard. We should play chess sometime." His lips curve up and his brow quirks. "Winner gets a prize."

The man screams sex, while my body screams please.

"I'm more game for Monopoly," I deadpan. My face fights to remain serious.

His nose scrunches up in disapproval. "That game has

absolutely no strategy from a business standpoint," he scoffs, shaking his head back and forth.

The song changes and we continue with the new rhythm.

I smile a wicked grin. "Just teasing. Although, I'm surprised you don't like it more."

"And why is that?"

"You seem well versed in the whole notion of the buy-everything-and-conquer-the-world aspect of the game."

His eyes go wild from my analysis, gripping me even tighter to his firm body. "I am good at conquering," he agrees, putting the sexual spin on his words as if just to make me blush. "If we played Monopoly together and you owed money, I am sure we could work out a deal." His eyes dance with mischief.

"Sexual favors as currency?"

Graham bursts out laughing at my newfound boldness. He spins me around, pulling me back tightly to his body. "And you would then own all my assets with that strategy, hotels and all. To think that the game I like least may become a new favorite." He brushes his fingers up my ribcage, tickling my sides and making me jump.

"Something tells me you wouldn't play fair."

He shrugs. "Life is not fair."

"That we can agree on," I respond, meeting his smoldering eyes. I am here at this event now because life isn't fucking fair.

Graham continues to stare, his gaze burning holes in the walls I built around myself for protection. I feel naked and vulnerable standing before him. His intensity guts me.

"You missed me, didn't you, Miss McFee?"

I shake my head. "No, not really."

"You are the world's worst liar."

After a minute to recircuit my brain, I am able to think more clearly. "Um, what are you doing here, anyway?"

"I thought for business. But somehow, you turned it into pleasure." His eyes rake down my body, soaking in my curves. When I don't say anything, he sighs. "I'm not a complete asshole, Angie. I do give to charity."

"For a tax write-off, I'm sure," I taunt.

Graham shrugs and flashes a cheeky smile, making me giggle. I just can't stop laughing around him. He brings out a playful side that I thought I kept buried over years of pain.

My eyes catch Zander's as he watches us dance. He is chatting with Ethan, so I doubt he is bored. Yet, a pang of guilt hits me hard. "I need to get back to my—"

"Date." Graham's words are laced with a harsh undertone.

"Friend."

"Ha," he huffs, "there's no way that you can actually think that boy isn't fawning all over you. You are insightful enough to know the signs."

"What? No." I shake my head for added emphasis. "We are friends."

Graham's fierce eyes force mine into a hold. "When's the last time you took a man?"

What.

The.

Hell.

"Come again?"

To the prom? To the movies? To a charity gala?

"Angie. You know precisely what I mean. Quit playing games."

"I'm not the one playing games." I continue to move to the music, although my heart isn't able to maintain the slow rhythm. It feels like it will beat out of my chest.

"The last time you fucked someone? Ballpark estimate is fine. You already mentioned your ex, Russell. So summer?"

As soon as the words reach my ears, I gasp in shock, quickly diverting my eyes around the dance floor to see if anyone showed any signs of overhearing his crude question.

"Excuse me? Are you really doing this right now? Right here?"

"Do you really need me to repeat the question?"

My head shakes involuntarily. "And how is this any of your concern?" I ask boldly.

A slower, more intimate song starts to play. I've completely lost track of how many songs we have danced. I pull away and get the urge to leave this inappropriate conversation. I do not want to talk about this. Not now.

Hands pull me to taut muscles, and I am enveloped in an iron casing of arms. The tightness of his body makes the tension rise in my shoulders, all the way up to my neck.

We are so close, I can feel his hardness push against my lower abdomen. He smiles down at me as my expression changes on my face to enlighten him that I feel his erection. How could I not feel it? The rigid length is pressed up against his suit pants, straining to spring free. Realization hits me that he wants me to feel it. He is being deliberately flirtatious and forward. And fuckable. I pull away from his hips to keep from grinding against his cock with every small movement. His hands grip my waist and prevent me from putting space between us.

"Everything you seem to be doing concerns me. You have me intrigued, Miss McFee," he whispers into the shell of my ear.

Wait.

Did he just lick my lobe? I jerk back a little at the dampness that chills and excites my body, sending pulsating blood throughout my limbs. Yes, he most definitely licked me.

"I'm not buying what you're selling," I state simply, trying my best to express disinterest.

"Isn't that ironic?"

"Shut up, you arrogant bastard." One more jab at my job and he will be wearing the imprint of my fist instead of a smirk.

"You are quite sexy when you're mad."

"And you are quite annoying when you miss social cues."

His chuckle makes me even more flustered. He's enjoying this, that much is obvious.

"Yes, give me feisty. I can handle it."

"Quit saying things like that to me." I try to sound convincing.

"And the question I need an answer to," he starts, completely ignoring my plea, "is a gauge for me to see how slow I need to go with you."

"You do not need to go anywhere with me."

"If you only realized how much self-restraint I have been using with you. You are the first person I have wanted to go slow with. Ever. But my desire for you has grown. Angie, I want to fuck you tonight."

"What?"

"I tried to stay away. I swear I tried. I tried to be noble. I tried to do what is best for you and back off. But not even a five-day business trip to Europe could squelch my desire for you. It just made the flame grow stronger."

Well, that explains his lack of communication this week.

"Let's date, Angie," Graham suggests.

"Huh?"

"My intentions may be unconventional. But," he says with a pause, "I am a bit traditional, after all."

"Righhhht."

He smiles, showing all of his teeth. "So, I will buy you dinner and then spread you out on my b—"

"You are seriously crazy." Traditional? Telling me that he wants to fuck me is not what I call classical romance! But then again, the books I like to read are contemporary with a bit of kink. Word porn with a plot.

"If you seriously think I'm going to let another man beat me to the punch, then you are the crazy one. Every man who has the honor of sharing space with you ends up fantasizing about fucking you senseless."

"You can't possibly know that," I mutter, still trying to make sense of this nonsense.

His breath is warm on my ear. "I can read it all in their come-fuck-me eyes. My eyes do the same thing, for your information."

I pull back to look at him. "And you are conceited enough to think that the feeling is mutual? Mr. Hoffman, I am sure that there are many other women in the database who are more suitable for your antics. Blonde and redheaded ones who might flaunt their bodies and be more your type. Ones who might lie down easily and allow you to have your way with them. Make out with you in hallways. Ones who will—"

"Enough!" he whisper-yells, still careful to keep his tone low enough for just me to hear, although I'm starting to have my doubts.

His voice startles me from my speech. I take a step back but only am able to move an inch. I fix my eyes onto Graham's and hold them in place while the words pour from my lips. "I do not trust you."

"Why not?"

Because every one of my instincts tells me you are hiding something. "You are a player."

The melody of the next song starts, but I am too wrapped up in the conversation to care how we look to the public.

"I have never given you a reason not to trust me. I thought last weekend would have proven to you that I will never hurt you. That I will take care of your needs before my own. And Angie?"

"Hmm?"

"My list of desires is one long list."

"Thanks for the rescue. It was nice. I still don't trust you."

A pang of jealousy rattles my core. I know Graham has a past with Sophia, and she is actively trying to pursue a present with him. As much as I am attracted to him, I do not have the energy nor the time to compete with a supermodel.

"Follow your heart, Angie. You feel this undeniable chemistry."

"Hearts are wickedly deceitful."

His mouth touches my lobe, and then presses into the spot behind my ear, sending rockets of pleasure throughout my body. I arch my back and thrust my chest out. Shit, he's good. His fingers play with my hips, moving them on his own to the music. "Angela, take a ride with me."

"That sounds ominous."

"One night with me and my words that you think are all talk will come to fruition."

"Graham—"

His piercing blue eyes stare into me, as if I'm the only girl right now in his world. "Come back to my place with me tonight." His tone is seductive. "I still haven't given you the grand tour."

His voice turns me inside out. My mind shakes with just the possibilities of what going back to his place with him would mean. "I don't trust you."

"You keep saying that. Yet, I find it so unnerving that you seem to trust everyone else. Freely. And with little hesitation." He looks over to the table where Claire, Ethan, and Zander are chatting. "Hell, you don't even question your own male friend's intentions. You don't see that you are a very desirable woman. You go out on dates with douch—"

"It's business. Work," my teeth grind out my words.

"Yeah, about that, you need to quit."

"The hell I do! Who do you think you are?" My finger pokes at his chest. His amusement reflects in his blue depths. Damn him! "And Zander is a friend. One who wants me to be respected, which is the opposite of how you are treating me at this very moment."

"When's the last time you fucked someone, Angie? And I warn you, if your response remotely resembles the time frame of a mere week, I will carry you out of this hall whether you like it or not and show you just how ruthless I can be."

My mouth gapes open like a fish. "The hell you will. You want to carry me out of here whether I like it or not?" I ask, nearly swallowing my tongue. I vaguely remember him suggesting a similar act outside of The Shack.

"Oh, you will definitely like it," he whispers in a raspy voice. "Beg for it, actually. Something tells me that you are a naughty girl underneath all of the good girl facade you wear around like armor."

"How dare you!"

"You need to be dominated. Plain. And. Simple. You crave it. You want me to boss you around—to have the opportunity to not have to think for once in your life. You try to package yourself as a feminist… Why can't you be both? Let me control things in the bedroom but still love yourself as a strong woman?"

Excuse me? "You are unhinged!"

"Keep your voice down," he warns. "Your body is already causing a scene. You want your mouth to cause one as well? Let me take a guess at your story, since you are reluctant to share. Men in your past and present have broken your trust. You now have a warped view on your self-worth. Maybe some underlying daddy issues? Sweetheart, give me a chance to—"

"Sweetheart? Really? You call me that after talking

about wanting to fuck me? And dominate me? If you are looking for a quick lay, I'm not your girl. I'm not a slut! I have a brain!"

"When was the last time you had sex? Answer the question, dammit." His eyes turn to a storm of dark blue.

My heart races as the rage inside the pit of my stomach bubbles into a whirling flame.

"Never!"

17

I see the emotion change on Graham's face to confusion, and instantly, the tears sting my eyes at the embarrassment of the reveal. I was never expecting to air out my dirty laundry tonight when I stepped foot inside the venue, but that is exactly what he is forcing me to do.

"Happy?" I ask angrily, as heat slithers up my neck.

"Depends." His simple shrug piques my curiosity. His hands tighten possessively on my back, as he leads the dance.

"On what?"

"You are exquisitely beautiful. Surely, you have some type of sexual history. What experience do you have?"

At this point I have nothing to lose. The wall is down. "Not much," I say with a shrug. "No one has gotten past a few dates. My most recent breakup was the longest guy I dated, and most of the summer he was out of the country. While I was a senior in high school, I met a guy, became friends, and started dating. He was in college already and that made things a bit challenging—but yet easier to hold on to my virginity." The death of James ended the relationship for good. I wasn't in the right state of mind to continue what had barely started moving beyond just being friends.

I share a summary of the non-intercourse past sexcapades—awkward hands, painful fingers, and jerky motions. In conclusion, only one participant got off.

'Twas not me.

His narrowing eyes watch me closely. Analyzing. Judging.

"Well, you got the answers you wanted. Can you leave me alone now? Surely this revelation should deter you."

"You think finding out you're a virgin makes me want to stop pursuing you?"

"I'm no longer easy prey to you. Right?"

Graham's eyes burn into mine. "I want you. More so now than ever. I'm enchanted by you, Angie, and I think that I'm appealing to you as well. Have any men hurt you, sweetheart?"

His hands caress my cheek bones tenderly.

"No," I whisper shyly.

"I'm just trying to figure out how such a diamond can remain undiscovered for so long."

"Why do you even care?"

"Any man who is in your past or present is viewed as a potential threat to me. Including your sing-songy friend," he says using air quotes around the word friend.

"You have got to be kidding me!"

"Oh, I am not in a joking mood."

"Are you ever?"

His chuckle is contagious and works wonders on my

tense posture. I instantly relax. "I think I might have underestimated you, Miss McFee."

"Better than being overestimated, I suppose."

His laugh grows. "My charm seems to work on everyone but you. You are immune."

"Is that why you're so interested? Because you can't have me? So, if I were to give in that would make you back off?"

"I have a feeling that if I were to have you once, then I would never be able to resist again. Does that scare you, Miss McFee?"

I swallow hard and nod in response.

"Despite what you might think, I do not want to scare you."

"Too late." My voice is barely a whisper.

"Let me fix that. I have a proposition for you. How about we discuss it in private?"

"Not interested."

"You haven't even heard it!" he snaps, pulling me from the crowd toward the back of the room. My protests fall on deaf ears.

"Quit treating me like a child," I sneer.

"Then quit acting like one."

I follow behind Graham, his hand firmly holding mine. As we pass some of the charity officials in suits, his name is called out in greeting, as if everyone that looks to be of high importance knows and respects him. I can only follow in his shadow, as he tries to open the doors in the hallway, finding them all to be locked. He pulls me down another corridor, where a red cushioned bench is located. Frosted wall sconces provide a warm illumination, casting a muted glow about the space. We are far away from the excitement in the ballroom; only the hum of the muffled music can be heard.

"Sit," he says, taking a seat himself.

When I hesitate, he tugs my arm, sending me surging right down into his lap.

"What is your problem?" I demand.

"I want to proposition you."

I scoot off his lap and turn my body toward his, resting my side against the wall.

"Oh, I'm sure you do."

"I had a whole week away from you. I tried," he says, running a hand through his hair, "to stay away. Trust me, I did. But it's as if you have a magnetic pull that is keeping me from pulling away from you. We will be horrible together, and yet I can't stop myself from wanting to push past the feeling of impending disaster just to see where this goes."

I swallow hard. I feel the force too. I missed him this week, and no amount of reasoning will help me to understand why.

"How much can I pay you to quit the agency?"

My heart stops beating for half a second. "You want me to quit the only job that I have right now? A job I literally just started?" A job that will soon pay all my bills. A job that will hopefully further my investigation skills.

"You will still get the money. It will be like a job you get paid for but don't actually have to do anything."

But it's more than the money. It's the connections and networking that will help me with my career. This underground world of the elite might be full of nefarious people who I need to investigate and explore. "I'm not quitting."

His eyes bore into mine. I can see his wheels turning as to how to get me to agree to his proposition. "I don't like being told no."

"I don't like being told what to do."

"You accepted Mark Tanner's dates."

"So. What's your point?"

"Angie, you do not want to be near that man. He is dangerous. He's using you as bait to get to me."

This is exactly why I need to be near him. He might be hiding something huge. Something that I can uncover and write about. The more Graham tries to force me out of the agency, the more I want to stay in. The more Mark Tanner tries to cover up his business conversations in my presence, the more I want to find out the reason why.

"How, Graham? What does he want from you? You make it sound like it's more than just business."

My investigative journalist instinct is to figure out their connection. The chance of a good story is slim. Most chases lead to nothing, but I have no leads at all. Nothing. And the one time I had an amazing story, it was snatched out from under me. Not again. This is my second chance.

His eyes twitch, and I know that I am right. He usually doesn't give me such a tell, but for some reason, I hit a nerve.

"Just stay out of it, Angie. And for heaven's sake, stay away from Tanner. I can't protect you if you do things behind my back. Do you understand?"

"I don't need protecting," I insist, but it comes out more like a whine.

"Said the last girl that—" He pauses and looks straight

at the wall. It's as if he is in a different place. At a different time.

"That what, Graham? Finish your statement."

"He's dangerous."

I put my chin up in defiance, not backing down from him. "I've been told the same thing about you."

"I can be dangerous, that is a fact. But I always protect what is mine."

"I'm not yours. Thus, your protection isn't necessary."

His hand moves to my left knee, running his palm up and down, while pulling the fabric of the dress up to reveal my legs, encased in silky thigh-highs. His movements are intentional and purposeful.

"Tell me to move my hand, Angie."

I close my eyes to savor the feeling of his touch. It feels so good, unlike any touch I have felt before.

"Tell me, Angie. Tell me to stop."

Graham pauses for a few seconds, waiting for me to say the words. When I am silent, he swiftly takes both of his hands and grabs hold of my waist, lifting me to my feet. He guides me to stand in front of him. I am pulled between his legs, which part to accommodate me.

"Graham—"

The pad of his finger touches my lips. "Shhh…"

I close my eyes at the feel of his hands sliding up my legs again, this time making it to the exposed part of my thighs. It has been such a long time since anyone has made me feel this wanted, this desired. But like every other guy in the past or present, they always have an agenda. Something they want.

"If you don't like what I'm doing then stop me. Tell me to stop, and you have my promise that I will."

I urge my mouth to listen to my brain. I should tell him to stop. I need to tell him to stop. Nothing good can come out of blurring the lines.

"Yes, baby, moan for me," he whispers. "Give in to me."

My eyes flash open at his words. Certainly I'm not moaning?

When his hand reaches the material of my satin panties, I fall forward at the sensations. Then I recognize my own wanton sounds of deprivation.

"Easy, baby." I can feel his smile penetrate the darkness of my thoughts. "Oh, you are very wet for me. So responsive. Tell me you like my touch. Tell me."

I hesitate for several seconds, feeling Graham's determination evident with every stroke over the fabric. He is chipping away at my reluctance to admit what he already knows; the proof of my arousal is all over his fingers.

"Tell me," he coaxes. "Angela?"

"Hmm?"

"I'm waiting."

"I like it. A lot, dammit."

"Such a good girl."

The simple words send a rocket of pleasure down to my core.

"I can't wait to see your pretty little pussy, sweetheart. Will you show it to me?"

I open my eyes and stare down into Graham's hooded gaze. We are both sexually charged and panting in breathless gasps. I feel intoxicated. Drunk off the energy he exudes. Over the frill of my skirt, I can see his erection, straining against the confines of his pants. To an outsider it would appear that I'm in a position of control. But I know better. Graham is calling all of the shots, and I'm too weak to resist.

I hike one heeled foot up onto the bench. Graham's groan spurs me on, my rational ability to make good decisions decreasing at epic speed. I flip my skirt over my elevated thigh, using my elbow to keep the fabric back.

"Such pretty panties too."

My lips curve up. "Thank you."

The pink satin panels tie into bows at my hips like a string bikini. Thin lace trims the border, creating a very modern look. They were a splurge purchase, so it feels good that he approves.

I look down at the crotch, seeing the darkened spot from my wetness. Graham does that to me—like no other man has done before. I am wanton and haunted by his commands. Graham's fingers pull at the ties on the side of my hips, undoing the panties. The fabric falls onto his lap, exposing my core.

Graham grasps the material in his hands, pulling the inner liner up to his nose and inhaling, never taking his eyes off my center. He gives them a lick of his tongue and it is the most erotic thing I have ever seen.

"Hmm." He lets out a deep growl. "Delicious. Just like I knew you would be."

His approval makes me melt even more.

"You are glowing, sweetheart. So beautiful. A feast for my eyes. And my hands and tongue are violently jealous over which gets to explore you first."

Graham's words make my legs weak, and I stumble

forward, using my hand against the wall above his head as support. He takes that hand and moves it to his shoulder, caressing my fingers before departing. My heart rate increases at the anticipation of what he is going to do next. With infinitesimal speed, he takes his right hand and uses two fingers to spread my folds, staring right into the source of my moisture. My head falls to the side at the simple feel of his touch on my most vulnerable parts. He is calculating and deliberate in his movements.

I am thankful that I thought ahead enough to trim and groom my nether region. It isn't like I ever expected to be in this position. I have never been in this position. Or this turned on before now.

Keeping my lips open, Graham uses his other hand to drag a finger up and down my slit, gathering my juices in its wake. The slow torment nearly drives me over the edge. I want to scream and push his hand on me harder. He is being too gentle, too respectful. I want pressure and—

More.

"Shhhh. I want to take my time. I want this memory burned into your mind forever."

I push my body into his hand, making him pull back.

He shakes his head. "Uh uh, so greedy, Angie."

"Please."

"Such a pretty little cunt."

He removes his finger from my inner lips, lifting it for me to see.

"See how fucking hot you are?"

"Yes," I breathe.

"Ripe and ready. Like a peach."

He places his finger on his lips, spreading the moisture

over his skin like balm. His tongue slips from his mouth, licking up the juice like it is liquid candy. Humming and moaning penetrate my ears as I watch him suck on his sodden finger.

"You are delicious, kitten. I am so hungry for more."

He moves his finger back to the center of the heat, repeating the same gathering and spreading over his lips. He is taunting me. Teasing me. Only giving me the barest of pressure. I am the one wanting more.

Graham takes my foot that is balancing on the bench and slips off my shoe. He caresses my foot with his expert fingers, making me grasp both of his shoulders for support.

"Feel what you do to me. Feel your effect on my body," he urges, taking my shoeless foot and moving it over the crotch of his pants. He presses my sole up and down his erection. He is so hard. Tense. His arousal is nearly my undoing. I can feel the pulsating blood travel even faster to my clit—a spot he very strategically avoided touching. "I want you so badly, Angie. Give in to me. I am going to make you come so hard."

"Hmm…"

"You want that, baby?"

Yes. Yes, I want that. I need that.

I tremble and shiver at the sensations and emotions that Graham elicits from me with expert ease. He puts my foot back in my shoe and places it on the ground before yanking me down to straddle him. My knees relax against the cushion, my naked crotch an inch away from his concealed cock. The smell of my arousal fills the air.

I use my knees as leverage and grind my crotch over his lap. I am wanton. Possessed by pleasure. His groans spur me on. I circle my hips and feel his fingers dig into the meaty flesh of my bare ass. I can feel my moisture soaking into the fabric of his pants. He guides my movements, taking back the control. He pushes me down hard onto his straining cock. I thrash my head back as I am about to reach the ecstasy I so desperately want.

Suddenly, Graham halts all movement. "Fuck," he growls. He snatches my sodden panties from the bench and shoves them into the pocket of his pants. His fingers move behind me to straighten out the back of my skirt.

"Sir," Collins's voice snaps me out of the erotic trance. My heart actually skips a beat in alarm from his presence. "I tried your phone," he clarifies as a defense.

Shit. I turn frantically and see his suited body in the shadows against the back wall. He keeps his distance while Graham rearranges my outfit for me. Collins is polite enough not to stare or comment on our public display of inappropriateness. "What is it?" Graham asks tersely. He keeps hold of my waist, despite me trying to slither off his lap.

Collins looks intimidated at my obvious embarrassment.

"It's"—he stops and shifts his weight—"Penny. You wanted me to give you an update right away, sir."

Who is this Penny I keep hearing being mentioned? Mark brought up her name, and now Collins has brought her up twice within the week.

"Do you have the coordinator on the line? Or a time to be reached?" he asks, rubbing his hands up and down my spine in a rhythmic motion. It is strangely soothing, and I find my heart rate simmering down to a healthy pace.

"I have him on the line, sir."

Graham stands, holding my body flat against his. He tucks me under his strong arm, pressing me into the side of his torso. For some odd reason I feel more vulnerable now than I did just minutes ago. We crossed a line, and there is no turning back. No redoing it. Now my body knows his touch, craves it, and senses its loss. The fact that I have little control over it is what scares me to my core.

"Please accompany Miss McFee to get some refreshments." Graham anchors me to him, steadying me from the numbness of my legs being in one position for too long. He tilts up my chin with gentle fingers, guiding me to look at him. "Angie, I'm sorry, but I have to accept this call. Please let Collins get you something to drink and eat. I will join you shortly."

My mind catches up with the situation. "I'll be fine, really. I have my friends to get back to." Penny is obviously more important. Is he in a relationship with another woman?

He uses his hand to push back a strand of my sweaty hair from my forehead. He reaches into his pocket, stopping my heart instantly. The panties. Instead he removes his cell phone, while giving Collins a knowing look. They exchange devices and nod at each other, transferring some message without any words spoken.

I am speechless.

"I'll catch up with you in a bit. Please let Collins escort you out into the main hall."

My mind fogs with the hot-cold personality of Graham. One second he is kind and accommodating. The next he is icy and calculated.

I humor him enough to stay next to Collins's side while I walk down the corridor of shame. Maybe it's for the best that he stopped the scene. The last thing I need is to get emotionally involved with another man who is incapable of giving me what I need. While my lower half says "yes," the more rational upper half says "hell no."

"Ma'am, there's drinks and snacks in the limo," he offers, talking at a higher volume to be heard over the buzz of the crowd mingling. "The event is coming to an end, and I will see that you get home safely."

"I'd rather stay and be with my friends," I counter.

"Mr. Hoffman woul—"

"Damn good thing I do not answer to Mr. Hoffman." I turn and move to go back to my friends, ignoring him. I feel Collins's presence behind me, patrolling me. Seriously? The man has a fatherly aura to him, although he isn't in the same age range. I find my thoughts ironic, considering I haven't had a real father figure in my life for quite a while now.

I see Claire and Ethan dancing together, but no sign of Zander. Ugh, why did I leave him alone? My eyes scan the room until I spot him sitting at the reserved table, drinking some type of dark liquid. Making my way over to him, I plan out my apology.

"Hey you." I give him a lopsided smile. "Sorry if it seems like I ditched you."

Zander holds up a hand to stop me. "It's fine, Angie. No need to apologize."

"Well, it was not my intention."

"I know."

I find my handbag that I hid under the table with all my essentials tucked inside. "Do you want to go look out at the water? I think the back doors lead out onto a viewing platform. Then we can get out of here."

"Sure. Sounds great."

As we walk toward the rear exit, Collins addresses me from the corner with his eagle eyes, making me halt.

"Go ahead, Z. I'll meet you out there in a minute. I need to use the restroom," I lie. He accepts this, and I watch his retreating form.

"Ma'am, Mr. Hoffman is not going to like this."

I turn to look at Collins, who seems on edge. "Okay," I say matter-of-factly. "Mr. Hoffman pretty much disapproves of most things I decide to do. He'll eventually figure out how to get over it." I shrug. "My life, my rules."

"He would rather take you home himself after his conference call. If you would rather go home now, I can drive you myself."

"Tell your Mr. Hoffman that I had fun today. I'm sure that he will make it a point to find me and make things more complicated. Until then, I'm going to enjoy my freedom."

As I turn to walk away, I feel powerful. Damn straight. I walk confidently through the doors and brace myself for the cold air that bites at my exposed skin. The lady bits sure are feeling the repercussions of forfeiting my panties over to Graham, making me wish I had the foresight to pack an extra pair in my handbag.

"Nice evening," I say to Zander, as we gaze out at the reflection of the moon on the river.

"It is." Removing his suit coat, he wraps it around my arms.

"Thank you," I say, as a shiver runs through me.

"So, I was thinking," he starts, "that if you are free sometime this week that maybe you can come by my place and we can do a video game tournament with the guys?"

I giggle. "Only if we don't play any type of racing game. I suck at those."

"Okay."

"And no time limit games," I groan.

"Deal. Any other stipulations?"

"And only games I'm good at."

He chuckles. "So you want to play Tetris."

I nod happily. "Great idea."

Zander playfully rolls his eyes. "Fine."

After several long minutes, I don't think my body can handle any more of the cold. I'm so not ready for winter. "Ready to head out?"

"Yeah."

"I'll meet you at the car. I need to go say goodbye to Claire and tell her we're leaving."

"Sounds good."

I go back in the same way and round the corner to get inside the ballroom, only to spot Graham in the corner with a camera crew, giving what appears to be an interview. He looks like a celebrity with his polished looks. I assume that he has donated a decent chunk of money for the cause. Everything about the man seems rich and overly extravagant. When the camera guy moves, I catch who is standing at Graham's side. The undeniable blonde tresses are perfectly styled in an elegant side do.

Sophia.

Anger boils in my blood, and it takes everything in me not to go over and claw his eyes out—and hers. The smile on his face and his eyes twinkling with laughter make me want to throw up. He's playing with me and her at the same time. Maybe he even has another side chick, Penny.

Damn him.

Sophia is dressed in a pale pink floor-length ball gown, adorned with tiny reflective beads. The dress only has one side strap, completely leaving her left shoulder naked. It is not a functional dress. She is here solely as arm candy.

Pangs of jealousy poke at my confidence. She looks like a walking star, sparkling in the spotlight like a professional.

I stare in silence as if I'm in some sort of warp zone trance. The male reporter asks Graham about his jewelry company and his employee—Sophia. So they work together for business and for pleasure. Lovely. Graham takes his hand, the same hand that took off my panties just a half hour before, and gently pulls at the necklace around Sophia's delicate neck. The beautiful diamond pendant sparkles in the lights of the production area, making me want to yank it off. My eyes fixate on the movement of his fingers. I watch a shiver run up her arms, knowing firsthand just how mesmerizing Graham's touch can be. It feels like I am observing an intimate moment between lovers, and the jealousy building inside me bubbles with the start of a fresh life.

How can he tell me one minute that he wants me and then the next be all over Sophia? This looks to be way more than just business.

I force myself to move a few steps closer to hear the actual questions being asked. Everything else is blocked out, and my entire focus is on them.

"Can you share any details on Jealousy? The line seems to be taking off and gathering fans exponentially. My wife is one of them." The male reporter makes a quirky face into the camera. "Sorry, honey."

Graham smiles at the reporter, diverting his eyes momentarily to his feet. Is he being shy? I never thought I would see this with my own eyes. He chuckles and reverts back to his impeccable stature. "The particular line is one of my pet projects, one I take great pride in, so thank you for acknowledging it. The only thing I can promise in the future is innovative products that appeal at the multisensory level."

"And there you have it, folks, the enigmatic owner of Jealousy, Mr. Graham Hoffman and his partner in crime Sophia Chantel. You can find these two—"

The voices fade as I continue to stare. I can't believe I let him touch me. In a public place! I fell for everything that spewed from his mouth. I am an idiot. But it wasn't like I wasn't warned.

When the two laugh with the reporter, who is eating up their on-screen chemistry, I am sent over the edge. I bypass the ballroom, bumping into a few people on the way out of the building.

I suck in air through my teeth, as I try to calm down my frantic heart. What is happening to me? Why am I this upset? Tears drip down my cheeks in angry streams, as I try not to hyperventilate.

Just breathe.

I shield my face from anyone exiting the venue and focus on staying calm—but it is useless.

Momma, I could really use you right now.

18

"Are you okay, Angie?" Claire asks, as I make my way through the door to our townhouse. "You should've been home an hour ago. Where did you go?" She stands up and gives me the biggest hug, which only makes me cry even more.

"I just had a moment. That's all."

"What happened? You were fine when I left the fundraiser."

I give her a squeeze back and then pull away. "It's just been a rough day. I really don't want to talk about it." Not with her nor with Zander, despite him asking multiple times in the car what happened. I wish I knew what was really wrong. My meltdown just seems over the top when I try to explain it to even myself. "I think I was just long overdue for an ugly cry. The cancer charity gala just happened to be the location of said freak-out fest."

I can tell she wants to pry, but I pray she honors my wishes.

"Want to watch a chick flick?"

I sigh with relief. "Yes, please."

Claire runs to the TV and grabs the Blu-ray case for our go-to favorite, *Ten Things I Hate About You.*

I can probably come up with a couple dozen more things I hate about Graham. But no matter how strong my hate is toward the man, the passion I feel for him is immeasurable to anything else I have ever felt. I want to hate him. But I mostly hate myself for liking him. I cannot afford another distraction when I am so close to finishing this last semester of school and hopefully getting an internship lined up. This is my last chance. There are no more re-dos.

I daydream during the entire movie. It is great background noise to my chaotic thoughts.

"Angie?"

I feel a soft tapping on my shoulder. "Hmm?"

"You fell asleep," Claire whispers softly. "Time for bed."

"Okay," I moan, trying to gain back my senses. I sit up and hoist myself off the couch.

"Oh, I completely forgot to tell you. There was a package for you on the doorstep when I arrived home. I put it on your bed."

"Okay, thanks," I respond, making the ascent up the stairs.

Entering my room, I see the perfectly wrapped pink present on my bed. It is the same shade of pink as Sophia's dress. It takes everything in me not to hurl the thing out the window.

I tear through the paper in a hurry to get the whole thing over with in one quick motion. I flip open the lid and toss layers and layers of tissue paper on the floor. In the box, I find roughly thirty pairs of designer panties, perfectly folded and on display for my eyes. Some with silk, some satin, some lace, some with just string. Some red, some white, some black, and some with intricate patterns. The styles range from an itsy-bitsy thong to a more conservative boy short. All classic, yet sexy. A very beautifully eclectic selection. It's so fucking perfect that I want to throw the entire box in the garbage.

I hate him.

I hate them.

I hate that I love them.

I hate that they are pretty.

I hate that he has a pair of mine.

Underneath the array of panties, there's a note. I clutch the paper in my hand and whisper the words out loud to myself in a scorned tone.

Feel free to dirty these, kitten. -GH

My anger bubbles over the sexual need I have for this man. I want him. Even when he drives me utterly crazy with desire and jealousy.

Feeling frisky, I hop online and find the corporate address for Jealousy. I browse the Internet for several minutes and find the nicest silicone vibrating cock that twenty dollars can buy and ship it to his office addressed to him. I include a cheerful note.

Go fuck yourself. -Kitten

Sunday morning can be summed up as uneventful. I wake to the sounds of sex coming from down the hallway. Apparently the rich, divorced suitor prefers small townhouse bedrooms—riddled with clutter—over his bachelor pad. I wonder if he has bizarre habits or a secret woman hiding out in the attic. Perhaps he is living in less than stellar conditions after his first wife wiped him clean. Claire doesn't seem to mind the situation—her moaning evidence of her approval. I chalk it up to home court advantage, but I can't help but wonder what it feels like to hit that level of pleasure.

I use my iPhone to start the 30 Seconds to Mars playlist of songs to drown out the ohs and ahs and yes pleases. Apparently Claire's alter ego is very polite in the bedroom, a vast contrast to how she acts in public. This Ethan guy has her unraveling at the seams. For a brief moment, I contemplate grabbing my novel, but then think again at how dirty that would make me feel if I decide to get turned on by chick-lit while my roomie is banging next door.

I make my way downstairs and find the Sunday paper—most likely belonging to Ethan—on the coffee table. The Life & Style section is on top, purposely arranged and left there, I assume. Several dried rings of stains damage the perfect image of Graham Hoffman and Sophia Chantel on the cover. I want to do more than just tarnish their perfection with some coffee.

I stare at the blonde bombshell, sporting the sparkly diamond necklace—easily costing a fortune. Even in the photo, the quality of the classic gemstones shines, but not more than Graham's smile. And that is what pisses me off the most.

He looks happy.

I throw myself into the cushions of the couch and submit to reading.

Local Love Cashes in for a Cure

By Violet Storm - *The Headliner Exclusive Interview*

GRAHAM HOFFMAN IS HOT, RICH, TASTEFUL, AND APPARENTLY UNAVAILABLE. I SAID IT, LADIES (AND GENTLEMEN); DON'T HATE THE MESSENGER! THIS LOCAL HEARTTHROB SAT DOWN WITH US FOR AN EXCLUSIVE INTERVIEW ON THE NIGHT OF THE CANCER FUNDRAISER AND GAVE US THE DEETS. WHILE HOFFMAN IS TECHNICALLY CONSIDERED A TRANSPLANT TO THE PORTLAND AREA, HIS BUSINESS ROOTS RUN DEEP UNDER THE ENTIRE CITY. BESIDES PROSPERING IN THE REAL ESTATE END OF THINGS, HOFFMAN HAS FOUND SUCCESS IN THE JEWELRY MAKING INDUSTRY, OWNING A TRENDY BOUTIQUE CALLED JEALOUSY. NO WONDER THE MAN WAS ABLE TO CONTRIBUTE A MILLION DOLLARS FOR THE CAUSE!

WHEN ASKED ABOUT HIS PRESENCE AT THE GALA, HOFFMAN STATED, "CANCER AFFECTS ALL FAMILIES, REGARDLESS OF SOCIOECONOMIC STATUS, RACE, OR BACKGROUND. NO ONE IS IMMUNE. I AM PRIVILEGED TO TAKE A HANDS-ON APPROACH TONIGHT RATHER THAN JUST TO BE THE ONE SIGNING THE CHECK. IT'S THE LEAST I COULD DO."

IN ADDITION TO THE HEFTY MONETARY DONATION, HOFFMAN ALSO CONTRIBUTED SOME OF HIS SIGNATURE JEWELRY PIECES FOR THE SILENT AUCTION.

OKAY, SO I DIDN'T STOP THERE, MY FRIENDS. AFTER STALKING THIS MAN FOR FIVE YEARS, I HAD TO ASK THE TOUGH QUESTIONS—THE ONES INVOLVING A LOVE INTEREST. I MEAN, SERIOUSLY, HE HAD A GORGEOUS SUPERMODEL OF A WOMAN RESTING ON HIS ARM. WHAT DID HE EXPECT ME TO DO? "I DO NOT KISS AND TELL," HOFFMAN CHUCKLED, SQUEEZING THE BEAUTIFUL SOPHIA CHANTEL—WHO LOOKED VERY SMITTEN WITH OUR EYE CANDY. WHILE CHANTEL IS EMPLOYED UNDER HOFFMAN'S COMPANY IN THE MARKETING DEPARTMENT, SOMETHING TELLS ME THAT THIS RELATIONSHIP GOES BEYOND THE PAYCHECK.

TIME WILL TELL.

-V.S.

I toss the paper aside before I lower myself to drawing a mustache and a set of horns on Sophia's face. It would give me instant gratification, but then leave me feeling empty and very alone. I have no claim on Graham. None. On most days, I want the man to stay out of my personal space. Then he goes out of his way to make time for me or buys me luxurious gifts or says things that make my heart melt. Clearly, Sophia is not out of his life. She seems to be an intricate part of his jewelry business. So even if we were to go on dates, Sophia would always be in the back of my mind taunting me.

Picking myself up from the rut, I vow to make today my catching-up-on-Human-Behavior-assignments day. I need a distraction, and nothing is better than burying myself in layers of schoolwork to detox my body from thinking about Graham.

I drive to the campus library and use the facility's desktop computer that has a better keyboard than my laptop. For a Sunday, the building isn't very crowded with college students. One study group uses the back conference room to have access to the white board and a few girls utilize the circular tables to spread out their work. I stay there until the workers remind me about the six o'clock closing, wanting to shut the doors for the night. Satisfied that I gathered enough information from the Internet, I save my work on my flash drive.

On my way home, my phone rings for the first time all day. I check to see that it is Mark before answering.

"Hey, Mark, what's up?"

"Angie. I'm glad I got ahold of you."

"Yeah? What's up?"

"I saw that you accepted my dates for this week. But then they all got canceled, and I wanted to know if I did something to offend you."

What is he talking about? "Um, I have no idea what you're talking about. I did not cancel them."

"Hmm, that's really weird. Also, when I went to check on your profile a few hours ago, it was disabled. I couldn't even see that you existed. It's as if you vanished from the site. I can contact the tech support team tomorrow during office hours and see if there is something wrong with the system."

"Okay, sounds good. I'll fill out a help-desk ticket when I get home."

"Well, can you still go out with me tomorrow? I have an appointment with some more associates. Your presence would be appreciated."

"Oh yeah, I can still go with you. What time?"

"It's earlier than usual. We are meeting at four o'clock. Does that work for you?"

I run through my mental schedule of classes and research obligations. "That works for me," I respond, accepting the date, happy that I can still partake in the Monday night ritual of watching reality TV.

"Awesome. I'll just write you a check since I can't put the money in your account. Can you wear something like what you wore on our last date? Your legs looked absolutely amazing."

"Um, thanks," I say shyly, shifting in my seat. "Yeah, I can find something that will work."

"Good, see you tomorrow."

When I arrive home, I find a short note left by Claire on my bedroom door stating that she is spending the night at Ethan's place and that she left me some leftover zucchini noodles in the fridge from her lunch. I smile at her thoughtfulness and take her up on the food offer. I am starving after skipping lunch.

I spend the rest of the night going through the week's mail and organizing my online finances. I flip through three magazines that Claire subscribes to and make a shopping list for groceries on one of the renewal insert postcards. At nine forty, I crash into bed.

Human behavior class is bearable due to Bryce's witty comments and his delivery of my caramel frozen latte with fresh whipped cream. Although our banter turns raunchy about ninety percent of the time, it's in good fun. He's harmless.

"You're sporting a different type of smile, Teach. You get laid?"

My cheeks light up with warmth as I'm sure the shade has turned an embarrassing crimson. My head tilt and raised eyebrow conveys the message of "hell no" efficiently.

"I should have guessed. You can still walk. If we were to f—"

"Bryce!" My squeal blends with the professor's raspy greeting to the class.

"Do you think she would go for a guy like me?"

"Who?" I ask, taking a sip of my beverage. Wednesday will be my turn to pick up the drinks. Thankfully, frequent flier punch cards alleviate some of the expense for the weekly ritual.

"Miss Pencil Skirt."

"You seriously have a thing for her, don't you?"

"I have a running list of things I could do with that scarf around her neck."

"Maybe she is hiding one of those old lady turkey necks." I try my best to keep a straight face. "The ones that can only be fixed with plastic surgery." I laugh at the horror displayed on Bryce's face. He shakes his head "no" repeatedly. You would think I kicked his puppy.

"But do you think it's even possible?" he asks again.

"If she starts wearing turtlenecks...ones with holiday-themed patterns...oh, and shoulder pads...I think you might actually have a chance with her."

"Wow. Thanks. You are cruel, Teach."

I giggle quietly and continue to write notes from the slideshow. My phone buzzes with an incoming text, and I check it when the professor is not looking in my direction. Despite everyone else having their phones in view on their desks, I keep mine concealed in my tote. The Entice date text flashes on my screen, and I open up my profile to see who reserved me. Apparently my profile got put back up on the server after being disabled. When I find the calendar button on the small screen of my phone, I search for the blinking numbers to indicate a date warning. I find nothing.

As Mark informed me yesterday, I am unable to see his name reserving the dates for the week. I send him a quick text asking him if he talked to the agency's tech support. He responds quickly that he will fill me in over the early dinner.

Mark's driver picks me up solo at twenty to four. He drops me off outside Parkhouse Plaza, informing me that Mark is up on the ninth floor at Chantilly's. I make my way through the lobby and find the elevators—remembering the layout of the building from the trial date with Graham.

Emotions flood through me as I wait for the car to stop on the floor for the restaurant. Part of me feels like I am cheating on him by being in the same building where we shared such an intimate meal and conversation. But then again, maybe it is fitting since he had Sophia wrapped around him for a very public interview at a fundraiser I faithfully support.

I shake off the feeling of guilt, chalking it up to my fluctuating hormones—even though my period is over a week away. It must be a girl thing.

"Angie, I'm sorry that I didn't pick you up myself," Mark says, standing upon my arrival at the table to kiss my cheek.

"No problem. I got here just fine." I smile. He looks great in a sharp black suit and bright red tie, contrasting against his pure white shirt.

The other businessmen have not arrived yet. Mark hands me a peachy cocktail that he already ordered.

"Your profile was tampered with," he says, cutting to the chase.

"What? Really?" I ask stupidly. "How do you know?"

"It appears you are booked by someone else for the next five months."

"You have got to be kidding me!" I shout, quickly softening my voice at the stares I receive from some of the workers. The venue is a bit more casual than El Pastel, but still posh and upscale. "Do you know who reserved me? I looked today and couldn't tell." Nor did I take notice on the calendar.

"Apparently, it is private, and the worker in the technology department is 'not at liberty to say.' He then proceeded to recite some doctrine on the protection of privacy yada yada." The annoyance in Mark's voice is evident by the way he quotes the worker with a mocking voice. "I have my theory though."

"Graham Hoffman," I whisper.

"Yes."

His words from the other night float to the forefront of my mind. *That's why I'm just going to handle the situation myself.* At the time I didn't understand what he could do or how much power he had. But now, I can see the man doesn't stop until he gets what he wants. He doesn't play by a different set of rules. No, that man makes up his own.

I take a deep breath and exhale loudly. "Son of a bitch."

"It'll all work out, Angie, don't worry," Mark soothes, rubbing his hand up and down my exposed arm.

I keep my emotions in check and vow to myself to relax until I am in the comfort of my own home.

Benjamin and Samson arrive together. They are dressed in suits and appear on a mission to discuss business.

I fiddle with my handbag and pull out lip gloss to moisturize my lips. However, I really am just trying to turn on the recording feature on my phone as discreetly as I can without drawing suspicion.

The men barely show me any attention throughout the appetizer and main courses. Nearly their entire conversation is in a blend of several foreign languages—which is again a huge red flag for me. Maybe Russian? Arabic? Mark periodically rubs my shoulder and refills my water glass, however, his focus is on business tonight. I play the dumb girl act and just smile and look as clueless as I can.

At the conclusion of dinner, awkward hugs and kisses on my cheeks are given despite my body language screaming "no, thank you." I just suck it up and hope that my audio file is worth it in the end.

When I make it through the door of the house, I throw my coat and clutch on the couch in a heap. I dash up the stairs, pulling the pins out of my hair as I go. Once in the bedroom, I undress and toss the purple minidress over the chair.

I am so spitting mad over the Graham situation that I can barely see straight.

He cannot interfere with my work by overbidding and monopolizing my schedule. Why was I not given the opportunity to accept or reject his offer? The nerve of him! Oh, if the tech support department was full of females, then that would explain it. He can stuff his charm up his own ass and let it marinate there. He probably already did it to their asses to get his way.

What does he want from me that Sophia—or any other girl—can't offer? Or perhaps this simply is just another way to get under Mark's skin. There definitely is bad blood between those two. Am I a pawn in this corporate game of cat and mouse?

I scrub the makeup off my face—my skin tingling at the vigorous rubbing—and slip on a freshly washed set of comfy fleece pajamas. I have an hour until guests arrive for the Monday night reality show ritual. I grab my laptop and log in to my account. Although the dates appear to already be reserved, without my approval, I click on the money manager button and my fingers nearly knock the device on the floor.

What the actual hell?

"You have got to be kidding me," I groan out loud. I look at the number that shows the current earnings from "accepting" the next five months' worth of dates. Two hundred fifty thousand dollars.

My mind races with the idea of suddenly being out of debt. The thought of not having to worry about when my next paycheck would arrive and if it would be past the deadlines for the bills.

No. Absolutely not. This is not right!

I did not earn this money nor do I plan on earning it. The amount doesn't even calculate to two hundred dollars an hour. I grab a calculator and start punching in the hours per day for each week and for the certain number of weeks. My mouth gapes at the per hour rate.

No. Freaking. Way.

This amount of money is more than just wanting my company. No, this goes deeper than that. This money is meant to dictate—to control me. It is a lockdown to keep me from networking and to ensure that I will be there to warm his bed, while figuratively slugging Mark in the balls.

Every ounce of me screams at how wrong this situation is becoming. I cannot do it. I race downstairs, nearly slipping on the steps in my fuzzy socks, and grab my phone out of my bag. I find the number for Graham's cell in my list of contacts and click on "call." I wave at Claire who enters the house with a fabric reusable grocery bag in hand.

"Well, hi there," she says.

"Hey you. Chat later. On a mission," I explain.

"Seems like it."

I stomp back upstairs and flop down on my bed, pulling the quilt up to my chin. A shiver runs through me while I wait. The phone rings twice before a sultry male voice clouds my judgment from the other line. He has the tone meant for wicked phone sex. Perhaps he would make it big on one of those hotlines that they advertise on sleazy website ads.

"To what do I owe—"

"You bastard!"

"Hmm, you are extra feisty this evening, kitten," he drawls. "It's turning me on."

"Shut up!" I feel like a loon but cannot seem to get myself under control. "Asshole!"

"Tell me, which panties are you wear—"

"Stop it! Just stop it!" He keeps trying to throw me off my game. To mess with my mission. Does he really expect me to submit to whatever he wants? "You tampered with my account." I am harsh and blunt. I hear him hum, and it makes me want to go for the jugular.

"I am a man of many things, but hacker extraordinaire, I am not. But I like your level of confidence in me. Thanks, baby."

I huff dramatically over his unashamed attempt at flirting. "Mark's dates got canceled. Yours got added."

"You don't say."

Damn his sarcasm! "Cut the crap, Graham. It's not fair. He reserved me first."

I can hear a creak. I picture him leaning back in a deluxe leather chair to rest his body away from his desk. Is he still at work?

"How about we discuss this in person? Are you free now? I can stop by your place."

I look at the clock and see that I have thirty minutes until the show starts. "I can't tonight."

"You better be keeping your ass at home and not whoring it around the city."

"You did not just insinuate that I am a slut. Again. Oh, the nerve of you! This is getting old."

"Hanging out with Tanner will give you that reputation, Miss McFee. Keep that in mind whenever you are trying to keep up a good reputation. When can I see you?"

"I'm done with class at eleven tomorrow."

"I can rearrange my schedule for you. I'll have Collins pick you up in the visitor 2B parking lot on campus at that time."

Conveniently, I park there on Tuesdays. Of course, stalker man would know that. "I can drive if you give me an address."

"You'll be coming to my office during my break. To avoid the security protocol upon entering the building, I would prefer if you were escorted. At least for your first time."

"But I—"

"Angela." His voice vibrates with an understood warning.

I shiver at his pushiness. Even at my height of anger, a small part of me is turned on.

"Can't you just give your staff a photo of me and tell them not to shoot?" I am only kind of joking.

"All members of my immediate staff are very aware of what you look like and who you are to me." I swallow hard as I listen intently. What am I to him? Not even I am privy to that type of information. "But I want you in my office promptly upon arrival tomorrow."

Where does he work—a fortress?

"Thus, Collins will need to be there to bypass some of the levels of security."

"Oh," I answer dumbly. I am very glad he cannot witness my mouth gaping like a largemouth bass. Why the hell does this man who makes jewelry need so much protection? What is he hiding?

"I'll have lunch catered. You seemed fine with everything the night we went to El Pastel. But do you have any dietary restrictions? Types of food you don't like?"

"Um. No. Not that I can think of. I like most food, unless it is some weird Asian delicacy." Like grilled insects and animal digestive system organs.

His laughter lightens my mood. "So, no jokbal, hongeo, or balut. Got it."

"I have no idea what those things are. But it is probably safe to say I would not be that willing to chow down on them. But I rarely refuse to try anything at least once."

"Whenever I travel to Thailand and South Korea, I make it a point to try one cultural delicacy per visit."

Wow. I can count the states I have been to using my fingers. Three of them were the "just passing through" states, so they don't really count. As for being out of the country ever? Nope. I don't even have a passport.

"Anything else I need to know?"

I think for a few seconds. "Oh, and I do not like the taste of mayonnaise." I avoid the stuff at all costs, surprising myself that I almost forgot to mention it.

"Is that so?"

"Icky."

"I think I can accommodate you."

My insides turn to mush at the tone of his voice, making

me think the topic of food turned into something a bit more risqué. I hear commotion downstairs and high-pitched giggling, which lets me know the party has started. "I have to get going. I'll see you tomorrow to discuss the situation with my calendar and how we're going to remedy it."

"I look forward to negotiating with you." His response is smooth and full of mirth.

Does he think I am going to back down and allow him to bully me into doing whatever he wants? No, we will be discussing this tomorrow. He can call it negotiating if it makes him happy. But tomorrow, I plan on laying it out on the table for him with crystal clear detail.

Organic hummus and a tray of raw vegetables take up nearly all of the space on the coffee table, as the gang gathers around for the show. The drink of the night consists of freshly made Bacardi mojitos, courtesy of Blake's mixology skills. Apparently his trip to San Juan last spring break unlocked his genius when it came to drinks with raw sugar cane, key limes, and sprigs of mint.

"I grew the mint myself. A little YouTubing and a trip to the local nursery," he says, plucking off a sprig to smell it, "and voila. Fresh herbs for the beverages."

"Very cool," Claire adds.

"And Angie?" Blake says getting my attention. "You can basically count the greenery as a salad."

I laugh hard at his snarky comment. It's the truth. "Hey, I ate zoodles yesterday."

Blake gives me a goofy grin, making me giggle. "Glad to see your palate is maturing into adulthood."

I turn on the TV and settle onto the couch beside Zander. He is unusually quiet tonight, making me feel a bit on edge.

"How is your journalism stuff coming along?" he asks softly.

His eyes don't meet mine, and I wonder if he is mad at me.

"Right now, I plan on pretty much giving up. I have yet to find anything worth investigating. And the couple of leads I have currently going are taking longer than usual to explore. I might just run out of time to fully construct something worth reading."

Zander turns to me and studies my face. "That's unlike you. You're not a quitter."

On the contrary, there was a dark period in my life where I quit caring for months. I had zero passion for anything. I promised myself I would do everything in my power not to get to that low again, despite how easy it is on some days to get near that downward slope.

"I'm just not cut out for this business. It's too unpredictable. And even if I somehow manage to pull myself out of rock bottom again, there is no guarantee that the next chase will produce anything worthwhile."

I often think back to how I decided this route for my future. It was James and my quest for justice. However, my brother will always be gone, and I don't want to be chasing after the unattainable forever.

Problem is, I have spent the past four years working toward these goals. Turning back now would shatter the sunk cost fallacy, but also leave me without a real path to financial freedom.

"I think you are being too hard on yourself. Not everything needs to be an epic story. You can write well enough without everything being a headliner."

"True. But in order to get my foot in the door, I need an internship. And those are competitive and hard to come by. Thus, I need to be stellar and a standout."

Zander brushes his wavy hair off his forehead. "Or what?"

"Or I am simply a graduating student with an English degree and no goal or job in mind. I mean, what would I seriously do with just a degree in English?"

"Hey," Claire interrupts. "Where is Resa?"

"She texted me earlier and said she would be a little late," Blake answers. "Was grabbing a smoothie and going to walk here."

"She better hurry if she wants to see the drama," Claire laughs.

"I can't believe the season is nearly over," I whine, sipping my mojito.

"Well, at least we can count on rejected girls being on the spin-off," Claire interjects.

I wonder silently if I will turn into one of those rejected girls after Graham has his way with me. Despite what Claire has already shared about Sophia, I am not convinced of her heartbrokenness. She and Graham look so perfect together that not even Photoshop can enhance them. I am pretty sure that in the end, I will be the one that ends up broken.

The show is a quarter of the way over when an out of

breath Resa bursts through the front door. She quickly turns and fidgets with the deadbolt to get the lock to click.

"What's wrong?" Claire and I ask in unison, bolting upright over the sound.

The guys jump up from their seats and move toward Resa. They check the window to see what has happened that has gotten her so rattled.

"I…he…there…them…" she trails off, pointing out the window toward the sidewalk.

I make my way over to Blake and Zander to try to look outside. I see nothing out of the ordinary. Just some cars parked in the lot and a college-aged female walking her dog under the streetlights.

Claire directs Resa to the sofa and offers her a drink of water. The show is playing in the background, but no one seems to have an interest in it now.

I kneel down in front of Resa on the floor. "What happened out there, Resa? Did someone hurt you?"

Resa puts her elbows on her knees and bends over to rest her head in her hands. When she goes back to sitting up, tears streak her face, marring her makeup.

"I"—she sniffles—"was trying to get a workout in and decided to just walk from the Campus Smoothie Cafe after I grabbed a green drink."

I frown at her. The cafe is miles away. This whole needing to please her boyfriend has me worried.

"Go on," I encourage.

"Well, when I turned the corner for your row of townhouses, I noticed a car was following me. I have no idea for how long, but I just had that creepy feeling. You know, when the hair on the back of your neck stands at attention?

I took off running. And a couple of guys jumped out of the backseat and started to chase me. I didn't even get a chance to look at them. I was so freaked out that all I could think about was getting inside where I knew it was safe."

Claire hisses. "Holy shit."

I am speechless. This could have been any one of us. This is the block I live on, and my once safe haven is now bringing me to paranoia.

"Should we call the police?" Zander asks.

"Nothing illegal happened, though," Resa says sadly. "I don't even have a description of the vehicle or the men."

Zander pulls his phone out of his pocket and moves into the kitchen.

"But maybe the police can question our neighbors and maybe someone has a security camera or something and could have caught a license plate or a face or something," I counter.

"We're poor college kids. No one can afford cameras," Resa cries.

"Something needs to be said so that if this happened before, there is a record."

"Angie has a point," Blake agrees. "This might be a pattern."

"Zander, did you call?" Claire asks when he enters the room again.

"Yeah, they should be here in less than five minutes."

I grab the remote for the TV and shut it off. Claire grabs a blanket from the back of the couch and wraps it around Resa. Blake makes hot herbal tea for her and serves it with lemon and honey.

It's nine p.m. when two officers—one male and one female—arrive to take Resa's statement.

"So, this is our fourth call tonight in a three-mile radius," the female officer explains.

"Fourth?" I exclaim.

"That's correct," the male officer answers. "All female victims."

"That's crazy," Claire says. "Just stalking?"

"No, three out of the four were drugged," the female officer says quietly. "Resa, do you think you were drugged?"

"No, I feel fine," she says softly. Tears stream down her face at the thought that something worse could have happened to her.

A knock at the door startles me, and I turn toward the sound.

Zander looks out the peephole and then unlocks the door. "Resa, your boyfriend is here."

He steps inside the warmth and gives Resa a big hug.

"I'm so sorry this happened to you, hon. I should have been there with you, but I can't have my cell at work and had no idea you were in trouble."

Resa clutches onto him. "How did you find out?"

"Zander texted me, and I came over right after my shift ended."

"Resa," the male officer continues, "where were you tonight prior to heading here?"

"The Campus Smoothie Cafe," she answers, "for a smoothie."

The officers look at each other, and the female one jots a message down on her notepad.

"Coincidence or not?" Claire asks, noticing the same interchange that I just witnessed.

"We're afraid not," the male officer responds. "All of the victims have the cafe location in common."

"Really?" Resa asks in shock. "Do you think this is an isolated thing? Like I was in the wrong place at the wrong time? Can I see the photos of the other victims to see if I remember seeing them there?"

"We are doing a full investigation into this matter, so releasing evidence would not be allowed. Also, most cases like these are isolated and often are not resolved."

"What should we do then?" Claire asks in a rush. "Just sit by and allow things to happen to female students?"

"Until we are able to find out who is drugging college females, it would be best to walk in groups," the female officer advises. "And always let someone know where you are going. Even if it's just a simple text. Texts are great because of the time stamp."

The officers take down Resa's personal information and then head out, followed by everyone else.

Claire flops down onto the couch and gives me a puzzling look. "Do you think there's a connection between tonight and what happened to you at The Shack?"

"I don't know," I answer solemnly.

My situation was different because mine was self-inflicted, and I don't know if I will ever have it in me to admit my weakness.

"Do you think this is an isolated thing?" she prods.

"I think there is a target, yes. But whatever is happening, something tells me it is more than just some random isolated occurrence that will never happen again."

"Yeah, I agree. So what are we going to do?"

"You are going to stay out of this. I mean it, Claire. I'll dig around and see if I can uncover anything that would be worthy of the police knowing. But this is serious."

"I get it," Claire huffs. "I just feel so helpless, and Resa looked so fragile. I just hope they track down the bastards who are terrorizing women. Last thing we need is to be caught in the crossfire."

"Trust me, I feel the same way."

19

"Miss McFee, being an investigative journalist does not mean interfering with an active police investigation," Dr. Williams sternly warns me, after hearing my thoughts on the campus drugging incident.

"I realize that, but what happens if this is a conspiracy that extends way beyond the campus walls? This could be a huge uncovering if I were to focus my attention on it. I can interview the girls and try to—"

"I am warning you now that it is illegal to tamper with an open investigation that is already on the police's radar. Leave the professionals to do their job. They might be providing their own set of private investigators, ones with decades of experience to figure out what is going on."

"Or they might just be doing the bare minimum because they think it's not a serious problem," I counter.

"Regardless, your job as a student is to write an actual article. Not to paint a conspiracy picture for the public's eye. You need actual evidence. Actual interviews. An actual story."

"Yeah and I had that last spring." It was epic too.

"Are you going to keep living in your past or push forward to the future?" Dr. Williams asks.

He is right. I need to stop dwelling on the what-ifs and move forward.

"Thank you for your guidance, as always," I say, getting up from the chair.

He places his glasses down on his polished desk. "I have faith in you, Miss McFee, that you will have a breakthrough." He points a pen at me. "I can see determination in your eyes."

"Yup, it's not like anything major is riding on it," I respond sarcastically. "Just my entire future career."

I am ten minutes late when meeting Collins in the parking lot, due to my conversation with Dr. Williams about my assignment. I am nearly ready to give up and needed his pep talk to snap me back to my life goal. Claire thinks I have OCD when it comes to deadlines, but then I just remind her about "The Purge"—as I so eloquently like to call it—and she snaps back into not being such a brat. If anyone has OCD, it is her. I blame the Internet for Claire's problems involving food. And Oprah.

"Good morning, ma'am," Collins greets with a smile and a small nod of his head.

I stare at the new black vehicle in front of me. It is bigger than the Mercedes, with shiny hubcaps and tinted windows. The length is longer but doesn't have the old-person vibe. I slip into the backseat with help from Collins's strong hand. As always, his attire is professional and his hair is well-groomed.

"Just how many cars does Graham own?" I ask, looking around the luxurious interior. The privacy screen is down, and Collins can easily see my facial expressions in the rearview mirror. I can see his smirk and his gaze wandering up to do the mental calculation.

"Well, if we are counting his summer cars and the winter ones, I would say five, ma'am. Maybe more."

"Such a waste for one man to have so many cars that he barely even knows how to drive himself." Graham drove me home after the hospital fiasco. However, he usually relies on Collins to escort him.

I catch Collins's snort at my joke, but he quickly recovers to hide behind his stiff statue-like persona. "I suppose, ma'am. But I assure you that Mr. Hoffman very much loves to be in the driver's seat."

Oh, I bet he does. A euphemism doesn't exist for categorizing Graham; he is blatantly controlling.

"Does he have a family?" I ask. As soon as the words leave my mouth, I am surprised at how much I care. I do want to know more about the man. He is very intriguing.

"Mr. Hoffman doesn't ever mix business with family."

"But he has one?" I pry.

"Don't we all?"

A sadness rushes over me, and I am transported to a time when that was true. I used to have a family. I had a brother who adored me and whom I adored as well. I had a mother who chose to suffer in pain just to have another coherent memory with her kids. I had a dad who was sober. It was the all-American family.

"Miss McFee, are you okay?"

I brush a tear from my eye and suck in a deep breath. I will never be okay.

"Where are we going? Where does Graham work?" Focusing on everyone but me helps.

"He is at Hoffman Headquarters Incorporated today, ma'am."

"Is that where the jewelry place is located?"

"The design, testing, and marketing departments, yes. The manufacturing facility and storefront are on opposite sides of the city in a more industrial area."

"So, what can you tell me about it?" I ask innocently, trying to keep the conversation going. I know whatever is said will be boss-approved. Collins is too aware of who he answers to for him to slip up and reveal too much.

I watch as he swallows. His Adam's apple is distinct in the reflection of the rearview mirror. I can tell he is uncomfortable only because his ears turn a rosy shade, while the rest of his skin stays a perfectly even tan. His throat clears, and he meets my eyes in the rearview mirror again.

What in the world is he trying to hide?

"Mr. Hoffman is the CEO of his own company which involves the buying and designing of jewelry. The headquarters harbors the research facility that tests and experiments with various minerals and ingredients. In addition, Mr. Hoffman has part of his building allocated to the use of marketing his chain of stores. Modeling, online advertisements, and social events planning are some of the departments that take up floors in the building."

"Wow. That's pretty impressive." His monologue seems very rehearsed, but impressive, nonetheless. "How can someone so young acquire so much capital to start their own company?"

Collins twitches, barely. If I wasn't concentrating on his reactions to my questions so much, I might have missed it. "Jealousy is the name of the jewelry line," he responds, ignoring my question.

"He didn't go and rob a bank or something equivalently illegal, right?"

"No, ma'am."

Something seems off. The more I am around Graham, the more I want to figure out what he is hiding. Why is he trying to buy me out of the agency? What does he not want me to find out?

I watch Collins maneuver the vehicle throughout the heart of the city, trying to share my attention between the scenery and watching for subtle changes in Collins's facial features.

"You mentioned that he has a chain of stores?"

"He plans to open a bunch in the next six months," he volunteers. "Some are already up and running."

Collins is very attractive for someone so taciturn. I imagine that his script does not waver into small-talk niceties. I could easily make it my mission to derail him into untouched conversational territory. Could be fun.

Before I can torment him, Collins pulls up under a walkway where two buildings are linked. I look up at the reflective glass exterior and am in awe of the rectangular prism structures joined together to form a capital H. How fitting. I marvel at the sheer size of the construction. I am intimidated, definitely.

The parking garage attendant scans Collins's identification badge as he hands him a folder from the passenger seat. The pop sound of the trunk opening resonates against the concrete pillars.

"Mr. Hoffman is expecting Miss McFee at half past eleven."

The attendant takes the file and peruses it, using a portable device to scan the document that I am unable to see. I crane my neck to see what is happening, my curiosity working overtime. Collins places his hand on some type of electronic screen. What is that? A palm reader? Seriously? We need to enter a parking garage, not the White House. Next up, strip search? I refrain from adding my snark to the mix.

Suddenly the window on my side slides down, and the attendant takes a good look at me and looks back at the file. The female worker manning the booth walks out to me and hands me my own magnetic badge on a lanyard that has the same picture that I used on my driver's license. I mumble a "thank you."

"Can I have your palm, Miss McFee?" the attendant asks politely. I watch intently as he presses my palm to the reading device that was used on Collins just minutes before.

Once done, he walks to the trunk and then shuts it. His nod to Collins is stiff. The metal gate rises to allow us access. Whatever happened to the little wooden barriers that looked like railroad crossing arms? Or the classically cool spikes for the tires?

"Do you typically smuggle illegal immigrants into the

garage via the trunk?" I am being a smartass, but I can't resist the urge.

My window rolls up by the push of a button from the front seat. I look at Collins in the mirror, and he answers my unspoken question. "Mr. Hoffman is very diligent when it comes to security. He doesn't put up with any breach. His concern of leaking trade secrets drives his handling of everyone entering the facility."

"Still seems a bit"—I struggle to find the right word—"excessive."

"One of those workers you just saw is new."

"So you were testing them?"

A single nod. "Mr. Hoffman is always testing his employees. You don't get to be as successful as he is by being careless."

"But you should be on a free-fly list," I comment softly. Surely, Graham trusts Collins.

"In case I am being compromised through threats and blackmail, all security detail for the building must treat everyone the same. All employees undergo a scan search upon arrival each day. All cellular phones and picture taking devices of any kind must be left in the vehicle or checked in at the front lobby each day. You have a badge now, so you'll be able to enter the front of the building without me."

"How did you get my picture on it?"

"You had your license on you the night at The Shack."

Of course. "What happens if I lose my badge?"

"Don't."

"Obviously, I'll try to keep it safe. But what if—"

"The palm scan should be the first line of security, if you seek entry into the garage."

"Should I leave my phone here, then?" I ask as Collins takes the ramp down into underground parking. He parks in a spot labeled with a star on the concrete, directly beside the set of elevators.

"Mr. Hoffman has made some concessions for where you are concerned, ma'am." *So much for treating everyone the same.* "We will not be checking in at the lobby. All security guards in the CCTV room are made aware of my attendance upon the palm reading device. They get an alert about me."

"Well, what about me?"

"Mr. Hoffman has briefed all of his employees in regard to you, ma'am. If you need to get to Mr. Hoffman in any of his buildings, there is a specific protocol and instructions on how to handle the situation. If I am unavailable to drive you, simply enter the front and show your badge. Ask anyone for assistance, and they will be more than happy to guide you to where you need to be."

I have no idea why any of the employees need to be aware of my presence or even my existence. I get the whole security issue, but the way Collins describes it makes me feel like I am getting the royal treatment.

I sit up in my seat and gaze out the window at the adequately lit garage. Even this is beautifully structured with architectural detail. I find it expensively unnecessary.

"He has multiple buildings?"

I am very aware of the cost of property in the state of Oregon, even when just renting with a roommate to lessen the blow to the wallet. I can't imagine the cost of actually owning an entire building. But having multiple ones? That's ludicrous.

"Mr. Hoffman is a very wealthy man, Miss McFee."

"Wow," I breathe.

"As for today, I'll be escorting you. I have special privileges once inside." I expect a wink to form from his eye at his proud declaration, but it doesn't occur. "Stay put, Miss McFee, and I'll help you out."

Oh.

He trusts me to skip some of the security measures he has in place? That doesn't seem very smart for keeping things consistent in business. But what do I know? Bakery cashier entrepreneur enthusiast rocks the top of my resume credentials. Business mogul and CEO, I am not. Aspiring investigative journalist? I can only dream.

I unbuckle my belt and gather my school items, mentally kicking myself for not leaving them in my parked car at school. I swing the tote over my shoulder as the door opens. Collins offers a hand, which I graciously take. He pulls me to an upright position.

Once in the elevator, Collins inserts the plastic badge as a key card into the slot in the wall, punches a five-digit code that I secretly memorize, and waits for the car to start moving before pulling it back out. While we ascend, he straightens his navy tie that looks great against the light blue of his starched dress shirt.

"Has anyone ever snuck into the building or been caught as a spy?"

He snarls, as if remembering the event on a personal level.

"Wow. Holding a grudge, eh? Care to elaborate?" I hedge, shifting my tote to a comfortable position on my shoulder. I dig blindly for my cell to shut off the power. The last thing I need is to draw attention to my special favoring amongst his coworkers.

"Not at liberty to do so, ma'am."

"You can really call me Angie. I won't tell your big boss man."

"I would rather not, ma'am."

"You fear Mr. Hoffman? Because I am here today because I am going to tell him to back the hell off. And I may just outright punch him." Collins straightens his posture and flexes his fingers in a nervous gesture at my statement. "So, I would stay on standby if I were you, just in case I need a ride in a hurry back to campus. Otherwise, I'll be hailing a cab."

"That will not be necessary, ma'am. I'll take you wherever you want to go regardless of what happens between you and Mr. Hoffman."

Protocol. "That's very kind of you. But, I doubt you will be so nice after I rip your boss a new one for his actions over the past couple of days. I swear the man has a personality disorder. Oh, and I have a reputation for acting before thinking when it comes to violence." I smirk at the memory of hitting the man at The Shack for getting fresh with me. Jerk.

Collins makes the attempt to loosen his tie—although the thing never moves even a millimeter. An ahem from deep in his throat is heard, and I can easily mistake it as a chuckle. The heat from his embarrassment meets his ears, turning them red.

"Do you have a wife and kids?"

"No, ma'am." I should really stop harassing the poor

man before his ears burn off and fall on the floor of the elevator car.

When the doors open, he heaves out an audible sigh of what I assume is relief. Before I ask how many women he has had to escort in elevators to Graham's office, he leads me to the glass doors at the end of a reception area that's furnished with a few couches, chairs, and magazine stands. I spot one of those cool coffee makers with the milk frother attached. A tray of pastries is set up adjacent to it. Collins uses his badge to gain access through the locked doors instead of using the doorbell. He escorts me toward the pretty woman sitting behind a modern white marble desk.

Huge poster ads in black frames are mounted behind the receptionist's desk. One features a mountain of ice, with a large diamond shining brightly in the mix. The name "Jealousy" is plastered elegantly across the top in golden letters. Another ad features a pair of red lips that are almost reflective. She has perfectly white teeth. Her tongue is stuck out with an elegant heart charm bracelet dangling from it. The entire display is highly sexual. I feel a bit naughty looking at it.

"Hello, Collins," the pixie-haired brunette with cherry lips greets cheerfully, taking my attention away from the wall of sexy photos. "Miss McFee." Her head nods in a soft, feminine gesture, acknowledging us. "I'm Hanna White," she chirps, flipping over the name plate that reads someone else's name. "I'm taking over for the previous woman who is on leave," she explains, reaching out her hand invitingly for me to shake.

I meet her smile shyly as we connect hands. What does she know about me already? I watch as her eyes linger on

Collins a little longer than I think is normal for a casual greeting. She hops around her desk, showing off her below average height and fuller body, ushering us toward the back of the office space. She has a Minnie Mouse vibe going on with her black-and-white polka dotted dress. She has a very classic but retro style. Her little bow barrette completes her look. She is adorable.

"Mr. Hoffman is waiting," she responds, more as a filler to the quiet air. I have to smile; it's not like Collins would ever help with the awkward silence.

I follow them down the corridor, looking at the magazine and newspaper clippings along the way that are enlarged and encased in frames featuring articles about the jewelry line. I pause and catch an article that I swear I read a few months ago. I scan over the typed print, trying to jog my memory.

We reach the frosted glass windows of a room at the end. On the plaque to the right, the words "Graham Hoffman, CEO" are etched into the flawless metal sheet. I marvel at the elegant calligraphy script and guess at the amount of people on payroll who are in charge of polishing such a piece of art. My scoff earns a raised eyebrow from Collins. I smile and recover in the best way I know how—through shameless harassment.

"Pixie likes you," I whisper, as she presses buttons on the wall outside of the door, probably in effort to alert Graham of our arrival. She is completely oblivious to my comment, concentrating on her posture and professionalism.

Collins nearly chokes on his tongue. Wow, for someone who strives to be composed in all situations, he fumbles the ball on this one.

"He'll be right with you," Hanna says with a smile, turning to walk back to her desk.

I point over my shoulder without looking, not caring if she sees me or not. "Minnie Mouse. She has a thing for you," I huff. "She was eyeing you like I eye a chocolate display case at the candy store. With want, longing, and mouthwatering desire. Totally digs you."

His laugh earns a heated glare from Graham as the door to his office is flung open. Shit. Did I get Collins in trouble for having a half second of—dare I say it—fun? I swallow hard at Graham's demanding stare.

"Miss McFee, you made it." He smirks at me with wickedness. "Collins, you can leave now." His voice turns gruff.

I glance at Collins, whose eyes are turned to the floor in deflation, and back to Graham. In an instant, Graham's arms wrap around my waist, and I am tugged into the room. The door slams rather loudly behind me.

"You really didn't have to do that."

His confusion is evident in his deep V between his brows.

"Collins didn't do anything wrong," I defend, pushing out of his grip.

"Oh, really?" He seems unamused.

"We were just chatting, and I can be pretty funny," I confess, trying to lighten the mood that is brewing.

"I think you want me to go to prison," he snarls, turning his gaze on me, pinning me still with his fierceness. His hands open and close repeatedly, as if he is warming them up for a fight. My breath picks up in short shallow pants. My confusion makes him growl. "You keep flirting with my most trusted employee, I'll immobilize him and fire him right on the spot. You got that, Angela?"

"I wasn't flirting. I was being friendly."

"Semantics."

Oh, the nerve of him!

"I was not flirting!" I snap, resisting the urge to make suggestions on how he can deal with his mood swings. I am pretty sure Collins has zero experience flirting anyway. "You should apologize to Collins right now. He has been nothing but respectful to me and accommodating. You could learn something from him, you know!"

"I only apologize when I do something wrong."

"Which is probably never, since you are so perfect."

"Quit rolling your eyes at me, Miss McFee."

My hands are animated as my temper rises. "You were wrong out there."

"Considering the exorbitant amount of money that I shove his way, he can refrain from getting friendly with you." He reaches for my hips, thrusting me into his body. I can feel the firmness of his taut muscles. My mind is fuzzy with the need to melt into him and the desire to slap him all at the same time. He lets out a sigh. "He cannot do his job, Angie, if he is emotionally invested."

"That's not true," I huff. "Besides, throwing money at someone doesn't give you the right to be a jerk. Plus, his job was to collect me from school. Mission accomplished." Just when I think I have said my piece, I remember the reason why I am here in the first place. "Oh, and do you think that throwing a quarter of a million at me will get me to bend to your whim and be at your beck and call?"

I try to twist out of his arms, but he holds me still. I feel safe, despite the growing anxiety in my belly over the whole situation. I am here to discuss his barbaric tendencies. I am not here to give this man further assurance that his methods are working.

Graham exhales, moving one hand from the small of my back to run through his thick hair. "We should not be arguing over this right now."

"You brought it up," I mumble, focusing on his sensual actions. He's too close to me. Every time we are this close, I lose control.

His arms release me and gently turn me around so my back is to his front. He helps me set down my bag and get out of my green coat. "You look very nice in jeans and casual clothes. Very pretty."

I whisper my thanks, noting his smooth ability to change the subject. *I am on to you, Hoffman, and your antics.* I guess I did look better than I do for a typical school day, forgoing the Uggs and sweats for dark-washed skinny jeans, an ivory bell-sleeved sweater, and heeled brown leather ankle boots.

I turn to examine his space. The office is very large with a huge desk and leather chair. Floor-to-ceiling windows line the entire back wall, making the room appear open and inviting. A small table is situated near the center window with what looks like our lunch on it. On the other side of the room, a sofa rests with end tables. Behind it, a large conference table is located with twelve chairs surrounding it.

Graham makes a comment that I don't quite hear. He looks very much in control in his charcoal three-piece power suit. Too bad for him, I am not his employee. Lucky for me, he is not entitled to boss me around.

I make one more scan of the room and then meet his eyes. "You look good too."

"Why thank you, Miss McFee."

"Ready to discuss how you are going to end the shenanigans of tampering with my job?" I jump to the chase, not wanting to waste any time. This is why I am here today, after all, right?

"Let's eat first before it gets cold."

"But—"

"You are more pliable after you are fed."

I snort over his silly comment. In a way, I guess it is true. But now I am not really hungry—the excitement of the day lessening my basic need for nourishment. "You think you'll get your way if I'm fed?"

I am shot an intense look as I follow Graham over to a table set up near the window, the skyline of Portland at his disposal. "It's always worth a shot."

We are on the top tier of floors of the west wing of his building. The view is spectacular, even in the bright light of day. I stare out, looking for the distinguished Parkhouse Plaza and Hoffman Hotel signature structures. Since mingling with Portland's elite, my appreciation for architectural design has been sparked, with a newfound enjoyment for the art and architecture of a building. *Geek.*

"So you own a jewelry company."

"Yes," he responds with a shrug.

"One that is growing exponentially and becoming pretty famous. I think I read an article about it in *The Headliner* several months ago. But I just can't remember for sure. You weren't mentioned in it, though. I would have remembered you."

He smiles a self-satisfied grin, showing off smooth white teeth. "I keep under the radar as best as I can. But the chain is taking off and soon I'll no longer be able to sneak past the reporters and photographers. I'm relishing my privacy before my publicist has it her way and I can no longer hide out."

"You seemed in your element being interviewed at the charity gala."

"I can be good at acting."

"Part of you has to love the attention."

Graham rubs his chin and pauses. "Perhaps a little. But I'm a very private person, Angie. My publicist and marketing manager have been on my case for weeks now. Thus, my name will be splashed soon enough."

There's more than just a name being splashed. His face happened to make an appearance on the local news and in the local paper. Pretty monumental, if you ask me.

I turn my attention to the outside, catching my reflection in the spotless window. "We all have secrets, I suppose." My mind drifts until Graham's image joining mine monopolizes my attention. I turn to stare up into his formidable eyes. "Is that why you were doing the interview at the gala?"

"Part of the territory for throwing down a hefty amount of money. Media channels always want to back it up with the origin. While I wanted to remain anonymous, I have a business to try to keep afloat with a depressing economy. And my marketing manager is pushing for the launch of more stores. There are a certain number of boxes that need to be checked. It is not just about me. There are stockholders, and my employees have equity shares. People are invested in the success of the company and are relying on me to lead."

He guides me to a seat and softly presses down on my shoulders to get me to sit. He hands me a cloth napkin and a glass of sparkling cranberry juice that my tastebuds savor. Under metal dome keepers, he reveals an arrangement of three different types of fish tacos, grilled corn and mango salsa, pico de gallo, and fresh guacamole. My hunger takes over without much warning, and I dive into the dish.

"I had this brought over from the hotel. If you like it, I can have some delivered to you in the future. It's one of the few dishes that can withstand not being eaten the instant it comes off the fire."

I nod, my mouth full of sweet mango salsa and fish. He stares at me in amusement, a smirk adding a sexy emphasis to all of his masculine features. Why is he watching me instead of eating? I grow self-conscious and take a sip of the sparkling juice, putting down my half-bitten taco.

"I find you irresistibly sexy when you eat. Call it an oral fixation if you want, but I find your mouth delectable and the way you use it even more alluring."

I wipe my lips with the napkin. My feet fidget back and forth.

"Please do not slow down on my part. I'm just enjoying the show." His words are highlighted with his flashing blue eyes.

My blush flames over my skin like wildfire. He says the most shameful things in the most shameless manner. My new black lace thong absorbs the heated moisture—the unmistakable result of Graham's slow burn seduction. If the panties he purchased for me weren't as pretty as they are, I would have avoided wearing them out of principle. But damn, they feel good—even when I literally have a strip of fabric stuck between my cheeks. My inner thighs itch to be touched. I try to rub them together to create the friction that I so desire, but the denim is too thick to give me what I need.

"That's another thing I find hot." His eyes travel up from my crotch while his hand reaches up to touch the side of my cheek. Fingers press and caress my burning skin. "You're so desirable. I don't even think you understand the magnitude of just how much." Releasing my face, he grabs my mahi mahi taco from the plate and holds it up to my lips. I bite off a small amount, chewing it slowly—savoring the mix of sweet and savory flavors—before swallowing. His eyes move seductively to my throat, then to my lips, and then back to my throat. I hear a moan escape his mouth, sending shivers of warmth up my body from my toes.

Snap out of it.

I return to feeding myself, and Graham manages to do the same. We eat in relative silence until the food is gone. Without the illusion of a barrier, I feel the pressure of the situation that is about to unfold.

"We have to talk," I start, jumping in headfirst again. "You can't—"

"I owe you an orgasm, sweetheart. I'm sorry that I had business to handle on Saturday at the charity event."

I ignore his comment and start plowing to the root of the issue at hand. "You canceled my dates with Mark."

Graham's sudden movement from the table stops me midsentence. He pushes his chair back and rises to pace in front of the wall of windows. One of his hands rubs the muscles at the nape of his neck; the other rakes through his dark locks from the front to the back.

"I warned you. Did I not?"

"Warned me? You pressured me to quit my job multiple times! That's not the same thing." I am speaking to the back of his head. He won't look at me.

"I warned you to stay away from Tanner. You refuse to listen to me. I did something about it." He reaches up to place his right palm flat against the window, smearing the pristine glass with the oils from his hand. "For your safety."

I move my chair back, nearly knocking it down in the process, walking over to stand in front of Graham's towering body. The man has several good inches on me even with my heeled boots. I tilt my head up to meet his smoldering gaze.

"Please don't interfere. I am asking you to contact Dominic to fix your error in judgment. I know you two are business associates. But he's my boss. And you are making things very complicated for me."

"I don't see the problem. I reserved you. I'm a paying customer. Keep your job and go out on dates with me. We both win."

"I never accepted the dates," I correct, my chin ticking with defiance. "It's not fair." After several long minutes of neither of us backing down, I ask the question that baffles me. "Graham, what do you really want from me? Surely, it is more than just physical competition or a quest at an easy lay. What do you want?"

"I want you."

"Okay..."

"All of you, Angie."

"What aren't you telling me?"

"I don't share."

Um, excuse me? "Did you skip that lesson in kindergarten?" My eyes dart to his and narrow into little slits.

"Probably," he says with a shrug, "considering I was homeschooled until third grade."

"Okay, so you have some extreme bouts of jealousy."

"I like to be in control. Always."

"That is obvious."

It is not his first time alluding to this notion. Each time he does it, it freaks me out even more. I am officially shocked and scared at the ambiguous word, each emotion fighting for the winning spot.

He stares at me with hunger in his eyes. "I really like to be in control, Angie."

"Okay, Graham, what does that mean exactly?"

"I would rather know what you think it means, sweetheart. Surely you have some sort of idea floating around in your pretty head."

"Well, as bossy as you seem to be, I imagine your need for control goes beyond the walls of just the office or the bedroom. I guess you do not become a CEO by taking orders, but rather giving them. Probably makes you all squishy inside too."

Graham moves over to the conference table, leans his backside against the smooth polished surface, and crosses his arms over his broad chest. He looks powerful. Unmovable. "Perceptive, despite your need for sass. Please go on," he persuades.

"Mr. Hoffman," I say, turning my attention away from the skyline, "what is left to say? You have to understand in your pretty little head that most people do not throw a temper tantrum every time someone disagrees with them. That most people have their own brain. Make their own decisions. Have civil discussions in the face of adversity. So, maybe—"

His blue-topaz eyes darken to the richest shade of sapphire stopping me midsentence. My eyes blur with a flash of color. His body charges and lunges toward me. Several sounds penetrate my ears—a growl, a whoosh of air, and my own yelp. His arms scoop me up and carry me over to a sofa, ignoring my weak protests. We descend together, and I try to wiggle out of his vise-like grip. He flips me over his knees, and my hands are swiftly pinned behind my back, confined by the strength of his unyielding fingers. I struggle, only to discover the rock-hard protrusion of his cock pressed against my lower belly. My thighs clench to hold back the molten lava burning inside me. I silently thank my intuition for deciding on the confining outfit over something flirtier, with fifty percent less material. I grimace at my reaction to being Graham-handled. My breasts heave against the side of his thigh. I am trapped and paralyzed in the shock of my own want and his own physical reaction to my close proximity.

"What the hell, Graham?" I yell. "What are you doing?

"What I should have done as soon as you stepped foot inside my office."

"Let me go." I try to keep my voice even and calm, but the little hiccup imperfections in my pitch give away my struggle.

"No. That's not what you want, Angie. That's not what your body needs."

I shake my head back and forth as best I can from the confining position he has me locked in.

"You just keep lying to yourself, sweetheart. Trying to convince yourself that you don't feel this attraction. You make me powerless. You're the one who is making me out of control."

"Oh no, do not blame this on me," I say, wiggling to get free. Big mistake. It is just causing friction to where I crave it most. "I swear your bipolar ways need to stop. You go from calling me sweetheart one second and then going all caveman the next. It confuses the hell out of me."

I can feel his appraising eyes all over every inch of me, soaking up my vulnerability. I feel naked under his gaze. He's enjoying the show—of this I am sure. His free hand smacks my butt with each squirm that I make. I am primed and sexually charged. I hear a string of unintelligible expletives spew from his mouth. The clapping sound hits my ears first before the sting warms my behind.

It is dirty.

Raw.

Sexy.

The swat is hard enough to invoke a small whimper, but light enough to shoot sensory pulses to my toes. My breath leaves my lungs in spurts, keeping my vocal tendencies at bay. I fume on the inside at how affected I am by this simple, inferior position I am in. None of my erogenous zones are intentionally caressed. I am fully clothed, yet my mind focuses on the pleasure of the nonsexual-sexual act. Graham is testing me. And I am submitting to his will, giving him exactly what he wants, exactly what I told myself I wouldn't do.

The sensations of the pleasure-pain pulses fool the rational centers of my brain. At no time has anyone ever put me in this position, not even as a small, defiant child. I have seen my fair share of time-outs, but other than that, refusal of toys and privileges topped the list of punishments growing up. Here, Graham is extracting pent-up emotions that I didn't even know I was holding on to. I knew that taunting him with my sassy mouth was playing with fire, but out of bottled-up curiosity, I wanted to test the boundaries to see how far I could push. And keep pushing before he would snap. There is something in him that thrills me and entices me to want to be bad and to make him lose the control he claims he must have.

In a matter of seconds, I am lifted up and helped to stand while Graham remains seated comfortably on the couch.

"Show me how turned on you are, Angela."

"What?" My legs quiver with the directive. I stare back while he runs a hand down his stomach and cups his erection straining to break free.

"Undo your button and zip down the jeans that must have been painted on you, they fit so well."

"I—"

"Do it, Angie. Fucking show me how saturated you are. Prove to me that I am not a delusional asshole. That this is not all fabricated in my head."

My thighs clench at his strong words. It's as if he is angry at himself. And for some unknown reason, I am compelled to listen. To take my trembling fingers and unbutton the button of my jeans. To pull the zipper down. I stand like a statue. My hands are down by my sides, and the front panels of my jeans lay open like a mounted butterfly, barely revealing my lace thong.

Graham leans forward, grabs the pieces of denim and uses them as handles to jolt me forward a few inches. He peels my jeans down so they are resting at midthigh. His growl is low in his throat. “I can smell your beautiful pussy from here.”

His unfiltered words cause my skin to heat. I don’t think I will ever get used to this level of comfort with someone.

My eyes close as he continues to trail his all over my body. My knees are about to buckle.

“Eyes on me,” Graham demands.

I open them and see the smoldering passion in his.

“I fucking love seeing you wear what I have picked out for you.” He moves his mouth to hover right at my apex, continuing to push my jeans farther down my legs. His warm breath makes my skin tingle. I want him so badly to stop teasing me and to just take me. He needs to just end this dance that we keep finding ourselves in. His full mouth connects with my lace-covered pussy, and I arch my back at the sensations.

“Ohhh,” I moan, as his arms snake around me to keep me from falling on my ass. He continues to feast on me, his saliva adding to my already-leaking juices. His tongue licks long paths from the bottom to the top, deliberately missing my most sensitive area. I am so close to losing control just from his simple tongue motions. “Please,” I beg. I grind my hips forward, trying to get more pressure from Graham’s nose on my clit. I need more.

Just when I think he is going to rip the fabric from me and give in to what we both appear to want, he stops suddenly. His body pulls back enough to break the contact. My eyes glare down at him in anger.

"What the hell, Graham?" I snarl, throwing my hands up in the air. "Is this some sort of sick and twisted game of shits and giggles for you?"

"Watch your tone with me," he warns.

I yank up my jeans and zip them up. Next, my button. I square my shoulders and bare my teeth. "Or what?"

"Or I will tan your ass so red that wearing clothes will seem like a job you hate."

My mouth gapes open like a fish. I don't even need to ask if he is serious, because I can already tell he most certainly is.

"And, Angie? I would love nothing more than to buy you clothes just so I can tear them off you or make them uncomfortable to wear."

I close my eyes at the image. Instantly I get wetter between my thighs. I can feel the moisture leaking out of me. It is these moments of bantering and his dirty words that send electricity straight to my pussy. My biggest fear during this whole tirade is coming true.

I am starting to like it.

Graham's eyes narrow with understanding. "You love that idea too. You want to be my bad girl. Tease me. Make me want to go utterly insane for you."

I gulp. I can feel the heat hit my cheeks and then run south to the juncture of my thighs. Everything about Graham screams sex. His ability to talk about it so confidently and without any embarrassment is attractive, as much as it is alarming. My body is drawn to his, and I don't know how much longer I can go resisting something that I so desperately want. I can't fall for it though. I can't get emotionally involved with a man who will be nothing more than a fun fling. My heart will not be able to survive it.

I walk over to the row of windows, leaving Graham on the sofa to simmer. I need some distance between us.

I have a bad history of picking the wrong men. It is a curse. I pick men to date who are emotionally immature or unavailable or tell lies. I pick those who can never put me first. Those who have ulterior motives.

Plus, I have an internship to focus on. Graham is a distraction. One I cannot afford.

I turn back and stare into his eyes. "What do you want from me?"

He lifts himself from the cushions and makes his way over to me. "Angela, it is plain and simple. I want to make you mine. To provide you the balance, and framework, and discipline that your body craves. I want to make you beg for release."

"That's why you stopped? You want me to beg?"

"Right now, I simply want you to do as you are told. But you have this inability to follow directions."

I scrunch my nose at his comment.

"But at least you are freaking cute about it."

I scoff.

"Angie, sometimes a little kink or edge play helps add life to something that seems routine. Trust me, we would not get bored. Ever. I was just giving you a preview of what we could be like. But before I give in fully, I need you to know my expectations."

"So, you want a BDSM thing?"

"No. I am not into labels or conforming to a certain lifestyle. I just want to be in control."

I roll my eyes. "Shocker."

Graham's eyes narrow. I try to cover up my amusement with a cough. I know he is itching to do something about my sass. And my new hobby is teetering as close as I can to the line without crossing over.

"So no tying me up or collars or whips or yes-sir-no-sir?" I ask.

"You watch way too many movies," he chuckles.

"Also known as porn," I interject, making his eyes narrow but his lips smirk.

"I mainly want control. It is that simple."

There's that two-syllable word again. The one that we keep dancing around but never really define.

He continues, "None of those things you listed out are off-limits to me, th—"

"So you are a sadist?"

"No, Angela."

"But you—"

"Nor am I a masochist or a dominant or a submissive," he interrupts. "I don't identify with any of those titles."

"I guess I don't understand."

Graham gives me a warm smile. His eyes soften and have a calming effect on my anxiety. "What I am saying is that with the right setting and mood, those activities can be fun. However, this is not something I want to conform to or limit myself with."

"So your kink you speak of is solely having control."

"Sure. But it is more of a need than a kink."

"But you have yet to tell me what that means."

Graham guides me back over to the sofa and pulls me down to sit beside him. He props my legs over his and then grabs my hands. He lazily massages circles into my palms with his thumbs. It feels divine.

"I never had to put it into words before, so give me a moment to collect my thoughts."

"Why is that?" I ask softly.

His eyes blaze with heat. "Because I have never encountered any woman in my life before you who has driven me so crazy with the need to want to control her." He swallows hard and looks out toward the windows at the city. "It is irrational and over the top. It is something that I never expected would happen. But from the moment I saw you by the pool, I knew my life would never be the same again."

A smile breaks out across my face.

"Angie, I need to know that you are safe. And warm. That you are taken care of and eating well. That you have money to spend on the things you need and want. I want to make sure that you do not surround yourself with assholes who I guarantee will hurt you. I want to know where you are—at all times. And understand the need I have for you to pick up the phone when I call or at the very least text back. I need to trust that you would never put yourself in situations where you could get hurt or be hurt."

This is all too much. My brain cannot keep up. "Graham…"

"Sweetheart, these are the things I think about while I am making multi-million-dollar decisions. While I am hiring and firing people who answer to me. This is what I think about on business trips to Europe. What keeps me up at night. You are driving me absolutely wild, like no one else has done before. I thought pushing you away would be better, but it was easy to see that it did the opposite."

My brow furrows as I absorb all of this new information. I pull back my hands, swing my feet to the floor, and rub at my temples. My head is spinning, and I feel a migraine coming on.

"I want you in the worst way possible. Like I have never wanted anything else. Including other women, business ventures, or inanimate objects. They are all frivolous things. I want you, Angie. Give us time to figure out what this thing is between us. I know you feel it. Let me date you."

The thought of him having other women makes my stomach roll with nausea. I do not want a relationship per se. But I sure as hell don't want to witness another girl getting all oh-Graham-yes-Graham in front of me either. Flashes of Sophia's perfect image cross my memory like a strobe-light show. I suppose I am just as possessive. However, my fear squelches all movements toward long-term intimacy.

I have waited twenty-three years, holding on to the last bit of control. It's all I have left from before everything in my life crumbled at my feet. I have managed to inevitably keep guys at a safe emotional distance. It was easy. But not anymore. I contemplate whether or not I can hold out long enough. Graham doesn't seem like the wham-bam-thank-you-ma'am kind of lay. His interrogation and confession prove that much. No, I have somehow, unknowingly, piqued his interest with my illusion of impassivity. Now I have a madman in my presence. Conquer and destroy are the things I see in his beautiful eyes. I am weak, and he wants to rescue me.

"But, you see," I say lifting my head, "we have a big problem, Graham."

"And what is that, my dear Angie?"

I stare him point-blank in the eyes. "I hate to be controlled."

"I beg to differ," he sighs, getting up to pace. "I think you are rightfully scared. But I know deep down inside you are intrigued over what I can offer you. Physically and emotionally. Financially."

I shake off the past thirty minutes of eye-opening erotica and use my quivering knees to lift my body off the sofa and stand on my own two feet. I cannot allow a little fun and fantasy to mess with my goals.

"I don't need to be white-horsed."

I turn to catch a small, crooked smile pulling at his lips at my wording. "It's more than that. I think we would be good for each other. Compatible even."

"I'm sure your bedroom skills are top-notch."

"Are you deliberately trying to piss me off?"

"Only if it's working."

"You, my little pyro, are going to get burned. You are in no position to play."

"Maybe I'm a masochist and will revel in it. Wouldn't that be a turning point?"

He runs his hands through his hair, pulling at the roots. His frown mars his perfectly chiseled features. He stops his movement suddenly and faces me again, towering over me but looking vulnerable and lost—a perfect contrast to his usual composure. "I do not want to hurt you. Quite the contrary." His matter-of-fact attitude unnerves me. He is back to the cool confidence, and it pulls at my gut instincts, dissipating my run-the-hell-away warning chant.

"You do things to me, Angie. You force my hand in matters and bring out possessive emotions and urges that I can't ignore anymore. I have seen it in your eyes. I didn't see it the first time we met. You had a wall up then. But in the elevator at Entice, it was there. I wanted to do things to you then. Very perverse and wicked things to you. And I still do. My desire has not dimmed. It has only gotten stronger."

"Why me?"

"Why not? You respond to me, just as I do to you. We have so much to discover about each other. It is exhilarating. You are pure. Endangered. Rare."

"No." I shake my head for added emphasis.

"You sparkle."

"So you have a virgin fetish, is that it? Conquer, destroy, get bored, then move on."

"If I wasn't so interested in getting to know you by talking, I would gag that sweet, sassy, defiant mouth of yours. I have an Angie fetish."

My eyes fly open at his threat/promise/fantasy. Could they possibly be mine too?

I straighten my back and bolt my feet to the floor. "Graham, we need to address the reason why I came today in the first place. You keep sidetracking me every time I try to get to the root of the problem."

He appears bored. "So, why did you come here, Angela?" He is simply humoring me.

"You tampered with my Entice account."

"Technical glitch." He shrugs.

"I need you to cancel your dates, since I am unable to do so on my end. All of your money can be refunded."

"I don't care about the fucking money, Angie," he shouts. "I want you. And you want me. It's easy to see. I have no idea why you are putting up such a fight to deny yourself something that you obviously want."

"Bullshit."

His innocent half grin makes my anger boil. "I see that I'm going to be graced with the presence of your sassy mouth again."

"Stop laughing at me, dammit!"

"I'm sorry, please forgive me," he says, chuckling, his hands raised in self-defense, "but I find it very amusing. I can't figure out when it will come into play or not. So, the waiting game is very exciting."

"I so want to hit you right now," I admit, my fingers balling into tight fists. I press them against his chest, pushing him back a few inches. "You know better than anyone that I have it in me."

"You aren't in the position to deliver punishment, Angie." His sexual innuendo and promise are evident in his tone. The man is impossible. "And from what I can tell, what we just did on the couch wasn't punishment at all for you. No, kitten, you enjoyed yourself very much."

"Go fuck yourself," I snarl.

I watch as Graham saunters over to his desk and opens the top drawer. I stare in confusion as he rustles some documents and office supplies.

"With this?" he asks, holding up the most ridiculous dildo. It is the size of my forearm.

I burst out laughing. The sight of him holding the shiny

neon-pink cock is too much. It looks heinous. "That"—I giggle—"arrived"—more giggles—"faster than expected." I blurt out the last words with a rush.

"Oh, the joys of the postal service," he responds sardonically.

I can't stop giggling.

His smirk lets me know he is not mad but rather entertained by my gesture.

I walk over to him and reach for the dildo. I hit the power button and am alarmed at how loud it is. I quickly drop it onto the desk.

"Holy shit, that is loud," I say, watching the thing pulse and jump over the polished wood.

Graham grabs the cock, turns it off, and places it back into the drawer. I can tell he is amused.

"Glad it arrived in one piece," I say with a huge smile.

"You forgot to read that the shipping box would not conceal the contents," he responds bitterly. "Why a company that sells sex toys would not package them more discreetly still boggles my mind. It was a lovely surprise when my personal assistant delivered my mail."

"It was not an oversight," I giggle.

He turns and rests his body against his desk, staring at me with mirth. "In front of several of my employees," he clarifies with a head shake.

I laugh even harder to the point of tears.

"What am I going to do with you, Miss McFee?"

"Nothing," I say confidently. "Because I'm not yours to worry about. And as much as I am drawn to you, I know that you don't play by the rules, and that scares me. So I'm not going to date you, Graham."

"You already are. Unless you want to quit the agency. Pick a better type of job."

"You can't cancel dates that I've already booked."

"I already have. It's done."

"Technically I suppose." I shrug matter-of-factly. "But I'm not going out with you when you play like this. Even if just out of principle. Plus, I still have someone on the back burner who deserves to have my time since he plays by the rules."

"Stay away from Tanner!" he shouts, reading my between-the-lines message clearly.

"Why?"

"Because you don't know him! You're a means to get to me. He saw that the first night we went out. He's using you. He doesn't have your best interest in mind!"

"Oh, like you do?"

"Here are your choices, Angie. Keep your job and date me. Or quit your job and date me. I am not going to sit back and watch you gallivant around the city with a bunch of men who are going to take advantage of you. Damn Claire for getting you involved in the first place. She has no idea what she has set into motion."

"Leave her out of this," I defend. "It was my decision."

"Make up your mind."

"What about the option of keeping my job and going about my business as usual?"

"Not an option. You have already refused my proposition. Now I'm removing your choice and doing things my way."

"You don't have a say!"

"Why won't you date me?" he asks, moving from his

perch to stand in front of me. "You obviously like the aspect of the agency to never want to quit voluntarily. I have provided you with a generous stipend. What's the problem? You want more money?"

"Screw you!"

He throws his hands up into the air, glaring down at me. "You drive me crazy, woman. Utterly crazy!"

My hands move to my hips, as I stand my ground. "You are stripping away my independence. I don't think you understand how hard I have worked to stand on my own two feet. You don't get it because you didn't know me before now."

"Tell me." His voice softens from his outburst. "I want to listen and learn."

I shake my head in refusal. I'm not ready to expose my heart like I have already exposed my body.

"Sweetheart," he soothes into my ear. "You don't understand how ruthless the world is, and I would hate for you to get hurt by trusting someone who isn't worthy of it."

I start to pace again. I'm so on edge that I think I'm about to go crazy.

He pulls me close—halting my back and forth walking—crashing my hips into his thighs.

"Graham…"

"I want you, baby. To take care of you. You have me slowly losing my mind with worry as you continue to go out on these dates with men you do not know. Yes, they have been background checked with the agency. But that doesn't mean that they don't have ulterior motives. I have boundary issues, and you test literally every one of them."

"Am I even your type, Graham?"

"What's that supposed to mean? Of course you are, baby."

"You sure you don't prefer blonde girls? Ones who are better candidates for what your wealth and persistence can deliver to them?"

"If you are referring to the article in the Sunday paper, I can explain. Sophia and I go way back. It's business. Quit looking at me like that. Let me explain. My publicist insisted on getting more exposure for the jewelry line. Sophia is the exclusive model for the marketing team. She has been on payroll for several months and is under contract. It is all for show. The media eats up that kind of crap and loves to spin their wheels, making something out of nothing."

Wait. Sophia is the face of this company. I am an idiot. Realization hits me, and the pieces start to come together. I pull away from Graham and take a step back. If they aren't sharing beds now, it will only be a matter of time before they default back to their old habits. She has fire in her eyes, and her conversation that I eavesdropped on inside the restroom basically spelled out her desire to get Graham back. Plus, working together in close proximity is the prime method for starting work-related relationships—or rekindling them. I glance over at the sofa that I sat on five minutes ago and cringe over the thought of them having sex on it in the past. After nearly throwing up in my mouth, I shake my head as if trying to exorcise the thoughts.

"You don't need me to be your companion, Graham. You have her. And even your business associates are supporting that idea. So run with it. Embrace it. Otherwise, I'll just feel cheap if you continue to pursue me."

His frown forms on his lips, wrinkles creating ridges around his eyes. "I never want you to feel that way. I just want to ensure that you are safe and to be with you. Only you. I can't change what happened in my past. But that is what it is—the past. I want you to be my present and who knows, maybe even my future. I have no idea how to explain this need to keep you from harm. It is irrational yet real. You do something to me that I cannot comprehend in full capacity. I can't pretend how you affect me. You control me."

What...I control you? "I don't need to be rescued. I can take care of myself. This isn't going anywhere," I confess, frustration pouring out into my words. "I need to go. I need space."

"I would love for you to stay. I can get Hanna to change my schedule. Angie, please—"

"No." I take a deep breath. "I'm going to give you twenty-four hours to remove your money from my pending account and put my profile back in its original condition before you tampered with it. If you don't do this during the time frame I have suggested, I'll go to Entice's HR department and cause a newsworthy ruckus. You don't need to agree or disagree with this. Just know that it will happen."

He takes one step toward me, and I back up two. "Don't do this."

"Twenty-four hours."

I make my way over to the chair where my bag and coat lie. The exhaustion from the mental stress of the day incapacitates my energy levels. I feel his presence on my back. The heat from his body only reminds me that I am playing with fire and that I could very well get burned. He lifts my coat with one hand and eases each of my arms into the sleeves. I sling my bag over my shoulder and make a beeline for the door.

"This isn't over," he whispers. "I'm not backing down."

I acknowledge his statement with a nod and exit the office through the heavy door. I find Collins on his feet. I wave to Hanna on my swift walk toward the exit, averting my eyes from the red-lipped poster, knowing now who the model is. My movements are all physical and meaningless, as I am unable to be genuine when I feel so lousy and overcome by confusion. Collins senses my dismay and maintains his strictly professional demeanor, avoiding eye contact. For that, I'm glad. If he looks at me, I'm not sure I will be able to keep from crying. Despite acting like I have the upper hand with Graham, I know that deep down I am a fragile mess. My heart presses against my chest, mourning the loss of yet another person who has made an impact in my life.

Without a word, Collins drives me back to the university and helps me out. He waits in the parking lot to ensure that my car starts and I am safely on my way before pulling out of the lot himself.

My mind races at what to do about Graham. Today's meeting didn't help solidify my wishes. Instead, it ignited a fire inside him that cannot be tamed.

20

As soon as I unload my bag at home, I hear the ping of my phone signaling a text, and I quickly turn it over to read the message.

Zander: Feeling bored and want to come over and hangout?

Angie: Sounds good. I can be there in 10-ish.

Zander: I'm leaving the lab, so I can just swing by and pick you up.

I freshen up and wait for the doorbell to ring. Zander greets me at my door with his boyish smile, and I instantly relax after an intense day. I need his company and carefree spirit more than I initially thought.

"Hey you," I say.

"Hey yourself." He studies my face. "You look like you have a lot on your mind."

My shoulders droop. "Yeah, it has been one of those days."

"Same here," he says as we walk to his car. "I'm regretting the help desk job even though the pay is steady. I just feel like my brain cells are getting killed by every person who could have fixed their own problem by a simple restart. There are only so many 'shut it off, count to ten, and turn it back on' directives I can say in a shift without completely cracking."

"You're so much better than that, Z. You really need to find something more fulfilling until you can apply for the real jobs."

He starts the engine and backs out with ease. He gives me a lopsided smile. "Do you ever just sit and watch the sun rise and set and wonder if you just wasted an entire day of your life? One you can never get back?"

"Yeah. But until recently, I wished the days would go by. That is what sadness will do to a soul. It will try to rush time. As if time is the enemy. I have so much pain still inside that each day I have to entangle it from what I need to accomplish. Otherwise, I would never get out of bed."

Zander reaches over and gives my hand a gentle squeeze. It is platonic and sweet.

"I'm tired of waiting for life to just happen," he sighs, placing his hand back on the steering wheel. "Nothing just happens…at least nothing that is worth living for."

I turn in my seat to look at him. Something is bothering him. He always has a sensitivity about him, but this is more than just having a rough day at work. He pulls into his parking spot and we exit. The music blaring from the townhouse vibrates my core, nearly making my teeth chatter.

"How can you live like this?" I grumble.

"I'm usually gone during the day," he laughs. "Plus, they chill the fuck out when I show up and are actually human when you arrive."

"Maybe I should stop over more often then."

"You are always welcome here, Angie. You know that."

Zander unlocks the door and we step through. He grabs the remote from the top of the TV and turns down the music to a non-deafening level.

When the roommates leave for a bar gig, Zander and I enjoy some beers and the leftover pizza he has in his fridge. We play some old-school video games together and laugh until we cry. It feels so good to just relax and rest my mind from all the chaos.

"Have you heard from Resa?" he asks, drawing back his beer.

"No, but I text her daily to see if she is okay. Her roommate checks in with me and says she's been staying over at her boyfriend's place. I won't be surprised if she doesn't withdraw from school and go back home."

"Why do you say that?"

"I think she was pressured into attending college in the first place. Her mom basically encouraged her to come to find a husband," I sigh. "We aren't that close. She mainly keeps to herself. But from what I know, her mom is pretty traditional and puts marriage up on a pedestal. Maybe this whole thing isn't for her, and she is just going through the motions to please her family."

"I really want you to be careful. No walking alone or

taking chances," he warns. "Not until these bastards are caught."

"Yeah, I know. I'll be careful."

My mind starts to become fuzzy after the second beer, and I rest my head on a sofa pillow as Zander chats about potential internships and job prospects. I love how passionate he is about programming. But I just cannot keep my eyes open.

The sound of screeching tires echoes in my ears. My mouth falls open, but the sound does not penetrate over the crushing metal vibrations and the blare of the horn. Hissing. Crackling. Popping. I scream, but I have no voice. My heart stops in my throat as I try to move my neck to the side. Then I see it…

Blood.

It is everywhere. On the dash. On the steering wheel. On the ejected air bags. I can't breathe. The image debilitates me, and my stomach twists to violent heaving. Red crimson splashes the leather and broken glass. Liquid drips off my brow, hitting my eyelids and traveling in a stream down my cheeks. A coating of stickiness covers my exposed skin. I blink.

Darkness.

I can hear my name. Over and over again. But I am not there. Gone. The old me washed away with the blood of the tide.

The air reaches my hair before it does my lungs. Panic

rises as I try to find my stability. My foot catches in fabric and—

Thump.

I fall forward onto the area rug—gasping for air. Finally, I can breathe. Like a cold slap on the face, it does the trick. I am awake. Alive. Tears pour in symbolic rivers down my flushed cheeks like déjà vu trickery. I close my eyes tight, trying to shut off the valve for the dam—just until I can function. Rapid footsteps resonate, and the vibrations of the floor shake my body.

"Angie! What happened? Are you okay?"

It takes me a few seconds to realize it is Zander's frantic voice. But why is he here? His warm hands pull me up and wrap me in a blanket. I am in a safe cocoon.

"Angie, answer me, please," he pleads. "You're scaring me."

He pushes me into the softness of a couch, and I start to remember my whereabouts. He reaches over me to turn on a lamp. I squeeze my eyes shut as they adjust to the sudden change in light.

He shakes me. "Angie?"

"Yeah, I'm okay," I lie. "It was just a bad dream." Only problem is, it's not a dream. It is a memory. One I lived. It is not some fabrication my mind made up. "I must have fallen asleep here, huh?"

"You were so tired after gaming. I kept asking you if you wanted me to drive you home to finish sleeping and you kept groaning and telling me you just wanted to lie in a cloud. Do you want to talk about your dream?"

"No, I just want to go home. Please."

Zander studies my face. I can tell he's resisting the urge to argue or persuade me to talk. "Okay, grab your stuff and let's go."

We arrive at my townhouse a little bit before five a.m. I sneak into the house to not wake up Claire and tiptoe up the stairs. I am wide awake and on edge. Twitchy.

I stand in front of the bathroom mirror and tremble with the chill that overtakes my body. I feel sick. Nauseous. It's as if my body wants to purge itself from the pain and memories that are stockpiling in my head.

I open my music app on my phone and select Linkin Park to play the *Hybrid Theory* album that got me through my pre-adolescent years—another dark era of angst and a turning point.

I put the phone on the counter of the sink and start the shower to get the water to warm. I strip down and get in, feeling the water cascade down my back, cleansing me. I saturate my hair with salon shampoo that Claire bought for me, enjoying the creamy smell of warm vanilla. I drop the bottle twice before being able to place it on the shelf's ledge, my trembling hands making me clumsy.

I tremble as I towel dry and wrap my hair in a makeshift turban. I grip the side of the sink to keep from falling. But I am falling in the figurative sense, one spiraling ball of anxiety plummeting down a steep ravine.

I rush into the other room—completely naked except for my hair wrap—and snatch my purse from the chair. Going to the bathroom counter, I tip my purse over and expel all of the contents into a heap. I dig through to find the small plastic case. It's the one that holds the key to my calm—like a protective treasure chest.

I take a deep breath and glance in the mirror to see the desperation and the pain reflected back. I shuffle on my unsteady feet, debating. My growing need outweighs all logical reasoning as to why I should stop. But I can't. I press on the plastic case's lever to pop open the lid. It doesn't move.

Frustration elevates. I smack the case on the hard countertop. Nothing. The rattle sound inside taunts me. Beckons me. It begs me. My mouth salivates toward the memory of the bitter taste. I crave that nasty taste and crunch under my tongue and teeth.

My impatience grows as I try to pry the container open. My struggle drives my ambition. My want hijacks my logic.

With all my strength, I slam my palm over the case, popping it open with a loud cracking sound. My eyes close with delight, but when I open them my nightmare is in vivid, HD-quality color. Through the mess on the counter, the pills have scattered with the violent exit from their safe haven.

All seven of them.

Lost.

Gone.

No…

"Sh…shit," I stutter, unable to make my hands and arms move.

My vision turns to spots and then clarity as I push my body forward, hovering over the search area. Panic rises like a heated sparkler, sending my mind into overdrive.

It takes me seconds to sweep lip gloss and spare change and travel tissues and credit cards onto the floor with the swipe of a hand. I spot two of the pills nestled inside an open pack of gum. My hand grips the little white beads, holding them like they are the most precious items in the world—an anchor, keeping me from floating out to sea.

"Fuck," I groan as the pain refocuses my attention. How did I get on the floor?

I slip farther onto the tiles with some of the disposed purse items, rummaging through the wreckage in search of survivors. I frantically fix my hair wrap, to clear my eyesight from the damp locks spilling out of the sides. Along the bottom baseboard of the cabinet, I find another one. I have three total. Three out of the seven made it to safety. My mind cannot clear. It's as if I am in an eternal fog.

Sweat beads on my forehead. I can hear the thump-thump of my heart beating wildly as I try to pick up the pieces that resemble my pathetic life. And that's what it is.

Pathetic.

I crawl on the floor for at least five minutes. I lift up mats, check behind the garbage can, and run my free hand along all borders and trims. I just can't get myself to stop, to give up hope.

Hoisting myself up from the floor, I spot three pills through the reflection in the mirror, concealed behind the soap dispenser. Carefully, I reach my shaky hand out to move the holder away from the fragile victims.

Slowly.

Steadily.

I extend my fingers to—

Nooo!

I watch in horror as tears escape my eyes and an

agonizing whimper escapes my mouth as two plummet to their death in the dampened sink. I snatch up the dry pill still behind the dispenser to add to my collection, and then I make quick work to try to scoop out the other two from the basin.

One rests in the bottom part of the drain, dissolving almost instantly into the small amount of pooling water and soap residue. I scrape up the other one from the inclined wall and try to dry it before it becomes paste.

Mine.

I wipe the semi-damp pill on my tongue, licking my fingers to try to capture all of the effectiveness before it is too late. I turn on the cold water and cup some in my palm, slurping it up into my mouth. Once I get enough, I splash some on my face and start the countdown until I will start feeling better again.

I slide my back against the wall and shimmy down until my butt rests on the floor. A burp escapes through my throat, and I get the chemical soapy aftertaste instantly. I lean my forehead against bended knees and can once again hear the music, as if all is magically right in the world.

It takes my bottom going numb to decide to move. I scoop together all of the lost items and pack them back into my purse. The music gets muted and my four rescued pills find a new home in an empty Altoids mint container.

I make my way into the closet. On tiptoes, I reach up for my black leggings. I pull an oversized periwinkle cotton top off a hanger, knowing that the length will cover my butt to make the tight-fitting leggings less inappropriate.

The moon glows through my window. I can't keep my

eyes off it. It is the one thing that provides me comfort in the night. The soft illumination, lighting the darkness whenever the sun is gone.

I grab my hairbrush and sit at the window seat. I detangle my hair and wait for the sun to rise.

"Angie? You in there?" Claire yells a while later. "I woke up with a text from Zander. Everything okay?"

I look at the clock. It is already after eight. I lost track of time.

"I'll be right down!" I yell back, feeling the throbbing in my forehead with an oncoming headache. I feel drained. I hear Claire mutter a few lines I cannot make out. "I'm fine!"

I hoist myself off the bench cushion and turn off the light. I finish up on the touches to my outfit and clean up the chaos that seems to follow me around.

Downstairs, I eat and drink what Claire has prepared, going through the motions.

"You don't want to talk about it, huh?" she asks, pouring me more coffee from the ceramic pitcher.

I shake my head.

"Have you thought about visiting the campus psychologist again?"

"No," I snap.

"Um, okay."

Shit. I overreacted. "Sorry."

"It seemed to do you good when you had regular appointments."

"No, I would rather not."

"Maybe find someone else off campus? Someone to talk

to about these nightmares? Maybe prescribe some medication?"

I can do this on my own. I just need a little time to get things settled. Then I will be fine. I can survive. I am good at that.

"I just…" I start, pausing long enough to piece together my words. Claire's attention turns from wiping up a small spill to me. She looks hopeful, as if I am going to let her in. Pangs of guilt flush through my body. She's my best friend too. We would have never met if the car accident didn't happen. I was content at Baker City Community College studying General Education and playing it safe with minimal risks taken. I wanted to be a voice coach and utilize some of the talent that my high school teachers raved about. James had the raw talent though. I just didn't know what else to do with my life but knew that getting some type of degree was my only way out of the town. I would have never needed to start fresh in Portland. "I…I…"

"You don't—"

"I just haven't had a dream that graphic about James in months."

Her eyes soften. "Yeah?"

"I thought that they were going away. Guess not." I say more than I usually would. The lasting effects of the pill relax me enough to not have a panic attack over the discussion.

"Angie, you're having them more often than you think."

I glance up from my bowl of oatmeal.

She stops fiddling with the dishes on the counter and finds a seat next to me at the table. "You have an episode about every other week."

My bottom lip drops down in shock. "What? Really? Since when?"

Claire gives me a half smile. "Since forever. But mostly over the past four weeks."

"I'm sorry that I wake you."

"Oh, no. You don't. I am getting ready by that time and on my way to the gym."

"Oh."

"I always just check on you and call your name a couple of times. You don't even fully wake up or realize that it's happening. Then you go right back to sleep."

"I just have so much on my mind. James's anniversary is coming up in a few weeks. My dad is back to his old tricks. And I miss my mom so much."

"I wish I could make things better." Claire moves closer, pulling me into a warm hug that I didn't even know I needed until I was draining my reservoir of tears onto her shoulders.

"My…my dad…he hasn't call…called you? Has he?"

Her hands move over my back, soothing me. She pulls away to look into my eyes. "Only that one time. And I told you about it and we handled it together. Is he asking you for more money, Ang?"

"Not yet. But I just have a bad feeling about it. I'm ignoring him right now." It's my coping method of choice when it comes to him.

One side of her mouth lifts up. I know she wants to say the famous filler words "I'm sorry" but knows better than to use them on me.

"It's like being happy is not honoring James's death," I admit.

"Angie, don't you think he would want you to go on with your life?"

"My head tells me that I should honor him by living a full life. But my heart can't understand how I can be full ever again when my other half was ripped from me. There are pieces of that night that I don't even remember. I have a box of memories buried deep in my closet that I have been avoiding for the past four years. But what's the point of even looking? Not even the medical reports have details to help me understand why we were on the road so late that night."

"It's not your fault someone else was on the road at that time."

"I know."

We sit in silence for a few minutes, watching the sun shine through the back glass door. I refill our coffees, keeping Claire's black and adding cream and sugar to mine.

"So, what's been going on with you and Graham?"

Typically I would be glad for a subject change at this point in the conversation, but talking about Graham causes me stress too.

"He tampered with my work account and is basically trying to get me to quit. Or get me fired."

"Wow. He can do that?"

"The man thinks he is above the law. He seriously has no set of rules that he lives by. Just does whatever the hell he wants, no matter who is in the way."

"Yeah. I can see that. Men like him don't get to be where they are unless they can take charge. He's a brilliant businessman after all."

"Yeah, he definitely likes to be in control. That's the problem. So do I."

"He likes you, Angie. I've never seen or heard of him being like this before. Trust me, I am hearing an earful from the other agency girls."

"Well, I caught him kissing Sophia. Full-blown making out. He managed to get photographed with her for the newspaper. I am counting my blessings that I had enough self-respect not to stay up and watch it broadcasted all over the local news. Oh, and the best part of all of this is she is the face of his jewelry line. The solo model designed to increase profits. Even his publicist is pushing them together. So why does he need me?"

"He probably doesn't want Sophia," she says with a shrug. "Maybe the whole business-with-pleasure thing is a turn-off for him."

"Well, she wants him."

"Takes two to tango," Claire agrees with a smirk.

"Why did she leave? And more importantly, why is she back?"

"She apparently left to handle some family issues. Rumor has it that she was on some form of contract before she left, securing her agency job, so returning might have been mandatory? It's all speculation, though. Graham ignores my questions when I badger him about her."

"When are you finding time to do that?"

She shrugs. "Oh, whenever. I did it at the hospital when you were admitted. Sometimes I see him at the coffee shop downtown. That man can talk his way out of anything, you know?"

"He's a smooth operator, Claire. Sophia is currently under contract with the jewelry line. I didn't sign up with the agency to add stress to my life." I signed up for the easy money and for the chance to further my career. "And Sophia being the main advertising model for all the ads for Jealousy is just a reminder that Graham is out of my league. He plays dirty and takes whatever he wants."

Claire gets up from the table and goes into the living room, but still talks to me. "He's extremely private," she hollers. I hear her rustling around on the shelves.

"But doesn't respect anyone else's privacy," I yell back.

She returns holding a couple of magazines in hand. She flips through the pages in a hurry. "You sure it's Sophia in the ads? I would recognize her face."

"Unless they're just photographing an individual body part. Then I guess it can be anyone."

Claire stops on an ad featuring a plain gold chain dangling from the petals of a long-stemmed red rose. The only human part of the ad are the pink lips that kiss the necklace and the beautifully manicured fingers that hold the rose. Regardless of the amount of airbrushing I am sure goes into a magazine page, the picture is beautiful. But there's no guarantee that is Sophia's hand or lips.

"It's pretty, that's for sure," Claire adds.

"He basically affirmed my suspicions today. She is a huge part of the marketing campaign. It's her."

"But he wants you, Angie. He is chasing after you."

"He can say the right things at the right time. As far as I'm concerned, he's very dangerous. Lethal. I don't think my heart would be able to handle him breaking it." I slouch into the chair, feeling the weight of a turning point on my shoulders. "I like him. I do. He does things to me that no one else has ever done before. Makes me feel alive. But I can't fall for a man like Graham."

Claire frowns, "I'm afraid it's too late, Angie. You have already fallen."

21

I arrive to Human Behavior exactly one minute before class starts, with two overpriced barista-made drinks in hand. I silently wish that whipped cream could be packaged separately somehow, because as soon as it gets pumped onto the surface of the piping hot beverage, there is no way of saving it from its demise.

"You better like it because the girl making it kept giving me angry looks over your list of specific requests. I swear you do this for shits and giggles."

Bryce shoots me a boyish grin. "You caught me."

"I mean, what man with active testicles orders smoked paprika in their coffee?"

"Spice with the smooth milk. The world is missing out on this phenomenon. It really should be on the menu." He takes a sip of his drink and closes his eyes as if he is having some holy religious experience. "The one with the lip piercing?"

"Huh?"

"Cafe girl."

I nod, as I think back.

He flashes me a cheesy grin. "Angry broads turn me on."

"Of course they do," I laugh. Bryce loves to challenge my tolerance. Luckily, his sense of humor matches mine and we can both laugh at each other. "How's life?" I ask, changing the subject back to neutral territory.

"Sexless."

And I fall apart. It only takes one word from Bryce to have me in stitches. I keep trying to convince him to drop out and join an on-the-road comedy act.

"You laughing at my state of need is offensive."

I giggle again, "Sorry. No harm intended." I put my hands up to show my innocence.

"I'm onto you, McFee. Your fake apology doesn't fly with me. You need to work more on your teacher-face."

"But I don't want to be a teacher!" At least not anymore.

"Too bad. It's in your blood."

"Whatever." He barely knows me, aside from how to make me blush.

He fiddles with his phone, making mine vibrate from my bag. He nods his chin toward the sound. "Go on. Check it."

As soon as the picture of human genitals loads on my phone, I can't look away. "What the hell, Bryce!" I sneer. And there they are, of all shapes and sizes, and diseases. Ugh! "Why? Just why?"

"Payback."

"For what?" I ask.

"For not taking better notes. I'm barely scraping by with a C."

"You are unbelievable."

After class, I grab a quick sandwich at the campus deli and eat it in my parked car while listening to The Fray. I enjoy the serenity while watching students walk along the sidewalk in front of me. I wipe my mouth and dispose of my napkin into my sandwich bag. I glance up through the windshield just in time to see Mark Tanner hand over a small package to a male student passing by. Neither stops. Neither shakes hands or says a word to each other. It is such a subtle incident that if I didn't actually recognize Mark, I would not have noticed anything peculiar.

Mark is dressed in casual clothes and aviators. It isn't even sunny out. I have never seen him dressed down. I might not have recognized him, but I know expensive shoes when I see them. And Mark likes his shoes. I quickly duck my head and act like I am texting. I open my camera app and snap a picture of his retreating form, as well as the student that he brushed into. I email the pictures to my secret address and type into the subject line "Mark Campus Handoff." How did I even get by before with just a flip phone? I never want to regress back to my archaic ways.

I turn the key in my ignition, and it putters a few moments before finally starting. Great. I pray that I don't need to get any repairs done anytime soon. I don't have time to be without a vehicle, nor do I have the money to pay for the service. The money from the few dates I have been on has paid rent, food, car loan, and insurance. Of course, if I accept Graham's proposition, I would be set for a while.

I twirl my hair into a messy bun and secure it into place.

I slip on a pair of sunglasses and cover my ears with a fleece headband. I back out of the parking spot and follow the direction of where the student went. He travels between buildings where there is not a paved pathway for vehicles. I can see that he is making his way to the other side of campus, so I drive around.

I park at the side of the library and wait to see if I can get a front view of the student. I consult my picture I took to make sure I am actually following the right person. Designer jeans, gray hoodie, and Chucks. When the guy rounds the corner, I snap another picture of his front, even though everything about him seems nondescript. He does have a unique way he trims his facial hair, but the cell picture does not capture these details.

Adrenaline runs through me as I shut off the car and hop out. I feel invigorated, as if I am on the verge of a breakthrough. I open the back door and grab a novel from the backseat. I cringe at the cover models. The guy has his hands directly over the woman's breasts. He is shirtless and overly sexualized. Lovely. It is like I am broadcasting porn. I take a deep breath and pretend I am absorbed in my steamy romance as I walk along the sidewalk and follow the guy in Chucks.

He walks along the path and fiddles with his phone. I keep my distance but instantly regret not being closer when I can see him hold the phone up to his ear. His other hand is animated, and I can tell by his sudden stops and nods of his head that he is stressed. He places his phone back into his side pocket and picks up the pace on his walking. When he trots up to the door of the Campus Smoothie Cafe, I debate on whether or not to enter or turn back around and go to my car.

I wait several minutes on a nearby bench, actually reading a page in the novel. After my nerves settle, I reach into my coat pocket and grab the ten-dollar bill I had left over from the coffee shop and decide it's fate. Removing my headband, I give my head a shake to fluff my hair back to life. I jog up to the store front and enter the warm air. Several muted televisions highlight sports and local news. Techno music is playing through the sound system as groups of students gather around the smoothie bar and high tables waiting for their drinks.

I squeeze into a free spot at the bar and am greeted by a worker within seconds. Him. He has removed his hoodie and now has on a green T-shirt with the cafe logo on it. His name tag reads Paul. At least now I have a name. And a work location.

"Hey," he says brightly. "What can I get you?"

"What's the best option?" I ask smoothly.

"Well, now," he smirks, "that all depends on your mood."

"I'm feeling, hmm, adventurous," I respond with a cheeky smile.

Paul smiles back at me and gives me a once-over—as much as he can with the bar top in the way. "Then I would suggest the Power Dragon smoothie. It has dragon fruit, peaches, fresh red raspberries, chia seeds, and apricot nectar in it. All organic."

And sugar, I quietly hope.

"That sounds amazing." I try my best at a throaty groan

that isn't too sexual. Pretty sure I fail. "I've been here a few times but never saw you working before."

"Yeah, I recently got hired. Sometimes new employees make it through the training fine, but they fail at serving up the actual drinks and then quit."

"Makes sense," I say, trying my best at small talk.

"Do you live on campus?"

"Nah, I am slightly off in a townhouse with my bestie. You?"

"Frat boy house," he says with a grin, "with eleven of my besties."

"Sounds smelly."

"Oh, it can be on party night when everyone whips out the AXE."

I laugh over his response, earning a smile. I watch intently as Paul adds ingredients to the blender and then closes the lid to start the machine. I fidget on the bar stool and try to see if anything seems "off" about Paul or the facility. Resa was at the gym and here the night she came barreling into the townhouse in fear from being followed. Is there a connection? Did the police officers investigate this facility?

In front of me, Paul grabs a clear plastic cup and shakes the contents from the blender into it.

"Why don't you join me in a sip?" I ask, pointing to the extras left in the pitcher.

"Sure, why not," he says, grabbing a smaller plastic cup from the stack. He carefully pours out the rest for himself. "Whipped cream?"

"Absolutely."

Once my drink is garnished, Paul secures a bubble lid to the top. I lift my beverage to cheers his.

"To…" he starts.

"To Magic Dragons."

"Power Dragons," he corrects.

"Sure, whatever," I laugh.

"And to love at first sip."

"Presumptuous, are we?"

"Confident."

I take the first drink, and Paul is right. It is love.

"This is delicious," I moan.

He stares at my lips and drinks some of his own. "Yeah, it's my favorite."

I check my phone for the time and realize that I'm going to need to run. "I'm going to have to go. I have an appointment."

"Can I at least get your number?" he asks, hopeful.

This whole detour was a way to find out more information. I still have no idea what his connection is to Mark. Having his number though would be a great way to do follow-ups if I need to dig up more information in the near future.

"No."

"No?" Paul asks, shocked. I must be the first girl that has ever turned him down.

"But you can give me yours," I say sassily.

"Hey, Angie, what brings you here out of the blue?" Dominic asks from behind his desk, looking as dapper as ever in a beige suit with a crisp white dress shirt. "I feel like it has been ages since I've seen you."

It's a risk stopping by unannounced. As big as the agency seems to be, it's selfish of me to think that his schedule would allow for such breaks in time to talk with newbie employees.

"I'm having a problem with a client," I blurt out. "With one of your valued clients, I assume."

"Please sit down," he says, gesturing to the chair.

"If this is a bad time, I can go, I shouldn't have sprung this on you all of a sudden. I am just frustrated and I don't know what to do and I have tried to handle things on my own and they don't seem to be working." Pauses and literary punctuation are forgotten in my verbal vomit of the mouth. The simmering stress of the day comes to an epic climax—right at this minute—in my boss's office.

His eyes widen and his posture straightens even more—if humanly possible. I have his full attention as he closes his laptop and shoves file folders in the top drawer of his desk. "Did someone hurt you?"

"No," I answer with a hard swallow. He scans over my face and limbs, and I am instantly glad that I decided to wear a little makeup under his scrutiny. I shift my weight to my left hip and then back again to my right. "If this is a bad ti—"

"No. Please, Angie. It's fine. You can always come to me with problems, and I'll do my best to handle them. Would you like a drink? I have something stronger than water."

"Oh, no. Thank you." I can see the anger simmering in Dominic's body, as I watch the rise and fall of his chest.

"Please start at the beginning. I might take notes as to determine the best solution or course of action. If necessary, I might need to further the documentation process as I see fit. We can fill out an appropriate form and talk about legal advice if necessary. I need to know what has you in my office frazzled on a weekday afternoon."

The rigidness of his muscles, pushing out against the fabric of his clothes causes me to quiver. The biting tone of his chosen words radiates with contempt and malice. He can't possibly be mad at me, I reason. I am the victim after all.

"Wait, legal assistance?" I blurt.

"Correct me if I'm wrong, Angie. But you bear the signs that someone has done you wrong, and I want to make sure the situation is handled by the books. If I need to fire someone or end a membership or call the police, I need to know. It is my responsibility to protect you and the company from scrutiny. Thus, a paper trail is warranted."

"Oh, well, I don't want anyone fired." I sigh. "I just want to do my job—which I happen to enjoy—in peace. And there's a client hell-bent on ruining all of my opportunities, and quite frankly, sabotaging any type of networking I am working hard at doing." Oh and he's a control freak and a blunt bastard who does not have a mouth filter. But he's smoking hot with sex appeal that should be classified as illegal.

I barely catch the sigh that Dominic releases from his lungs. He drops his pen onto his desk with calculated coolness and seems to have relaxed a bit. "I see." He gives me a look that means "continue."

"A few days ago, my profile disappeared from your

servers. I tried to check it to see why I stopped getting updates. I know that sounds conceited, as if I get booked every day, but I felt something was amiss when previously scheduled dates were getting canceled without the client having a choice in the change. In fact, said client thought I had changed my mind when I had already accepted a string of back-to-back dates. I dug into the issue more and saw my profile was taken down by an unknown source."

"You contacted the IT department?"

"Yes, the client did too. I filled out a help-desk ticket and got confirmation that my request was received. So, the next day, my profile is up and running. However, my next twenty-one weeks are booked. By a completely different client. Dates I never agreed to accept."

"Wow."

Wow? That's all that he can say? Doesn't this border on criminal insanity? A different version of OCD: Obsessive Control Disorder? "Boat loads of money are now reserved in my account. The client is buying every night for the next twenty-one weeks, and I have plans on some of those nights. Some were even marked as unavailable on the calendar. Well, apparently he does not care. He is keeping me monopolized away from any other suitors. I never had a chance to accept or reject."

He scratches his chin and eases back into his chair. "I see. Continue. Get it all out in the open. You will feel better," he persuades, oozing of laid-back power.

I lean back in the chair, crossing my feet at the ankles. "So, I did the math." I snicker inwardly at how frustrating it was for me to play with so many numbers at once. I nearly had to call in the cavalry for help with the crunch, before hives harvested on my skin. I pull my phone out of my bag and find the notes section where I recorded the numbers. "Twenty-one weeks times seven days a week brings it to a total of one hundred forty-seven days. The client reserved four hours each night. So, a total of five hundred eighty-eight hours. The lump sum before agency cuts is two hundred fifty thousand dollars. That's a quarter of a million!" I pause a moment and wait for some sort of expression to form on Dominic's face. I get nothing. Not a gesture, a gasp, nor a groan. Nothing. He remains stone-faced. Now it's my turn to react in surprise. "It works out to be four hundred twenty-five dollars and seventeen cents per hour!"

"Nice."

What the hell? "I beg your pardon? 'Nice'?"

"Sorry," he grumbles, playing with his gold ring. "Well, after the agency cut with escrow and all, you would have significantly less."

"Dominic, this man is clinically crazy. I do not care what his background check and medical records claim. I know. I can tell. He's lost his damn mind." And I am starting to lose mine for fantasizing about him every chance I get.

"Did you talk to the client? Discuss matters?"

"Yes."

"And?"

"He is an unbudging prick!"

"Would you like to have a formal meeting with…" He taps three fingers against his jaw line. "What did you say his name was?"

I didn't yet. "Graham Hoffman."

"Ah, yes, Mr. Hoffman." There is no surprise in his expression—a complete poker face.

"What all do you know about him that you are allowed to share? Is my life in danger? Should I upgrade my ten-buck tube of pepper spray?"

He stifles a laugh. "I don't think that will be necessary." At the beginning of the conversation he was on board for arresting the man himself. But now… Why is he not taking this more seriously? Is it because Graham's jewelry business has connections with the agency? Is it because they are friends and not just acquaintances?

"Oh, and am I allowed to refuse these dates that he has hijacked? Do I even get a choice in the matter?"

"All of these questions can be answered at the mediation that I'll set up. I will make sure the head of HR is present. I can have you use the company lawyer as well. Unless you have someone else in mind to represent you." When my expression screams of course not, he continues. "I'll have an associate contact you. But, Angie, I assure you, Graham—although eccentric in his measures of communication—will not hurt you. If he does, I'll personally kill that fucker."

I jerk back in my seat at the expletive. "Thank you, Dominic. But aren't you two business associates? I saw you two—"

"You questioning where my loyalty lies?" he asks with fierce eyes.

Whoa. He's mad. My bones rattle my insides, shaking ice through my veins. I gulp in an unladylike manner, utterly thrown off guard. I straighten in the seat, halt my fidgeting fingers with the hem of my shirt, and put the finishing touches on my strengthening composure. "I know that ultimately, it comes down to the digits. And Graham is bringing the agency some heavy-duty capital. Pissing him off will not be good for business. I get that." So why give a hoot about me?

"On the contrary, Miss McFee, you have it wrong. Pissing you off would not be good for business. Do you have the slightest inclination as to how much power you hold among all these men vying for your attention?"

I shake my head slowly, even though I am sure the question was rhetorical.

"I'll put forth the protocol set in place for such things, but with all due respect, Miss McFee, you simply have an admirer at your disposal. A very lucrative, unrelenting, and possessive one at that. Somehow I doubt this meeting that I'll set up will provide you with the outcome you are expecting. And I wouldn't be a good boss if I didn't warn you that Graham sees you as a challenge. As with most powerful men, he doesn't like to lose. Thus, he'll fight and fight dirty. We can only try to predict his moves before he makes them."

"I'm not a prize. And I am not for sa—" I choke on my words. Shame warms my face at the realization. I am for sale. I can't bring myself to look at Dominic. My head sways in the downward position, hair falling around my cheeks in desperation to hide from reality.

"Angie. You can't possibly see yourself that way. You are not doing anything wrong. Let's work this out together. Find a happy medium. This all can be resolved."

I shrug, unable to make my eyes meet his waiting gaze.

"We can go to HR today and set up a meeting that works with your schedule. I'll personally make sure that Graham can attend. Graham and I are friends, Angie, but I'm on your side. Before we go, please at least drink some water and calm down a bit. You are visibly stressed."

No shit.

I am freaking out about a man who seems to have some immeasurable and unexplainable interest in me. I feel like I am caught in a web.

Most of my waking moments are spent thinking about Graham and the effect he has on my body. He is breaking down my defenses—one by one. Soon, I will be lying on my back in a king-sized bed, giving up my virginity, and then waking up the next day with nothing but a memory—and the feeling of defeat and loss all over again. Because either he will leave or I will. Men who have everything are usually quick to search for the next best thing. I do not want to be his girl on the side while he continues getting closer to Sophia.

I am a challenge. One that when met, the obsession will end. Should I just submit and get it over with? From that point of view, that seems to be the most logical thing to do. Can I do that to my body? Put out just to get out? Can I be a hit-it and quit-it type of lay? I suppose the crazy amount of money serves as a good pillow to lessen the pain.

"Here. Drink this."

I take the glass container of water and twist through the safety seal to open the lid. "Thank you," I mutter, taking a sip. It is going to take more than water to make my worries go away. I lift up from the chair, signaling that I am ready to talk with HR.

I follow Dominic out of his office and down the hallway until we are at the office of Human Resources. Once inside,

I talk with the assistant director and retell my story. More notes are taken—followed by nods and small smiles. The more I tell my side out loud, the sillier it sounds. I am complaining over the extreme amount of money and the fact that I have job security for the duration of my short-term contract. Of course, to the average human, this sounds like a dream come true. Maybe Dominic is right. This meeting might not do any good for fighting my point and giving my perspective. In the end, Graham might just have succeeded in pushing me into a corner and twisting my arm. Damn him.

"So, this Friday at ten o'clock works for you, Miss McFee?"

"Yes, that works fine for me." No class on Fridays so I am free all day.

Dominic walks me out and toward the elevator. "You have my cell number if you ever need me to intervene. Please do not hesitate to call me."

"Thanks, Dominic. I appreciate you taking the time out of your schedule to meet with me today."

"Anytime."

When I get back to the car, I turn my cell phone back on and find that I have a missed call from Graham. What does he want? I listen to his simple "I miss you" statement and groan at the effect his voice alone has on my body. I am screwed. My messages filter in after the power is on for a few minutes. I am then able to read the text that he sent.

Graham: If you wanted a date on Friday, you could have just called. Beating around the "bush" is the fun part of MY job. And yours is very pretty. ;)

A winky face? And a sexual innuendo? He's too much! Ahhh…I resist the urge to type back something sarcastic or insulting. He can wait to hear from me on Friday. I will not give him what he wants.

I open another text, this one from Zander, and read the message.

Zander: Thinking about you…hope you are okay. Please let me know.

I toss my phone on the passenger seat and pull out of the parking spot in the garage. I pull up to the local health clinic before I have the chance to change my mind and chicken out. Once inside, I use the kiosk to select the service I want and choose the option for a "walk-in" visit. I enter in my personal information and then wait to be called back.

I check my email and answer a few *Bad Advice* questions while I wait the twenty minutes until it is my turn.

"Angela McFee," the nurse announces.

I grab my phone and follow her back into a private room where a staff member is typing in a few notes on her computer.

"Hi, I'm a nurse practitioner specializing in rehabilitative therapies."

"Nice to meet you," I say, taking a seat in the chair in the corner of the room.

"What brings you here?"

"I was in a car accident a few years ago and received physical therapy on my leg and shoulder. However, the pain from my injuries is returning, and I am in enough discomfort where I would like a prescription filled to help me cope."

She types notes on her computer, accesses my health file that I uploaded on the kiosk, and wheels her chair over to me to examine the range of motion for my shoulder and leg.

"I can prescribe you a series of exercises and a physical therapist who can either come to your house or you can meet for therapy in their office."

I frown at her recommendation. "I've done all of that before. I just need some pain meds to get me through the next couple of weeks so I can even be able to go back to stretching. Right now, I'm in agony."

"I am sorry, Miss McFee. You're not a candidate."

I get up from my chair and head toward the checkout window. I pay my waste of a copay and head back out to my car. I shouldn't be surprised. This is not the first time I've been denied what I desperately need.

It takes me longer to get back to campus due to rush-hour traffic. I park in the visitor lot and walk toward Livingston Hall. The top floor of the building has the computer labs. I make a beeline down the corridor to the help desk and IT support center.

A girl with purple hair removes her ear buds at the sight of a life form. "Whatcha need?"

"Is Zander Worthington working today?"

"Yup, he's actually updating all of the machines in L205 to the newest release of Fedora." She smiles, her eyes lighting up with the technical talk—even though it is one-sided. "It's a flavor of Linux," she adds, as if that is enough to make me understand the jargon.

"Oh, okay." I swallow and nod politely. That sounds intimidating just thinking about it. Zander is probably having a field day getting his mind deep in computer softwariness.

I make a hasty retreat before I am sucked into a discussion on the importance of encryption and how to identify a secure website. Nope. Not in the mood for that today.

I find Zander in his element in the empty lab. One computer plays Sum 41, while he runs from machine to machine, updating the operating systems.

"Hey, what brings you here?" he asks, losing concentration at the creak of the door. "I've been worried about you."

"I know. But please try not to. I'm fine. I came to work on my research for class. I figured that I would see if you were on shift. And you are." I make my way over to him to get a closer look at the screens he is working on.

"Cool. I can set you up with one of the computers in here if you want to hang out."

"Can you make sure that it looks like what I am used to? You know how I get freaked out over change." I narrow my eyes at him. "Are you laughing at me?"

"Of course. You crack me up with your misguided repulsion." He chuckles and flops down in front of one screen to stop the update process to preserve the familiarity for me to complete my task.

I replace him and remove my flash drive and notes from my bag.

"I forgot to tell you the other night that I saw in *The*

Headliner that the charity gala exceeded last year's earnings and hit an all-time record."

I smile. "Yeah, I saw that too. It's awesome that the community supports such a worthy cause."

"I'm glad you asked me to be a part of it this year. I had fun, Angie."

"Me too."

"I happened to see the photo of Graham with some blonde, as I'm sure you did," he says softly, carefully walking on ice.

"Yeah. They work together. Apparently it was a publicity thing for his jewelry company." Am I actually defending him? And most importantly—why?

"I just don't want you to get hurt."

"I don't want to get hurt either," I admit. But something tells me that is going to happen no matter how I slice it.

Once all of the machines are updated, he shuts them each off, and we walk down the stairs to the main exit. He walks me to my car and then enters his.

"Bye, Z," I wave.

"See ya, Ang."

I watch as Zander pulls out of his spot and leaves. There is something off about him tonight that I just cannot put my finger on; he seems sad. I turn my key, and my car sputters and struggles to start. I rev the engine and it gains life. I back out and pull onto the road. Raindrops sprinkle my windshield and glisten under the streetlights. I swipe them away with my wipers.

Fog settles over the ground, making everything look gray. I come to a stop at the intersection, and when I press down on the gas to move forward, my car shuts off. I switch my hazard lights on and check my gas level—which appears to be half full. No dash lights come on. I turn the key again and nothing happens. Silence.

I shift the car to neutral and turn the steering wheel to the right. I step out and move behind the trunk to give a firm push to the frame. Slowly, I guide it to the side of the road, into the shale. I shut off the caution lights, retrieve a white plastic bag to put in the window, and grab my purse. I lock the doors and call a towing company to come move it to a nearby shop for an evaluation.

Being just a mile away from the townhouse, I decide to risk the weather and walk the rest of the way. A little rain won't make me melt.

I pull the hood on my jacket up over my head. I use the light on my cell phone to help guide my steps as I trudge through the mud until I see the first row of townhouses in the distance, where the sidewalk begins. The moving fog makes the entire area seem creepy—or it is just my overactive imagination playing tricks on me. I pick up my pace as the rain droplets get more frequent. My jacket absorbs most of the moisture from soaking into the next dry layer.

An incoming text diverts my attention from my focus on getting back home, and I accidentally drop my phone onto the gravel. I quickly pick it up and wipe off the dampness. The number is unknown to me, and I open the message app to read the complete message.

Unknown: Girls like you should be careful.

22

My hands shake as I try not to drop my phone again. I read the words one more time to make sure I am not seeing things. Is someone watching me? My eyes dart around my surroundings but can only see darkness and the vague outline of streetlights in the fog of the night. I start to jog and am relieved when I make it to the sidewalk. It's as if stepping foot on it makes me somehow safer. At least now I am near a bunch of homes.

My lungs scream for air as I keep up my pace. I am just a couple of rows away. Maybe a fourth of a mile, if that. I will myself forward and transition into a run. And I run and run.

My throat clenches as my foot slips, and I am airless. Gravity drops me to the cement. Pain sears through my knees and palms. The wind is knocked out of me, and my phone gets propelled forward. It takes me a few seconds to realize I've fallen. The rain is now beating down in a violent attack, stinging my exposed skin. My hair is soaked despite my hood, and the drops are streaming down my face. I pick myself up and rub at my sore knees. I am sure they are bruised and bleeding underneath the fabric of my pants. My palms are skinned but nothing is broken. For that I am thankful. I find my phone a couple of yards in front of me and rub it against my wet clothes—only to just smear moisture all over the screen. I attempt to jog but cannot get my legs to cooperate. I am in pain.

I need to make it a few more houses. Ironically, no one is around. It's as if the entire area is deserted. I focus my attention on getting home, up the steps, and to my door. I rummage through my purse for the keys and realize they're in my pocket. I unlock the door and push my drenched self through the threshold into the entryway.

I peel off my jacket and throw my soaked purse onto the floor near the rack of shoes. I remove my boots and toe off my socks.

The sound of loud masculine laughter coming from the kitchen bombards me and helps awaken my senses.

"Claire, I'm home!" I yell loudly—giving warning to my presence—to avoid witnessing naked body parts.

"Okay! Be there in a few minutes!" she giggles. "Just finishing up dinner. Do not come in here."

"Make sure you sanitize the space," I call back. "Changing clothes and will be down."

I slowly crawl up the stairway, feeling the pulling skin of my knees with each bend. Ouch. I resist telling Claire what happened. At least for now. She will freak if and when I do tell her. I just don't want to kill the happiness right now that Ethan seems to bring out of her in abundance.

When I enter my room, I quickly discard my wet attire

and examine the damage done to my knees. Just some mild swelling and a brush burn. I clean the open areas and place bandages over the wounds. I wash my hands and decide to forgo covering the skinned flesh on my palms. The blood has already clotted and scabbed over. I open my dresser and settle for a set of pink fleece pajamas with the words "Girl Power" printed across the front. I slip on a pair of fuzzy red socks and brush out my wet hair.

Settling in on the sofa, I find a medium sized package on the coffee table addressed to me. Seriously, again? What is with the random packages?

Claire's voice penetrates my ears with her shushing and exaggerated stops.

"What smells so good?" I yell, giving warning to my reappearance.

"Ugh, um, homemadebutternutsquashsoup," Claire answers suddenly, blending her words together in a rush. The sound of rustling and falling plastic cups fills the silence. "I had a craving."

"Yum! I can smell the nutmeg and cinnamon. Smells like fall in here. Love it!"

I hear a few umpffs, and I stifle a giggle. I really am just hoping they clean up after their sexcapade.

Claire's head peeks around the door frame between the kitchen and living room, giving me a sly smile. "Um, can you close your eyes for just one minute?"

"Sure." I shut my eyes, moving my palms to cover the lids for added effect. I hear two different sets of footsteps running past the coffee table and up the flight of stairs to the second floor. The laughter heard from the top of the staircase lets me know instantly that I am safe to look. "Please tell me you two Clorox wiped all of the surfaces! I just cleaned them the other day!" I holler, only sparking their giggles.

Three minutes later, Claire emerges, fully clothed in loungewear. "Sorry about that," she mutters, her face actually producing a blush. It must have been some good sex for her to react like that. "I'll disinfect everything. Promise."

I shake my head back and forth in mock disapproval. I cannot hide my amusement. Maybe living vicariously through your roommate's romps is the way to make it through college unharmed by overzealous billionaires.

"You shower already?" Claire asks suddenly, looking at my hair. She flops down on the couch.

"Car broke down and I got caught in the rain," I explain.

"What? And you didn't call me? Especially after what happened with Resa," she scolds.

"Yeah, I know," I say with a frown, "but I figured you were busy."

"Angie! You can be so dense sometimes. What if something happened to you?"

"I'm fine. Nothing bad happened."

"You are hiding something. Spit it out. Now."

I guess the downside of living with each other is that we pick up on each other's emotions and signals. "So, I got a weird text from an unknown caller."

"What type of text? What did it say?" she demands.

"'Girls like you should be careful.'"

"Holy shit. What does that even mean?"

"Not sure. I haven't gotten any more texts. May have just been the wrong number."

"Regardless, that is super messed-up. No idea who it's

from? Was someone following you? Where's your car now? Why the hell did you think it was a good idea to walk home alone at night in the rain? I could seriously tackle you right now."

"Easy, hun, go easy on her," Ethan chimes in, joining us in the living room. His expression is that of what I assume to be a satisfied man. "Hey, Angie."

"Hi." I push myself up from the couch and switch to the solo chair, curling my feet under my behind.

"You don't have to move for me," Ethan says suddenly.

"It's fine, really."

"Answer the damn questions, Angie," Claire snaps. "Are you listening at all to this, Ethan? Someone may be after her!"

I let out a sigh. I knew I should have kept this one random act to myself. I knew she would blow this out of proportion. "My car was towed to the shop. I have no idea what the text means or who it's from. Obviously. I don't just give out my cell number, so the person must have lifted it from a document or got it from someone I know. My contacts list is small, so I doubt the person who texted me is someone I am in good standing with…plus, it is an unknown number. Probably a burner phone. Or maybe it was a wrong number. A silly mistake."

"You have many enemies?" Ethan asks softly.

I answer "no" as Claire yells "yes" over top of me. I turn to glare at her.

"But you do, Angie. You have that douchebag Russell who is pissed at you for trashing his precious douchebaggy stuff. And you probably have enemies from the night at The Shack. Top that off with this fierce competition for an internship." She lets out an exaggerated exhale, obviously bothered. "You probably irritated some classmate and don't even realize it."

I turn to Ethan. "I have no known enemies. I keep a low profile in classes and stay under the radar with my research and coursework. No one should really view me as a threat. I have not dated many people, and Russell was the one who dumped me. But he is a trust fund baby and can replenish his stupid supply of clothes and tennis rackets. Or his daddy can."

"But a text seems like a targeted attack on you. This is not a random act," Claire reminds me.

"Yeah, I know, and trust me, I am freaked out too."

"Now I am afraid to even leave you this weekend," she whines.

"What's going on this weekend?"

"Ethan and I are taking his son, Finn, camping at his cabin in Goldendale."

"Washington state?" I ask.

"Yeah, so you will have until Saturday free of us," Claire responds, prancing around the room like a fairy.

I try to contain my frown at being granted a weekend without the company—even if it is sporadic at times—of Claire. They will be two hours away from Portland. "Sounds fun. Take pictures, especially if you have to hunt for your food and cook it over an open flame." I watch as she stops her dancing and stares at me, mouth gaping. "I would pay to see something like that," I continue, stone-faced.

She turns to Ethan with bulging eyes, making him chuckle at her fear. "I promised you, babe, it's not your average camping. Full kitchen, master bedroom, and bath. Even electricity."

Claire and I look at each other and say in unison, "Glamping."

"Sure," Ethan says, "with mall shopping a town away."

"Whew," she exhales, "that sounds much better than my daytime nightmare I was having right now."

I giggle.

"The only downfall is that cell phone service is tricky out in the wilderness," Ethan admits.

"We'll be leaving after I finish my afternoon shift at the gym tomorrow," Claire reminds me. "Who will help you pick up your car from the shop?"

"Don't worry about me. I'll text Z or something."

"Want to borrow mine?" she offers.

"Nope, too fancy. Last time I drove it, I scraped the hubs on the curb."

"Ugh, I pretty much do that every time I try to parallel park," she laughs. "I want one of those parking push buttons where the car just does the job itself. You sure you'll be fine here?"

"Yes. Go, enjoy, relax," I respond. "Quit worrying." The first meeting with Ethan's son could be the making or breaking point of the relationship. For Claire's sake, I hope the weekend runs smoothly and without any awkward moments. I think she actually enjoys dating one person—even if it is from the Entice database.

"Ready to eat?" Claire asks, disappearing into the kitchen after Ethan and I agree that we are indeed hungry.

Three minutes later, she sashays back into the living room holding a tray with three bowls of soup and sliced bread in a pile. I move the mysterious cardboard box to the floor so Claire can place the tray onto the coffee table. We all grab at the food and watch trash TV.

Whenever Claire's snoring becomes louder than the volume on the TV, I leave Ethan to take care of her and go upstairs with my package in hand. It is light, and the professional label is one from San Antonio, Texas. Nothing from the print gives away what it could be or who it could be from.

I place the box on the bed and dig through the medicine cabinet in the bathroom for a small pair of scissors. I cut through the packing tape with ease. I keep the packing peanuts inside and pull out the elegantly wrapped box. The gold paper is thick and embossed with swirls and circles. Shiny reflective gold ribbon is wrapped around both sides of the box, making a pile of random threads at the top—all curled to perfection. The gift looks professionally wrapped and too artistic to tear apart with nimble human fingers. I weigh the shirt-sized box with both hands. Shockingly it is a mere eight ounces or less; the outer packing box actually seems heavier.

A little gold envelope is taped to the top with my name printed on it in black calligraphy ink. Not a single splatter or misprint. I pluck the card out—careful not to damage the wrapping.

I hope you find this a suitable alternative to my once promise. I am eager to find out from my own personal experimentation with you. A manual should be enclosed. Dream easy, sweetheart. This should assist. -GH

I stare at the professionally typed words. What promise? Graham sent me something with a return address from Texas. Why? I sit with my beautifully wrapped package for a good five minutes before making any sort of movement. Should I even open it? I am furious with him. I need to remember that. Maybe to send my point home, I should bring the gift to the meeting on Friday and make him take it back. Whatever it is, I don't want it. I slip out of bed and use my nighttime routine as a great coping mechanism and a distraction.

I scrub and wash my face. I brush and floss. Then I give myself a pedicure, complete with deep red nail polish on my toes. Nothing is left to do. I have exhausted all of my possible distractions.

I stare at the bed and find the golden treasure waiting in the same place I left it.

Don't be a coward. Open it!

I walk hesitantly to the bed. I sit on the edge and plop the box on my lap. Deep down, whatever it is, I know that I am going to like it. Graham picked it out just for me. Part of me is sad that I am going to have to refuse it, just to prove a point.

I tear a piece from the side of the box, removing the perfectly angled paper that wraps underneath. I continue until all of the paper is off and all I am looking at is a plain white box. I slide the lid off and push back the tissue paper over the edges. What are these?

Rings? Like jewelry?

Inside a delicate velvet-lined display case, I find six silver rings behind the plastic protective shield. I open the case and pluck one of the rings from the little individual compartments. I place the pretty grape-embellished ring on my right pointer finger.

Wait. It doesn't fit. Crap.

I try the other fingers, but the band doesn't get past my first knuckle. Why would he send me something that doesn't even fit? I try the others—which are all different in decorative style—and find that none of them fit. My phone buzzes with an incoming text.

Graham: Surely by now you have opened your gift. You must be "busy." ;)

Angie: None of them fit…

I scold myself for sending the message before announcing that I have decided I am not accepting the gift. I wait less than a minute for his response.

Graham: One size fits all…did you break your fingers today?

Um… What the hell does that even mean? And what type of ring fits all? I play with the arrangement of rings again, looking for an adjustment mechanism on the bottom of the silver loop and finding nothing. I run my fingers over the silicone, feather, and metal designs that adorn each of the six rings. Am I putting them on wrong? Maybe my intuition is broken… My phone buzzes again.

Graham: Want me to come over and show you how to use them, kitten?

Graham: Nothing would please me more. :P

Okay, the tongue is too much! He's laughing at me. Doesn't he mean "show me how to wear them"?

I dig to the bottom of the box and find the manual. The cover has the company logo JEALOUSY in blocked letters across the top. The signature ruby-red lips stare back at me like reflective mirrors. I want to puncture holes through them, now that I know the model. Inside the shiny-paged brochure, a picture of all six rings appears in an artistic display. The print "For Her Pleasure Collection" is featured at the bottom of the page. My stomach flips, making my heart feel pressure.

Umm…what?

My attention goes to the first page, and I read a paragraph about how women are often shy when it comes to self-pleasuring and that eighty percent of women need clitoral stimulation to reach an orgasm. On page two, there are testimonials about women who have bought the rings and loved them. They oohed over how luxurious the rings look—like they are classy sex jewelry.

"He bought me sex toy jewelry." I say the words out loud slowly—as if I am a two-year-old—pronouncing each syllable carefully and hesitantly. What. The. Hell.

Graham bought me sex toys. And apparently his online company specializes in this type of fetish. I remember the silicone cock I sent to his office and wonder if this is some sort of retaliation. These rings are way more elegant than my purchase. They are classy. Sexy.

I flip to pages three and four, which illustrate the benefits of each type of ring. It is not until page seven that I am able to find the diagram that shows where on the finger to place each device.

I hope you find this a suitable alternative...

To what? Just my fingers?

I owe you an orgasm, sweetheart.

The words spoken to me in his office filter into my memory. Holy shit.

I slip the ring with two identical rolling spheres on my pointer finger. I turn the ring so that the 3D part is on the underside of my hand. I rub the balls over the exposed part of my other arm. Feels cool and interesting. But to put this on my clit?

I lie back onto the bed, remembering the amazing feel of Graham's fingers on my sex at the charity gala. Nothing can possibly be better than that. Except, however, when he licked my panties in his office. I almost exploded then. Perhaps this will be a suitable alternative to the real thing. My moisture gathers between my thighs as my excitement increases with the anticipation.

I read more about the rings, discovering that each ring is waterproof and they can even go in the dishwasher in the utensils bin, using the vented silicone sleeve that is provided in the box. That part makes me laugh.

I put three rings on one hand and three on the other—examining each carefully. I am enthralled at the detail of each design and structure. Well, I have never even heard of such a thing, let alone had my own set. Music starts playing from my phone, and I jump up from the bed with a startle. What the hell? I frantically grab it and see that Graham is calling—and must have made a custom ringtone all for himself. "I'm Too Sexy" by Right Said Fred seems egotistical but accurate.

"How in the world did you manage to hack my phone and customize a ringtone?"

"Hello to you, Angie." He chuckles. "I have my ways. Am I interrupting?" His tone is smug. I can picture his face lighting up with amusement and wonder.

"You wish," I snort.

"Come on. I need to know if you like the new items that my company will be launching in four weeks. You have an exclusive set with the bonus rings. A deluxe collection." His pride bubbles out with his words. "They are not even on the market yet. But if they were and if having nude pictures in advertisements was viable in the states, I would have your pretty pussy as the pamphlet centerfold. Hands down," he chuckles.

"I thought you sold jewelry."

"They are jewelry." He sounds offended. "Mighty fine with multiple purposes," he adds proudly. An image of him wiggling his eyebrows pops into my head. "You don't like your gift?"

"No…I…um…"

"So I am interrupting. Are you on your bed right now? What are you wearing?"

"Graham…"

"Or are you naked? Hmm."

"Stop."

"Floor? Bathroom counter?"

I don't answer.

"Wow, living room? Dirty and risky." His husky voice coos.

After a long pause, I can hear his breath catch.

"Angie?"

"Ya?"

"Tell me."

"I'm on my bed." This is none of his business! Why am I even entertaining him?

"What are you wearing?"

"My most un-sexy pair of fleece pajamas."

"Hmm…lucky pj's. I would love to see you right now, sweetheart. Spread out on your bed," he instructs. "Your fingers wearing my designer jewelry?"

"Yeah," I choke-cough. How embarrassing!

"Good girl. This is a huge fantasy of mine."

"Grah—"

"We should FaceTime."

"No!" I snap.

"Shhh…touch yourself." His voice washes over me, warming me from the inside out. I think of his fingers gliding over me—the same fingers that had a hand in making such an erotic female-friendly toy. "I'm about thirty seconds away from night shipping you a new laptop with a top-of-the-line webcam installed. I need to see you, baby. Tell me what you are doing. Paint the picture for me."

"Graham," I warn. "This has to stop."

"Touch yourself, Angie. Try them out." His words sound like a moan to my ears, lighting a flame deep from within, pushing me to the edge of insanity.

I have no idea what possesses me. Maybe it is his voice. Or maybe deep down inside, I enjoy when he bosses me around. I slip my fingers into my pants and rub the devices over my sensitive spot—trying each one out to see what I like and don't like.

"The one that has the little silicone spikes and balls is supposed to be pretty powerful. Take your time. Go slow. Keep that one external only," he warns, his voice strict and powerful. "The last thing I need is to be hauling your pretty little ass to the ER to remove my gift from your pussy."

I suck air through my teeth, following his directions—more out of curiosity.

"When's the last time you jilled off?"

What language is he speaking? "Jilled?"

"Masturbated?"

I let out my nervous laugh. It is more to just fill the silence with anything other than a real explanation.

"It's just an expression."

"Oh," I breathe.

"Guys jack off, girls jill off," he explains calmly.

Ah. "Jack and Jill."

"Focus. Last time, sweetheart?"

My mind goes fuzzy over his endearment. He can be so sweet. Normal. "Oh. Um…" I think back to last week of my mental calendar. "Um…the day after our first date." I instantly regret my choice of words.

"Hmm. And to think I didn't have a profound effect on you at that time. You are one confusing woman, Miss McFee."

"You touched me at the charity gala, though," I remind him, hung up on the timeline.

"And I owe you an orgasm from that night. So I am trying to pay you some restitution for my leaving you high and dry that evening. Although, you were never really dry."

"Funny. What about leaving me on edge at your office?"

"No, Angie, that was intentional denial of orgasm. For your choices."

"What choices?" I snap back.

"Your lack of being able to choose what your heart and body want."

"Whatever," I huff.

"So you think about me while you touch yourself?"

I blush at his comment, thankful that he is not here to witness the effect he has on me. "How do you know I was thinking of you? I could have been reading my novel."

"That's fine. You can rely on your smut book. But something still tells me your mind substitutes me as the hero. Hmm…and by your moan, I would say I am correct. So your orgasm was epic?"

I swallow, steadying my playful fingers. My touch feels great—as it always does—but sadness gnaws at my conscience, sending guilt on a rampage.

"I'm waiting for an answer, sweetheart."

"It never occurred." My voice is barely a whisper.

"Why not? You get interrupted?"

"No."

"Then why no orgasm?"

I don't know. I never know. "I just didn't."

"And you give me yet another reason to worry that you aren't taking care of yourself properly. Finding sexual release, baby, is healthy. When was the last time it actually happened?"

I gulp and bite at my tongue. Is there no end to the humiliation?

Bed, swallow me now…

"Angie?"

"Hmm?"

"Answer me." His words are clear and precise. His command over me scares me. He makes me want to please him.

I remain silent, not wanting to divulge any more than I already have.

"You know what happens when you push me," he warns.

"Never," I breathe, barely able to hear the word myself.

"Never?"

I nod.

"Angela?"

"You heard me," I snap in frustration. The words come out in a whoosh, my emotions buried deep in my gut.

"Yes, I heard you. But what do you mean by never?" He pauses to wait for my answer and then sighs. "As in you do not know what one feels—"

"Yes, yup. Correct. You got it," I stutter.

Oh, how mortifying!

"How the hell do you expect me to believe something so shocking? You said you dated some men."

"That is true."

"And?"

"And it just never happened. We never got to that point."

"And with yourself?" he probes. "You just don't try to get there? Out of fear or shame or what misconception?"

"Trust me, I try to get there."

"Then why can't you?"

"I get close and then I have no idea." I want to cry, I am that frustrated. "I just can't. Maybe I'm broken."

"Shit. Well, this situation has to be remedied. You are missing out on life, with or without a man."

"I try. I continue to try." Shut up, Angie. Shut. Up.

"Sweetheart, I know I got you that gift. But I would rather you put it away in your nightstand drawer for the time being. Do you understand what I'm saying?"

"Why?"

I want to play! Tonight might be the night it works.

"I was a little overzealous and missed some valuable information where you are concerned. In due time, you can use them. Just wait for now. Can you do that?"

Okay, this is confusing. "Sure."

"Oh, and Angie?"

"Hmm?"

"Come downstairs and let me inside."

"What?"

"I'm at the door, kitten."

23

A muffled squeak escapes my mouth, and I do sound like a cat.

At the door? What is Graham doing here? I end the call abruptly and hop around the room, trying to calm my nerves.

I nearly throw myself down the steps to get to the door fast enough, afraid to make the beast wait too long out in the cold. I glance into the living room and say a silent thank you that Ethan and Claire are locked in her room—hopefully asleep. My shaky hands unlock the door and pull it open to find Graham standing there. He is wearing loose fitting jeans, a dark maroon V-neck sweater, and an opened black jacket. He looks yummy and dangerously sexy.

Graham's eyes rake over my appearance. "You almost look"—he smirks—"innocent." His voice comes out sharp. "But it's just an illusion, I'm sure." Both his brows rise with his forehead, and his eyes give me the stern, authoritative look. It's the same look I would often get when disobeying my elders as a child. I want to turn away from the awkwardness, but I don't dare break the contact. He has officially put me in my place with a single look. Talent exemplified.

"What's got you in such a bad mood?" I ask, moving back to allow him into the warmth.

"It's called hunger."

"So you want dinner?" I ask stupidly.

He shakes his head and looks to be holding back a comment.

"I'm still mad at you," I remind, "for not putting my profile back to normal, you know?" My own stern look is reflected back in his.

"Good. I like you angry," he says in a relaxed tone, softening his eyes. "I'll take great pleasure working out some of that hostility in you." His fingers dust behind my neck, pushing my hair away to cascade in soft layers down my back. "Nice socks."

I stare down at the red fuzz and smile at the compliment—despite knowing that it was full of snark. "Why are you here?"

Graham's caresses travel up to my chin and come to a stop on my cheeks. If they weren't a rosy hue before, they are now. I can feel the electricity passing through my skin like a torch in the night.

"To remedy your dilemma." The words fall off his lips like melted butter. "Think you can be a good girl and take some direction?"

How can I resist him when he phrases it just like that? My heart quickens, and it's as if I am once again caught in his web. I nod in agreement, but it isn't good enough. "I need your words," he insists.

I want nothing more than for Graham to ravish me. To tear off my clothes and have his way with me. This is why he came tonight, right? The charity gala preview only whetted my appetite and made me hungry for more. Tonight, I hope to get more.

"I'll be good."

"Oh, baby, I am equally fond of you being good—and bad. We'll see which side of you wins tonight. Now, for the instructions, I am going to give you three tasks. Do you think you can handle them?"

Depends. What are they? "Y-yes." The sound of the simple word quivers with my nervous vibrations of my vocal cords.

"Yes, sir," he corrects.

Ohhh, he is playing a game. "Yes, sir," I echo back the words, trying hard not to giggle like a high schooler.

"Good girl. First, I need you to go upstairs to your room and close the door. Do not lock it. Second, I need you to kneel on your bed facing away from the door. And third, I need you to think about how turned on I make you."

I slowly nod to show that I understand but am greeted with an intense look of expectation. "Yes, sir," I murmur.

"Your cute shy act will not work on me tonight, kitten. Now go and wait for me."

I turn on my heel and dart upstairs, careful not to slam the door to wake up Claire and Ethan. Shit. What if they hear me yelling during the night? That will definitely make for some awkward morning-after discussions over an organic fruit smoothie in the kitchen. As soon as I am safely in my room, I start to freak myself out over following the directions to the letter. Did he want me to get naked? I can't remember! I run through the list in my head, playing his words back as if coming from a recording device. No, I don't think he mentioned anything about my clothes.

Instantly, I grow self-conscious of my blemishes—something I have never felt before, even with previous boyfriends. Walking toward the bed, I pull the waistband of my pants and panties down to reveal several scars on my hips. What if Graham is disgusted by the whitened streaks over even paler skin?

I stare at the scars as if I am seeing them really for the first time. Some are curved. Some are a series of straight marks. I trace the ugly lines with my fingertip, visually erasing them. I was barely conscious when the glass was being pulled from me after I was admitted to the hospital. James had glass in him too, but it was too late to try to get it out of him in a hurry.

Oh, James, I miss you.

What if Graham asks me about these marks? The few times we have been in intimate positions together I have not been naked. But if I am, he will notice. He always notices the details. And I don't want to talk about it. Talking about it doesn't help.

I listen for any movement on the stairs or in the hallway. My own heartbeat distracts my senses. The thump-thump sound lulls me into a state of comfort; it is the calm before the storm. I suspect he is making me wait, just because he can.

I use my alarm clock to keep track of minutes as I carefully kneel on the bed as instructed, cringing at the feel of the fresh scabs on my knees. I rest my butt against the heels of my feet, not knowing how formal to be. It takes seven minutes before I hear the telling creak of his weight hitting the middle step of the staircase. He's coming. Now.

My pulse picks up rhythm, and I raise my posture to a full-on kneeling position, scolding myself for being so eager to please and hoping I didn't open my wounds again beneath the bandages. The click of the door and the soft pads of his feet hitting the floor are the telltale signs of his presence. However, it is the energy that fills the room to capacity that makes every cell in my body awaken. Graham has that effect on me. His confidence alone commands the room to bow down at his feet. I, on the other hand, am kneeling on the bed, desperate to turn around and see him.

"Close your eyes."

I do as I am told—not out of fear, but out of trust. Expecting a blindfold to cover over my vision, I am surprised by the warm breath at my ear. I get the impression that nothing about tonight is going to be what I predict, and that alone is exhilarating.

"Submission can be a powerful aphrodisiac, Angie," he purrs. The velvety smoothness of his voice intoxicates my senses. "But it involves mutual trust. Do you trust me to give you the ride of your life tonight?"

"Good luck with that, Graham. I trust that you'll give it your best try."

"Hmm…I'm going to have so much fun with you. You are the perfect combination of sexy and cute. A rare blend of defiant and submissive."

I want to respond with something sassy but decide to just keep my mouth shut. If he thinks he can break my bad luck streak then more power to him.

"This room suits you, by the way," he says upon survey.

"A mix of classic and modern. Maybe I should keep you with your eyes closed so I have ample time to snoop around."

"Hey!"

His laugh has a calming effect on my butterflies. It is like he is their master and can tame even the wildest one.

I feel the press of the mattress in front of me, toward the headboard. My chin is gripped strongly, making my eyes pop open in shock of the suddenness of the motion—but not from any pain. It's just surprise. Dark sapphire eyes stare into mine, making me quiver from the sheer force of the intensity. Graham has one knee on the bed and the other leg on the ground, keeping his height dominating above my kneeling form in a position of power. I swear the man could be laid out flat on the floor and still have the aura of command and control. Every breath he takes is planned. Calculated.

His hands adjust my curling hair behind my shoulders and then slide down my arms to rest on my hips. He tugs me forward and captures my lips between his own. I melt into his kiss and forget about everything around me. It is just the two of us.

Graham thumbs at the waistband of my fleece bottoms, toying with the elastic. I suck in a breath as our lips part. The anticipation is causing me to unravel.

"Tell me you want this, Angie. Make me believe you."

I want something that I have never had, but in the back of my head know it exists. But do I want to continue this with a man who is repeatedly stepping over the boundaries? He is someone who might prevent me from finishing my second chance semester if I cannot catch a break.

My chin is nudged by gentle fingers. "Angie, I am waiting."

"I want this." At least for tonight. I'll worry about tomorrow when tomorrow comes.

Graham's steel-blue eyes penetrate mine. He studies me for a moment and then nods once. His warm hands tug upward at the bottom of my shirt hem, revealing my bare abdomen. A shiver runs through me over the anticipation of what's to come. I lift my arms as my shirt finds its new home on the floor.

"Cute," Graham mouths in reference to my pink lace bra, "and sexy. Just like you."

"Thanks," I shyly grin. I was not planning on anyone seeing it, although I'm not sure it would have altered my selection.

He kisses my shoulder straps and uses his teeth to tug them down. His hands cup my breasts for the first time, feeling their weight. I moan and tilt my head toward his mouth until our lips meet again. He sucks on my bottom lip as he unfastens the clasp in back, discarding the article to join my shirt. I wonder why he is starting on top, instead of going straight to my source of pleasure. This slow play is driving me into a hazy daze. When his mouth captures my right nipple, while his other hand pinches the left, I realize that I know nothing about foreplay. A tremor hits me, and I nearly convulse off the side of the bed.

"So responsive," he says breathily over my dampened flesh.

I fist his hair and tug. I want more. So much more.

Graham chuckles at my reaction and peppers kisses

down the valley between my breasts until he suckles my left nipple between his lips.

"Ohhh," I moan, throwing my head back.

He releases his hold and locks eyes with mine. "You better not come until I tell you to."

"Huh?" Come? I have spent the better half of the last decade trying to get there. I sincerely doubt he could get me there without even taking my pants off.

"You heard me."

Yeah, I heard him. I just don't believe him.

"And if you think I can't get you there just from this," he says, tweaking both nipples with his thumbs and index fingers, "then that will be a fun challenge for another day."

I stare at him in disbelief as he guides me off the bed to stand in front of him. He shifts his body on the bed so that he is sitting with his knees spread.

"Strip."

"Excuse me?"

"Angela," he says in warning.

My shaking hands grip the waistband of my fleece pajama bottoms and gently pull them down. I shimmy my hips side to side allowing the fabric to pool at my feet. I step out and kick the garment to the side. I am in just pink lace bikini-style panties. Panties that were part of the collection sent to me from the same man who is ogling me with hungry eyes.

"What happened to your knees?" Graham demands, his voice gruff.

He gently touches each bandage and flicks his eyes up to mine with concern.

"I fell." It's not a lie.

"When?"

"Tonight."

"Dammit, Angie. You should have told me."

"It's not like you have given me much of a chance," I defend.

He lets out a curse. "I should not have had you kneeling on your wounds."

"I'm fine. Really, I am."

He grabs hold of my hips and jerks me toward him. "Next time, you tell me. Understand?"

"Yeah. Got it."

"Now show me your pretty pussy."

I stare down at the only piece of fabric I am wearing other than my socks. Why does this man make me feel so vulnerable and yet so confident? I lock eyes with Graham and thumb down my panties. I bend at the waist until they are around my ankles and then kick them into the growing discard pile. I take the liberty of removing my socks—knowing that they will not make the cut.

"Breathtaking," Graham exhales. "You are exquisite. My diamond in the rough."

He stands to join me and cups my ass cheeks between his hands. He squeezes to almost the point of pain. But I like it. I grind my core against the roughness of his jeans making him snicker. I need the friction. It is primal and instinctual. He leans down and bites at a sensitive spot on my neck, directly below my ear. I gasp at the chills it causes. Pleasure and pain are all packaged into one clear emotion—desire.

Graham lifts me up from the floor, and I wrap my legs around his waist. He guides me to my bed, laying me flat. I release my hold and watch as he removes his jeans and sweater. He stands in just his boxer briefs, and I can see the outline of his erection. He is just as turned on as I am.

"Like what you see?" he asks seductively.

I smile and nod. "Yes, sir."

He joins me on the bed with a quick kiss to my lips. I moan at his fleeting form but am soon met with a kiss to my navel and then to my clit.

Holy. Shit.

I jerk my body off the mattress and am quickly held down with strong arms.

"Scream all you want. But you do not move, Angie. You stay put. You endure all that I am about to give to you. This is payback for the torture you have caused me these past few weeks. You move without permission, I stop. Understand?"

"Yes."

"Yes, sir," he corrects.

I echo his words and will my body to stay still. But I somehow know that I will fail.

Graham's thumbs part my dampened lips, while his tongue starts lower at the sensitive skin below my entrance. He licks all the way up until where my patch of hair rests. I whimper at the sensation and try not to move an inch. He flattens his tongue again and travels the same path. Tears well in my eyes at the concentrated pleasure. My hands massage his hair as he continues his relentless torture on my body.

After a series of several swipes—I have lost track of the count—he centers in on my clit and sucks it into his mouth as if it were the pearl of an oyster. His mouth maintains the pressure, while his tongue runs laps around my sensitive bundle of nerves.

"Graham!" I yell, resisting the urge to bolt up off the bed.

I can feel his smile as he releases his hold. He travels lower and flicks his tongue back and forth over my entrance, joining it with one finger. He slides it in and scrapes along my slick flesh. The penetration feels wonderful. I am so ready. He pumps in and out with one hand, while the thumb of his other hand presses on my clit. His eyes meet mine and dance with satisfaction. He knows that I am at his mercy. He gives me a sexy smirk, and I melt into the bedding. Why does he have to be so good-looking?

Graham's finger exits, and I immediately mourn the vacancy. I feel empty. He then brings his dampened finger up to his lips and sucks my juices off—staring deeply into my eyes. He adds another finger to his mouth and slides it in and out, wetting both. He then rubs my folds, as he presses both fingers into my opening. I feel stretched to my limit and tighten my muscles involuntarily.

"Relax. You are so fucking tight. But you can take it. Your body will stretch to accommodate me, but you have to relax."

Easier said than done, mister.

Graham pulls back just enough to reach my clit with his thumb. His other thumb joins and both work at getting me to relax. When he thinks I am ready, both his fingers probe me deeper, curling up toward the anterior wall of my pussy. He uses a slow rhythmic pattern of thumbing my clit with one hand, while pulsing his fingers in a "come here" motion.

I grip the quilt between my fingers to keep from coming undone. I am on the verge of exploding, and my breathing is frantic and irregular.

"When you are ready, let go, baby. Give me all you have."

"I don't think I can," I say.

"Yes, you can. You just need to stop thinking about it. Just feel."

I shake my head "no." I am close. But I always get close. It's as if I am stuck. Stuck in this never-ending loop.

Graham growls and leans his head down to rest on my left inner thigh. I scream out in pain and arch my back off the bed as his teeth sink into my flesh. And then I let it happen. I let my body take over. I forget about everything but the pain and pleasure. I give in to the waves and waves of the orgasm.

Unintelligible sounds spew from my mouth. My hips lift off the bed until Graham has to use his elbow to hold me in place. I want to move away from the pleasure. I want to get away from his fingers. It feels too good. The rush of sensations infiltrates every area of my body. It is like I am charged.

When I come down from my high, I sink back into my pillow and close my eyes. I tug at the quilt, trying to get it around me.

"Do not hide from me, Angie," Graham warns.

He gathers me into his arms and leans back against the headboard, keeping me in between his outstretched legs. We stay just like we are for a while. I don't have any sense of time. Graham whispers in my ears how much he wants to explore with me and how he has never felt this way before now. I melt into his arms and drift off into a mild sleep, still able to hear his murmurs but too weak to answer in any coherent way.

The nuzzling of my ear makes me fidget under the blanket. I blink and focus my eyes on Graham's piercing blues.

"Would love to know what you were just dreaming about," he says softly.

"It was just a continuation of what happened earlier. Except you go further."

"And we will…but I want to take things slow with you. For the first time in my life, I want to savor this."

For the next twenty minutes, my shoulders, back, and neck are massaged into a puddle of goo with expert fingers. I feel boneless and pliable. Graham knows the perfect amount of pressure to apply to be effective, but yet never hurting me.

"You know I'm not thrilled about this whole waiting thing."

"In due time, sweetheart. Patience."

"Overrated," I groan.

He rests his palms on my belly and rubs along my waist, making me squirm with anticipation. It's like he is touching me for the first time all over again.

"Shifting your hips up into my hands is not going to change my mind, sweetheart."

Oh. I slump my body back down, not even aware that I moved in the first place.

"When I take you, you will be capable of giving me every part of you."

Not if, when.

"I'm still mad at you, you know."

"Oh, I know," he responds with a smile. "But your job and my job have nothing to do with the chemistry we have for each other. I refuse to stay away from you, Angie."

His phone buzzes in his pocket, and he shifts to check the source. I give him a puzzled look as he rejects the call, allowing voicemail to pick up the message.

"What about you?" I ask.

"What about me?"

"Don't you"—I gesture toward his cock—"need to…release?"

"Tonight was about you. I can wait. Plus, edging is a way to make everything more intense when it finally does happen."

"Oh," I mouth. He did mention something in his office about it. I just thought it was an expression and not an actual practice.

Graham kisses my forehead and then my lips. He smacks my ass and laughs over my jumpiness.

After spending at least an hour cuddling, we browse through women's magazines and give each other the cheesy quizzes that are featured in every issue until our tummies growl.

"Do I need to make you a snack?" he asks, pretending his didn't growl along with mine.

I reluctantly get up from the bed and throw on a thick cotton robe. Graham puts his pants back on but forgoes his shirt. For that I am thankful.

I lead him downstairs and into the kitchen. From the fridge, I pull out a variety of cheeses, olives, cured meats, and crackers to snack on. We sit on the island stools and munch on our food, laughing at each other's silly jokes.

The sound of Graham's phone stops me midgiggle. He curses under his breath and fishes out his device for the second time.

"I have to take this, I'm sorry," he apologizes, and then swipes his finger across the screen to accept the call.

I hop upstairs to grab my own phone and check my messages. When I pad down the stairs, Graham is still on the phone. His posture is stiff as he paces the living room. I settle my butt on the stairs and do what I'm not supposed to do. I listen.

"Borrowed license and tags? Yeah, I figured as much. Fuck," he growls. "I knew that this would happen as soon as it was printed. Yeah. Yeah, I know she is freaked out. Put her on the phone."

Who is he talking to? A family member? Sophia? The mysterious Penny? And what has him so stressed?

"I'll be there shortly. You need to calm down. I have my men assigned to this; we will figure it all out. Yes, you are safe. I won't let anything happen to you, you know that. Proceed with your daily routines. We will find him."

As Graham is about to end the call, I sneak back upstairs and gently close my bedroom door before taking the flight down a little bit louder than usual.

"Hey," he smiles at my presence.

"Hey," I answer, trying to read his body language. Something is definitely wrong, and from his stance, he does not want to talk about it. His focus is over my shoulder at some spot on the wall.

"Something has come up that needs my full attention."

I give a short nod.

He goes back upstairs to retrieve the rest of his clothes, and I wait from the bottom step.

He pulls me against him and looks me straight in the eyes. "Tonight was one of the best nights I've had in a very long time."

I can't help but get the impression that he feels guilty over it or that it will be the last one.

"Me too," I agree.

Deep down I know that the call was about Sophia. She is in trouble, and he will come to the rescue. Choosing to be mad at him for caring about her would be selfish. While lately I have been those two things, tonight I want to be different.

Tonight is another turning point. I got to see a different side of Graham. A fun side. A normal side. I catch myself falling even deeper for him. But lurking in the background, there's someone else vying for his attention. And she is everything that I am not.

24

There's something to be said for the power of a full night's rest. Medical studies have been done for decades over the importance, need, and quest for sleep. Every morning that I wake up without the recollection of a nightmare is classified as decent. And this morning has the sun shining, and despite having Graham's stay cut short last night, I feel positive and dare I say—perky?

It is comforting waking up and knowing that I have a plan for the day. Sometimes it's the simple routines that keep me balanced. And on today's agenda, I think I will add a walk to the mix.

I wrestle my hair into submission long enough to pull it back into a ponytail. I throw on yoga pants that barely fit my booty and an oversized sweatshirt. I make my way downstairs to search for my sneakers that I use for these rare occasions. It has been a while since I've gone for a basic walk, but today just seems like as good a time as ever to make a change.

I grab my keys and mini pepper spray, and then lock up. Claire and Ethan must still be asleep, so I try to be as quiet as possible. They leave for their glamping trip today and are probably just catching up on rest.

The air is cold but I know that once I get a pace going, I will warm right up. My knees rub against the spandex and cotton fabric blend, producing a mild ache. The good thing about living relatively close to the university is that there are tons of sidewalks around the community. I turn left and walk along in front of the row of townhouses. A few people are out walking their dogs, and I get sniffed a few times in passing. The grass is still wet from last night's rain, and despite the little scare with the text message, I feel safe with all the morning walkers out. Who knows, some of them may be just coming home from a night out partying.

I turn the corner and pick up speed, feeling my muscles warming up. I use my phone to track my distance and get lost in the movement and my steady breathing. I wonder what it would be like to be in Claire's situation where waking up next to a man is the most normal thing in the world. I have never done that. Ever. Last night was the closest I have gotten to that happening. When Graham stopped over unexpectedly, I fully expected to fall asleep next to him. We have gotten very close in a short period of time.

Do I trust Graham? I know he would never intentionally hurt me. He seems very overprotective. He just takes things to the extreme.

I step from the curb to cross the street, and a light hits my periphery suddenly and—

I jolt myself back. My ankles hit against the curb of the

sidewalk. I lose my balance and fall to my butt, as I stare at the car speeding past.

"Asshole!" I yell, picking myself up off the street.

I dust my hands down my pants and look both ways before continuing to cross. I didn't even hear them coming or see them. I can't remember if I was paying that much attention but still. As highly populated as the area is, surely the driver should have been more careful.

I use the adrenaline running through my veins to propel me home. I find a note from Claire attached to the door letting me know she and Ethan are going out for breakfast and then leaving for their trip from there. I check the phone and see that I made a three-mile loop. Not too bad for my first time out in months. I let my lungs cool down and make my way into the house for something to eat.

I blend frozen fruit, milk, and ice—leaving out the sawdust tasting chia seeds and ground flax. Claire and Ethan are gone and the townhouse already feels empty. I could get used to this Ethan guy hanging around because it has been translating to Claire being at the townhouse more. The sound of my phone draws my attention away from the *Vogue* article, "How to Drive a Man Crazy (In and Out of Bed)." Somehow this article was hidden from last night's perusal with Graham. He had too much fun as it was with the quiz "Which Disney Princess Matches Your Sexuality?" Apparently I am a cross between Cinderella and Belle. Go figure. Eek, the phone continues to buzz.

"Hello," I answer, checking the clock on the microwave to budget my time.

"Angie. It's Mark Tanner."

"Oh, hey, Mark. What's up?"

"I have some good news for you. An acquaintance of mine, Steve, from Seattle is visiting town in a few weeks. I told you about him. He's a recruiter for Pacific Press."

I get up from the stool and do a half dance in excitement as he continues to talk.

"You mentioned wanting to be an intern in your area of study. Want to discuss it over a late lunch?"

"Wow! Really? That would be awesome. I'm free after twelve." Back on the first date, he had mentioned something about an old college friend having ties to some of the news outlets that might be offering internships. Considering that most well-established positions are attained by knowing the right people at the right time, I jump at the chance to explore the possibility. Plus, being closer to Mark helps me decide if he is worth pursuing regarding my research.

"There's a diner on the corner of Alhmed and Sixth. I can meet around twelve thirty. My treat." I can almost see the smile that has to be playing on his lips.

"Cool. See you then. Oh, and Mark?"

"Yeah?"

"Thanks." I nearly squeak.

"My pleasure."

I twirl around while drinking my smoothie—excitement taking the lead emotion role. River Valley gives free rein to students to find their own internship—even if they are out of state. While the Student Services Department will assist, it usually falls upon the student to avoid getting a poor position as a last resort. I do not want to rely on chance. Not for something this big. If the internship is a success, most likely the company will hire internally. Thus, I can have a job directly reserved for me after graduation. It's definitely a student-loan-friendly move.

I float through my morning routine with even more pep in my step. Maybe it's the walk or the call from Mark or the sun actually shining or the fact that I am riding the coattails of an amazing orgasm. But I don't need to overanalyze it. I feel great.

Betty's buzzes with the lunch crowd. Despite looking like the typical diner, the clientele consists mainly of suited businesspeople. I'm thankful for my instincts being correct when I decided to wear my khaki wrap-dress and brown heeled ankle boots.

"Angie, you look lovely," Mark compliments, leaning down to press his lips to my cheek. His boldness shocks me speechless. I blink at the overly friendly gesture but brush it off as being such. "I reserved us a table. This place is always busy during the lunch hour."

"Thanks." I follow him into the back of the diner, passing by animated conversations and skirt-wearing waitresses with trays of homemade pie in hand. "Oh, that looks good," I moan, not even aware that my words are out loud.

Mark turns to look at what I am talking about and grins. "Sweet tooth?"

I give him a sheepish smile. "Guilty."

"Coming here and not getting pie is grounds for immediate dismissal."

I laugh at the remark, happy that my sugar needs will be met. We slide into a booth facing each other. I order lemonade, and Mark gets a sparkling water. After our orders are taken, we jump straight into business.

"So, my acquaintance, the one I mentioned before, is coming into the city for a conference two weekends from now. He needs to first touch base with a few of the job fairs that are sponsored by local hotels. If you want, I can set up a meeting where we can all have dinner and discuss the options of you possibly scoring an internship. Maybe even bypass the list usually gathered at the fairs."

"Yeah, of course, I would love that."

"He's pretty much a hard-ass when it comes to recommending people to the hiring crew. But I put in a good word for you."

"Wow, you barely know me. I really appreciate you backing me."

I can't help but think about the reasons why Graham hates him so much. While Mark is a bit handsy and flirty, he has not shown me any indication that he is vindictive or malicious. He has gone out of his way to help me with my choice in careers and voluntarily offered his resources. Does Graham see him as a corporate threat? As far as I can tell, both men have different interest avenues. If they both just stick to their lanes, why would it ever be a problem? Graham is very established already. I just can't put my finger on it. The rivalry. The hatred. The drama.

While I have been recording business conversations with Mark and his associates, I am coming up empty-handed.

"Well, I'm sure there will come a time when I need your help or a favor. If you send me your resume and transcripts of what you have done up to now, I can forward them to him so that he can peruse them ahead of time."

"I can do that. Sure, no problem," I eagerly agree.

"So, if you are free that Saturday, I can make a six o'clock appointment at Fortune."

"The trendy restaurant at the Parkhouse Plaza?"

"Yes." His smile is contagious.

My mind runs through my plans, quickly remembering that I have no dates or obligations due to Graham's invasion over my free world. "Works for me." I smile with gratitude. "Thank you."

"No worries."

"So, Angie, did you get the Graham situation figured out? You seemed pretty upset about it when I told you about your profile."

Big understatement. I was and still am raging mad. The point is that Graham is out of line. And I am helping to blur all of the edges.

"I have an HR meeting tomorrow morning with the agency reps to discuss the issues." I stress the word issues as being plural.

"If you want help to piss him off, I can assist. Show up at the meeting unannounced to put in my two cents"—his eyes gleam with mischief—"might do the trick."

Oh, you are doing a great job getting Graham to blow a gasket already. No need to add fuel to the flame. Plus, if Graham finds out about this lunch, he will probably hit something—or someone. The man seriously needs to cool his jets. "I can handle him." Who am I trying to convince?

Mark's phone vibrates on the table and he flips it over to see the caller. "Sorry, I have to take this," he apologizes to me before turning his attention to the person on the other end. He steps out of the booth and snarls, "I told you never to use this phone."

I play with my straw wrapper and look as stupid as I can. It takes everything in me not to show emotion on my face. Who is he talking to? I hear Mark get off the call, only for another one to buzz in.

"Has terminal con la entrega?"

I hear the Spanish and quickly dig for my phone to start the recording but the words are coming so fast.

"Mover el producto para su prueba," Mark demands, his tone stern. "No puedo chatear ahora debido a los oídos."

There is a long pause, and I can tell Mark is anxious. His breathing picks up and his eyes refuse to make eye contact with me—which is unusual for him. Several phrases are spoken rapidly in a language other than Spanish. The words are slurred to the point that I cannot even commit any of them to memory, let alone find confidence that my cell picked them up.

"Paul esta en eso," he responds, back in Spanish.

Paul. That name I know now.

I am able to catch the last couple phrases on my video but have no idea the quality of the recording. But one thing is clear. Smoothie Guy Paul is involved.

"Is everything okay? You seem stressed," I ask as soon as Mark hangs up. I try my best at looking light and carefree, when in reality, I am about to shake right out of my skin.

"Trying to conquer the world is a challenging task," he jokes.

It is fake. A diversion.

But I play along. "I'm sure. How about we try an easier task and try to conquer some dessert?"

After lunch and a heaping slice of triple-chocolate mousse pie, I am running on carb-overload fuel. With a few bites, I have completely balanced out the calorie deficit from the morning workout. I say goodbye to Mark and we go our separate ways. I spend some time wandering around the streets of the city, window shopping and exploring.

I don't even realize the huge building looming over me, casting the sun away by its sheer size, until I spot Sophia across the street leaving through the double security doors of the back of Hoffman Headquarters. Her blonde locks blow in the wind, only making her look more beautiful.

I move against the side of a boutique shop and stand still long enough to catch Graham exit his building and join Sophia on the street. He cups her elbow and bends to whisper something into her ear, making her laugh and move her hands up in an attempt to fix her hair. Instead, he does it for her when he sees her struggle. My heart rate plummets as he helps her across the street, his hand at the small of her back. He shakes his head at something she says, while opening the door for her as they slip inside a cozy little Italian restaurant. If I didn't hate her before, I definitely do now. Every bone in my body is jealous that Sophia and Graham have a past. And from the looks of it, a present too.

Scraping myself off the side of the building, I turn right and force my legs to move. I deliberately walk in the opposite direction, taking the route of avoidance. I use my phone as a distraction and check the couple of new messages.

The first one is from Zander.

Zander: How are you doing?

I text him back a quick message and open the next message.

Unknown: I know where you work. Can't wait to meet you.

The cryptic message causes my blood to run cold. I text back a response and try to gain some information.

Angie: Oh yeah? Well, if I don't know your name, it will be hard to meet up.

My attempt at flirty is always awkward. I wait for a response but my phone buzzes with a "Not Delivered" message. My heart sinks over the fact that within twenty-four hours, I have received two mysterious texts from two separate unknown callers.

I look around the street and shiver in the breeze. People brush past me as if I'm not even there. I feel invisible, but also feel watched. My phone vibrates again. Another unknown number, from a different thread.

Unknown: Love your tan dress.

My heart stops. I am wearing a dress. However, it's concealed under a lightweight trench coat. I suck in cold, crisp air, and my lungs burn. I scamper into the first building I see and try to catch my breath. It is an apartment building with a set of double doors and a security system to protect the inhabitants from intruders—like me. I am too anxious to take a taxi back home so I pull up Zander's number and give him a call.

"Hey, Angie," he says cheerfully.

"Hey, I don't mean to be a pain, but my car is still in the shop. Can you pick—"

"Yeah, of course, where are you?"

I give him the address and wait on the floor in the entranceway for him to arrive.

It takes Zander twenty minutes to pull up in front of the apartment building. He idles illegally and hops out with a concerned look on his face—I am assuming from my distraught appearance.

"Angie? You've been crying. What the hell's wrong?" he asks, gripping my arms gently.

I sigh and sniffle. "Just a rough day."

"You've been hiding something from me for weeks now. Just tell me what's been going on with you. Are you in some kind of trouble? I can help."

He guides me into the passenger side of his car and flips off the few cars moving around him blaring their horns over his bad parking. He climbs into his side of the car and weaves into traffic with ease.

He glances over at me, and I can feel his eyes burning holes into the side of my face.

Fine. I am tired of lying to him. "When I lost my job at the bakery, I picked up another job. But it is secretive. Don't ask me for more details, please. I need the money."

"Okay…"

"Well, I am starting to get some weird text messages. I think they are related to the job."

"Well, then quit."

I shift in my seat. "Did you not hear me? I need the money."

"When have you been about money, Angie? This doesn't make any sense."

He's right. Money is just for survival. I am not an extravagant person. "And it's about potentially lining myself up with someone who might be able to further my career. Whether it be connections or research. I am grasping at straws, I know. But this is my last chance to be an investigative journalist. And not settle. I'm desperate."

"Will you show me the texts? Maybe I can try to trace the phone numbers."

"I'll email you the screenshots of the texts and the phone numbers. But I think the sender is using burner phones."

"Or they may be setting up a proxy or using an offshore IP address to conceal their location."

"Based on the actual messages, the person is local."

"Well, I'll see what I can do. But in the meantime, I'm worried about you. What are you going to do?"

I stare down at my need-to-be-polished fingernails. "Keep doing what I always do. Keep on keeping on."

Zander gives me a sad smile.

When I arrive back at home, I run up the stairs and change into sweats. For dinner, I pull out a frozen single-person entrée from the bottom back of the freezer. If Claire was home to witness this, I would hear about sodium content and the harmful effects of high fructose corn syrup. If her research on microwaving plastic—regardless of whether it's bpa free or not—is completed, I would probably be hearing about that as well. I still count to three before opening the door. Just for superstition's sake. Apparently having a plastic tray and cardboard box that can be recycled is not sufficient enough to keep me from exposing my food, unprotected, in our shared freezer. After the soy incident, I tread—and hide—carefully.

How does the saying go? Scold me once, shame on me…scold me twice…then, I'm an idiot.

Regardless, I miss her lurking around the townhouse, ready to pounce.

After dinner, I pull open my recorded video from lunch and get to work at trying to decode the conversation Mark was trying desperately to hide. From my memory of certain recognizable Spanish words, I am able to discover that Mark and his associates have a product to move. And that Paul is helping. The part of the conversation that has me the most intrigued is the part where Mark talked about ears.

It's funny how the mind works. Just when I think I am drifting off to a peaceful slumber, my thoughts pull at me, anchoring my conscious mind back to stable grounds of reality. All I really want to do is fall. I roll on my bed, pulling my legs up and to the side in a fetal position. I wrap my arms around the comforter, pulling it up and under, preventing air from getting under it.

I think about the past few weeks and all of the changes I have had to endure. Despite the new added levels of stress pressing on my shoulders—keeping me from much-needed rest—I have a renewed strength that I didn't have before.

Tomorrow, I plan to show Graham that I am an independent woman that he cannot push around with his demands and attempts at control.

Just thinking about the different layers of Graham is enough overload to cause any brain to act wayward. The man can turn on the sex appeal like no one else I have ever met. He can be soft and tender at the right times. What irks me the most is when he calls me sweetheart—an endearment that no one has used on me before—and melts the ice from my heart and my panties right off my behind. He makes me feel things with just his words alone. That is something I never felt before, even when the physical stimulation was done. With Graham, it is just…

Easy.

The bad thing about the whole situation is that I want him. I do. But I can't have him the way he wants me. He is a roadblock keeping me from what I need to do. I just can't figure him out. Why is he the way he is with his possessiveness, strong opinions, and overpowering personality? He makes it his mission to be secretive, and I find myself wanting to do the same. I catch him bringing out the best and the worst in me, often at the same time. That's what truly scares me and the main reason why I need to put my foot down when it comes to tampering with my job. I need to solve my own problems because in the end, I can only rely on myself.

25

I wake up the next morning with a wet pillow, wet hair, and a wet shirt. I roll out of bed and hobble to the bathroom to see the bloodshot eyes staring back at me with confusion and pity. I do my morning routine and get dressed.

I make my way downstairs to force myself to eat a granola bar and drink a mug of tea to keep my nerves at bay. Today, I meet with Entice Escort Agency's Human Resources department and go head-to-head with Graham. I have no idea what to expect as far as his reaction and behavior and can't help but feel guilty with mixed emotions of my own. I need daters to have access to my profile. I need to continue to see Mark so I can see what he is hiding. I need Mark to choose me to escort him—even if his motivation is just to piss off Graham. If he doesn't want me, then I cannot easily uncover what he is trying to hide. My future career depends on it, and I put the only eggs I have in that basket. I need to find out who keeps texting me. Maybe if I date enough people, I will be able to find out who he is. But at what cost?

So Graham and I are at an impasse.

I finish my granola bar and debate whether or not to spike my tea.

I distract myself by organizing the stack of mail that rests on the island. Claire must have brought it in before leaving for her trip, taking all of hers out. I order the pile from least-important-looking to most-important-looking and start opening. I scoff at how much paper is wasted in sending out garbage to residents. Apparently, the whole Go Green initiative only applies to some businesses, while others still find that postal mail is their best way of advertising.

I blindly throw away three real estate fliers. I actually receive four credit card applications—which I find hilarious that I would even be offered them in the first place with my credit score. Nope, having three almost maxed-out cards is enough for me to attempt to manage. I slow down through the rest of the weeding, opening an official envelope with an embossed logo informing me that they got my application and are grateful for my interest in their Los Angeles facility. I scan the rest of the document and then settle my eyes on the expected recipient's name. Claire Nettles.

I stare in confusion at the words, like a mental patient. It takes me several seconds to comprehend that Claire must have missed this envelope while she was taking her mail out of the stack. I spend the next few minutes reading the entire document—overcoming the feeling of guilt for violating her privacy—to understand that she applied for the same internship that she has in the past. Only this time, it appears to be a more permanent position, not just a summer thing. I quickly unclench my fingers, before I completely destroy the piece of paper.

Calm down, Angie. It's not like she got accepted or like she has made up her mind either way. I can't help but feel like someone has pulled the rug out from under me. The oxygen in the room feels thicker. Claire never mentioned having a desire to go back to California to work. I mean, I knew she had a great experience and did a great job there, but I thought she was happy here.

My fears are irrational. We are both going to graduate. We can't stay roommates forever. Not everything can stay the same.

I scoot down from the stool and make a beeline for the fridge to grab my emergency stash of pastries I picked up from the coffee shop. I select a cinnamon roll and a danish. I feel like making bad decisions, when inevitably I will experience bad outcomes. Seems fitting. I lick the icing off the cinnamon roll and then chow down on the rest. The sugar rush will make things temporarily better—despite being short-lived.

I can't help but think that Claire tried to shelter me from her decision to apply to the facility. She probably didn't want to make me sad unnecessarily in case they rejected her. Just another reason to love her more.

I munch on the second bad decision and stuff the thank you note into the envelope, debating on whether to slip it under Claire's door and explain the mistake or not. It's not like an acceptance letter. It's just a note stating that they received her application.

While getting ready, I decide that taking two pills will

be better than just the effects of one. I swallow them down carefully with tap water, knowing that preparing myself ahead of time is best. After this Graham drama is over, I am going to need to figure out how to replenish my supply.

I can tell that nothing about today is going to be easy—as if the path has already been set, and there is nothing I can do to change the course.

It takes twenty minutes for my taxi driver to arrive at Entice. It is my first time actually entering through the main doors of the building. As expected, the lobby area is pristine and beautifully decorated with modern art. I take the lift up to the eleventh floor. Under the soothing lights, I am guided politely to the back of the office space by a staff member—limiting all talk to just directions—and into the conference room.

I fidget nervously in my beige skirt and suit jacket ensemble, instantly turning chameleon-like and blending into the pale walls. Claire would definitely not approve of my lack-of-real-color choice for this occasion, but it was all I had available that would fit and still look semi-professional. Pretty sure the last time I wore it was for the Sugar Butter interview—which just goes to show how outdated it really is.

I am nearly positive that the wilderness will keep Claire and me from being in contact for the next few days. Knowing that there's a possibility she might be leaving the state makes my heart hurt. I could really use her support right now. I try to avoid thinking about her to keep myself from being sad. I cannot be sad if I plan to go up against Graham publicly.

The conference room is set up for functionality only. There is no artwork on the walls and the color scheme is considered bland at best. A huge television is set up along the west wall. The privacy blinds are opened to the outside; however, the windows are tinted enough to keep the sun from causing a glare. The room could use a little bit of greenery—similar to the plants in the waiting area. Perhaps even a sculpture or conversation piece.

I step deeper into the room, where I am greeted by a professionally dressed woman.

"Ms. McFee, I am Martha Pitman, director of HR. It's a pleasure to meet you."

I accept her handshake and give her a small smile. Martha Pitman personifies grace, elegance, and control. Her smart red pantsuit commands others to pay attention to her. I can't help but feel small—insignificant, really—standing beside her.

"Ms. McFee, as promised by Mr. Crawford, your representative Rich O'Neill has looked over your file and has already contacted you via email to touch base as to how today will run."

I nod my agreement and take the seat around the long conference table that she gestures toward. Rich did shoot me an email, but it was extremely impersonal and didn't boost any of my doubts as to finding an amicable outcome. Regardless, I know that I am not at fault and am the innocent one in this whole mess. It is the job of the agency to straighten out the mix-up with the reservation of my dates.

It takes a couple of minutes for Rich to join us. He is in

his fifties and has the "uncle" vibe with an eighties mustache and navy blue polyester suit. His red-and-blue-striped tie rests over his pressed white dress shirt. I frown. He looks patriotic at best but definitely not powerful.

Martha steps out of the room while Rich and I spend some time going through my paperwork that Dominic recorded, as well as the copies of the email that I sent to the technical support team summarizing the situation. We discuss strategy—basically me being honest—and go through the highlighted points of my case.

Once Martha reenters the room, we start the preliminary proceedings, and I sign my name on a few documents referencing that the meeting did in fact occur. I feel Graham's presence in the room before I ever see or hear him. Butterflies wreak havoc in my tummy, practicing multiplication. I turn my attention to the doorway and see the strong-willed man, who has been known to make appearances in my fantasies. He is dressed impeccably in a tailored black suit, crisp white shirt, and black tie. His look is modern and fresh—the exact opposite of my legal representative.

"Mr. Hoffman, Martha Pitman, Director of Human Resources," she informs, shaking his hand smoothly.

"Nice to meet you," he charms. He directs his attention behind him as a middle-aged man fills the space with rivaling confidence. He motions toward the man. "This is Gary Shippens, my legal counsel."

Gary looks like a real shark out for blood, and if this was anything more than a mediation, I would be intimidated. His gray suit is equally as sleek and his receding hairline only makes him look more mature—experienced and cutthroat.

Martha smiles at the greeting and motions for Graham to take a seat at the table. Great. Even she is infatuated. And he knows it.

For a mediation meeting, it feels more like I am in court.

Graham's eyes sparkle with a fine line of playfulness as they land on me for the first time. It was as if he deliberately ignored me until this very moment. From an outsider's perspective, it would appear that he is nervously attentive; from someone aware of his many expressions like I am, it implies that he is amused. His smugness irritates every cranky nerve in my entire body. I resist the urge of crawling over the expensive conference table and smacking the smirk right from his perfectly poised face. Why can the man never have a bad day in the looks department? And why the hell is he not intimidated and embarrassed by his overbearing behavior that landed him here in the first place?

Is it because just days before he gave me my first orgasm that rocked my body? Is it because he knows that despite my efforts, I cannot resist his charm?

I can't understand how everything involving this man is back and forth. One second we are pawing at each other. The next we are having a meeting to discuss boundaries. I could seriously get a case of whiplash. But, I honestly cannot figure out who is more at fault with the mixed messages. I know that I share in the blame. But today is entirely different. Today is about gaining some control back, at a time when my life desperately needs it.

I watch as Graham pulls out a chair directly across from me and sits down. His fluidity of movement makes me add to my list of the things he does that pisses me off.

"Okay, let's get started, shall we?" Martha smoothly

announces. "Mr. Hoffman, as director of Human Resources, it is my responsibility to follow-up on any complaint about clients at the agency. Do you know why we are having this meeting?"

"I understand the need to have protocols in place."

Suck up.

"I guess I am here because Miss McFee is"—he directs his attention over at me—"upset with me?" His hand gesture is that of complete dismissal. He has better places to be.

Upset? Damn straight, jackhole.

Graham flashes his sparkling smile as a muffle of snickers erupts. "Jackhole?" he asks with mirth.

Shit. What I thought was only said in my head must have escaped my mouth. Rich squeezes my hand under the table to keep me in line. Greatttt…I am eating right out of Graham's hand. He knows he is getting to me, and he is enjoying every second of it. I pull my hand away, not welcoming the physical contact.

Rich leans into my side. "Miss McFee, control yourself."

Okay, okay, I get it. I will shut up.

Graham's legal counsel writes a note on his pad and angles it toward Graham, who can't hide his grin. He gives a single nod, and instantly it feels like there is a secret meeting happening where I am not invited. Am I some kind of joke? It's as if he isn't taking this meeting seriously at all and it just started. What are they doing over there, drawing stick figure cartoons?

I catch myself sliding my pelvic bone into the chair, despite trying to be mindful to maintain a confident posture.

Meeting with Dominic a few days ago gave me the impression that something could change, that my rights as an employee would be considered. I got the illusion that my free will is still valued, despite the job being about customer satisfaction. Will Graham win in the end for the sole purpose of keeping up with the appearance that Entice honors the elite clientele?

"Ms. McFee, would you like to express your concerns to Mr. Hoffman?" Martha asks, refraining from taking a seat.

I swallow hard. I don't really see the point—besides now having it officially documented. He knows my concerns. I have told him several times to let me do my job, to quit interfering. Today is about restitution.

My hands entwine and twist against the surface of the polished table. I feel small and silly. Just the other night, he was pleasuring me with his hands, respecting me and honoring my body with careful precision. Now we are in a meeting that neither of us is enjoying. Instantly, I regret going about it this way. Perhaps, I could have struck a deal with Graham, negotiated better by giving him a little of what he wanted to reach my own goal in the end. Or at least give him the illusion of such a deal.

"I, um," I stop midbreath, looking around at the room of faces. I only know Graham. The rest are strangers. Just people who I have met in person today, who have no vested interest in my case. Or my best wishes.

"Cut to the chase," Graham demands.

His words cut to my throat, making it hard to speak. He seems cold all of a sudden, uncaring. Ruthless.

"Why am I here?" he asks. "What rule did I break from the client contract that I signed over a year ago?" His voice resonates with power; he is in full business mode. I instantly feel sorry for any of his own employees who ever have the unfortunate occurrence of getting on his bad side.

I stare up into the eyes of the Human Resources director for support. Obviously my spokesperson beside me is useless. It's like someone put a pin in him and deflated him. He is basically invisible. And apparently Graham showed up today with his lawyer just for decoration. He doesn't need someone to speak for him when he is doing a mighty fine job all on his own of commanding the room.

"Mr. Hoffman, the employee is distraught over the length of time you reserved her services," Martha interjects, looking at her file folder for guidance. "And the exorbitant amount of money you put down over this timeframe."

His smile is condescending. "Let me get this straight." He steeples his fingers, and I am instantly drawn to them. "I am meeting the time requirements. I am meeting the pay requirements. And I am meeting the employee's contract limits." He uses his fingers to count off each listed item for added emphasis. "But, instead, I am sitting here today because I am paying too much money? That's why I am here? Entice is getting a huge cut of that money too. So, why is anyone here unhappy? Spin some alternate scenario where we all win. I guarantee you can't."

I glare across the table at his cold eyes. He's making me look like a lunatic, and he's smug about it. Damn him.

My throat tightens up. I try to push the knot forming in my throat back down. I feel ridiculous and irrational for causing a fit over a quarter million dollars.

I tap Rich's arm and lean into him to whisper. "I never had a choice. My profile was tampered with." His nod lets me know he catches my quietly spoken words. Graham's posture and determination pull at the threads keeping me together. He has his "I am going to win" face on.

I can't help but wonder if Mark didn't reserve me for an extended amount of time if we would even be sitting here now. If it wasn't Mark—if it was anyone else—would Graham even try to throw money at me to prevent me from going on agency dates? I know he hates Mark, but to what extent? He won't tell me the details, so I am walking blindly into the situation.

"Mr. Hoffman, Miss McFee claims she never had a choice," Timid Rich interjects.

Graham leans into his counsel and talks loud enough for the whole table to hear. "Ask Miss McFee if she would like to go to breakfast or lunch or dinner today. I do, after all, still have her reserved. The time of said meal can be her choice. She can choose what she wants from the menu. Heck, I'll even allow her to drive." His mockery boils my blood, making my temper rise to the point of speaking my mind.

"Listen, Mr. Hoffman." I can feel my nostrils flaring. "I do not want your money." I slam my hand on the table and feel the sting instantly. "I do not want your overbearing self to grace my presence either," I snap. Regardless of how said body turns me on like an electric switch is flipped. "Not now and not for the next twenty-one weeks."

"You want to keep your job—the one I continue to suggest is not suitable for you—but you don't want my money? How is my money any different from any other person's money?" he asks with a snarl.

Martha shifts her weight and holds her hand up. "Okay, let's all just calm down and talk about—"

"Correct! I don't want your money!" My voice dominates over Martha's.

"Whose money do you want, Miss McFee?" He says my name with such slowness that it chills my insides.

"Mr. Hoffman? Ms. McFee?" she tries again.

"Not yours," I grind out of my teeth. "You can shove it up your—"

"What is the fucking difference? The money has to come from somewhere. Why can't it be from me?"

I stand up from the table and hover over the surface to glare at him.

Rich grabs hold of my arm, yanking me to get my attention. I wince as he squeezes my skin to try to get me to sit down. Graham's face turns murderous, as he flies up from his chair. "You do not need to grab her like that! Remove your arm or I will."

Rich releases me, as I slump back down into the chair. He pushes back from the table and growls under his breath that I am ruining everything.

Gary clears his throat and looks at Graham. "Let's take a breather, Mr. Hoffman. Out in the hallway."

As soon as both men leave the room, I am able to inhale. My lungs burn with the deep influx of oxygen. I feel like I have heartburn from my breakfast of champions, and I instantly regret thinking that eating anything at all was a good idea.

"Let's discuss where we should go from here," Rich insists, while we have a moment of privacy. "For starters, you need to settle yourself down. Conduct yourself like a lady." His tone is curt and condescending.

My stomach twists. "I, um, need to use the restroom." I don't wait for permission. I dart out of the room and down the hallway past Graham and Gary who are whispering to each other.

I hear Graham call after me but am too focused on not throwing up all over my suit. As soon as I am safely in the restroom, I throw open the stall door and double over the bowl. I expel the contents from my stomach.

I don't want to go back out there. I want to lock myself inside and disappear.

"Angie?"

It's Graham. It's always Graham. Since meeting him, he has completely infiltrated every section of my life. He is so embedded in my daily thoughts that avoiding him can no longer be a solution. I need to face him head-on.

"I'll be right out." I try to sound put-together, even though I know I am falling apart.

I wipe the tears from my eyes and only look in the mirror long enough to make sure I am decent. I rinse my mouth one last time, careful not to get damp spots on my outfit.

When I make it back into the conference room, everyone turns to stare at me. I find my place next to Rich and pop in a breath mint from the little ceramic bowl that serves as a centerpiece in the middle of the table. Martha guides us back into a discussion. Graham's eyes lock onto me, and I try to avoid his gaze. I do not want to cry anymore. He will see right through my emotions and be able to pick them apart one by one—using each to his advantage.

That's what businessmen do, right? Find a weakness and then exploit it.

"I don't want his money," I express. "I just want to continue my job and get my profile back in working order."

"So go to lunch with me, and I will not pay you."

"No. You can't blackmail me into doing what you want."

"Here's the problem, ladies and gentlemen," Graham announces, achieving everyone's attention, as if he owns the room. "I am a paying customer. Miss McFee does not want to break her contract. But somehow, I am rejected without—"

"I never accepted or rejected! I had no choice!"

"So, you'll have lunch with me?"

"No."

He tosses his hands in the air flippantly. "Sounds like a rejection to me."

"I…I…please…I—"

My heart races and my body feels like it is in an MRI machine. Every muscle fiber is begging to flex and contract and wake and rise and escape. I feel a bit dizzy over the lack of nutrition from breakfast and losing it all a few minutes ago. The two pills I downed hours ago seem to have had zero positive effect on my mood and my anxiety. I feel crummy.

"Angela," Graham hisses. "It's not a big deal."

"Five months," I choke out, eyes welling with tears at the realization that I am reserved for a job I do not want and kept from getting other jobs in the process. If I'm going to adequately investigate Mark and his line of business, I cannot tie myself down to only one client who is hell-bent on getting me fired.

"Give us a moment alone." The simple spoken words from Graham cause everyone to rush and scurry off like ants fleeing a stomped mound. Weird. He takes the remote from the table, clicks a button, and suddenly the glass windows in the room turn frosted giving us the ultimate privacy.

"Angie, please don't cry. I can't stand it when you cry. Please, sweetheart. We'll come to an arrangement on our own, without an audience."

Tears stream down my cheeks. He moves to my side of the conference table and kneels down below my chair. His fingers caress my skin, bringing chills to my arms.

"Keep the money. It means nothing to me. I just want to keep you safe."

"I feel like it's more than just that," I sniffle.

"It became more, yes. I know you feel the attraction. You are just scared."

"I don't want the money. Not like this anyway. I never earned it."

"Take it anyway."

I shake my head frantically. "No, I can't."

"It's very sexy to me that you went through all the trouble to call this meeting. You are very ambitious, and your feistiness is a quality I look for in employees. Come work for me at Hoffman Headquarters. You can do better. Why are you so set on staying here? I can give you a better job. Pay you just as much."

"Why do you care?"

"Because I know how ruthless the business world can be, and forgive me if I would like to protect you from it."

"But it's not for you to decide."

He hoists himself up from the floor in one fluid movement. His hands clench into fists as one slams onto the table. "I could wring Claire's neck for getting you involved," he snarls.

"It's not her fault!" I defend.

"The hell it isn't!"

"She would have never suggested this job if the bakery I used to work for was still operating."

"This is one hundred percent her fault," he insists.

We glare at each other in a standoff. Graham turns his back to me, running his fingers through his hair.

"Is that what it is?" he asks, whipping his body around again.

I look into his blazing blue eyes with confusion.

"The recruitment bonus?" he demands.

"What?"

"Her bonus for bringing on new employees. She gets a hefty check," he explains. "I'm sure it's in your contract."

I feel the blood washing out of my face. "This isn't about bonus money."

"Hell, I can pay her triple the bonus if that's what it takes to get you to not feel guilty about quitting."

"She didn't force me. She quite frankly likes the line of work. She thought that if I were to put myself out there in a noncommittal way, I would—" I stop before I say too much. I take a deep breath and wipe at the wet trails of tears.

"She's also more experienced than you. Less innocent."

"How the hell do you know?"

He gives me a look of disgust. "Men talk just as much as women do. Her name gets around."

I am dumbfounded. "Wow. Just wow."

"Don't try to act surprised."

"She's not a slut! She's way stronger than I'll ever be," I interject.

"That's where you're wrong. Women like Claire are a dime a dozen. Easy to find. You, sweetheart, are what every man fantasizes about. A rarity."

"Whatever," I say with an indifferent shrug.

"Angie. Just quit. Keep the money. It's yours."

"I need to work. I lost my last job because of the economy." And I need a link to Mark.

"All the more reason to accept my deal. Quit and take the money. Or keep the job, take the money, and date me solely."

"Did you tamper with my profile? You did, right?" I ask again, even though I know he did. He pretty much admitted it back when it happened.

He shrugs and looks away.

"Graham?"

"I might have exerted my technical skills to my advantage."

"You told me you didn't hack it."

"I didn't. But I have connections."

"You really hate Tanner that much?"

"I hate any guy who puts themself in my way of getting what I want. Tanner wants you because I want you. I saw the sparkle in his eye the very moment he saw you with me. He's obsessed. This is not chance. And the fucker—" He cuts himself off, tilting his neck to stare up at the ceiling.

"What? Tell me," I urge, curious to get some insight on his overprotectiveness.

"Nothing."

"I feel like we are where we were before this meeting happened. Nothing has gotten accomplished."

"Because you are so damn stubborn," he huffs.

"Because you are so pigheaded."

"And you make horrible decisions."

"And you make me crazy."

"And you're so feisty."

"And you're so controlling."

"And careless."

"And overbearing."

We both laugh at the insults being thrown freely, without reservation, from the heart of the matter. It is true. Everything. One hundred percent the truth.

"I'm calling off this meeting, and I'm taking you home. If you argue with me, I'll carry you over my shoulder and down the sidewalk in broad daylight. I don't give a flying shit what anyone thinks."

"Please, Graham," I plead. "I can't. I can't keep doing this…this. Whatever the hell this is."

"No. Angie. You are exhausted as hell. You didn't even sleep last night, did you?"

How does he know? "It was a rough night."

"Exactly. You need some rest. And I can bet a grand that you didn't even eat much today."

I swallow the lump down in my throat and tremble as he stares me down. Without a better alternative, I follow Graham out of the room. He grips my hand in his. Part of me thinks it is only to stick it to HR. But, nonetheless, it feels good to have him at my side. I refuse to make eye contact with Martha, Gary, or Rich, embarrassed that I unknowingly wasted their valuable time. I am making a name for myself here but in the worst of ways. I am surely going to be pegged as being that girl, the one that causes unnecessary drama.

"Don't worry about them." Graham comforts me. "They are well paid and this isn't your fault. Dominic should not have persuaded you to having a meeting in the first place. He gave you false hope that I would back down when he knew full well that I wouldn't."

I stop short of the end of the corridor, resting my hands on my hips. "What should he have done, then?"

He gives me a relaxed shrug. "He should have told you to give in to my wishes."

"Of course," I respond, my tone sarcastic, "you would suggest that."

"Yep."

I shake my head and bite back a smirk at his confidence and follow him on the elevator leading to the garage.

"Do you remember your parking spot number so I can have Collins deliver your car back home?" he asks.

"I got a taxi. My car is in the shop getting repairs."

Graham gives me a nod and starts his polished silver Lamborghini from the key fob. I imagine that the car has never had to spend a night in the rain or cold. It is stunning.

My phone buzzes with an incoming photo. I quickly open the message app and wait for an image to enlarge. No! My vision blurs, and I feel my body floating like a feather to the ground as my fear takes over.

26

"Angie? Angie!"

I can hear my name in the distance but cannot find a way to the voice.

"Hell, Angie, wake up, you're scaring me."

Warm hands pat my cheeks and push my hair back from my face. The touch is so gentle and soft. It's like being caressed by a cloud. I want to stay wrapped in this security blanket forever.

"Dammit, wake up!"

My body is shaken, and my eyes pop open at the force.

"What the hell happened?" Graham demands. "Are you ill? Hurt?"

My eyes search for my cell phone frantically and find it upside down on the concrete in the parking garage. I am wrapped in Graham's arms on the cold cement.

"My phon—"

"Who cares about your—"

"No, look!" I demand, pointing at the device.

He follows my vision and grabs my phone. He turns it over and sees the picture that was sent to me.

"Who sent this?" he asks in disgust. "How did—"

"I don't know. It's from another unknown caller."

I stare at the display on the screen and feel my stomach clench. There I am, ass bare and grinding all over Graham like a slut. There is no denying that it is me. We were on the bench at the charity gala. It is obvious from the angle that the photographer had a clear view to capture us in action. But why? And how?

"What do you mean by another unknown caller?"

"I have been getting some creepy text messages. I think from a client at the agency but I'm not sure. They are all from different unknown numbers."

"I'll find out who is at the bottom of this," Graham promises.

My phone vibrates, making me jump. I hear his snarl before seeing the reason. I take my device from his hand and read the message.

Unknown: There are more.

"Why am I being targeted?" I ask.

"I have no idea. But I'll have some of my security people look into it. I promise you, we'll find out who is blackmailing you." He takes a deep breath and pushes his hair off his forehead. "Or me," he snarls.

Graham helps me up and opens the passenger side of his car for me to enter.

I look up into his troubled eyes. "How do you know it is blackmail?"

"There would be no other explanation for the torment, other than to have some type of demand. I imagine that will be coming next."

He slips into his seat and starts the engine. The purr soothes me and unnerves me at the same time. He leans over in his seat and squeezes my hand gently. "Please don't stress, Angie."

I give him a weak smile. I would be lying to myself if I told him "okay."

"Let's just wait and see what this crazy person wants in return."

I stare at my shaking hands and know that no matter what I do to comply, there are digital copies floating about the Internet. The picture will never disappear. It will always be lurking in the back of my memory—even if any demands are met.

My eyes close as Graham weaves his way through the heavy lunchtime traffic. My head throbs with all the baggage that seems to be stacking up at my feet. And for what reason?

"Angie?"

I turn to meet Graham's concerned eyes. "Yeah?"

"Do you want me to take you home?"

We are nearing the Marquam Bridge that would take us back to my townhouse. Thoughts of being there by myself, without Claire, make me not want to go. I don't want to be alone.

"No," I exhale.

"Then where?" Graham asks. "What do you want me to do?"

"I don't want to be alone," I admit. "I just want to forget

about everything that has happened today. Make me forget, Graham. Make it all go away."

"Angie…"

"Please."

I watch as he makes a sharp left and follows the route parallel to the river north. When we are just blocks away, I know that he is taking me to his place, and a thrill runs through my core.

It might be a mistake. The timing might be off. But right now, I need to make this mistake.

My hand reaches for his thigh, and he jerks at the sudden touch.

"I mean it," I start, "I want to just—"

I don't even know how to finish. I'm not thinking clearly. And for once, it feels amazing.

Graham expertly parks his car into his assigned spot, jogs over to my side, and pulls me out into the stale air. I shut the door with my butt and turn to push him against the side. My lips crash into his, and my stomach presses into his groin. I can tell he wants to pull me away and talk, but I don't want his words right now. I just want to be reckless. Uninhibited.

"Ang—"

My mouth continues to explore his, and I chip away at his self-control. Hands knead my ass and jerk me upright so that my legs can wrap around his waist. He turns me midair and sets me on the front hood of his car, grinding his hips into mine.

My mouth rips away from his reluctantly. "Yes," I breathe.

Graham's hands explore my sides as my body trembles over the feeling of being desired.

"Let's get you inside, shall we?" he asks with a smirk.

I give him a nod and a yelp when he scoops me into his arms and hauls me over his shoulder.

"Stop, people will see," I squeal.

"Funny how you didn't seem to care just minutes ago about anyone other than me when you attacked me."

"That was not an attack," I giggle.

"It most certainly was."

Graham gives my ass a playful swat. Soon we are in the elevator, and his keycard is pressed into the penthouse slot. Once inside his foyer, he sets me down and helps me remove my shoes and suit coat. He discards his own. He then scoops me back up and carries me into the living room, nearly tossing me onto his couch. He follows me there. His body towers above me as he runs his fingers through his hair, while balancing his weight on his elbow. It's as if he is having some internal battle with himself.

He bends down, capturing my lips, as my fingers thread into his hair. He takes my breath away. I grind my core upwards, trying to get the friction my body needs.

Pulling back, Graham smiles and then kisses my forehead. "You need to eat something."

I prop my weight up on my elbows and let out a whimper. "What? Right now?"

I watch in disappointment as Graham runs both hands through his hair and then peels himself from my body. He walks into the kitchen and opens the fridge, peering inside.

"How does a turkey and cheese sandwich sound?" he calls out to me.

"Sounds like avoidance if you ask me."

His eyes dart to mine. "I'm not going to continue this line of conversation until you've been adequately fed. Taking care of you will always be my first priority, Angela."

Problem is my sexual needs outweigh my hunger needs at this moment. I sit upright and cross my arms over my chest as I watch Graham toast me up a sandwich. His eyes catch mine, as I can't help but stare, and wiggle with delight as he finishes up his task.

Carrying the plate to me with a glass of juice, he sits down on the opposite end of the sofa and watches with excitement as I take the first bite. It's good.

"I feel like there's a secret ingredient in here," I say, lifting up the top layer of bread to inspect what's inside. "It's really delicious."

Graham's smile is warm. "I put a little Italian dressing inside."

I nod and sip some of the cranberry juice, placing the glass back down onto the table. Every bite of my sandwich brings huge overwhelming feelings to the forefront of my brain.

Graham cares for me—even if it is a bit over-the-top at times.

And no matter how hard I've been trying to push him away, maybe it took all of these struggling moments to realize that he is who I needed the whole time.

Placing my empty plate down beside the glass, I crawl toward him, curling up on his lap like a kitten.

Graham is warm, and the calmness that he brings to me is like a soft blanket, enveloping me when I need it the most. Feeling safe for the first time in so long, I let down my guard and allow my body to relax into a peaceful slumber, tucked into his side.

"Angie..."

"Hmm?"

I press my chest against his, as he wraps me in his arms. My lips start at the base of his neck, kissing the smattering of stubble that's just started to form. I can feel his pulse change, as I work my way up to his ear, where I nip at his lobe. His thighs shift as I continue my sensual assault without a word.

"Are you flirting with me?"

My eyes adjust to the light in the room, as I force them to open. The sun is now setting, casting a warm glow to the entire penthouse.

The nap is making me feel bold, and I have zero regrets about it. There are so many things happening in my life that I'm unsure of, but Graham isn't one of them. This time I'm sure.

"Maybe."

"I don't think you are ready," he says slowly. "Let's have dinner."

"I'm not hungry for food, and I don't need you to have a conscience right now. Right now, I need you to be the bad guy you have been warning me about from the very start. Either be up for the challenge, or I will find some—"

"Italian food?"

I growl. Partially out of frustration and partially out of deprivation. And the man laughs at me. He fucking laughs.

"Apparently, I'm the only one here who is lustful. Fun times," I mumble.

"Angie…"

"I need you to be my bad choice."

I know that he is thinking he is taking advantage of me right now in my emotional state, but I don't give a fuck. Right now, I want him. All of him.

Graham smirks. "And I will be—but first, food."

Wrestling his way out from underneath me, I watch as he meanders into the kitchen to pull out takeout menus and then proceeds to place an enormous order for delivery.

"I hope you don't expect me to eat all that."

Making his way back to me, he bends and places a kiss to my forehead. "I know how cranky you get when you're hungry."

"You are confusing my horniness for hunger."

I yelp as he flips me onto my back.

Graham's eyes drop as he stares at my trapped body. He has me sandwiched between the cushions of his sofa and his torso. When our lips collide, it is like we are breathing the same air into one another. I lose myself to his taste, allowing my tongue to explore every part of him it can reach.

It isn't until the food arrives that we detach ourselves from one another.

I rub at my swollen lips, as I watch Graham dish up way more pasta than I can possibly eat. But I try. I try to enjoy these small moments in time, instead of constantly trying to rush ahead.

"It's really good," I admit, taking another bite of the ravioli. And another.

Graham nods, giving me a calming smile. But when we

are both done, his eyes turn serious. He clears his throat. His Adam's apple bobs to his increased breathing. "If I start, I might not be able to stop," he admits. His words hold so much meaning, and I understand his message fully.

"Good." I bite my bottom lip and maintain eye contact with him.

Graham's animalistic groan makes a shiver run through my body. He leans down and nibbles on the sensitive skin below my ear, licking back and forth over the softness. My heart drops into the pit of my stomach, and I slouch a bit in the comfort of the sofa, exhaling a moan of pleasure through my parting lips. My simple movement gives Graham a sliver of access to the inside of my mouth. He sucks. He explores.

Sliding his tongue around the corners of my mouth, he slips into the heated passageway. His hands snake around to my behind, twisting me up and around to be on top. He pulls me over him in a straddling position in one swift move. I feel the satin inner layer of my skirt slide up my legs, exposing the lacy edge of my thigh-highs. I sit down harder into his groin, feeling through his suit pants the thickness of his erection, waiting to escape. I swallow as his mouth assaults my tender flesh, taking his tongue and sliding it across mine. I bite down a little, causing him to smirk.

"Tease," he grinds out, pushing my hips up off him and then pulling them against him hard—my body slapping against his roughly.

I break the kiss, throwing my head back, hair flying wildly in layers over my shoulders. He pushes his head into my chest and moves it from side to side over my camisole as if he is unsure of where to find refuge. His mouth moves up to my neck, sucking and biting and licking and tasting along the base. I gasp and groan at the onslaught of pleasure, feeling like my panties will explode off me if he continues his ministrations.

The feeling of being airborne makes me grasp his shoulders. My eyes fly open, and I realize that Graham is lifting me and carrying me up a flight of stairs. I push my face into the side of his neck, tightening my legs around his waist. I giggle at the sound of his string of curse words. Part of me is pleased that I am not the only one being affected.

"Glad you are entertained by my utter loss of control," he grumbles sarcastically, pressing my back against the first wall he comes across, halting my giggles with the shock of his change in mood.

My eyes connect with his, and I see the caged animal finding his prey—me. The next moments are a blur with the flutter of hands and grinding of hips and gasps of wordless moans.

Graham's tongue drives into my mouth in exploration, swirling around the insides of my cheeks, tangling with my own. I am pinned, unable to move. I feel like a trapped butterfly getting mounted to the wall, and it is everything that I secretly told myself I didn't want. I wiggle to create the friction that my pulsing sex demands. The electrical sizzle of trapped need fills the silence of the air, almost crackling in my ear.

My thighs squeeze tightly together, and I desperately attempt to gyrate my sodden crotch against his and to loosen the hold of my confining skirt. His hands find the exposed bare flesh at the tops of my nylons and slide inside the back of my skirt, slipping over my satin panties. He pushes the material between my cheeks, kneading my naked flesh with his palms. My fingers rake through his hair, mussing up the order in the heat of the moment. With one hand groping my behind, he takes his free one and sweeps both of my hands from his hair up above my head, pinning my wrists to the wall. He has me squished against the wall, panting and moaning into his mouth as he takes complete control over my defenses. For someone who thinks he is the one who lost control, he has me fooled. Everything about this man paints the picture of the power he commands. In vivid, living color.

His growl sends a shiver down my spine as he straightens himself, tightens his hold on my bottom, and then totes me farther down the hall. He turns his back against a door and uses his weight to push it open, revealing a master bedroom with a huge king-sized bed in the center. He lowers me gently to the duvet-covered mattress, aligning himself over my body, maintaining the kissing and biting. My lips pucker with the pleasure-pain of his teeth and are then soothed by the sucking. He pulls away to nuzzle his face in my chest, moaning as he moves his mouth over the peaks.

He moves up off me, balancing his weight on his forearms to stare at my face. "So pretty. You are such a sight." He bends down to swallow my bottom lip into his mouth, nipping and tugging at it—tasting me. Devouring. Feasting.

"I have waited so long to finally touch you like this. To really touch you. And baby? You are so worth the wait." With one hand, he fans my hair out from behind my head, spreading it over a cranberry-colored satin pillow. He rolls off me, grabbing a pillow for his own head, never taking his eyes off mine.

My heart bangs against my chest at the turn of events. I knew he was bound to make a move. However, I didn't expect it to be so…

Delicious.

I watch with anxious anticipation as he reaches into the nightstand drawer, pulls out a remote control, and then uses it to soften the silence with some music. I lay back and will myself to relax as David Gray's haunting instrumental version of "This Year's Love" plays through the hidden sound system. After adjusting the volume, Graham slips out of bed to light some candles around the room. While very romantically cliché, I surprise myself by liking the gesture. It warms my heart that he is going to all of the trouble to make this experience less stressful for me—even if it was unexpected. After the numerous missed opportunities to achieve an orgasm, my belief was restored in myself when Graham helped me let go in my own bed. Maybe all along it was my self-doubt that was holding me back from enjoying that level of pleasure.

Now I lie on his bed, staring up at the glorious man who has taught me that I deserve to be happy and that it is okay to trust someone else while being broken. Despite all the chaos going around me, I can stop my world from spinning out of control for just this moment and enjoy the feeling of losing my inhibitions.

And that's the turning point for me.

Graham is my equilibrium. He sees me exactly the opposite of how I see myself. He sees me opposite of how most males have ever viewed me. To everyone else, I am damaged. A challenge and a conquest. But to Graham, I can just be me. Angry, sad, foolish, or—

Happy?

My eyes blink back tears at the realization that for the first time in over a decade, I can honestly say that I am just that. I am happy. Balanced.

Yes, I might lose my chance at a real internship again. Yes, I have a lurker sending me crazy texts and pictures. Yes, I am potentially being blackmailed. Yes, I might have my best friend and roommate leave me for a dream job.

But ever since Graham has crashed into my life, everything has been different. Out of the shadows of any preconceived notion of how I would live the rest of my life alone, Graham forced himself inside the fortress of my stubborn walls and changed the game.

It is like starting over. I am not the same Angela McFee I was before. I have evolved and figured out that when there is darkness, there is still the hope for light. Happiness is the hope. Hope for a brighter tomorrow. Hope for a better future.

The feel of tingles traveling from my scalp to my toes sends me spiraling back to the present moment. Graham continues to run his fingers through my hair as he settles in beside me on the mattress, inviting me to snuggle in closer to his side with each stroke.

"I am going to touch you all over, sweetheart. I am going to drive you deliriously wild."

"Yes, please," I purr.

"I am going to give you so many orgasms, and you are going to beg me for more. That, I will thoroughly enjoy." His eyes twinkle with promise. "I will give you pleasure."

My mouth gapes open, and I just focus on breathing.

"We are going to need to get you on some kind of birth control regimen. I'll schedule a doctor's appointment for you this week."

"I'm on the pill," I offer sheepishly. "For cramps and such."

His brow furrows, a frown on his lips. "Depending on the type, you have to take it the same time every day. No skipping. And you cannot be on any antibiotics or the effectiveness will be lost."

Well, then. I swallow hard and blink up at him from my reclined position on his massively big bed, dumbfounded that he knows this much about the female body and the regimen of contraceptive dosages and effectiveness.

I clear my throat and prepare to provide him with the information he is obviously waiting for. If he wasn't lying in the bed, I could see him tapping his foot on the floor in an effort to speed up my response.

"I have been on the pill for about four years to help manage the pain during my…"

"Don't start being shy now." He kisses my nose. "I'm about to see every inch of you. Up close."

"I take it for regulating my period." I feel my face flush at the mention of my monthly cycle. This can't possibly be normal conversation with the person you are about to sleep with, but I don't have past experiences to use for comparison.

His expression changes and his features lighten. "Okay. Good." I watch as he reaches into the top drawer of the nightstand on his side of the bed, handing me a stapled packet of papers. "My health screening, dated last week. I know that you are free of any diseases since the agency already checks into that before contracts are signed."

I nod and swallow hard, panic starting at the fast-paced feeling of the events that are about to unfold. I am not naive enough to think that this is not going to hurt.

"Are you sure you want to continue?" Graham asks, locking eyes with mine.

I stare at the stack of papers listing out the word "NEGATIVE" in bold print on every test performed.

"I'm not going to lie here and be dishonest to you. I am scared a bit that I will not measure up. That we will have to stop in the middle because it hurts too much."

"Shhh…don't be afraid of me, sweetheart," he says with a warm smile, playing with my hair. "I am not some type of monster. Yes, it will be uncomfortable, I am sure. But I will give you pleasure. That I promise. I just wanted to provide you with the necessary paperwork now. Because when I am ready to ravish and claim you, you won't have time to question the sincere concern I have for your safety."

"Okay."

"You have to relax and trust me. Understand? I will not hurt you and I will take my time. And you don't have to worry about owing me anything. This is about you. I will take pleasure in pleasing you. I can make my demands at another time," he responds with a wink. "Now, I need to see more of you."

I watch as he kneels on the bed, pulling me up to kneel with him—his strength obviously apparent against my weakened form. He maneuvers himself behind my back and starts peeling my camisole up and off my torso, exposing the lacy fabric of my white bra.

"Lift your arms."

I do as I'm told and watch as the material gets pulled up over my head. A pile is started on the floor.

The next song plays through the sound system and has a calming effect on my nerves. As much as I want him right now, I am terrified to get swallowed up. I am not sure if my emotions can handle the stress.

At no time do I question whether or not Graham approves. His feral intentions are evident all over his face. I part my lips, licking at the dryness. I hear a deep, guttural groan escape his. Although I have found myself in similar compromising positions before in the past, I have never felt the magnetic pull as when he touches me—or even looks at me. Ever since our first meeting, I have been intrigued and drawn to the mysteriousness behind the blue orbs that pierce me and probe me into giving more than I think I am capable of giving.

I surrender to his touch as he pulls me into his body, groping my skin, tugging on my hair to spark my moans of pain-pleasure. I didn't think I would like the rough play, but I do. I very much do. And he knows it.

Graham guides the shift in my position to give him access to my legs. I lie back on a mound of pillows and abandon my naive thoughts of staying concealed from his appraising eye. My skirt is slid from my body, making its home on the floor. One by one my nylons are slid down each thigh. At each passing inch of newly exposed skin, Graham caresses and kneads his palms into my flesh. His attention goes to my breasts, squeezing them through the material. I moan and my chest heaves with the pleasure of having someone other than me touch them. At the unsnapping of my white bra, I shyly move my hands up to cup my globes. He has seen me naked before but right now, it feels different. Like I am baring my soul to him for the first time. I receive a disapproving gaze and a shake of the head from him.

"Do not hide your body from me. You are beautiful. Let me see you."

I slide my hands down and lift my body up on my elbows, freeing my naked breasts, making them bounce with their weight. Instantly, his hands and mouth find refuge between the peaks. My nipples are tweaked, making them stand in proud salute—shooting pleasure signals throughout my entire body. I watch as he licks between both globes, finally finding a pink circle to suck into his mouth, making me nearly fall over the edge from the unrelenting pleasure.

"You like that, huh, sweetheart?" he asks between closed teeth around my nipple. He sends a warning of sexual promise directly to the apex of my thighs like Morse Code—letting the rest of my body know how much I want to be devoured.

I close my eyes with the sensations and grow impatient for attention to be given to its twin. I don't have to wait long. Every time his hands leave, he replaces the exposure with his mouth. Back and forth my breasts are worshipped and caressed into submission. I don't even know the point in time in which I rest my back entirely against the bed. My sense of time and my surroundings are clouded—leaving my decision-making skills incapacitated. My mind wants to slow down and get a grip on what I am really doing, so I don't miss a moment of the long-awaited journey.

Graham releases my fingers from his hair. I giggle; I

didn't even realize I was holding him helplessly to me. His body retreats from mine, making me groan in disapproval. He grins over me with hooded eyes.

"I'm not done with you. Don't worry, my little sex kitten," he teases with a husky whisper. His voice alone causes me to get even wetter between my thighs. His words act like kindling to my smoldering desire, and my body clenches at the promise behind them.

I watch as he removes his buttoned-down shirt and undershirt in expert fashion. He unlatches his belt, pulling the strap from his jeans. Then, he leans over me with just his pants on, completely naked everywhere else—including his feet. What is it about him wearing just pants that I find so incredibly sexy? His tanned body looks natural in the glow of the lamp, and I revel in his muscular form. His shoulders look huge compared to the narrow V of his waistline. His abdomen is sculpted, leaving an arrow of muscles and pelvic bone extending beneath the front of his pants. I want to lick the path that leads to his cock. His hairless skin—except for the naughty trail running due south of his navel—glows and ripples with every slight movement. I struggle to keep my drool in my mouth, sucking in a deep breath as I admire the man before my eyes. What a sight of steel.

Holy fucking cannoli.

"Such a pretty, but dirty mouth," he coos, his eyebrows raising with wicked intentions.

Crap, I need to get a muzzle or something. I don't even realize I am speaking out loud before it's too late. No wonder my mouth often gets me into trouble.

He runs his fingers through his hair as he evaluates my vulnerable form laid out over his mattress. He pulls the duvet from underneath my butt, tossing it to the floor, revealing the cranberry sheets that match the pillowcases. I am held still with his gaze, as if he has me shackled to the bed posts with just his sheer will alone.

"I love how creamy and perfect your skin looks against the solid background," he whispers. "I'm so lucky to have you here with me, baby. So lucky."

My heart catches. A ball of nerves forms in my stomach, growing in size, as I watch his hand move at infinitesimal speed toward the lace trim of my matching white satin panties. I pant with each passing second, anticipating the feel of his fingers on me. I forget about everything.

The scars…

If I trimmed enough…

How embarrassingly wet I am…

"Spread your legs for me," he instructs in his sultry half whisper. "Good girl."

I feel the moisture pool in the layered fabric, knowing that I have never felt this wanton before in my life. He kneels then sits back on his heels, pulling my feet up to bend at the knees, opening me even farther. My crotch is inches away from touching his erection through his pants. I am straddling him, with my butt elevated against his thighs. He massages each foot with careful ease and attention. Who would have thought that a foot massage could produce the same type of electrifying pulses that escaped from my breasts? I sure as hell didn't. I feel like my body is being taken over, and the control I once had has disintegrated, leaving me at the altar of Graham.

"Lie still," he warns, his tone serious and concentrated.

I keep my twisting body steady, trying to breathe

through the pleasure of his touch. If my feet could do this to me, what am I going to do when he is in me fully?

"Please," I moan.

"Please, what? Tell me."

"I want—"

The pausing of his caressing makes me moan in wantonness. I am charged and ready to go, and he is teasing me now. "Tell me or I'll stop."

Is he for real? I glare at him, knowing by the tension in his jaw that he definitely is serious. "I want you to touch me," I implore.

"Where?"

"You know where," I seethe, not wanting to say the words. He damn well knows where. Need a freaking road map?

"Show me, baby. Show me where you want it."

My hesitation meets his stern gaze. He shifts himself in his pants, stifling a moan at his obvious need. His self-control is frightening and admirable. I can tell that he is struggling with his restraint. However, I know that he will rein it in.

I huff and move my eyes away from his, sliding my fingers down past my navel.

"No."

"Hmm?"

"Look at me."

I blink hard and move my head back to look at him. I trail my hand over the front of my panties, closing my eyes only briefly as I savor the feel.

"Rub yourself for me, baby. Show me. Let me see what you want."

I shake my head in refusal, not wanting to embarrass myself anymore. I watch as he leans down, using his nose to clear hair away from my ear.

"Angie, be a good girl and listen to me."

Did he just bite me? Shit. He just nipped my ear, making me feel even more pleasure under my resting palm. I can feel the blood pulse through my sensitive bud, jumping with the slightest stimulation.

"Show me, my dirty girl," he growls, moving back up to get a better look. "Use your fingers. Touch yourself. And keep your eyes open!"

I pry them open again, meeting the sapphire ones that glaze over with need. His eyes divert their attention down to my apex, as I rub over the fabric, soaking up the leaking moisture with each press of my fingers. I move my hand back up to my belly and then slip it under the lace trim, finding my scorching sex in its puffy, desperate form. My moans mix with Graham's, as he switches between watching what I am doing to looking into my eyes. He closes his lids and when he opens them, I see another level of intensity present. His determination to seduce me and make me succumb to his will is evident in his dominating position and his words.

"You look so fucking hot right now. Do you know that?"

I groan and continue to spread my moisture over my lips underneath the thin confining layer of satin. I straighten my legs, while my bottom perches comfortably on his thighs, elevating my hips off the mattress. I use my free hand to squeeze and pull at my breasts, sharing the attention between the twin globes. After hearing the primal sound escape his lips, I snap out of my fantasy world and find

Graham penetrating my crotch with a gaze that could burn my panties right off the bone. In a swift move, he reaches down, gripping fabric in each hand. With little effort, he pulls in opposite directions, shredding the material from my flesh. A complete waste of money. But the satisfaction expressed in his features is priceless. He slides his warm hands up my smooth thighs and peels off the remaining scraps of satin and lace.

"I liked those ones," he responds with a smirk.

"You didn't act like you did," I counter with a roll of my eyes.

The scent of my sex fills the air, and I tense with embarrassment at the uncontrollable moisture seeping from my thighs. I give Graham a shy one-sided grin as his eyes widen and then narrow with emotion.

"I can't wait to make a meal out of you. You look and smell divine." He moves my legs back into position, surrounding his hips. "Good girl, keep touching yourself for me. I want to see you get yourself nice and ready. Although, your dampness indicates that you are already there. You getting ready, kitten?"

I purr my response, unable to form words. He's teasing me, and I'm loving it.

He tugs my legs firmly, lifting my bottom even more onto his thighs. I can feel and smell the liquid heat melting from my folds, most likely leaving a nice damp spot on his designer pants.

"Do you usually insert one finger or two?"

"Only one. But I am able to take two."

"Hmm…you can take a lot more than that, sweetheart. We just need to get you ready for something bigger. Yes?"

I nibble my bottom lip between my teeth as I stifle a groan at my rubbing and circling of my clit. I can feel the tension building—as it has every time in the past. I push my lower back into his knees, pressing my shoulders into the mattress firmly. It takes everything in me not to squirm away from his grasp and hide under the covers to conceal the intimacy of the act. He has fingered me himself. But there is something about masturbating in front of him that has me completely emotionally exposed to him.

I watch as Graham puts his hand into the pocket of his pants and pulls out a ring like one of the rings that he gave to me. He must have placed it there when he got out his medical forms from his nightstand.

"Here. Try this one. Do not insert anything inside. I want to be the one who has that privilege tonight."

He pulls my hand reluctantly from my sex, making me groan in displeasure, giving me a tsk tsk and a grin. I stare in utter shock as he leans down and takes my finger in his mouth—lapping up the juices with his tongue. He sucks the finger in and out in rhythm to my exaggerated breathing, nipping his teeth across the flesh. His eyes find mine as he releases my finger, moaning and uttering some unintelligible sounding curse words. He slides the silicone ring with several spheres attached to my clean finger, turning the multi-purpose jewelry to the inside of my knuckle. He places my hand back down on my heat, never actually touching it with his own flesh. His hand hovers over mine, moving it in lazy circles all over the primed region.

"That feels so good," I moan and buck off the bed, bouncing my behind on his legs.

"Easy, sweetheart," he warns. "I want you to relax and

focus on the sensations. Don't overthink anything. Just free your mind of any tension, and don't forget to breathe. I want you to keep your eyes on mine. Can you do that?"

I nod in agreement. He takes his time grinding the silicone over my folds, spending several minutes on my pulsing bud. I feel my hand with the ring being pulled away from my body. I keep my gaze on Graham's as I feel his fingers replace mine, and I throw my head back into the pillows, lifting my hips off his legs to gain more flesh-on-flesh contact. When he touches me, it feels so much better.

"Ohhh…"

"Shhh," he soothes. "Relax."

"But…but…"

"Shhh." He continues to stroke up and down my wet slit, spreading the moisture all over my folds and over my clit. He palms my trimmed hair, mumbling something that I cannot make out over my moans of ecstasy.

My heart races as I try to settle back down into the mattress. I attempt to make sense of all the foreign feelings that radiate from my fingers all the way to my toes. I have never gotten this worked up before. Even though Graham gave me my first orgasm, in my head it might have been a fluke. That maybe I will never get there again.

"Get out of your head, Angela," he scolds. "Quit thinking."

He places one hand on my mound and the other squeezing a breast. The flutter of the building tension rises within me, and my body begs for a release. Two fingers go back to my clit, kneading the little bud with an expert swirl. I scream out, pushing my hips up as an offering to him.

"That's a good girl." His coos warm me even more.

"You are close to having your release, sweetheart. It's up to you to enjoy the benefits of letting go."

His hand on my breast slides up to my neck, rubbing and squeezing around the base, forcing me to stay still. I feel pinned to the mattress. And I love it. The electrical charge ignites the flame that travels through every part of my body. I am so close but…

And then I feel it. It is pain mixed with pleasure. Graham pinches my clit, and I free fall over the cliff in an avalanche of desire.

"Ah! Ahh…ahhh…"

As I feel like I am flying, Graham removes his hand from my neck. He pushes a finger from his free hand into my entrance, hooks it along the edge, and pulls up. I thrash on the mattress, hitting another peak that I didn't even know was possible.

"Oh, Graham!"

"That's it. Scream my name, baby."

My mind empties itself of all coherent thoughts. I don't even know what words spill out of my mouth nor do I care about the details of the spillage. I can feel my inner muscles pulsate and clench with the leveling orgasm, reveling in the sensation of the much-needed release. Blackness hits my eyes—unsure if I close them or if that is a side effect of feeling too much too fast. I feel exhausted and rejuvenated at the same time. Before I am even fully down from the high, I feel my hips being lifted and Graham's fingers kneading my behind. I watch as he leans down, meeting my rising hips, and…ohhhh…yes.

"Hmm…" He moans—the sound muffled—as he takes a taste from the source.

I cry out in utter shock, tears leaking down the sides of my cheeks. Instantly, I feel the rising of my heart rate and the reenergizing of my sex. The tension builds, although the speed is instantaneously linked with each lick. It is like he is defrosting me from the walls of ice I have built around myself as an armor of protection. He makes me feel safe to let go.

I twist my upper body back and forth, trying to endure the levels of pleasure he is giving me, not sure if I can take any more.

"I can't…I just can't," I beg for him to stop.

"Yes, you can. Give it to me. Give in, baby." His words vibrate off my pussy lips, causing me more pleasure. As he licks and probes with his tongue, he slips a finger into my tight channel, filling me up all the way to his last knuckle. He wiggles his finger inside of me, stretching my barely touched flesh. He sucks on my clit and pulls his finger out, pumping it. I jerk with the full sensation. I arch my back, feeling him fingering me with now two fingers. I feel stretched to my limit. There is no way I can fit more.

"So fucking tight," he groans, matching my exact thoughts.

I give my body over to Graham as he pumps and sucks on me until all I am able to accomplish is trembling and screaming out his name, experiencing another tidal wave of an orgasm—even more intense than the first round. We both collapse on the mattress, Graham rolling me to rest on top of him, while I pant. I can smell my juices on his lips; his smirk shows me that he doesn't mind the mess. I hide my face into the hollow of his neck, shielding my eyes from his scrutiny.

"So, now you're going to play shy, kitten? Where did the tiger go?"

I cringe and tighten my muscles, curling into his side, shaking my head back and forth.

His chuckles fill the room. Both of our breathing patterns return back to normal.

"What about you?"

"What about me?" he asks, taking my head in his hands. He pushes back my veil of hair, revealing my vulnerable eyes. He is looking into the window to my soul.

I point to his still prominent erection. Surely, that has to be uncomfortable for him.

"Miss McFee, what did you have in mind?"

"I, um…" I can't keep my eyes off it. "Could reciprocate?"

"I have no doubt," he responds with a sexy half grin. "But, as promised, this is about you. We can have more fun tomorrow."

I glance at the clock and see that it is well past midnight. "It is tomorrow," I inform him. There is an innocent edge to my voice, yet my carnal thoughts are anything but. I trail my fingers down his rippling abdomen, resting over top of his confined erection. "And I want you, Graham." His cock twitches up into my palm, mirroring the need.

There is no mistaking the growl coming from deep within his abdomen or the way his eyes darken with hunger. "You can't say things like that to me, baby, and expect me not to react."

"I want you to react."

Instantly, Graham stands, ripping off his suit pants, tossing them into a makeshift pile on the bedroom floor. His black boxers are the only material keeping his beast of an erection firmly contained. He puts one knee on the bed, running his fingers through his hair in contemplation.

"I'm sure." I answer the silent question that he seems to be asking. "I haven't been sure about anything more in my whole life." I shamelessly reach out to rub Graham's cock, but he is faster and captures my hand in his before I reach my destination.

My words pull at his control, making him hesitate and question whether or not I am ready for this next stage of my life. The longer he waits, the more pressure I feel.

"If I have you once, I know without a doubt that I won't be able to survive without having you again. Regularly. So if you aren't serious about pursuing a relationship with me, then this has to stop now. I don't share. And I'm a demanding lover."

I pull my hand away from his and push myself up on my elbows to stare longingly into Graham's eyes. He's being serious. Every one of his words needs to be taken at face value.

"Okay," I answer blindly. I do not want this to stop, and for the first time in months, both my brain and heart agree.

I reach my hands up to cup his face, moving my thumbs in a soothing motion to show him that I am being genuine.

"If you think that I won't be good or if I'm not your type, then I can—"

"Stop," he growls, hovering over me with searching eyes. "I have never doubted what we could be together. But there's so much that we have to learn about each other. That will come in due time. Right now, I am going to take you, Angie. I want to warn you that your first time isn't going to be as great as you read about in your romance novels. I am above average. I am not saying that to brag. I am saying that so you can have another reason to back out."

For the first time ever, I see a shyness overcome him at the mention of his size. Of course he is freaking above average. He is huge everywhere else.

He runs his hand over his chin, struggling with his emotions and his protective instincts. "And inevitably, I am going to hurt you. It's your first time after all. But I promise to make it feel better again soon."

After that last orgasm, I have no doubt. I want this so badly. I lean into Graham, capturing his lips with mine. I use my feet to tug down his boxers, eliciting a laugh from him over my eagerness and deftness. His hard erection springs free, poking against my thigh in all of its glory. I run my hands down between our bodies, grasping his length firmly in my palm, barely able to get my fingers to curl around and connect. If I wasn't so sure of Graham's lovemaking abilities, I would be scared shitless over his massive size. I'm not naive enough to think that this isn't going to hurt. I know it will. But I also know that the pleasure will soon follow. It will be well worth it in the end.

"You are going to end things soon if you keep touching me like that."

"Oh," I mumble, letting go.

Graham leans back and pumps his cock a few times between his fingers, making my eyes grow wide with the anticipation of the entry. His free hand pulls at my pussy lips, spreading the moisture of my still flowing juices around the opening.

"I want you so badly, baby. I know that whenever I get inside I won't be able to last long."

Graham slips in two fingers, pushing against the walls, trying to prepare my insides for his girth. With his weight on his elbow, he leans over me, capturing my lip between his teeth. Despite how much I have mentally prepared for this moment during most of my adult life, I am tense and nervous.

He releases my lip and leans up to look at me. "Condom or not?" His words come out breathlessly, and I know he is feeling this intensity between us as well.

"Not," I moan, wanting to feel all of him naturally for the first time. We have both been tested recently, and I am already protected from getting pregnant.

Graham's fingers vacate me, and my muscles clench at the emptiness. I feel the head of his cock settling between my thighs, waiting for the right moment to push inside. He shifts his weight to his side, and he takes a deep breath.

"You need to open up your legs a bit more."

I follow the directive and try to relax. With gentle fingers, he pulls my pussy lips apart and rubs at my clit. He rolls back on top of me, putting most of his weight on his knees and elbow. With careful precision, he slides his hips forward to move inside just an inch.

"Baby, you are too tense. I need you to loosen up. I don't want to hurt you." His soothing words caress and iron out the knot forming in my stomach. My insides unravel from the gentle coaxing. He presses on my clit again, making me moan.

"If you don't like something, or if I am moving too fast, you tell me to stop. Understood?"

I hum out my response, trying to keep my eyes open so I can stay in the moment.

"Just say the word. I will respond to that and immediately stop. You have to trust me though, Angie. It is all about trust."

His hand slides under my lower back, and I arch my torso to give him more room. I am completely at his mercy. Every nerve ending charges with electricity, screaming for his body. I want him. Like I have never wanted anything before. I want to forget about everything in my life for just a moment. I want to soar. And the eyes staring at me with desire only tell me that I am going to get my wish. I can feel his cock pressing farther inside my tightness, stopping when met with some resistance.

While I own a collection of toys and have had fingers inside me, I know how extremely tight I am. No matter how many times I have fantasized about this very moment, I never expected the person who would be my first to be as big as Graham. I don't think there is a way for me to not be uncomfortable.

Graham slips his hand from behind my back, moving his torso off me to shift his weight over to his left elbow. His mouth captures mine, and he pushes his tongue deep inside my mouth. He slides his attention to my ear, sucking the lobe gently. At the same moment his right hand tweaks my nipple and his teeth clash against the sensitive flesh of my ear, his hips rise and push all the way forward. He thrusts into me with one fluid motion, filling me from tip to root. My back arches, and my mouth opens on a scream, but instantly Graham's lips are on me again, soothing me with gentle kissing. His hands slide up and down my sides, as his lower region stays motionless, allowing me to get used to the feeling of being so full. And achy.

My eyes meet his, and I feel the temperature once again rising between our gaze. I can see him struggling to stay still inside of me. He rests his forehead against mine, and we match our rhythm as we breathe.

"You okay? Did I hurt you too badly?"

"I'm good. I just need a moment to get used to it, that's all."

"You feel so fucking good, baby. It's taking everything in me to make this last."

After several minutes, Graham starts to pull out of me, and his pulsating cock scrapes against my walls. I take a deep breath and wait for him to push back in. His deliberately slow speed is meant to benefit me. His face is stiff with concentration, and his body is coiled tightly, ready to unwind in a spiraling speed. He pulls out again, and heat spreads through me. I run my hands up and down Graham's back, adjusting to the pace of his movements.

Graham's hand slides down my belly and finds the little pleasure bud that desperately desires his attention. And it gets just that. With expert fingers, Graham tugs and presses and circles the nerve bundle, making me jerk and thrust upward at the sudden jolts of pleasure that he produces from me.

The man knows what he is doing. He is learning my body, committing it to memory, and then executing his onslaught of pleasure.

We both moan in ecstasy as my orgasm grows, making the early pain that I felt become just a distant memory. Graham is delivering what he promised. He is mastering me, and I am just a slave to the pleasure that he gives. My hips match his thrusts, and I am able to stretch even more to accommodate him. Moisture leaks out of me, traveling down my crack and onto the sheets. I wrap one leg loosely around his back, urging him to continue. I am so close.

Our tongues dance and probe with each push and pull. My breathing quickens, and I know that the peak is just a few seconds away. Sensing my need for release, Graham changes his pace on my clit and presses even harder. I feel the drop in my buildup, and then the skyrocketing release as I throw my head back against the pillow and loudly moan his name.

"That's it, baby. I'm right with you. Give me your pleasure," he groans. "Scream for me."

As I am still soaring with my own orgasm, I feel Graham stiffen and push all the way forward, pulsing himself deep inside of me. His groan echoes in my ears, letting me know that he is feeling the same intensity as I am. The rush of warmth that fills me nearly sends me over the edge again for a follow-up release. His body wilts over mine, our limbs weak and our bodies drained of energy.

Graham rolls off me, his cock still twitching against my thigh, as moisture drips out of me. He pushes my damp hair back from my forehead, concentrating on my eyes.

"Are you okay?" he asks again. His fingers smooth against the sides of my face, searching for the truth. Through my fog of vision, I give him what he wants. I would give him anything in this moment.

"Okay is not a good description of what I am feeling right now. I am great. Wonderful. Exhausted. But I want to do it again."

A lazy smile brightens his features. He is so sexy.

"While I want to and am physically ready for more, you, sweetheart"—he leans over to kiss my nose—"will not feel the side effects until a few hours from now. Your pretty cunt is going to be sore and raw if we do not give it a rest."

I push out my bottom lip in a pout, not wanting to be denied the wonderful rush that I felt just moments ago. My body craves him, and the sparks of obsession trigger every one of my nerve endings whenever we are connected. I have waited long enough, and now I want more.

"Please…"

"You're so"—he kisses me on the nose—"adorable."

"But not adorable enough to give into my needs?"

"I don't plan on letting you go," he states, wrapping me in his arms tightly. "We will have plenty of time to explore each other and all the surfaces of this penthouse later."

I smile dreamily at his words, satisfied that he wants what I do. For the next twenty minutes, I let him pamper me and take care of me with gentle massages. He carries me into his excessively big bathroom—nearly the size of the entire first floor of my townhouse—and sets me on the toilet.

"Pee," he instructs.

"Yes, sir," I say sarcastically, but I don't actually do it. I don't think I can with him in the room.

"Pee, Angie, so you don't get a urinary tract infection," he says matter-of-factly. Of course he would know this. The man seems to be very current with everything sex related, as well as the female anatomy.

I surprise myself and am actually able to perform, even though his back is turned as he brushes his teeth. I watch in awe as he rips open a fresh toothbrush and puts minty cinnamon paste on it, handing it to me while I rest on the seat. He opens his medicine cabinet and pulls out a personal cleansing cloth packet, handing it to me.

I catch his reflection in the mirror and see his gaze shift from my eyes to my legs. I glance down to see the smear of blood on my inner thighs and quickly close them, blushing profusely at the intimacy behind the evidence. I look back up at Graham—my toothbrush hanging from my tightly closed lips—and catch his blazing predatory stare, burning holes into my skin.

He spits and rinses, spinning his body around to lean against the edge of the counter. "You never have to be embarrassed with me. You are exquisite," he says on an exhale, "and I am a lucky man for getting the privilege of being your first."

My skin flames, and I nod silently to his words. I change my focus and take care of my immediate needs. Tearing open the foil package, I use the hygiene cloth on my tender flesh, discarding everything into the nearby trash can.

Apparently I am an invalid, because Graham helps me off the toilet and over to the sink, where I spit and rinse my mouth out. He carries me back into the bedroom. Sliding one of his black T-shirts over my head, he trails his fingertips along my bare skin while slowly lowering the fabric. I smooth out the hem over my clammy skin, luxuriating in the expensive feel of it.

"Having you clothed will help keep me from having you again during the night when I know you are inevitably going to be sore," he comments, trying to make me understand his intentions. He kisses me on the forehead, pats my ass, and then guides me back into the bed.

Graham leaves the room, while I lie on his bed. He comes back with a glass of water and hands it to me.

I drink half and he downs the rest, setting the empty glass in the bathroom on the sink. He walks back slowly and joins me on the mattress, wearing nothing at all. No complaints will ever be heard from me. Realizing that the duvet is on the floor, he swings out of bed once again and pulls the blanket over top of us both.

When the lights are out, we snuggle close to each other. My back gets pulled into his chest and his arms wrap around me in a protective embrace.

I feel safe. Like nothing could ever touch us.

27

The feel of warmth surrounding my entire body wakes my senses and allows my eyes to drift open into narrow slits. The sheets are wrapped around me in perfect unison with Graham's strong limbs. I take a glance at the clock on the nightstand and see that it is nearly eleven o'clock. I have not slept this well in so very long that I can't even remember the last time it happened.

I try to turn my body, but the arms around me tighten, and Graham's sleepy murmur breaks the silence of the quiet morning in the downtown Portland high-rise. I wait a few minutes and make my second attempt. I lift one arm free and shimmy down toward the base of the bed to slip from his hold. When I am nearly free, the bed shifts suddenly, and I squeak at the flying body parts moving swiftly in front of me. When the movements stop, I find myself pinned underneath Graham's body. His incredibly sexy smile and raised eyebrow become my new focus, and the thought of escaping this beautiful man's grasp is furthest from my mind.

"And just what do you think you're doing?" he asks, holding my wrists tightly above my head.

I blink up at him, attempting to display my best look of innocence. "Going to make you breakfast?"

"Is that so?" he asks incredulously.

"Maybe."

"Has anyone ever told you that you are a horrible liar, Miss McFee?"

"Why no, I have never heard such a thing before."

Graham stares at me for a second, then releases me as he falls to my side, laughing loudly at my obvious lie. "You are something else, Angie."

"I've been called worse," I joke, loving the light airy feeling of the morning after.

He leans up on his elbow to study me. "How did you sleep?"

"Really well." My forehead wrinkles. "Great, actually."

He pulls my wayward hair from my face, gently dragging his fingertips over my cheeks. "So I wore you out?"

"Maybe it was the other way around. You were definitely not the first one up this morning."

I can't help but smirk over his grin. If I wasn't so satisfied, I would call it cocky, but the telltale signs of soreness are evidence enough of what that confident man is capable of doing to a woman's body.

"I stayed up late watching you sleep and listening to see if you were going to talk more." He nuzzles my nose. "You seem to tell the truth in your sleep."

"Oh, really?" Now he has me intrigued. And scared.

"Yes, ma'am."

"And did I say anything last night?"

"Hmm…yes."

"Well, that's"—I frown—"concerning."

"I nearly gave in to your demands for an encore performance. You make it very hard to resist when you do that breathy half whisper. But baby, you are going to be sore."

"What breathy-whisper thing are you talking about?"

"Oh, Graham, you are the sexiest man alive," he imitates with an airy feminine voice that sounds nothing like me—asleep or awake. "Mount me like a stallion."

I laugh over his attempt. "Wow, I sound like a bimbo."

"I can't describe it. But I'm going to now make it my life's mission to get you to do this while we are both fully coherent to act on it. Because, if you can do it while you are awake, I won't be able to stop myself."

I clear my throat and give my best attempt. "Does it sound like this?" I ask, rasping my voice and lowering my tone.

"Um, no. What you do in your sleep is adorably cute—not creepy and masculine."

I deepen my voice more. "What I just did was not creepy."

"I'm not interested in sleeping with an old man with laryngitis, Angie."

I playfully smack his arm and giggle, basking in the afterglow of the morning sun and the warmth radiating from Graham's smoldering eyes. I allow my fingers to walk their way down his chest, settling at his waist. I rub at his skin, enjoying the way his muscles ripple under my touch.

"Stop trying to seduce me."

"Is that what I'm doing?"

"Quit trying to pretend you are innocent. I now know the truth. While I would love nothing more than to take you again, I know you are sore and tender."

"I don't feel sore," I whisper softly. "But I am starting to feel deprived."

I stare intently at his eyes as his low growl vibrates through his vocal cords. His weight shifts and he tugs me back into the spooning position. His hand grips my top leg and pulls it up and over his hips, leaving easy access to my apex. His cotton T-shirt is little deterrence to his probing fingers, making me realize that the whole use of it was more of an attempt to make me feel comfortable about spending the night together post romp. My folds are pulled apart and the pads of his index and middle finger press into the entrance. My body stiffens at the intrusion, and I let the air I didn't know I was holding release from my lungs.

"I think I have made my point," he comments, pulling his hand from between my legs and moving it up to his nose. "But you smell divine. Intoxicating, Angie. You make me so fucking hard with just the thought of being inside you again."

"Then do it," I beg, wanting to feel that same explosion that I felt just hours ago. "I want you, Graham. My body wants you."

"Not at the expense of tearing you up. Hush, quit trying to tempt me, my little minx. We will have plenty of time to explore each other more once you aren't so puffy and inflamed."

I watch as he turns to reach into the nightstand drawer, pulling out a little container of ointment.

"This will help you heal better," he explains at my unspoken question, "and be ready for me faster." He twists off the lid and presses two clean fingers into the tub to gather a small amount of gel.

He is like a mobile pharmacy with all of his post-sex products. Between the special wipes and the ointment, I can only imagine what else he has tucked away inside drawers and cabinets.

"Open your legs back up, baby. Let me take care of you."

I obey and rest against his chest as he spreads the salve into my most sensitive parts, administering his loving after care to my body. Carefully, he inserts one finger inside my passageway, rubbing it into the warm pink flesh. The salve heats with the friction, and I can't contain the moan escaping from my parted lips. With the mix of pain and pleasure, it is nearly impossible to detect which is more prevalent. Each twist and turn of his finger hurt slightly, but the overall encompassing feeling is that of ecstasy. My insides start to melt, and I rock my hips upward against his finger, sucking it inside.

My left hand reaches back into the warmth of the sheets, searching blindly for the hidden treasure. I travel up over the firm length of Graham's thighs, through the tuft of soft hair, until I find his growing erection. A curse word slips off his tongue, and I laugh at my ability to bring out the crudeness in him, feeling powerful that I can at least affect him when he so passionately affects me.

I can feel the moisture slip from me, soaking Graham's finger with my juices. When I think that I am going to burst from the slow torture, I lift my body up and climb on top of Graham's legs in a straddling position.

"Angie?" he asks hesitantly, gripping the flesh on my hips.

I grind my crotch into his length, moaning at the friction created. "Hmm?"

"Baby, this isn't a good idea."

"I think it is the best idea I have had in a while," I whisper. I rub harder, tossing my hair back over my shoulders. "This feels so good that I may come from just grinding. Just lie still and let me enjoy myself." I smile softly as his eyes widen and then narrow. I must have done the half whisper thing that he seems to like, because his erection jumps, and I can no longer wait. I lift my butt off his thighs and line up my entrance with his engorged tip. His hands loosen on my waist and help to guide me onto him.

"Slow, sweetheart," he grinds out between clenched teeth. "I mean it. Go easy."

I can already feel the folds stretching around him, tugging at the inflamed skin as I move a centimeter at a time down his length. Graham's eyes are narrowed as if he's the one having the pain. His blood is pulsing through every inch of his shaft. I place my hands on his stomach to balance myself and then sit my hips down hard into his, sliding completely to the root.

Ouch!

Our mutual swear words mix in the air with a breathless harmony.

"What the hell does slow mean to you?" he asks, a bit angry at my suddenness of wanting to be filled.

"I thought"—pant—"the Band-Aid Approach"—pant—"was best." I bite my bottom lip into my mouth and suck on it to take the focus away from the raw pain that I feel deep within my body.

Once I am accustomed to the sensation of being full again, I start to move my hips up and down slowly, never gaining or losing more than a couple of inches.

Graham's hands slide to my back and push me forward. Before I know what he is doing, I am being rolled and once again am under the mercy of whatever he chooses to administer.

My shirt slides up, exposing my naked skin. Graham sucks on my nipples, biting them and kissing me through the pain. He has a rough side to him that I am loving. And craving. I don't last long under his ministrations and am howling his name throughout the bedroom as I see stars. Graham pumps a few more times and shoots his release inside of me.

While I have nothing really to compare it to, I know that Graham is an exceptional lover. He is all about taking care of me first and worrying about himself second. My needs come before his own, and while he often pushes me over the edge with his bossiness and his overprotective tendencies, I know that his heart is in the right place. I feel cherished and safe.

When his body starts to relax, Graham slips from my warmth and rolls to his back, pulling me to him. The proof of his orgasm is dripping down my thighs, and I couldn't care less. I am exactly where I want to be. I lay my cheek upon his chest and allow my mind to relax enough for my heart to follow. Hands wrap in my hair, playing with the softness.

"I don't think I'll ever get enough of you," he whispers.

"I feel the same way," I admit. "You have given me so many first experiences. First orgasm. First time having sex." I frown. "I don't think that there's anything I can give you that you haven't already experienced with someone else."

He tries to pull me up so he can see my face, but I press harder down into his chest.

"Look at me, baby. Please." He tries again, and I finally give up.

"Hmm?" I ask.

"No one has gotten as close to me as you have. No one. And yes, I have experienced physical acts with other women. But only you have unleashed the emotions behind those acts."

I nod, trying not to let the tears start pooling. He's so sincere and honest. I lean down and rest my lips on his for a chaste kiss.

"How about I go pick us up some lunch while you take a bath?" Graham offers.

"That sounds wonderful," I admit, just in time for my stomach to rumble. I must have worked up an appetite.

I watch the view as he rolls out of bed and saunters into his walk-in closet for a pair of loose jeans and a T-shirt. He then goes into the bathroom, and I can hear the start of the water filling up the tub.

"Go relax, sweetheart. I'll be back in a bit."

I crawl out of the nice cocoon I created in Graham's bed and make my way toward the sweet smell of almond coming from the bathroom. A layer of bubbles are popping at the surface of the water filling up inside the huge basin. I add a scoop of Epsom salts from the glass jar resting on the edge. I remove my shirt and settle into the huge tub. It is heaven.

Once I am done, I dry off and wrap myself into a luxurious white robe that is hung on the back of the door. I feel like I just had a spa treatment without the exorbitant cost.

I make my way downstairs and into the foyer in search of my phone. I have not checked my messages since leaving Entice yesterday with Graham. The reality of knowing that someone is out to scare me is pushing to the forefront of my mind.

My phone is dead, and I trot back upstairs in search of a charger. Surely Graham is prepared and has something near his bed. I search the nearby outlets and only find lamp power cords being plugged in. I open the top drawer of the nightstand and find the ointment container that Graham used on me just an hour ago. I see a wad of cash with a money clip holding it in its perfect place. I also find a set of keys tucked away in the back. A whole hell of a lot of keys, and none that look like house or car keys either. The second drawer has an opened box of condoms inside, but none are missing. Yes, I counted. Some of the Jealousy sex toy rings slide around with each jolt of the drawer, and yes, there is a charger.

I quickly plug the cable into the free wall outlet and attach my phone. While my cell rests, I make my way into Graham's closet in search of a clean shirt and pair of pants. Something about wearing a man's clothes always makes me feel extra sexy.

Graham's closet is as big as my entire bedroom back at the townhouse. Custom dressers are installed in the back with modern lighting. Rows of suits are aligned on the left-hand side, while his casual wardrobe appears to be to the right. I move toward the back wall and pull open a couple of drawers to peek inside. Belts, ties, and socks fill up several compartments. In the bottom drawer, I find two lock boxes.

What secrets are you hiding, Graham?

Beside the boxes, I find several sets of solid black clothes and a ski mask. Huh. Why would he need a ski mask? I finger through the dark clothes. Nothing appears to be designed for winter. Under the stash, I find dark ball cap style hats, a pair of binoculars, and three wallets.

Kneeling down, I leaf through the wallets and discover a different ID and credit card in each. All appear to be Graham in photo form, but none actually have his name printed on the license.

What the hell?

What is going on?

I trot back into the bedroom and grab the set of keys from the nightstand. I try each key on the two lock boxes but have no luck.

I can hear my phone come to life and the vibration sound of incoming voice messages and texts. I replace the items in their rightful places and walk back into the bedroom, keys in hand. I put them back into the nightstand drawer.

I put in the passcode to my phone and am overwhelmed with all of the notifications. Claire called me six times. Then she texted seven times. The car garage called. Zander left me a few texts. And one mystery number also messaged me. I open that message first.

Unknown: Looking forward to booking you as a date.

Unknown: Something tells me you will be a wild ride…

My skin crawls as my brain makes sense of the words. Who keeps taunting me?

With trembling fingers, I shut off my phone. During the mixer event at the mansion, I met several men who seemed eager to meet me. Why not just book a date? Maybe they tried. With my account being gridlocked with Graham, maybe someone grew restless and impatient.

I hear Graham shuffling around on the first floor and rush back into his closet to make sure everything is back in place. I grab a folded blue T-shirt from a shelf and slip it on. I slip on a pair of gray jogging pants and fold the waistband over twice to keep them from falling down.

"Angie?"

"In here, stealing your clothes," I call out from over my shoulder. I try to keep my voice steady. He needs to think I am calm and collected. That I can handle myself. And that is what I want.

I need to figure out these texts on my own. Maybe this will help further my career. Suddenly I go from having a no-profile to being a person of interest. And why? That is what I am going to find out.

"Hey," Graham says, squeezing me around the waist from behind, "I brought us back lots of food."

His touch warms me from the inside out, but I cannot shake the feeling that he is hiding something major. Why does he have a drawer of discreet black clothes? What about the lock boxes? The keys? The wallets with different identifications? There is no reason why a jewelry designer would need any of these things.

I turn in Graham's arms. "I'm hungry," I respond with a sly smile.

"Are you flirting with me, Miss McFee?"

The man does love to feed me. "Is it working?"

My ass gets a slap, and I gasp at the thrill of having such an effect on him. "Sure is."

"Then yes, yes I am."

Graham clears his throat. "You are playing with fire again."

"And for once, I don't really care if I get burned." The words are out of my mouth before I even comprehend the magnitude. What am I saying? Am I admitting to myself that Graham could hurt me and that I really don't care? What does that make me? A masochist, that's what.

I stand on my tiptoes and rub my crotch against Graham's thigh.

"You are sore."

"It's the good kind of sore. The one that needs friction and extra attention."

"Angie," he warns.

"Graham," I warn. "Either take care of me or I will take care of myself."

I yelp as he picks me up and hauls me to his bed, throwing me down in the center next to the takeout bag of food. His hands slide down my sweatpants.

"You look damn fine in my clothes." He squeezes the meaty flesh of my ass. "But you look better without them."

I lift my hips to assist in the discarding. His face nuzzles my neck, causing me to arch my back and mold myself to his body.

"You are mine," he growls.

My lower body jerks upwards to meet his thrusts, but he is wearing way too many clothes. I sit up and start pulling off his shirt. I admire his form with a hum. "There, that's better."

I lick along his neck, and out of my peripheral vision, I see the door move. My body jerks over the unexpectedness, and my stomach clenches with distaste.

Graham's body stiffens, and he looks over his shoulder to see what has my attention. "What the hell? Sophia? What are you doing here?"

"I'm sorry to interrupt," she says softly, staring right into my eyes.

"No, you're not," I mumble under my breath, but no one hears.

"You told me over lunch to let you know if I receive any more text messages."

So they just had lunch together? Lovely. I thought we were going to eat together here. And she is receiving texts too? What kind of texts?

I roll to my side, trying to tug the comforter over me while I find my pants. I retrieve them off the floor and slide them on ungracefully. Oddly enough, it feels like I am the other woman, and I cannot get out of this room fast enough.

He halts my movements with a gentle grasp to my arm.

Then he turns back to Sophia. "You could have called," he says coldly.

"But I figured that since I was already in the area, I would just show you in person."

I try to tug free, but Graham is blocking my way. "I'm going to go."

He ignores me, keeping his menacing eyes on Sophia. "How did you get in?"

I don't need to be here for his interrogation. I just want to go home.

"You know your doorman has a sweet spot for me. He let me up. Just like old times."

"He shouldn't have," Graham sighs.

"Let me go," I snap.

"Angie, I want to discuss this."

"Seems pretty basic to me."

"When I went to pick up our food, I ran into Sophia. We had a coffee and chatted. That's it."

I gather my belongings from a pile on the chair. This is awkward. I never thought after what we shared last night that I would be performing my first walk of shame.

Sophia clears her throat as I walk toward the door. "Old habits are hard to break. Just figured you'd want to make sure I was safe. You always take such good care of me, Graham."

"Angie, don't leave. I can explain. Please," Graham pleas.

"It's not a big deal, really," I lie. "I just think it's best that I go home." I turn the doorknob and walk into the hallway.

Graham follows me downstairs and into the foyer where

I find my shoes. I slip my phone into my handbag, clutch my dirty clothes to my chest, and hit the button for the elevator to let me down.

"Sophia and I have a past to—"

"And a present," I chime in with a big fake smile. "Don't forget about the present."

"She is an employee, yes. And an—"

"Girlfriend," I fill in the blank.

"Ex," he clarifies.

"One you share meals with and—"

"It was just coffee."

"One who has access to your apartment."

"The doorman made the wrong assumption."

I huff. "I wouldn't be surprised if Sophia had her own key."

Graham flinches, his jaw tense. "She is getting threatening messages like you are. She is terrified. Working as a model in the industry has opened her up to stalkers and male attention. I feel responsible. I am responsible. I have money, and anyone can see that I protect those I care about."

My eyes well with tears I cannot control.

"Not like that, Angie," he says quickly. "It was never like that. What I feel for you in no way compares to anyone I have had in my life before. I know you are mad at me. But you have to understand that it is you who I want. No one else."

He makes a move to touch me, and I dodge his advances. His face winces with pain from my denial.

"Graham…"

"Baby, I am falling so hard for you."

Graham's words jolt my heartstrings. I am so torn. Do I

allow myself to fall too? Do I allow myself to be vulnerable to a man who could potentially ruin me forever?

"I need time to think. Please give me some time."

The elevator car arrives, and I walk inside. The door shuts as Graham runs his fingers through his hair in distress.

"This is not goodbye," he promises.

It is for me.

28

I make my way out of the elevator, through the lobby, and out into the cold fall air. Looking around, I realize I don't have a car. I look down at my meager attire. I look like a street bum in designer male sweats.

"Miss?" an older gentleman calls as he rushes out of the building.

"Yes?" I ask, eyeing his suit uniform.

"Mr. Hoffman has requested that I have a car waiting for you." He takes a few breaths, visibly frazzled. "And I will in just a minute, if you would kindly wait."

"Okay, thank you." I really could use a lift right now.

When the black Lincoln town car pulls up, I slip into the backseat and rub my neck with the back of my hand before strapping in. So much has happened in the past twenty-four hours that it feels like the burden of stress weighing me down is unmanageable.

The man I thought I was getting to know is hiding things, and his ex-girlfriend obviously wants him back.

Have I been deluding myself all this time, clouding reality with my made-up fantasies?

"Where to, miss?" another kind gentleman asks from the front seat.

I provide my address and watch blankly out the window as all the buildings pass by. My phone vibrates with an incoming call. It is Claire. Shit. I completely forgot she called and texted numerous times.

"Hey you, sorry," I answer. "Don't be mad."

"Angie, good, you are alive," she mumbles in a frantic tone.

"Yeah. Barely. What's up? Sorry I never called you back or even looked at the texts. Got distracted."

"Three more girls got drugged on campus. It's all over the news. Did you see?"

"What? No, I had no idea."

"I kept calling you and texting you because you didn't come home. I was worried."

"I didn't think you'd be back home yet from your trip."

"Well, Ethan had to come back early. But where've you been?"

"I was at Graham's." Making more mistakes with my life. "I'm so sorry I didn't let you know. Everything is one big cluster right now." I feel sick to my stomach. "For sure drugged?" I ask.

"Yup. Just like you and almost Resa. This is insane." Claire turns up the volume on the TV in the background. "Sorry, the president of River Valley is speaking now. I think he's just trying to make it seem that the university is not connected to these incidences."

"Saving his own ass, I'm sure. This is not good publicity for any university."

"Yeah. He definitely is trying to convey sincerity. Probably for the cameras."

The night I got admitted to the hospital was also the night I took a pill at The Shack to calm my nerves. I just figured I had a bad reaction to all the alcohol I consumed. But this is now a thing. This is a big deal.

"Are the girls okay?" I feel stupid for asking it as soon as the words flutter out of my mouth. Of course they are not okay. Who would ever be okay from something like that?

"One girl is hospitalized at Portland General."

"Wow. This is crazy. And scary!"

"Yeah, and I know the girl. Remember Monica?"

I think back to where I have heard that name before. "The girl from the mixer at the mansion?"

"Yeah, that's her. She's a rather new agency girl too. She apparently was found face down in the bathroom at a frat house, and an ambulance was called."

"Which frat house?"

"Not sure. All of my information has been passed to me by Gossip Girl Tracy. If it was not all plastered over the news, I'd think she made it up."

"Hold on, Claire," I say and then put the phone on mute. "Hey," I call into the front seat, "can you take me to Portland General instead?"

"Yes, ma'am."

I switch off mute and put my phone back up to my ear. "What else do you know?"

"Every fraternity is under a huge investigation. But you

know how political those things get. No one ever is held responsible."

"Yeah," I agree. "Probably because the big alumni investors were also part of the same fraternities their sons belong to now."

"Yuck. Dammit," Claire yells. "I don't trust these people in authority positions to fix this mess."

Two years ago, several freshmen nearly died after a hazing ritual went wrong involving the consumption of vodka shots. The university completely disregarded the seriousness of what was happening during the initiations into these iconic groups. Articles were written focusing on the bad lifestyle choices that the victims led and did not bear light onto the fact that hazing was a real peer pressured norm on college campuses. Instead of trying to make a change with how students enter into sororities and fraternities and use the incident as a teachable moment, the victims became further damaged. So, Claire is right. Trusting the university to do something about these drugging cases is not very realistic. They have their own agenda to upkeep.

"I'm going to head to the hospital and try to talk with Monica. This is some scary shit."

"Okay, I'll see you when you get home. Oh, and Angie?"

"Yeah?"

"A bunch of cars were vandalized on our street. Mine was spared but only because I had it parked at Ethan's place while we were camping."

"Shit."

My phone buzzes again with another text.

"Okay, thanks for the heads-up. I'll see you in a bit."

I open the message up from Zander and backtrack to catch up on his texts. He is just worried about me after hearing about the drugging cases. I type out a quick response.

Angie: I am fine. Don't worry about me.

I flop back into the leather cushion of my seat and listen to the voice message from the car garage. I redial the number and get connected to the service technician. "Hey, this is Angela McFee. I received a voicemail message instructing me to call you guys right away. It was pretty vague, so I'm curious what is up."

"Oh yes, Miss McFee, there's a huge problem with your car."

I groan. "Great, how much is this going to cost me?"

"Hard to say, but you may need a new car," the technician replies.

"What? Why?" I ask in a panic.

"Our lead technician discovered that your car stopped running because there was bleach added to your gas tank."

"Bleach? How?" Is this the type of vandalism Claire just warned me about?

"It is a criminal offense to tamper with someone's vehicle. Bleach contains chlorine, which is a highly corrosive oxidizer."

"But my car worked and then just stopped."

"Well, your car probably had some gas in the tank, but when the gas wore off, the car stopped. Did you smell any bleach fumes while you drove it?"

I think back to the night it broke down. It was the same

night I started getting the creepy unknown number text messages. "No. I don't recall any weird smells."

"Okay. Well, we may have caught the issue early and can still save your engine and your car. But we need to keep it for another week to make sure it's safe. Or you will need a whole new engine. And at that point, I would take the insurance money and try to buy a new vehicle."

"Okay, thanks for letting me know."

"In the meantime, contact the police and file a report. We have never seen anything like this come through our shop. This was definitely a new one for the team here."

I get off the phone as the driver pulls up to the front of the hospital.

"Thanks for the lift," I say as I scoot out of the backseat and onto the sidewalk leading up to the sliding glass doors.

Once inside, I make my way to the gift store and purchase a get well card and a small bouquet of flowers with a tiny balloon sticking out of the top.

The ICU is located on the fifth floor on the west annex. I get buzzed into the unit just from saying I am a visitor. Since it is during visiting hours, no one questions my presence.

I quietly slip into Monica's private room at the end of the hall and try not to disturb her while she sleeps. It was not long ago when I was the one lying in a bed hooked up to an IV. Perhaps I was drugged too, and the side effects of the pill I took voluntarily was no side effect at all. Maybe someone did slip me something in one of my drinks at The Shack. Maybe I am a victim on the growing list of victims.

The squeaky sound of the chair's leather cushion jostles Monica awake in a semi-panic.

"I'm so sorry. I didn't mean to scare you," I quickly respond, standing up and moving toward the hospital bed. I place the vase of flowers and card on her bed tray.

Monica's eyes squint and adjust to the light in the room. She studies me for a few seconds and then is able to recognize me.

"You're in the agency," she whispers, as she sees the bracelet on my wrist.

I look down at it. I forgot I even had it on, since I barely take it off. It has become part of my normal look these days. "Yeah, I'm Angie McFee. We met at the mixer event several weeks ago. Claire and I are roommates, and she told me that you were a victim of a frat party drugging."

"So they say," she says softly. "I don't remember a thing."

"I'm so sorry," I say with a frown. Her eyes are sunken in, dark shadows marring her once flawless complexion. It's as if this incident has aged her ten years.

"Why are you here? It's not like we know each other well."

"My friend Resa was almost drugged. The night she was followed by some men was the same night three college students were drugged while dining at the Campus Smoothie Cafe. Now you are a victim at a Frat party. Plus two other girls."

"Wow, two more?"

"Yeah. Do they know what type of drug was found in your system?"

"There were several. But the standout one was Fentanyl."

"For pain?" I ask.

"Yeah. But that drug would not make me feel paralyzed."

"You said you don't remember anything from the night. You sure? Can you think back to any types of drinks you had? Anyone that stood out as being out of place?"

"I'm such an idiot for even attending the party. I never go to those types of things. But my roommate's crush was going to be there, so I went for moral support."

"Who was the crush?" I ask, earning a frown from Monica. "I promise not to share. I just need to figure out what is going on. I cannot trust the campus police to solve this mystery."

"Bryce. He's a frat guy."

"We have class together."

"Please, please, please don't let him know about my roommate."

"I won't," I promise.

I silently hope that Bryce is not involved in any of this situation. But to rule him out would be careless.

Tears well up in her eyes. "Am I in more danger? Did I end up in some type of crossfire, or am I being targeted?"

"I have no idea. But I'm going to figure this all out. I need you to hang low. Do not go anywhere alone. And do not drink anything that is not sealed."

Confusion flashes over Monica's face. "Okay," she agrees reluctantly. "Not sure why you have so much interest in all of this. But I guess any help to uncover why River Valley U girls are being drugged would be good."

"You're not alone. None of this is your fault. Please don't let anyone know I was here. I need to keep a low profile if I am to figure out what is going on."

"Be careful," Monica warns. "I'm so thankful some guy named Paul found me before someone could assault me."

"Wait, what?" I ask suddenly.

"Yeah, he's who came to my rescue. He found me and called an ambulance before I could seize."

Shit. Something is not sitting right with me. I need to find out more about Paul. And his connection to Mark. Until I can find out how and why campus girls are being drugged, no one is safe. Including me. "Let me know if you need anything. Get some rest."

I exit Monica's hospital room and make my way to the waiting room so I can type out some notes and email them to myself. *Wheel of Fortune* is playing in the background, and several people are drinking coffee while glued to their phones. I pull up the number for a taxi and call for a car to come pick me up. Between the strange texts and now my sabotaged vehicle, I am starting to feel like I am the one being targeted and not Monica. The closer I get to figuring out what is going on, the more I feel threatened.

The smell of woods and citrus fills my nostrils, and I glance up from my phone to catch the back of Graham as he travels down the hallway. He slips into Monica's room. I hoist myself up and follow quietly down the same hallway and hang out outside the room to eavesdrop.

"Who are you?" Monica asks in a shaky voice.

"My name is Graham Hoffman. I'm doing an investigation on what happened to you at the frat house," he explains.

I can hear the sound of the bed squeaking. "Yeah, I heard that one before," Monica exhales. "I know nothing."

Why is Graham trying to grill Monica? Why do we both have a vested interest? None of this makes sense.

I sneak downstairs in the elevator before Graham can catch me spying on him. My taxi driver is waiting at the curb, and I slip inside the backseat. I give him the address and make a phone call.

"Hoffman Headquarters, Hanna White speaking. How can I help you?"

Wow, I was not expecting anyone to answer and was going to leave a message. "Hey Hanna, this is Angie Mc—"

"I know who you are," she interrupts with excitement. "How are you? Graham isn't here right now if that is who you're looking for."

"I'm doing good. Why are you working on a weekend?"

"I like putting in extra hours while the previous assistant is away on leave. So much to catch up on, and I am usually bored on Saturday afternoons. What has you calling?"

"I'm calling because I need your help, actually. I'm kind of on a mission," I say in a jolly tone.

"Oh, do tell," she purrs. I can imagine her clapping her hands with excitement. Hanna always seemed to have a cheerful personality; someone who knows how to have fun. Part of me is sad with guilt that I am indirectly involving her.

"I want to give Graham a sexy surprise on Monday by coming to the office. But I need you to keep it a secret. Does he have any breaks in his schedule where he'll not be in his office? I need to set it up there. Trust me, he will like the surprise," I say with a voice as sultry as I can muster up.

"Oh squee! I love all parts of this idea. He's not a man who likes surprises, from what I can tell. However, something tells me he will welcome what you have in mind."

I give her a laugh. It is forced. "That's the plan."

"Give me a second to look over his calendar. This is so much fun."

I wait patiently. "Thank you so much."

"Okay, so he should be at a meeting from one until two on the other wing of the building. So you have an hour window of time to sneak in."

"Great," I respond, "I'll be there. Oh, and can you inform security to not contact Graham about my arrival? I really am looking forward to surprising him with my appearance when he comes back to his office. I need this to be special—if you know what I'm saying."

"Yeah, good idea," Hanna agrees. "I'll talk to the lobby and parking garage attendants as well. Oh, and those in the video room."

Of course he would have video surveillance in his own building. Why did I not consider that before? "Awesome. See you Monday."

"Bye, Angie."

By the time I hang up the phone with Hanna, I am at the townhouse. I hand over the owed money in cash and exit the backseat.

I use my key to open up the door and am greeted with the cozy warmth from the inside heat.

"Thank God you are home," Claire says in a rush. She peels herself from Ethan's embrace and gives me a big hug. "I was worried about you."

"I went to go see Monica at the hospital."

"Oh yeah, how did it go? How is she?"

"As good as can be expected. But there is something very fishy going on."

"Agree and it has me so freaked out," Claire admits.

"You both need to be freaking careful," Ethan warns from the couch. "This is getting serious."

I swallow the lump in my throat. "She remembers nothing."

"Please tell me you're not going to make this your little pet project, Angie. Please tell me that you'll let the police do their job. Please," Claire begs.

I shrug. "I needed a story. Now I have one. A legitimate one. And what better motivation can I possibly have other than to find justice for my own sake? I was a victim too. I'm invested in this just as every female should be who is on campus. It affects us all."

"You be careful, or you'll be a victim again," Claire reminds me.

"You both be careful," Ethan snaps. "Enough of either of you playing hero."

"Hey, I'm always careful," Claire responds with irritation. "It is Angie here who loves to put herself in all sorts of danger."

"Well, I don't want you to be part of the crossfire," Ethan warns. "Stay out of this, Claire."

Claire rolls her eyes at Ethan and earns a slap on her ass, making her yelp. I take that as my sign to head upstairs for bed. Every part of my body is screaming for rest. The adrenaline running through my veins over finally having a focus for my journalism class has me forgetting about Graham and Sophia and their on-again-off-again relationship. Screw them both. I have enough self-worth to not invest any more time in trying to have a romantic relationship with Graham.

My phone buzzes on the nightstand with an incoming text. I open the message from an unknown number and get another image of my bare ass on top of Graham. It is a visual reminder that someone is out to get me. Underneath the photo, the following words appear—*Fifty grand will make the pics disappear. I'll be in touch.*

So this is what blackmail looks like. Graham was right; there would be a demand. Unfortunately, it is one I have no capability of meeting.

My throat burns with the acid rising from my stomach. I have no idea how to fix this issue. Maybe the person blackmailing me is also trying to scare me by tampering with my car. The chances of two people trying to hurt me would be slim. This all has to be connected and not some wildly strange coincidence.

I flip my phone over and silence it from incoming message warnings. I need a clear head if I am going to start fresh on my investigation. I have a lot of catching up to do. Dr. Williams is going to want to see progress. I need to have something concrete and not just some made-up theories concocted from my vivid imagination.

As soon as my head hits the pillow, I am overtaken by sleep.

Monday morning, I attend class with Bryce and discuss the internal investigation into the university's fraternity. He seems his typical self, except upset over girls getting hurt—potentially by people he knows. My mind is elsewhere during the entire class, and I find it impossible to pay any attention to the instructor.

After class ends, I hurry home to shower. I blow-dry my

hair into a soft flowing wave, apply makeup, and slip on pantyhose and a mini-dress. I need to make this all look believable if I am to pull this off. I rummage through Claire's closet after getting approval via text and find her longest trench coat stuck in the back behind several other coats. I secure the tie around me. I enter back into my room and find my oversized leather purse in my drawer and start to fill it with my mini camera, my recording device, leather gloves, and a tiny notebook with a pen stuck in the spiral binding. I also throw in my tiny lock picking kit that I ordered online. I am ready to go.

Graham is hiding something. Between the animosity toward Mark and discovering him in Monica's hospital room, he seems to be in the thick of all the drama. Hopefully today, I will be able to find a few more pieces to the puzzle.

The taxi driver pulls up to the townhouse on time, and I slip into the backseat. It takes us fifteen minutes to get to Hoffman Headquarters due to there being little traffic on the roads.

"I need you to pretend to want to park in the parking garage," I instruct.

"Huh?" the guy asks from the front seat.

"I'll give you an extra big tip. Just pull up to the parking garage, and once I get out at the elevators inside, you can just exit."

"Sure, whatever."

When we pull up to the security officer, he instructs the driver to pop the trunk. He gives me a small knowing smile. Hanna should have warned him of my arrival so that some protocols get waived. I flash my identity badge and do the palm reader, just as I did when Collins escorted me the first time I was here.

Once through security, my driver goes into the entrance of the garage and drops me off at the first set of elevators. I pay and exit the car. The cool air runs up my nylon legs, under my trench coat, causing me to develop goose bumps. I pull the panels of the coat tighter around my front to keep my dress completely concealed. I quickly call Hanna to allow me remote access to her floor via a code.

In order to avoid the metal detectors, I had to be able to enter through the garage and not the main level's lobby. Even if the security officers knew I was surprising Graham, they would have been thrown off by my lock pick kit, camera, and recording device.

I take the elevator up to Graham's office floor with ease, courtesy of his personal assistant. She buzzes me in through the main doors and greets me with a genuine smile.

"So good to see you, Angie."

"Likewise," I say back. My heart is racing, and I am starting to second-guess myself.

"Graham is gone, so go on back," she responds with a wink, eyeing my sexy appearance. I imagine that she thinks I am naked underneath the coat. That is the illusion I am trying to portray.

I balance on my red stiletto heels and walk back to the office. Once inside, I manually lock the door. I slip out of my coat to gain better fluidity of movement and toss my bag on top of the polished desk. I plop down into the leather seat and set my cell phone timer for thirty minutes. That should give me plenty of time to search and get out of there before I get caught. I tug at the top drawer of the desk. Locked. I fish out the lock pick kit and go to work at getting the drawer to open. I have seen this done in the movies and got a kit online more as a hobby. It takes me a couple minutes but I have success. I rummage through some business documents and find nothing out of the norm. I lock the drawer and start on the second one. Inside, I find some mints, some bank statements, and a directory of employees. Nothing alarming.

When I unlock the bottom drawer, I nearly choke on my own saliva. An entire cardboard box is filled with cell phones. Upon examination they are burner phones—cheaply made and all having different phone numbers. I open up the flip phone from the top and search through until I find the message that was sent: "There's more." Holy shit. Opening up a second phone, I find the sent message to read, "Looking forward to booking you as a date. Something tells me you will be a wild ride..." The next phone—a lower version iPhone—was used to send a picture. To my phone. It is the same picture that was sent to me for blackmail purposes. I throw the phone back in the box and roll my chair back from the desk as if it is about to catch on fire.

I can feel the blood drain from my face, down into my neck, and settle in a pit, where it starts to boil.

I feel betrayed. Confused. It is like he is living some double life, and I do not know this man at all.

I pull out my mini camera and take photos of each burner phone's message. Why would Graham blackmail me for money? This makes no sense. Inside his bedroom closet, he had fake IDs and dark clothes that one might use for a robbery. Is he hurting for money? Surely he would know I have none. Nothing is adding up.

Once there is nothing left in the desk to explore, I find the filing cabinet—which is surprisingly unlocked. I pull open the drawers and leaf through the various files. Nothing seems noteworthy—except for one particular file. It is labeled Entice Escort Agency. I pull out the folder and finger through the documents until I find Graham's signature on the paper that names him owner. What the fuck? Owner? He owns the company? What about Dominic? I skim through every form and every paper until I eventually find Dominic Crawford assigned as a co-signer. A co-owner. And the date of the signature is less than a year ago. What the hell?

I take more photos and hurry to put the documents back in order just the way I found them. Bile rises in my throat, and I struggle to keep air in my lungs. Who is this man? A man with multiple identities. A man who I slept with—multiple times. A man who has warned me away from him from the start. A man I cannot seem to stay away from.

The bottom of the filing cabinet is locked. I grab my pick and go to work at releasing it. I glance at my cell phone. I have five minutes. Five minutes before I need to get my ass out of there. Five minutes to find even more dirt on Graham Hoffman. Or whoever the hell he is.

I twist and dig into the opening of the lock where a key would go. I turn and hear the telltale click and the release. Victory. I pull open the bottom drawer and find orange prescription drug containers. Eight of them. All with different labels. All with different medications inside.

Three minutes.

I snap pictures of each label. I open each bottle and take more pictures. I blink hard at the label that contains the same drugs that were prescribed to me after the accident with James. They are the same drugs that my physical therapist refuses to give to me now. I should be healed. I should not need them. But I do. I am in so much pain that it is hard to know when the crushing feeling will be too much to withstand on any given day.

Two minutes.

I pop open the protective lid and allow the chemical smell of the pills to infiltrate my senses. It is a high for me to just smell them. I feel the power they have over me charge through my body. My hands shake with the need. My mouth salivates with the desire. No. I can't. I do not need them. Every day I go without is a day I feel stronger.

One minute.

I run to the desk and snatch up my leather bag. I open it and toss the pills loosely into the cavern. I throw the empty bottle back into the bottom drawer and lock it. I slip on my coat and tie it tightly over my trembling body.

I rush out the door, allowing it to close behind me. I walk briskly down the hall only to be greeted by a wide-eyed Hanna.

"Angie, everything okay? You're leaving? Graham should be here soon. I can call and check?"

I want to throw up. I need air. "Yeah, I got my period. Can you believe it? What are the chances?" It is the first excuse to pop in my head to justify my departure. "Going to need to do a raincheck on this impromptu office surprise."

"Oh no, that sucks!" Hanna expresses. "I can't imagine Graham not wanting to see you though. Why not stick around?"

My eyes are glued on the elevator. I need to go. I need to

get out of here before Graham catches me. "I'm pretty sure I'll have blood dripping down my leg if I stay any longer. It came out of nowhere."

"Oh, ugh, okay, I hate when Aunt Flo visits," she says in a flutter. "Want me to tell Graham you stopped by?"

"Can you keep it a secret? I'll be back another day to give him an extra sexy office surprise post period."

"Okay, sounds good. He is on the fifth floor in the marketing conference room if you decide you want to see him. Otherwise, see you later."

I throw myself into the elevator and hit the close door button. I rest my back against the posterior wall and try to catch my breath. I slip down to the floor and pull my knees up to my chest. Holy shit. What is going on? Everything I thought I knew about Graham is a lie.

Owner of Entice? Burner phones and pills and blackmail and alternate identification and weird clothing. Why would someone who has always warned me against him want to blackmail me? Why does someone who appears to have unlimited funds want money from me? And all the victims? Is he behind the mess happening around campus?

Anger boils through my veins. I want answers. I want them now. Today.

I rip open my bag and shuffle through its contents in search of the little white discs. One is not going to cut it today. I fish out two and toss them into my mouth. I chew violently on the pills until the nasty bitter taste distracts me from the emotional pain that is slicing through my heart.

I know nothing about Graham Hoffman. And what I thought I did know is a fucking lie. I settle my head against my knees and allow the headache to consume me. I take five steady, calculated breaths.

I can do this.

I survived worse things.

My nose drips in accordance with the silent tears flowing down my cheeks. I use the sleeve of my coat to soak up the moisture.

Breathe. Just breathe.

I focus on the air filling and deflating from my lungs.

Breathe.

When I gather the fragments of strength I have left in me to fight, I crawl toward the number panel and slam my fist onto the five, making it light up.

Shit's about to hit the fan.

And Graham fucking Hoffman better brace himself for me.

Follow Angie and Graham's story in *Rush of Jealousy*, as their journey continues.

ACKNOWLEDGMENTS

To the bookstagram and online community: Thank you for allowing me to enter into the bookish bubble and for accepting me—flaws and all. I never dreamed that I would have found the level of support I have received since joining. So many people have reached out with enthusiasm over my future books, offered amazing advice, and have been the driving force in helping me to keep pushing forward with my passion and dream of becoming a published author. Your continued support means the world to me. I hope I made you all proud.

To my beta readers: Thank you for accepting my unedited work, offering constructive criticism, and helping me to grow as a writer. You all have been the first eyes that ever saw my writing. Thank you for giving me the confidence to continue with my passion project.

To my husband and children: Thank you for allowing me to be more than just a mommy. You all have been my safety net, through the struggles and the triumphs.

To my friends and family: Thank you for showing genuine interest in something that has consumed my entire life the past few years. I did it! I really did it!

To Andrea R.: Thank you for reading, editing, and cheering on Graham and Angie—even when their stubbornness drove you wild. You saw something special in these characters and helped me to progress toward publishing. You have been one of my biggest cheerleaders on this series, and I cannot thank you enough.

To Jenni R.: Thank you for messaging me in the wee hours of the morning just to yell at me over my characters. Your investment in my work and confidence in my ability have been monumental in pushing me toward the finish line. You helped spark a passion for reading within me back in college; never in a million years would I have predicted that I could be sharing a bookshelf with those same authors.

To Kristen L.: Thank you for reading my work-in-progress and making valuable suggestions on how I can improve. You have given me a lot to think about during the different writing phases, and I appreciate your honesty and desire to help me better myself.

To Jen B.: Thank you for listening to me rant, vent, and stress over the writing process for this book. Thank you for helping me with the struggle of finding the best-fit editors. You have been a great friend.

To Sawyer Bennett: Thank you for being a sounding board and lending a listening ear when I first made the decision to progress toward publishing. Your advice and words of encouragement have been life changing. You are my goals.

To Ann S. and Ann R. (Happily Editing Anns): Thank you for taking on a massive trilogy from an unknown indie romance author. You saw potential in my work and helped me polish it so well. I have learned so much during this entire process and appreciate you both taking the time to teach me the ropes in this industry.

ABOUT THE AUTHOR

Victoria Dawson is the creator of books with fiery heroines and possessive heroes. She thrives on writing stories that transcend the minds of readers, allowing them to get lost in the journey to love—and all the drama that entails. Prior to delving heart first into the romance writing world, she taught middle and high school students mathematics for ten years.

Victoria is a unique combination of hopeful realist and hopeless romantic. She is an iced coffee connoisseur, a reality TV enthusiast, and a habitual wearer of stretchy pants. If she is not chasing after her three active children, she is often found scouring social media for her next book boyfriend.

Having grown up in an itty-bitty town in Pennsylvania, Victoria is a little bit country. She currently resides in Maryland with her family.

Made in the USA
Monee, IL
05 June 2024